Demolition Queen

Champagne, Murder & Chaos

Betsy Cook Speer

Dedication

To my wonderful mom, who taught me I could do anything. She also read and edited this novel too many times to count and then encouraged, cajoled, and kept at me until I published it.

Special thanks to…

Andrew (who designed the cover), Michael, and Peter, my three sons, all incredible sources of inspiration and fun.

My great husband, Rick, for his editorial help, his support and for giving me the opportunity to write.

My brother Skip, who spent endless hours doing the most amazing job of editing.

My dad, who bought me my first tools, and gave me my love of hardware stores and music.

Kristin who always believed.

AWS Writers' Group: Adrienne Dines, Mary Albanese, Meg Gardiner, Susan Graunke, Kathy Montgomery, Tammy Huf, and Kelly Gerrard.

Jenny and my editors.

PROLOGUE

I knew Jake was unconventional from the start. It kind of fit. I wasn't too conventional myself. Otherwise, I wouldn't have been halfway up the steep Swiss mountain trail in a freak storm wiping clumps of snow from my wind-whipped cheeks and hopelessly tangled blond hair.

Couldn't see a thing. Not a single Grindelwald chalet in the disappearing valley below. Not the imposing Jungfrau Mountain across the way. Not even Jake who'd sprinted up the trail under beautiful blue skies. Brown chin-length hair in a blunt ponytail. Folded purple hang glider slung over one shoulder. Unmistakable extreme-sport glint sparkling in his Foster-beer-can-blue eyes.

No doubt, he'd headed up to play an insane game of "tag" where hang gliders darted and dove dangerously close to rocky cliffs and each other. I just hoped I wasn't too late to join in.

I was only ten minutes behind, carrying my own hang glider. I also had my ever-present plumber's bag. Never left home without tools. Hated getting caught out. My bag only held mini-binoculars, climbing rope, lightweight hammer, pocketknife, and my favorite long, red plumber's wrench. I should have caught up.

A half hour up the trail, I heard snow crunching under boots and my ears perked up. Then three men squeezed past me with disgruntled nods and sagging gliders as they headed back downhill.

Jake wasn't one of them.

If and when I found him and he hadn't got his danger fix, he'd be way more than just disgruntled. More like royally ticked off. Not the best time to share my recent revelation. One that shocked the heck out of me. One I wasn't sure how to phrase.

"Jake, you're the love of my life."

Ugh.

"You complete me."

Too Jerry Maguire.

"I want to spend the rest of my life with you."

Gawd, no.

I felt my lip curl as I pictured him fixing his intense blue eyes on mine, waiting for me to explain. As if I could. This sudden about-face didn't even make sense to me. I just wanted him, dammit, even with his insane stunts, like hang glider tag.

Although, I probably wouldn't have said the same the night we met just over a year ago.

***

I'd wandered into a Swiss après-ski bar at the base of this very mountain and spotted an extremely drunk, extremely cute guy swinging upside down from a deer antler chandelier.

Grinning, I tilted my head sideways to admire his body and rugged, unshaven face.

"I don't think we'll ever get ole Jake down," said the bartender.

Sounded like a challenge to me.

My grin widened. My turquoise eyes probably sparkled too.

About that time, one of Jake's blue-jeaned legs slipped from the chandelier. I lurched in his direction. Honest to God, my plan was merely to help him down. Instead, my hiking boot caught the strap of my plumber's bag, and I began to fall. Of course, to catch myself, I grabbed the only thing in reach: Jake's brawny, swinging wrists. So, as I regained my footing, I yanked him from the chandelier.

I felt a rush of air as his body plummeted past my face, an inch from my nose. The bar floor shook under my work boots as he crashed front first onto a table full of shot glasses and beer mugs.

He didn't move. Not right away. Neither did I. I'd done enough already.

It felt like an eternity before he gingerly lifted himself from the table and staggered backwards. Glass shards protruded from chest to groin. The guy looked like a bloody porcupine. A cute, *tall* bloody porcupine. I'm tall too. Five foot ten. But he had at least four inches on me, even with my thick-heeled boots.

"What's your name?" he slurred.

While visions of reckless homicide charges danced in my head, I contemplated using an alias. Finally, I said my real name, "Sam."

"Nice to meet you, Sammers. I'm Jake," he said.

He nonchalantly pulled the handle of a splintered beer mug from his palm while giving me a lopsided mischievous grin that made the most amazing dimple appear on his chin. Then he began to bend at the knees. I thought it was to look me square in the eyes. Not so. Jake and his punctured body had had enough and collapsed onto a chair.

Ironically, as he passed out, one of my favorite songs was playing. "Amnesia," by Pousette-Dart Band. As the line "I hope that it's only amnesia," played I was thinking if Jake had amnesia it would be a good thing. That way he wouldn't remember I was the one who'd maimed him.

At the hospital, Jake floated in and out of consciousness for an entire day. When released forty-eight hours later, we still hadn't had a real conversation.

Filled with guilt but mostly curiosity, I offered to drive him home. He slept the whole way even as we pulled up to his cozy Grindelwald mountainside chalet in the setting sun. I roused him long enough to help him across a suspended porch with a hundred-meter drop. Then I guided him into his rustic living room and onto the over-stuffed couch, where he passed out again.

No way could I have just left him like that.

Of course, his simmering gaze, mischievous grin, and muscular chest, glimpsed during a hospital sponge bath, had nothing to do with it.

First things first, I started a blazing fire in the broad stone fireplace. Then I turned and stared down at him. His breathing was even and deep. Perfect time to tiptoe into his bedroom and snoop, just one of many well-honed skills.

Guilt didn't enter my mind as I slid open his closet door. But disappointment did. No titillating insights here. His mountain climbing ropes, clips, crampons, and axes were completely unenlightening. Climbers in this expensive resort town were as common as the ten a.m. mom and tyke stampede at my London Starbucks.

About to move on, a white perfectly pressed button-down shirt caught my attention. Without hesitation, I discarded my not so clean black T-shirt and put on Jake's shirt. Its shoulder seams hit about four inches down my arms and its shirttail went to my knees. The kind of shirt I'd feel sexy wearing with nothing on underneath. *Hmm.*

Moving right along to Jake's antique pine dresser drawers, I found: Six side-by-side, evenly spaced identical black sports watches. One dog collar with a tag that had a GPS tracker in it, like my old lab "Clancy" used to wear. Tidy stacks of triathlon T-shirts from around the world. *No big surprise.* You didn't get a body like his without some major work. There were also expertly folded fleeces of every color. It was like a J. Crew catalog.

I recalled thinking, *This freakishly tidy side could be a problem.*

To say that neatness was *not* my strong suit would be a crime against, well, the truth.

Geez, Sam.

What are you on about?

Here you are in a remote cabin with a total stranger who, don't forget, has interesting bar habits and possibly dangerous qualities, and you're worried about housekeeping incompatibility?

I gave myself a mental slap.

I pictured my mom lecturing me with one of her "pearls of wisdom." *Not* talking to strangers. Even as I grinned about that, I quietly closed the drawers and hightailed it to the living room for another look at Jake, *my* stranger.

He looked angelic, harmless.

Firelight danced on his scruffy cheeks and closed eyelids.

Nothing to worry about.

I stepped closer. Close enough to see inside the collar of his red chamois shirt. I'd wanted to kiss that part of his neck for the last two days. Probably because it was one of the few body parts not bandaged.

But as he turned over, I stood still as a statue. His shirt had ridden up above green drawstring hospital pants. I saw the edge of a thin black line. I just had to see the rest.

Probably should have stopped there.

Of course I didn't.

I lifted his shirt to examine a swirling blue tattoo. With that, Jake's fierce, almost black, unseeing eyes popped open. His hand was like a vise wrench. It gripped my wrist, twisted my arm behind my back, and forced me to the couch.

Face-to-face with flared nostrils and puffing breath, I weighed my limited options.

Should I stay?

Should I head for my plumbers bag and tools?

Something in his charging-bull expression told me that moving would be a big mistake. I held my breath, stared back, and in seconds, his expression went from murderous to childlike.

Fascinating.

As if waking from a hypnotic trance, he blinked, grinned, and said, "Nice shirt." His gorgeous dimple reappeared and Foster-beer-can-blue eyes sparkled. His tongue ran over perfectly straight teeth, pausing on a diagonally chipped one at the front. He looked surprised, as if it was one of his multiple injuries not yet cataloged.

"So, Sammers, what do you do when you're not feeling up invalids?" he asked.

His smart-aleck question caught me off-guard. My cheeks went hot. All of me went hot. I felt disoriented and wasn't happy about it.

"I write, direct, and act in my own quirky demolition, rescue, action TV show. I wield powerful tools. I demolish walls. I empower women," I said, going for a cool, unaffected tone. "You?" I asked in an offhand way, like I didn't really care.

I expected a gruff, extreme-sport declaration. So, I was completely thrown as he gently took my right hand.

"How did you get this?" he asked, staring at a jagged scar on my thumb.

"Fencing," I said. "UK national champ three years running," I added with a grin.

He looked impressed but not surprised.

I liked that.

"And this?" he asked, pointing at a raised diagonal ridge that bisected my palm. He ran his finger along it. That tickled. I tried to arm wrestle my way out of his grip. I couldn't.

That, I didn't like.

Arm wrestling was my specialty. I was strong. It came with the job. Although most men would study my blond hair, turquoise eyes, and slim, curvy frame and not take me seriously. I beat them every time.

"Installing bathroom moldings for my mom when I was eleven," I finally said, answering Jake's question about my scarred palm.

His expression was funny. I wasn't sure if it was concern or professional interest, but since he didn't look at me like I was crazy, I kept going.

"After the bleeding stopped, my mom pretended to be a fortune-teller," I said.

Jake still held my hand as I ran a bent, shaking finger along the cut line like Mom had as she'd said, "You are lucky, my dear. This extended lifeline will help you cheat death. But that prize will come at the expense of other's lives." I paused, and then said, "Mom looked so shocked when she realized how morbid that sounded."

Jake didn't look shocked, but I blushed, wondering why the heck I'd told him that. "You haven't told me what you do," I said, shifting the focus back to him.

"Extreme sports," he said as he ran his hand over his shirt. He winced when it hit the bandages beneath. "Injuries too. Except not half as bad as the ones you inflict in bars." He frowned, but his tone was teasing.

"Hey, don't you ever mention that again," I said in a stern voice. I raised my fists ready for mock battle, and remarkably, his eye color intensified. Something else remarkable happened. He didn't physically move, but I felt as if he was all over me, inside my head.

That's when I *really* should have run.

"Listen, you're not getting off that easy," he said, tracing my bottom lip with the only unbandaged finger on his left hand.

Far from running, I sat there very, very still. That was *until* a toasty feeling began in my crotch and made me squirm in my seat. The heat roared to my chest and cheeks. With both hands, I collected the hot curtain of hair from my neck. I unconsciously *or* consciously left myself wide open and Jake leaned in. He brushed his lips across mine and with that, a sharp bolt ripped through my body. I dropped my hair, jerked away, and stood on shaky legs. I should have kept going, but the blood pounding in my ears was way too disorienting.

"Not the reaction I was going for," Jake said, grinning at me as he stood so that his red chamois shirtfront pressed against my chest.

"Hey, I'm not getting accused of invalid molestation again," I joked with a shaky half grin. I even put crossed arms between my breasts and his chest.

As if that would help.

Again with the dimple. Jake raised one eyebrow. "Unfortunately, that's not possible…right now," he said in a hoarse voice.

Registering his look of pure lust mingled with a large dose of disappointment, I scanned his injured groin-region.

"Oh *gawd*. I am so sorry," I said, blushing.

Mortified, I twisted toward the kitchen, but Jake grabbed my arm and grimaced as he pulled me tight against his bandaged chest.

"I'm out of commission, but I presume you're not," he whispered, peeking at my breasts, inside the white button-down I'd 'borrowed.'

The next day I got my matching tattoo.

***

I tapped that tattoo beneath my fluorescent green windbreaker and then pulled up my hood and shivered. The snowy wind howled and swirled around me. It blanketed everything, including my long, thick eyelashes. I tilted my head down, blinked to knock it off, and noticed the twenty-foot drop to the next snow-slicked ledge. I shivered. The twenty-foot drop didn't bother me. It was the *thousand*-foot drop to the valley and the humongous splat I'd make if I went over.

Where are you, Jake?

If Jake hadn't already taken flight, he was definitely too late now, and not just because of the snow. The sun was dropping fast. With the face of Jungfrau Mountain covered in deep shadows, total blackness was not far behind.

Seeing no need to take my glider any further, I wedged it into a crevice for safekeeping. I'd grab it on my way back down.

I took a deep breath and repositioned my bag's strap diagonally across my chest. Then I faced the next seven-foot-high boulder. About to scramble up it, I wiped new clumps of snow from my eyelashes and took another look.

It wasn't a boulder.

It was a man.

A very pissed-off-looking man. He also looked incredibly out of place with his exposed shaved head and overdone fake tan. Not to mention his dark boulder-gray Naugahyde coat and the nunchucks at his side.

I knew nunchucks. My favorite martial arts weapon as a child. Big difference though. His weren't made from yarn, masking tape, and two empty paper towel rolls. His had two ragged foot-long sections of hang glider pole connected by thick guide wire.

Where had he come from? And what was he up to? He didn't look like the politely-scooting-past-type. I had a very bad feeling about this Neanderthal.

With that, another of Mom's pearls of wisdom came to mind.

Everyone just wants to be heard. Try friendliness first.

Heck, what did I have to lose?

I shrugged and flashed my friendliest, most sympathetic smile. "Had to abort your flight?" I shouted above the gusting winds and pointed at his hang glider poles-cum-nunchucks. At the same time, behind my back, I slid out my heavy wrench and opened its spiky jaws with two quick twists.

Mom may have been altruistic, but she was no idiot. Brilliant backup plans were just as indispensable.

Well, either smiles were this guy's thing, or he had a short attention span, for immediately his furious expression left me and trailed across the snowy void beyond my left shoulder.

Well done, Mom.

I was pleased. That was *until* I followed his gaze, and then my jaw dropped. For, at that moment, Jake and his hang glider swooshed past as if tethered to a jumbo jet on a roller coaster.

My first thought?

Maybe this is a good thing.

This way I won't have to act on the whole "tell Jake now" impulse.

Probably would have been a huge mistake anyway.

Except, when Jake's glider leaped high in the air and then plummeted five-stories, I got a bad feeling about that too. I glared back at the nunchuck guy as if he was to blame. To my horror, his orange face and bloodshot eyes were mere inches from mine. I almost gagged at his stale coffee/cigarette breath but that was the least of my problems. His 'nunchucks' had begun whirring like helicopter blades near my ear.

So what was my *new* brilliant backup plan?

Lose those suckers and run like all get out.

I clenched my ice-cold wrench tight. Its metal-toothed jaws clanged as I swung it from behind my back, aiming for the nunchucks. Maybe it was the snow, maybe it was the wind, but I entirely missed. Instead, the wrench's jaws ripped through Mr. Nunchuck's orange cheek and then latched onto his exposed branch-sized wrist like a pit bull. He looked as surprised as I felt as he stumbled backward and tilted toward the edge. With cheek gushing like an oil well and arms swinging like lopsided pinwheels, he went over.

I blinked at the snow that maniacally swirled where he'd stood. Then I dropped to my jean-covered knees, leaned over the edge, and peered down through the dwindling snow at his body. Sprawled on the ledge far below, he looked like a gray snow angel. A snow angel with a gold gun in its waistband.

A gun?

I hated guns. I hated bullets too. I even hated the little cardboard boxes that bullets came packed in.

I couldn't fathom what Mr. Nunchuck's problem was and I didn't mind defending myself during his bizarre attack, but I was no murderer. He could die down there because of me.

Scrambling for my bag, I plucked out my pocketknife, opened its piton attachment, and hammered it into a crevice. I secured my rope and again leaned over the edge. About to throw it down, I stopped and frowned.

Mr. Nunchuck was gone *and* so was my wrench.

Darnit. That was my favorite wrench.

To make matters worse, Jake had probably landed in the valley already, which meant I'd be climbing down alone. *And* judging from the purple-blue shadows on Jungfrau, I'd be doing it in the dark.

I angrily jerked the long rope from the piton, coiled the rope around my bent arm, and was about to stow it when I noticed an orange light reflecting off my bag's side. I looked across the void to Jungfrau's sheerest side. I spotted a flare sending out a smoky trail that dissipated quickly in the shifting gusts of wind. If someone needed help, he or she would be there awhile. Climbers could take hours to reach that spot. Shifting winds could smash a two-ton rescue copter against the rocks like a kite.

"OK, let's see where you are," I said. My boots squeaked in the snow as I crouched and grabbed binoculars from my bag. Zooming in, I saw no one and/or no *thing*. I zoomed out and scanned Jungfrau's face in ever-wider circles. Still nothing.

I rechecked the darkest purple-blue shadows one by one and was about to give up when a shadow moved. Pushing the binoculars to their highest magnification, the flare's fading light reflected off something that had been stuck behind the jutting cliff, and I gasped.

Snagged on that cliff, Jake's purple glider frantically whipped back and forth, not far from becoming nunchucks itself.

Different words of wisdom, not Mom's but Jake's, seeped into my nearly frozen brain.

Stay with your craft so rescuers can find you more easily.

Then why wasn't Jake with his craft?

"If you're already climbing down, I'm going to kill you," I said *and* then jumped as a blinding lightning bolt zigzagged across the sky. *Oddest weather day ever.* My eyes followed its tail to a cliff above my left shoulder where a man stood surveying Jungfrau. *Good.* Another pair of eyes on the job filled me with hope.

Oddly, as another lightning bolt struck and quarter-sized raindrops started to fall, the man took *off* his baseball cap and stowed it inside his shirt. I considered waving and asking if he'd already called for emergency help but then my nunchuck-nemesis joined him. I shrank behind a boulder and watched as Nunchuck pointed toward Jake's hang glider. He even gave the stranger a congratulatory slap on the back.

Was Jake's crashed glider a cautionary tale?

Was the horrible Nunchuck congratulating the man for surviving? Didn't seem his style.

I wondered if more sinister motives were at work and tried to fathom how the pair on the cliff could have been involved in Jake's crash. But as the rain and wind suddenly died down, an unshakable sense of dread hit me. My skin prickled inside my coat as Jake's words repeated in my brain: *Stay with your craft...*

I aimed the binoculars at Jake's eerily still glider. I saw nothing unusual at the top.

In the middle, the sail had a few small rips.

Then I reached the bottom. I saw frayed guide wires and something else.

My eyes zoomed in jerky and fast like bad camerawork in a cheap horror flick. Dangling beneath the sail were familiar thick navy-blue socks and scuffed brown hiking boots. Ominously dark liquid dripped from their tips.

"No. NO. NO," I repeated as I followed the liquid trail down and down to where it had saturated a snow-mounded crevice.

It had soaked the next one too.

And the next.

I only got a brief glimpse of the mound after that because the flare sputtered and died. But I knew that all together those mounds held more blood than Jake had left on that bar floor a year ago.

A body's worth of blood.

CHAPTER ONE

One year later, a tall figure dressed in mask, goggles, and green coverall gave an ear-ringing whistle. With that, an all-female TV crew, including camerawoman, lighting, and sound technicians moved into place around the edges of a dark hay-strewn barn.

Lights blinked on. They highlighted the space just outside the open barn door where a ski-masked man, carrying nunchucks and a sword, towered over a petite woman dressed in a filmy pink gown.

"OK everyone, Demolition Queen, take sixty-five. Episode number fifty. Lights. Camera. Action," shouted the character wearing the coverall.

Immediately, the ski-masked man threw down his nunchucks. He shoved the woman against the rough doorframe and held her in place with the side of his broad shiny sword. Next, he tugged at the black mask around his eyes to leer at the milky-white breasts heaving against her bodice. He swung his black cape aside. He sheathed his sword but as he looked down to unbutton his pants the woman grabbed his shoulders, drove her knee into the vee of his stiff black pants, and shouted, "Take that."

As he hopped around in pain, she skittered her open-toed stilettos inside the dim barn, slammed the door, and bolted it. She looked around and spotted an open flame flickering on the far brick wall and a crafty smile formed on her cherry-red lips. Looking like a woman who knew what she wanted, she pushed away from the locked door and headed straight for the flame. It glowed through her filmy gown. It outlined her body as she swayed before it with an appreciative moan escaping her lips.

But not for long. The beautiful flame swiftly became a scalding, hissing mass. The solid wall trembled like a Richter-quality earthquake. Her sensuous grind ground to a halt.

"Get me the hell out of here," she screeched but she didn't run. Instead, she stared at four-inches of narrow saw blade that had just broken through the bricks near the floor and was powering up the wall.

"Hello!" she shouted, as the saw reached the ceiling's rough dark rafters, but it didn't stop. It turned and cut a line ten feet across, horizontal to the ceiling.

"Hello?" she tried again. The blade turned once more and headed for the worn wooden floorboards. Even with plaster dust and brick chunks flying, she merely fluffed her gauzy gown, did a sexy shuffle, and shouted, "I bet you're a hunk with bulging biceps, sculpted six-pack, and swirling tattoo."

She was sketching the imagined tattoo across her hip with shiny red fingernails when the wall emitted an earsplitting squeak. It also tilted her way. Calm as could be she backed up right before it slammed to the floor inches from her perfectly polished toes.

Coughing and hacking, she squinted through the swirling red dust and caught sight of her rescuer. It would be hard to describe the deepness of her red-lipped frown. But *why* she frowned was easy to see, for on her rescuer's frame not a bicep or six-pack was in sight. Mask, goggles, and coverall hid the lot.

Much more annoying than that, her captor reappeared. He charged through the dust, wielding sword and nunchucks.

"Watch out!" she shouted.

But her coverall-covered rescuer already had his long narrow saw blade poised and ready. Using the blade as his only weapon, he maneuvered the captor through the debris like a piece on a chessboard. He easily fended off each parry and riposte of the captor's sword.

The young woman proudly clapped and cheered during the fight's first minute or so. By minute three, she impatiently drummed manicured fingers against her thighs until finally, her captor gave up. As he fled back through the gaping, dusty hole, she locked shining eyes on her rescuer. She positively beamed as he peeled away the bulky green coverall. She alternated between biting and licking her lips as her rescuer's white protective padding came off. But as her knight in shining armor ripped away a sweat-soaked shirt, green goggles, and dusty mask, her lips formed a perfect red O.

He *was* pumped.

He *had* a very nice six-pack.

But he *was not* a *he*.

Removing a red baseball cap, the rescuer released a gritty blond ponytail. As it settled between sports bra straps and athletic female shoulder blades, the female rescuer shouted, "Cut!"

Or rather *I* shouted, "Cut!"

Immediately, I went from rescuer back to director. My all-female *Demolition Queen* film crew knew the drill. They relaxed around me and stayed put. After sixty-five takes, the damsel should too, but she'd already inched toward the cute one-man-cleanup-crew guy.

Couldn't blame her.

I shook plaster dust from my red baseball cap and then slid the small black fan belt from my ponytail to release accumulated brick chunks. I pulled a clean black long-sleeved T-shirt over my sports bra and moved across the barn. I headed straight for my camerawoman, Felicity, who'd been filming from the barn's darkest corner.

I felt light and happy. Battling masked captors and demolishing walls was my kind of thing. Plus I loved directing. Except maybe for today during takes one through sixty-four, when the evil masked swordsman either tripped on his cape or skewered things, like the wall and *me*.

Almost hoarse from yelling, "Cut," I was praying that take sixty-five was our last. I kept hold of my reciprocating saw just in case.

"Felicity, how's it look?" I asked my camerawoman, who corralled ringlets of ginger-colored hair into a black Chanel headband. *Not always a good sign.*

"Your nunchuck guy is still disturbing," Felicity said, pulling a face.

"Good," I said.

"I still don't understand. Why write in a character like that," Felicity said and gave me a sideways look. The look that friends and family had been giving me since the love-of-my-life bled out on that Swiss mountain a year ago.

And they didn't even know about my run-in with Mr. Nunchuck.

So why was I reliving anything about the day Jake died? There were so many unanswered questions. Like, what really caused Jake's glider to crash? Who was Nunchuck? Why was he there? Who was with him?

Was using Nunchuck's character my own sick form of therapy?

Probably.

"Felicity, how did his swordplay look?" I asked, without answering her question.

"The bastard finally nailed it," Felicity said louder than she should.

"You're not messing with me, are you?" I asked, but I was already feeling an excited buzz in my ears. There were not many things I enjoyed more than wrapping a *Demolition Queen* episode. *Well...things I could do in public.*

Holding my hair back, I leaned in to see for myself.

"I knew it felt good, but this is flawless," I said to Felicity, pointing at the screen with disbelief. "It's like the captor changed between take sixty-four and sixty-five," I added with suspicion creeping in.

Smiling, I moved from behind the monitor and said, "Everybody, our fiftieth episode, is wonderfully and miraculously wrapped."

Excited applause and whistles from the crew filled the barn.

"Sam?" shouted Felicity. "Before I forget, right before take sixty-four, the station chief rang. He wanted to discuss the *Demolition Queen* party."

I frowned. My crew definitely deserved a blowout but that wasn't why our tweedy station chief wanted one. Promoting the show was his only goal. It would be a circus.

"No surprise there. I'll call him later," I said. "Hey, if you're free tonight there's this black-tie thing up the hill with Conrad's cronies. It would make perfect footage for a *Demolition Queen* party episode. Felicity...?"

Felicity wasn't paying attention. I turned and followed her puzzled gaze in time to see the *still* masked swordsman do something I'd only seen one person do *ever*.

He swung his shiny sword in a high, wide arc. Then he slashed it clean through the neck of an acid-green *Demolition Queen* champagne bottle. With that, the neck flew out the door and the masked captor caught gushing champagne in tall, acid-green champagne flutes.

With eyes narrowed, I marched across the dark floorboards. A foot from the man, I hauled my fist back and then punched the heck out of his arm. "I knew it," I said, pointing at his black mask-covered face.

The broad, muscular man stabbed his sword into the wet floor and pulled off his mask to expose stern, straight lips, laughing crinkled eyes, and static-filled silver hair that flopped onto his forehead.

"Can't stand it when someone gets your goat, can you?" Silverblade's eyes twinkled as he pushed a flute of champagne into my hand and clinked his against mine.

I gave a grudging smile and leaned over to hug Silverblade, my fencing mentor/father figure. "Isn't your preeminent butt supposed to be in the morgue?" I asked as Silverblade peeled off four-inch-thick padding, worn so he'd appear as massive as my nunchuck-nemesis.

"The stiffs can wait, my lady," he said, bowing stiff and proper. "I could not stay away," he added as he straightened and chuckled.

"Right. You couldn't stay away from the set? Or my female crew?" I grinned and took my first sip of champagne. "Mmm. I needed that. Thanks."

The nickname, Silverblade, not only came from the swords he wielded but from the silver dissecting blades in his morgue. We became buddies there five years ago, when I helped identify an antique claw hammer used in a grisly tool-related murder.

Most recently, I visited Silverblade's morgue to identify the body of a deranged quasi-fan stalker. My minor celebrity status had attracted the weirdo. He bombarded me with hate mail all because he couldn't build the "beginner's table" featured in my "Crazy Chef" episode. His letters ranted on about my show empowering women while depowering men.

It ended as bizarrely as it started. He was crushed under his own adult-sized mousetrap basket, clutching a letter that framed me for his death when I'd only ever laid eyes on him once when he snuck into our Soho studio.

Darned if Silverblade or I could figure out how the beginner table stumped a man capable of constructing a full-sized Mousetrap game in his garage.

Either way, it cemented Silverblade's and my friendship.

***

With a start, I looked up into the rafters at my massive antique Waterloo Station clock. Seeing the time, I climbed on top a new rubble pile and shouted to my crew, "Guys, it's three fifteen." *And* Friday. "If you're headed back to the Soho office, you better get a move on." Instantly, caterers began stacking dishes. Felicity and crew unplugged equipment and began packing.

Driving from this Surrey barn on Conrad Albany's estate, to *Demolition Queen*'s London Soho offices, took an hour *if* lucky. Friday after four could take forever.

I could move our offices down here to Surrey, but I'd miss Soho's bizarre buzz. Punked-out art students balancing limo-sized canvases on their heads. Businessmen emerging from sex shops. Homeless women in Gucci shawls shaking Starbucks cups.

Anyway, trips into Soho balanced out the effects of Surrey-land, home of the mega-rich and original desperate housewives.

Plus, although Conrad called this *the barn*, he'd outfitted it to his 'first class or don't bother' specs. It was large enough to house a family of five too.

"Sam?" Felicity said, rolling a stack of her equipment toward the rubble pile. "I can make it tonight. What time and what should I wear?"

"Set-up inside Cranmont's foyer door. Eight-thirty if you can. Wear pink and formal if you've got it," I said.

Felicity nodded. "Good luck," she said knowingly as she left.

Her 'good luck' was for an extremely important phone call I'd make once everyone cleared out. "Thanks," I said and inhaled the calming scent of damp plaster. "Isn't that a wonderful smell?" I asked Silverblade as he joined me on the rubble pile.

Silverblade sniffed the air and dismissed my comment with a shake of his head. He also pushed some dangling speaker wires out of his way and I made a mental note to fix those tomorrow.

"To your fiftieth episode," Silverblade said. He clinked my glass again and then pointed at my new ten-by-twelve-foot wall cutout. "Nice job, by the by."

"Thanks," I said as I shook more plaster from my scalp. "Wish you'd been here from the start."

"Me too," Silverblade said, topping up our glasses with his broken-necked bottle. "Unfortunately, a particularly unusual John Doe kept me rather busy." He paused. "I'm ever so sorry about the swordsman I recommended. He said he'd done jobs like this before."

"Probably not against this," I said, gingerly lifting my saw from a chunk of plaster and wiping its blade on my dusty jeans.

"Not that I'm bothered, but..." Silverblade paused. He turned an admiring glance toward the open door. His 'captee' stood there in her clinging wet dress. The dress wasn't hiding much. "...what life lesson did we teach your *Demolition Queen* viewers today?"

"That women can fend off attackers, demolish walls, be rescuers, and..." I said, hopping down from the rubble. "...anything else we put our minds to," I added as I headed into my favorite room, my workshop. Home to my beloved three-hundred-strong tool collection.

Inside, I studied the pegboard above my workbench. As Silverblade entered, I was making room for my saw. I'd just taken down a framed front cover of my latest book, *It's Not About the Wall*.

"I really enjoyed reading that. Loved that title too," Silverblade said picking up the frame.

For some reason, he turned it around. *Who does that?* Had he felt the photo taped on back? Or seen the uncomfortable look on my face as I stared at it?

Either way, now he was staring at the photo, the only one of Jake and me. We'd been caving/spelunking and were surrounded by stalagmites and stalactites. I was wrapped strapless-gown style in a blanket. Jake was bare-chested with his swirling tattoo peeking over low-riding jeans. Mud smudges covered our exposed skin, and we both clenched big ole cigars between smiling lips.

"So you were saying, about today's lesson?" he asked, gently setting the frame down.

"Don't let appearances fool you," I said answering his question and flashing my wickedest grin.

"You've terrorized another unsuspecting hardware lad, haven't you?" He chuckled and picked up a hammer engraved with the words "Knock 'em Dead." It was a gift from my mom, commemorating my first *Demolition Queen* episode.

"Hey, it was his own fault. Treated me like I didn't have a clue what to do with a crowbar," I said. Grabbing the hammer from Silverblade, I simulated the twirl, toss, and catch I gave the ten-pound chunk of metal above the lad's buzz cut.

Silverblade closed his eyes, breathed deep, and attempted to suppress a grin like a disapproving father. I assumed he was remembering our one and only hardware store trip together. Somehow, my presence flustered the poor clerk. He knocked over his own tower of paint cans.

"You don't exactly look like a typical customer with your hair, killer smile, and legs that won't quit," Silverblade teased.

"My point exactly. Shouldn't have to," I said, pursing my lips.

"Touché," Silverblade said and bowed his head.

"Ha-ha." I rolled my turquoise eyes. "Speaking of fencing, that last take went well, don't you think?"

Silverblade snorted. His head rocked back, and his shock of white hair flopped up and down. "The Fencing Federation would strip you of your titles if they'd seen your fencing today. Parries were sloppy, timing was off, and you're out of shape."

I bristled. "I'm not coming back to Silverblade boot camp, so forget it. After last time, I couldn't lift my arms high enough to brush my teeth for a week. Anyway, I'm holding out for your unbeatable move," I said.

"Only taught one person that move. Got to want it bad," Silverblade said, with a teasing frown as he patted his heart.

With that, I dropped to one knee. "Master, entrust me with your secret so that I may conquer a worthy opponent," I said. Adding an evil laugh, I lunged at Silverblade's ribs with fingertips pointed like a sword.

"I pity that poor sod." Silverblade laughed and then parried with his own flattened hand. He gave me a peck on the cheek before heading out the workshop door.

CHAPTER TWO

Exiting my workshop ten minutes later, the barn was like a tomb. My crew, Felicity, and the caterer were gone. Silverblade and his captee were gone too and probably together. Oddly, the one-man cleanup crew, *who I might add had cleaned up nothing*, was missing in action.

How long was I in there?

I checked the clock—ten minutes tops.

Impressive.

I was ecstatic to be alone. It was time for my phone call with Helen Palmer, CEO of MedMaker Corporation, the industry forerunner in biotechnology. Helen was about to introduce her most exciting product ever to the world. Simply named the MedMaker.

I sat, centered in front of my computer and the two industrial wooden spools that supported my red slab-of-concrete desk. Tapping my steel-toed boot against the left spool, a camouflaged fridge door popped open. I grabbed two mini *Demolition Queen* champagne bottles and two straws. Then I rang Helen.

"Hello, sweetie, how's your day been?" asked Helen.

Helen just happened to be the most brilliant woman I knew and…*my mom.*

I turned on my webcam and wiped plaster dust from the computer screen. A Savoy Hotel logo came into focus and then Mom's beautiful oval, smiling face. She looked elegant in an impeccably tailored black dress. Chocolate brown hair in a French twist. I'd swear the woman could pass for *Breakfast at Tiffany's* Holly Golightly.

Science never looked so glamorous.

"Mom, you can't be this cool and collected, not today," I said, angling my screen to see her better. "I'm so excited I can't stand it." I grinned as I straightened my black T-shirt and wiped dust from my jeans.

"Is that what you're wearing to my launch?" Mom asked with feigned outrage.

Feigned, because I wasn't really attending. Mom was superstitious about that. *Go figure.*

At least she let me watch via phone. Although, so far all I'd seen was her donning killer four-inch heels. Mom preferred looking the men in her male-dominated field, square in the eye. Me? I preferred twirling crowbars above their heads.

"Did you get my gift, your good luck box?" I asked with a grin.

Mom smiled and pulled a brand-new box of crayons from her briefcase.

Mom began the crayon tradition by putting a new box in my Christmas stocking every year. Somewhere along the line, crayons also became our good luck gift to each other.

"How about you for your fiftieth episode?" Mom asked, as she laid down her phone.

I nodded and shook my crayon box. Mine always included my favorite crayon color, Wild Watermelon. I inhaled the waxy scent on their smooth, pointed tips. *Almost as good as wet plaster.*

Then I wrinkled my nose as the backs of Max Carlisle's sharp-creased trousers moved into view. Mom's sales manager was peeking through the Savoy ballroom stage curtain like a little boy. I preferred that view to the formal shot I got as he turned around. Starched hankie. Large, scholarly tortoiseshell glasses. Hyper-serious expression. At least I couldn't smell his gross cologne from here.

Why Mom had hired this thirty-five-year-old I'd never understand. Yes, he went to Eton and Cambridge. Came highly recommended and did an excellent job. However, he was a condescending prick. Reminded me of someone too. Just couldn't think of who.

When MedMaker Corporation had problems earlier this year (i.e., corrupted files, stolen funds, and jailed employees), Mom was adamant that Max wasn't involved. Personally, I still thought he was hiding something. When nervous, the guy built long paperclip chains. *Suspicious.* Right?

"Bloody nuisance," Max whined, peeking between the curtains again. "Last year, I could have swung a very large dead hedgehog around that ballroom without hitting a soul."

Nice. Pick on defenseless hedgehogs.

"We have one disastrous year, and we get this," Max said, turning again. He was fidgeting with his posh Windsor-knotted tie and his glasses, plus pulling at an eyebrow.

The guy's a wreck. I grinned.

"Helen, they are going to rip us to shreds," Max said.

What a wimp. Mom expected an unpleasant surprise or two today, but you didn't see her going all mental.

"Well let's go see." Mom's chirpy voice made Max flinch.

Then "we" (Mom and "me" in her phone) brushed past Max, moved through the curtains, and squared off behind the lectern. Mom propped her phone up, aimed at the audience, so that hundreds of expectant faces stared at me from my computer screen. Shoulder to shoulder, business-suited women and men filled every chair. They lined the back wall and spilled down the sides too.

No demolition, no matter how intricate, huge or messy could have pulled me from my screen as Mom began.

"Hello, I'm MedMaker Corporation's CEO, Helen Palmer and I've spent the last fifteen years working on one thing," she said, and then paused. "I guess that makes me a workaholic." Another pause. "Hmm, or maybe I'm just slow."

The crowd laughed.

Mom was great at laughing at herself.

I didn't get that gene.

"Before I go any further, I would like to recognize my biggest supporter, my daughter, Sam. I couldn't have done this without her or BB."

BB.

I smiled.

BB was not a person. BB stood for Buckeye Balls. The best peanut-buttery-chocolate treats ever. They fit perfectly with Mom's all-time-best words of wisdom: "A chocolate buzz is always the answer."

Over the years, we'd made and consumed enough to feed all of the UK *and* France. When Mom pulled all-nighters on tricky MedMaker dilemmas, I brought dinner and my Buckeye Ball tin. I'd perch on her desk stool and talk to her on a speaker until she had time to emerge from the other side of her anticontamination lab's safety glass. I'd also deliver pep talks and pipe in inspirational tunes like "We Are the Champions" and "Ain't no Mountain High Enough." Of course, for celebrations, I brought champagne. Like the night Mom began trials on her first MedMaker test subject *Suzy Q.*

Now, I turned up the volume as Mom's voice went from laughing to serious.

"For too many years doctors have had to make do with inadequate tools such as time-delaying blood tests and ineffective medications," Mom said.

I knew she frowned too because several people in the front row were frowning *her* frown.

"Did you know that oftentimes between performing a blood test and beginning the prescribed medication, body chemistry can change? Sometimes, changing so drastically that by the time the prescription is administered, the medication and/or dose can be incorrect." Mom took a deep breath, and her voice quickened as she said, "Well that's about to change, all because of this flat cream-colored chip called the MedMaker."

She must have smiled because the front row was smiling.

On my computer screen, Mom's hand appeared in the top right corner. It held a flat square chip. Onscreen the MedMaker chip looked Oreo cookie-sized but most of the audience wouldn't even be able to see the quarter-inch square.

"Not only will this chip eliminate our current system that risks lives, wastes time, and throws away money…"

Mom paused, and the room was so quiet, I'd swear I heard Max pulling at his eyebrows.

"When implanted under the skin, it makes your cells smart enough to combat allergies, diabetes, bipolar disorders, asthma, and heart disease. It also administers vaccines and controls pain in the event of injury or terminal illness. My greatest hope is that one day very soon it will cure cancer." Mom beamed as she mentioned curing cancer. It was her biggest bugaboo.

The applause was so loud, I almost turned the volume back down but then the audience went quiet as Mom asked, "How does the MedMaker do all this?"

A man five rows back waved his hand.

Nice suit. Clean shaven. Too bad about the oil slick on his head.

I leaned toward my screen. *Wait a minute.* I knew him.

Mick Tambour. *Obnoxious reporter, will travel.* I punched my palm with my fist, wishing it was his face.

This last year, he'd contributed to MedMaker Corp's problems by trying to discredit Mom's groundbreaking feats. Luckily, he hadn't succeeded.

Tambour waved his hand again. My super-smooth Mom ignored him and seamlessly continued, saying, "By constantly monitoring the blood, the MedMaker knows when it needs to stimulate the immune system or, when necessary, administer gene-coded medicines. Medicines which it builds with elemental ingredients that it extracts from the body's waste."

As Mom said "body's waste," I could hear a hint of a smile in her elegant American/Brit accented voice. The front row was even smiling. No one else I knew could make those words sound elegant. *Hilarious.*

"So will we still need doctors?" Helen asked.

Once more Tambour's hand flew up.

Once more Mom ignored him.

"That's a resounding yes," Mom answered her own question again. "Not only will doctors prescribe the MedMaker for their patients, they will access and monitor it with the help of dedicated remote controllers. Controllers protected by impenetrable access codes."

This time when Mom's hand appeared on my screen, it held one of her dark blue palm-sized controllers. It had black buttons and a three-inch screen.

I was one of the first to see it work the night of the trial launch. While *Suzy Q* was tucked up at her own home, Mom pressed one button on *Suzy Q*'s MedMaker controller and *Suzy Q*'s white blood cells, iron, potassium, and vital statistics filled Mom's computer screen. It was so cool.

"Hard to believe this little thing can do all that," Mom said. She paused to let that sink in and then added, "Now, I could throw lots of mind-numbing technical stuff at you…"

Mom's teasing tone meant she was wrapping up. *Always leave 'em wanting more.*

"But that would be no way to show you my appreciation for coming here today. Suffice it to say this groundbreaking technology will save lives. Hopefully yours and the lives of loved ones." She paused. "Thank you very much."

Again, the crowd went wild. I couldn't even hear the corks pop as I opened my two champagne bottles. "Well done, Mom," I said, clinking them together. Putting a straw in each, I sipped first from mine and then Mom's. I had the fleeting thought that sipping from both might be bad luck, but this was one amazing day.

What could go wrong?

Next, Mom and "me" were on the move toward the back of the stage. I could see the left half of the audience where Tambour sat. I also saw Max's left side as he approached the lectern, smoothed his tie, straightened his glasses, and cleared his throat.

"Salutations, fair ladies and gents. I am Max Carlisle, MedMaker Corporation's sales manager." Max readjusted his glasses, *again*. "I have a prepared talk, so I promise I will not be magniloquent."

Puzzled looks abounded.

I stuck out my tongue at Max's onscreen image. This was the Max I knew and *didn't* love. Always throwing in obscure words that I had to look up. I'd seen his speech on Mom's desk earlier this week, so I'd already looked up and knew that magniloquent meant "lofty and extravagant in speech."

Continuing, Max said, "But first I must share with you my concerns about the MedMaker."

I froze.

What?

Mom had expected surprises but not within her own ranks.

"Yes, I am concerned about this product..." Max paused. "Because..." Another dramatic pause. "It is so superlative that the MedMaker could sell itself, and then I will be sans travail." Pause. "Without work?" He translated his French words with a smug chuckle and shifted his glasses yet again.

"Wanker," I said to my screen. "If you touch those glasses one more time, I'm going to rip them off your face."

Obviously, he couldn't hear me. He shifted his glasses another time.

"In fact," Max said, "its impenetrable access codes alone would—"

"Codes-schmodes," Tambour shouted from the aisle. He shook his fist too. "Enough of this technical shite. Let's talk financial cock-ups."

Gasps sounded around the room. Open-mouthed guests and reporters looked between Max and Tambour, then back at Max, who no longer looked reserved and upper-crust-like. More fight-ready schoolboy, I'd say. He'd crumpled his £200 tie and was clutching the lectern as if he was going to leap over it at Tambour.

Without warning, my view tilted again. It took a second before I realized Mom was on the move without "me." I saw her calves, trim back, and French twist steaming toward Max. She maneuvered between him and the microphone. Then she leaned over the lectern to address Tambour. I didn't have to see her face to know her expression. Her stern yet quiet and disappointed one. *The worst kind.* It worked as well on Tambour as it did on me. The standoff lasted all of five seconds until Tambour, rather intelligently as I saw it, took his seat.

Although, the idiot wasn't done.

"OK then let's talk about a missing *Doctors For ALL* group," Tambour blurted out. "I would bet this group sponsored by MedMaker Corporation has been ambushed for the medicines you supplied. So what are you going to do about it?"

"We do sponsor *Doctors For ALL* groups but they give basic medical aide and dig wells for fresh water. We donate the vaccines and antibiotics they use too, but nothing worthy of an ambush," Mom said.

Her cheeks were slightly red. Her lips were pursed too. I knew that look. It was her little-white-lie look. If Mom did know something, she'd have an awfully good reason for not telling it.

"Is it true that you funded this group to beef up public relations after your disastrous year?" he asked.

"If only it were that easy," Helen answered with a wry smile. "We've supported *Doctors For ALL* groups in the best of times too—"

"Nonetheless, your charitable PR could backfire," Tambour sneered. "Perhaps one of the volunteers is to blame."

"*Doctors For ALL* volunteers are medical specialists, professionals, and teachers. Hardly loose cannons," Mom said in a low, controlled voice. She meant business. "And let me make this perfectly clear. Concerns about my company's PR would be miniscule compared with our concern for the well-being of any group."

"So what would you be prepared to do if the group were in danger?" Tambour asked.

"Whatever it took," Mom said.

"OK, then let's go back to MedMaker Corporation's financials," Tambour said.

Tambour's line of questioning was dizzying.

Without missing a beat, Mom said, "I believe you used the words financial cock-ups, and yes, we suffered a near-fatal blow at the hands of a small band of insiders. But our multibillion-pound company is back on track, thanks in a large part to WhistleBlown Corporation and one very special man."

One very special man?

Mom held up this month's *Forbes* magazine. "Conrad Albany: A Man Who Only Wins," she said, reading the cover. "If you will allow me, I would like to read from the article's memorable first line." The corners of Mom's mouth lifted as she read. "In his spare time, Mr. Albany slaughters ninety-year-old women…at croquet." Mom paused over the *dot, dot, dot* a lot longer than I did when I first read it.

"While on the business battlefield, he skillfully pulls international corporations from death's grip," Mom read and looked up at the audience. "Sounds like someone you'd want on your side, right?" Helen grinned. "Now please join me in welcoming Mr. Conrad Albany, CEO of WhistleBlown and a Business Excellence Award nominee." Helen began the applause and turned toward the stage curtain.

Conrad's there?

Well, of course, Mom would have a backup plan.

I felt a little betrayed. She never mentioned my husband would be there.

He looked incredibly attractive as he walked on stage with his thick black hair that just touched the collar of his hand-tailored gray pinstriped suit but I felt no surge of wifely pride.

Husband.

The word still shocked me. The fact that I married Conrad, a man thirty years my senior, who was twenty-eighth in line to the throne, shocked me even more. Marriage *and* to a way older man from the upper *upper* crust? *Not my style.*

Although, there were some pretty good reasons for it at the time. Some of which, in order of weight or influence, were:

> 1. The nightmarish fog I sank into after Jake's death. I'd lost my soul mate. Nothing made sense or mattered.
>
> 2. Mom's high approval rating of Conrad as he became her company's savior.
>
> 3. Conrad pulled some of his royal-ish strings and miraculously saved me from landing me in the slammer after the Mousetrap Stalker's death. I felt like I owed him.
>
> 4. He was thoughtful, sensitive, and wanted to see me through the fog. (See #1.)
>
> 5. The man was persistent and persuasive as all get-out. He could get Imelda Marcos to go barefoot. *He was that good.*
>
> 6. Last but not least, he was attractive and charming with a presence that made people, *especially women*, do what he wanted. I called it the Conrad "cause." You did things "cause" Conrad wanted you to.

So as a distraction (see #1 again), I agreed to one date. That one date turned into a blur of Ascot, the Royal Box at Wimbledon, croquet soirees, and believe it or not, polo lessons (see #5).

Four months later, when Conrad proposed at Sandy Lane, Barbados, I vaguely remember thinking, *What the heck?* (See #4, #5, and then #4 once again.)

Six months on, #4 and #5 had become suffocating and overwhelming. The absolute worst part was that I didn't feel like myself around him.

To top it all off, he wheedled his way into my fencing sessions with Silverblade. Another reason, besides needing my arms, that I avoided Silverblade boot camp. Although, Conrad continued going and got way too good for my liking.

Conrad was extremely jealous but other than a protective arm around my shoulder once in a while, he never touched me. Fine by me. What wasn't fine was how he tried to control my life.

What the heck? More like, what the heck was I thinking?

I re-focused on my screen as Conrad gave Mom a quick hug. She looked ecstatic. I was happy about that.

Next, Conrad flashed his wide, cocksure smile at the audience. He then checked his wristwatch, worth more than most people's homes. "Do not worry, I shall only take a few moments of your time, and then I must dash," he said, in his very proper British accent. "Now, you might be thinking that as Helen's son-in-law, I might have given Helen's company extra special attention. I can assure you it only got a little bit." Conrad winked at the audience.

"So, what does WhistleBlown do? Well, we help corporations avoid and/or recover from Enron-type disasters. We do it every day. Usually, we discover these impending catastrophes because of anonymous information from company employees, stockholders, and customers. And because we guarantee anonymity, our sources openly share knowledge and concerns.

"Sometimes their reports pertain to price hikes and package colors. Just as often, they are about the theft, record falsification, and coercion similar to what MedMaker Corporation employees shared with us.

"In this case, after we received reports of wrongdoing, we went straight to Helen. As CEO, she approved our action plan, and in days we annihilated the internal multileveled scam," Conrad said. He smacked his hand on the lectern and flashed a triumphant smile.

Next Conrad turned toward Max. "Unlike you, I am not worried about job security. There will always be vermin attempting to swindle companies," Conrad paused and stared at Max for a couple of beats.

Inside joke? Accusation?

Either way it was a little awkward. It sure supported my Max suspicions.

Conrad finally looked back at the crowd and continued. "WhistleBlown has tremendously bad news for these vermin. We know all their tricks so they do not stand a chance," he said, glancing at his watch again. "Now it is time for you to enjoy canapés and a bit of fizz on MedMaker Corporation, so I thank you for your time."

Conrad waved manicured hands overhead like a bloody rock star before exiting through the velvet stage curtains. "Me" and Mom followed. I couldn't see much but heard Mom's killer heels tapping down stairs.

"Conrad thanks so much for coming," Mom said. "I was right. You made the perfect diversion for that little confrontation."

I knew they'd reached the Savoy's foyer because I saw Mom's pointy shoes on its marble floor, facing Conrad's perfectly buffed solid-black wingtips.

"I owe you one," Mom said.

"I assure you that is *not* the case." Conrad's shoes shuffled and pointed toward the door like he was about to leave. "Don't forget to be at Cranmont Manor, eight p.m. prompt, for this breast cancer fundraiser bother."

Glad he said that. Mom was notorious for getting stuck into work and forgetting social engagements. Of course, *that* gene I got.

"I don't need a costume for this, right?" Helen asked.

"I don't think you even need to bring your own bra." Conrad's grumbling voice retreated. "By the way, your daughter is impossible," he shouted from somewhere across the foyer.

"I know."

I heard the smile in Mom's voice and saw it as she studied her phone.

I was psyched. Time for our traditional debriefing. Except, as Mom stared at her phone her relaxed, happy expression went serious. "Has Rock rung you today?" she abruptly asked.

"No…" I said.

Rock. Real name Duncan Rockney. Rock for short. Seemed a fitting name for a guy who chased jungle viruses for a living. Oddly enough, he was a self-professed geek and one of the biggest scaredy-cats I knew. He was petrified of spiders and snakes, as in what would climb out from under a *rock*.

He'd been on Mom's MedMaker team until two years ago then took off to fulfill his real love, field virus studies.

"Rock keeps ringing then gets cut off before I can answer," Mom said in a stressed tone. "I'm a little concerned. He's supposed to be meeting up with Gabby to investigate a new virus somewhere. I'm not sure where," Mom added.

"He's probably ringing to congratulate you. And I'd bet Gabby took off to check out a bigger virus outbreak like last time," I said.

Gabby, was an ex-MedMaker Corp virus specialist too. She now split her time between teaching Chemistry at Denison University and doing what Rock did.

"So Mom about your launch—"

"Sam, I've got to ring you back," Mom said.

My screen went black. I leaned forward and tapped it. Stunned, I fell back in my seat.

Mom hung up on me?

"How quickly we forget our biggest supporter," I said.

CHAPTER THREE

After Mom hung up on me, I got over it the best way I knew how, Buckeye Balls. Taking one peanut-buttery-chocolate treat from my tin, I popped it into my mouth. About to go for another, I stared suspiciously at the tin. I'm a half-full kind of gal *except* concerning my tin. Clearly, it was half-empty, and I was pretty sure the missing half hadn't passed my lips.

I was still contemplating my tin when Silverblade reentered the barn. "Where have you been?" I asked. "More importantly, have you been eating my Buckeye Balls?"

His wrinkled brow, at the mere mention of peanut butter, answered my question.

"Any luck?" I asked.

"With my captee?" he asked and pushed his floppy hair aside. "I'll never tell."

"I see," I said, smiling.

"While I'm waiting for traffic to die down, take a look at this. He propped his open laptop on the shelf above my desk, beside my pocketknife collection. "A buddy of mine found this on YouTube," he said and pushed play.

His videos usually had odd morgue humor and ghoulish laughs so I considered myself lucky when the video had no sound. It began with a white shirt cuff filling the screen. The cuff had a two-inch circle of blood on it that someone was trying to scrub off using a large yellow sponge.

"What is this?" I laughed, giving Silverblade a skeptical look.

"Give it a minute." Silverblade nodded toward the computer.

All of a sudden, the circle of blood shape-shifted. It looked like a satellite image of a tropical storm.

Then it got interesting.

The hairy wrist inside the cuff shook, presumably trying to knock the blood off. But the swirling blood started moving up the sleeve. As it neared the shoulder, I couldn't see a face, but the man ripped open his shirtfront like a Superman wannabe. He desperately tried to pull the whole thing off, but his still-buttoned cuffs held tight. Barebacked and bare-armed, he bent at the waist hopping around with the shirt dangling from his wrists like a hairy Chippendale reject.

Meanwhile, the swirling red tentacles of blood started back toward the cuff.

The man freaked out. He stomped at his shirt then pulled and pulled to free his wrists. His left wrist popped loose, red and chafed, but the right, closest to the blood, held tight. A hand clutching a scalpel moved in and began sawing at the taut sleeve between cuff and blood. Bizarrely, the blood sped up. The person cutting lifted the blade just in time as the blood jumped over the cut line.

With that, the cutter drove his scalpel into the sleeve nearer the cuff and frantically sawed. The charging blood was inches from the scalpel when the "Chippendale" ripped away the remaining sleeve and tossed it onto the worktop near the sink. Then the sleeve, *all by itself*, inched toward the sink, and jumped in.

"So what do you think?" Silverblade asked.

"Wow. That's the first one you've shown me that didn't look like a five-year-old made it," I said, laughing, but realized I'd been clenching my fists.

"It could happen," Silverblade said with a smile.

"Right," I said. I could never tell if he was just trying to creep me out or if he really believed what he said.

"OK. OK," Silverblade said, closing his laptop and picking up the yellow knife beside his computer. "Tell me, why do you collect pocketknives?"

"My Dad started the tradition. After he died, Mom kept it up," I said. "But if you're looking to start your own collection, you'd better look elsewhere," I said teasingly.

"A yellow knife? I don't think so." He put it down and grabbed an evergreen one. He rubbed his thumb across its gashed side. "I'd pick this one. Looks like it's had an interesting life."

My smile froze. I couldn't help it. I snatched the knife from him and pocketed it. Why of all the knives in my collection did Silverblade have to pick that *one*? The *one* I'd recovered after months of searching the base of Jungfrau. The *one* I'd given to Jake, shiny and new, on the same amazing day I got my tattoo.

I knew Silverblade was staring at me, but I wasn't going to explain. "So, is our captee still here?"

"No, but I got her number," said Silverblade with a smile.

"Darn. I wanted to congratulate her. She did a great job looking at me with surprise," I said then added, "I also wanted to apologize for the water explosions—"

I was cut off as a foghorn ringtone blared from my back pocket.

"What explosions?" shouted an angry male voice, *also* from my pocket.

A look of displeased recognition passed over Silverblade's face.

"Sorry. Got to take this." I rolled my eyes, pulled out my phone, and smiled apologetically at Silverblade.

"I must get going anyway. See you next week," said Silverblade. He planted a fatherly kiss on my forehead, extracted his sword from where he'd stabbed it into the floor earlier, and bowed.

I blew him a kiss as he left and then plopped onto my desk chair. I paused to inhale the calming scent of wet plaster again before saying, "Conrad, I told you the foghorn is only for emergencies—"

"What explosions, and where the blazes are you? You're not renovating my tower, are you?"

I didn't need a webcam to know that his mouth and cheeks were squeezed tight, and his half-angry/half-scared gray eyes had gone the color of wet cement.

"Conrad, I wouldn't touch your Cranmont Tower. You asked me not to." *Plus, he'd had a hissy fit when I asked if I could.* "Today, I'm filming in the barn. The explosions were merely small, controlled special effects."

Small, controlled special effects? I'd sliced right through hot water pipes. Along with that bald-faced lie, I twisted strands of hair around my fingers.

"What if you'd been hurt in that barn?" he sputtered. He hated the barn.

Not that I blamed him.

His mum's prized thoroughbreds used to live here. Evidently, the old bat paid way more attention to them than Conrad, her only child. Of course, I didn't help things when I chose "that barn" as my home office over a suite in Conrad's forty-room eighteenth-century pride and joy, Cranmont Manor.

At least he didn't mind if I pulled down a wall or two in here.

"I've been frantic," Conrad hissed. "But I breathed not a word of it to your mother so as not to mar her big day."

My mother?

Mom would never go ballistic like this.

He'd gone too far and knew it. So I wasn't surprised when he played the scared card.

"Samantha, darling, ever since those horrible bricks fell on you in the MedMaker annex, I immediately thought the worst—"

"Defective." I bristled. "Defective bricks."

The bricks were like dole valves. They let moisture in, but not out. Their insides became mush, so they crumbled like sand castles *except* for their mortar. Those rigid bits hit me like a ton of bricks, literally. My scalp tingled just thinking about how they'd knocked me out.

The worst part was that Conrad found me bloody and unconscious in the derelict annex building scheduled for demolition later this year. He was so hysterical, the emergency crew almost put him on the stretcher. So I didn't plan on telling him that Mom had given me permission to film a Demolition Queen episode there in a couple weeks.

Maybe an apology would shut him up.

"Conrad, I didn't mean to scare you—"

"Samantha, this *Demolition Queen* and carpe momo bollocks has to stop."

Here he goes again.

Carpe momo was a term Felicity and I coined after copious amounts of red wine on a Tuscan holiday. It meant "seize the moment." After that, carpe momo and empowering women became *Demolition Queen*'s mission.

Conrad's and my definitions of seizing the moment were worlds apart. Conrad's was smoking obscenely expensive cigars. Mine? Wielding dangerous electrical tools to demolish really big things.

"It is unseemly and highly embarrassing to track down my wife with a foghorn, and I won't do it anymore."

Good.

Rolling my eyes, I opened the yellow knife and hurled it at a dartboard fifteen feet away. I expected Conrad's usual "I am twenty-eighth in line for the throne" rant so when I realized he'd hung up, I was pleasantly surprised.

Plus, my knife hit the dartboard, dead center.

CHAPTER FOUR

Exiting the barn, I frowned at the sooty-gray clouds crowding the sky above Cranmont Manor. Not to worry. It wouldn't dare rain on a party at Conrad's pride on the hill, his baby, his most prized possession…

What the heck?

My eyes bugged out at his manor. Usually it resembled a huge sand-colored castle with soaring stuck-on Doric columns. Tonight, Cranmont was more of a "Pepto Bismol pink" gift box. It had one huge pink bow centered over the front door while wide pink ribbons hugged its columns and then stretched down the manor's sides toward the rear terrace doors.

Was that the true source of Conrad's foul mood? Or the multicolored hive of caterers, florists, and sound/lighting technicians swirling on his stone steps. Mrs. Party, the party planner to London's upper crust was shouting at its center. The woman's voice was worse than a nail gun without ear protectors. I should know. Her rapid-fire staccato voice gave me a headache at Lord and Lady Wolverhampton's thirtieth wedding anniversary a month ago.

To avoid it all, I jogged around to the right and was startled to see an ambulance, partly obscured by one of Cranmont's twenty-foot high hedges. Surely, it was there as a precaution for tonight's eight-hundred-plus party crowd.

No attendants were inside. Probably stretching their legs. *Going to be a late night for us all.*

Passing the ambulance, I squeezed through a small gap in the hedge and walked through a dark boulder archway into Cranmont's "secret" tunnel. With just four little words, I made it my personal playground.

"Lights," I said. With that, a hundred yards of sloping, cobbled, seventeenth-century tunnel lit up.

Then I said, "Music." Barry White's sexy baritone voice enveloped me. *Mmmm.*

"Zip wire," I called out and overhead, a leather strap buzzed toward my raised right hand.

When I renovated last month, the lights and music were essential, but this zip wire was pure indulgence. Especially its hyper-speed acsensor, suited more to black-ops missions. I just liked knowing I had an alternate and speedy escape route from Cranmont.

I grabbed the strap, slipped my boot into its stirrup, and flicked on the acsensor. With hair flying, I torpedoed along the zip wire, up the slanted passage. *Pure exhilaration.*

Cranmont's tunnel had a cool turning circle about midway up, which opened to the sky. I reached it in seconds. Daylight was fading and I was moving super-fast, but one of its steel-strapped doors looked ajar.

Convinced since day one that there were secret tunnels and mysterious goings-on, I was dying to get inside those doors. I'd even tried picking their locks, a skill I'd nurtured from a very young age. How else would I have kept up with Mom's super-secret work at MedMaker Corp?

So the fact that several of Cranmont's doors had not succumbed really ticked me off.

I'd slammed on the brakes to investigate that ajar door when *whamo,* a screeching Led Zeppelin guitar solo cut off my beloved Barry White.

Nothing against Zeppelin, just this particular song. It had been *Jake's favorite.* In the last three days, without warning, it had played ten separate times. Even after deleting it from my playlist.

"Zeppelin off," I shouted. My echoing voice sounded like a crazy person's, but at least Barry White came back and crooned once more.

I focused on the door. Close up it no longer looked open. I pulled hard on its handle, but it didn't budge.

Shoot.

I climbed back on, finished zipping to the tunnel's mansion end and hopped off at the old basement kitchen, the sight of a true lock-picking success.

***

My first day at Cranmont when I snuck inside that kitchen, it was *Great Expectations* personified. No mice ran in and out of wedding cakes. But there were eighty licked-clean soup bowls sitting beneath cobwebs that swirled like cotton candy pyres to the chandeliers. Decayed carcasses languished on dust-covered trolleys beside an out-of-order dumbwaiter too.

I was incredibly engrossed in my find. So when the Irish housekeeper's round weathered face appeared out of nowhere, it scared the crap out of me.

"How in blazes did you get in here?" she asked, pressing down her frizzy hair.

"It was open," I lied even as lock-picking tools pressed against my thigh. "So what's the story with this place?" I asked.

The housekeeper nervously looked toward the open kitchen door and then said, "Five years ago, Mr. Albany's mum, Wilhelmina, dropped dead in here just before the soup course. Guests were quite upset." She nodded gravely, and then added, "About the soup, not Wilhelmina. She was a right bitch." The housekeeper cackled.

***

I was standing there smiling at the kitchen lock, remembering that day, when out of nowhere came another voice. Although this one was deep and shaky, it too scared the crap out me.

"Madam."

I spun around and stared at Conrad's half-deaf nonagenarian butler. "James, my man, you've got to stop this whole lurking butler act. It really freaks me out," I said into his good ear.

Having said that, it also cracked me up. Straight out of central casting, James came complete with starched morning coat and spotless white gloves. He was hunched and squeaky, like Dick van Dyke's old banker in *Mary Poppins*.

Standing that close, I noticed for the first time that his earlobe had five small stitches. "James, do you have a wild side?" I teased.

James blinked watery eyes at me but didn't appear to have heard. So I shouted, "How about you save me a dance tonight at the fundraiser?"

"Regretfully, I will not be attending," James said. He eyed my jeans and T-shirt as if to imply madam should not attend either. Then he straightened and announced, "Mr. Albany wishes to see the lady of the manor in Old Mr. Albany's study."

Geez. He was forever reminding me of my lady of the manor status, as if I didn't take it seriously enough, which I didn't. I can only imagine what he thought of me, the brash American.

"Yes, sir," I saluted, leaving James to freak out someone else.

I took the basement stairs three at a time.

It was too late to impress James.

CHAPTER FIVE

Emerging into Cranmont's quarter-acre "den," or rather *our* den, I was relieved no party-helpers were around. Conrad went ballistic the last time non-Cranmont staff saw me looking "rough," as he put it.

I lurched across the room and peeked around the den's broad oak door into the art gallery. *Total chaos.* No one seemed to notice me as I darted behind a humongous pink thermometer, advertising the Breast Cancer Fundraiser's goal: "£25 Million!"

No one noticed me either when I leaped onto the grand sweeping stairway. Mostly because a thick curtain of pink helium balloons, tethered to the railings, went all the way up to the fourth floor.

I raced up a flight and then skipped along the upstairs hall where red sixteenth-century Tibetan silk walls absorbed all noises from downstairs. I peered inside Old Mr. Albany's study. Inside this quintessential country gentlemen's retreat, I saw wall-mounted deer antlers, hunt prints, and plaid nubby-wool wing chairs, but no Conrad.

I got that a lot. Being summoned to the study when Conrad wasn't even *in* the study.

However, he *had* been here. Quiet strains of his favorite Vivaldi violin duet floated in cigar-marinated air, and hundreds of bright multicolored Snood faces taunted me from his computer screen.

Snood.

Conrad was obsessed with this American computer game. Connecting three identical Snood faces to make them all disappear didn't fit his modus operandi. The game ticked none of his top priority boxes such as…

Improving Cranmont Manor
Making money
Collecting fine art
Networking with very, very important social and business contacts

It made even less sense to be playing when eight hundred guests were about to arrive at his stately manor. Curious to check out his scores, I barely touched his still-warm mouse when each and every Snood face morphed into a red, beady-eyed skull, and these words ran across the screen: "Game Over—Resume Life."

Resume life?

Boy, I would if I could.

CHAPTER SIX

The words "Game Over—Resume Life" still circled my brain as I raced into the expansive fourth floor guest suite. Except for a quick overnight business trip to her Paris office, Mom had stayed in the suite every night this week so we could hang out and catch up.

I was still hoping to fit in that de-brief before the party. Sadly, the only *Mom* things here were clothes, the Matisse line drawing she gave me as a wedding gift, and a five-foot-square painting that she'd started last year and added new lines and swirls to every time she visited. Both pieces of artwork usually lived in the barn but were here for safekeeping during the demolition.

I quickly straightened them and turned to go, but then I spotted a box with green-striped wrapping paper, smack in the middle of Mom's king-size bed.

Stepping closer I read its small gift tag.

Sam.

Living dangerously, Mom?

I grinned. I was notorious for opening gifts before their time.

I already knew it was not just a gift. Mom's gifts never were *just* gifts.

Any gift worth having is worth a hunt.

Her hunts came with clues.

I unhappily discovered this at age five when the clue solving and hunt for my Easter basket took six hours. At age ten, I was not impressed when it took a week to find my birthday present, a Dremel drill set, in our stables. By then my pony Tonka had nibbled it.

After years and years of Mom's clue training, I'd improved. Even enjoyed it *sometimes*. Mom still stumped me most of the time. Only once did I ever solve something before her.

***

We were at a Yankees–Red Sox game, sharing a box of Cracker Jacks. Its prize wrapper had a puzzle on it. I could still picture the instructions and diagram like it was yesterday:

You may move only one thing to make the ends of the matchstick U's touch each other. (See diagram)

The open ends of the matchstick *U*'s faced each other, spaced a matchstick length apart.

"Let's solve this together," Mom said.

She removed hairpins from her French twist to set up two *U*'s on my baseball program. Of course each time we moved a hairpin to make the *U*'s touch the other *U* was disassembled.

Until, all of a sudden, it made perfect sense to me.

"Do you give up?" I asked Mom.

Mom's surprised but skeptical look was priceless. I knew how to solve a puzzle that she couldn't.

My knowledge came from years of reading in bed. When my tired arms sagged and the book got closer and closer to my face, eyes relaxed. With that, the middle two inches of the line I was reading would 'disappear'. Words to the left and right of those two inches would merge, *touch*.

Grinning like a hyena, I showed Mom how it worked. I held the Cracker Jack prize wrapper eight inches from her face and told her to look at the *U*'s but relax her eyes. Then I slowly moved the wrapper closer and closer. At five inches, she still looked skeptical, but at four inches, she looked amazed.

"I see it. The matchsticks *U*'s are touching," Mom exclaimed.

She also said three words I'd never forget: "You beat me."

***

"Turn up the speakers," bellowed Mrs. Party from the terrace. "Five minutes to party time."

The woman was four stories down but so loud she could have been right outside. I looked toward the window. At that exact moment a flash of light reflected off the scaffolding poles atop condemned Cranmont

Tower. For the first time I noticed a gaping hole in the wall around the tower's top. One of the huge square stones was missing. *Not surprising.* Conrad said the place was dangerous.

"Well don't just sit there, get moving," shouted Mrs. Party.

Whom Mrs. Party shouted at this time was a mystery, but it got *me* moving.

I looked down at the ripped gift-wrap littering Mom's king-size bed. I'd done it again. I was staring at an intricate inlaid wooden box. Its lid had a thick dark border that framed a princess gripping a chisel. *Interesting gift.*

Of course, Mom would notice the empty bed. She'd also shake her head and laugh. Even so, I balled up the paper, grabbed the box, and raced out of the guest room like a naughty child.

As I hit the landing, balloons on the stairs were swaying as if someone, maybe Mom, was on the way up.

I wrenched open the walk-in linen closet door to hide the evidence. Just before I shoved the box under a stack of fluffy duvets, I spotted the words, *an eye for an eye,* in the box's frame. *Hmm.*

I also noticed a layer of soot on the top duvet and swatted at it. The tiniest lady-of-the-manor voice urged me to "tell the housekeeper about the soot." *Yes, definitely, later*, I thought as I backed out of the closet. I slammed the door, expecting to see Mom on the landing but it was empty.

Although, from the excited voices drifting up the spiral stairs, the art gallery was not.

Shoot.

I was late for my own party.

CHAPTER SEVEN

Dressed and ready, I leaned over the upstairs railing to survey the art gallery where the already raucous fundraiser crowd swarmed. It was an amazing sight. Guests screeched their hellos and threw air kisses. Popping champagne corks crisscrossed overhead. Every guest wore at least some pink in support of tonight's breast cancer charity.

It was highly entertaining, but I couldn't stop speculating about the inlaid design on Mom's gifted box. *What could the princess carrying a chisel mean? Was I the princess?* Her clue "an eye for an eye," written in the lid's border, sounded ominous. *Did Mom mean for me to start a scavenger hunt tonight?*

Well, it would have to wait for even though my good friend Lady Wolverhampton was running tonight's fundraiser, I had to give the formal onstage welcome and mention tonight's auction. The auction items were meant to be quite amazing but then so were the take home goodie bags. They held designer watches and perfumes worth several times what I shelled out for Mom's sixtieth birthday. *Incredible.*

Lady Wolverhampton was one smart cookie. She had to be to reach tonight's £25 million auction goal. First, she'd chosen Cranmont and Conrad. The perfect mix to draw masses of people. Conrad lived to show off Cranmont. With all these people admiring his home and his one-of-a-kind art collection, his mood should be euphoric.

Or not, I thought as I noticed that Mrs. Party had erected huge plasma screens that covered every single Monet, Turner, and Picasso. *Oh boy. Things could get ugly.*

Although, not as ugly as the dress I was wearing. Conrad bought it specially for tonight. Its tiers of net tutus from the knees down were so tight I had to waddle. The party could be over by the time I crossed the art gallery and the ballroom to teeter onto the terrace stage.

I was starving too. Every time my stomach rumbled every damn tutu shook.

At least Felicity had arrived. We could joke about my dress.

I watched her struggle across the foyer's pink-carpeted threshold. She was hugging a tripod and two cameras to her chest. She also lifted the hem of her vintage designer gown to edge around Mrs. Party. Luckily, the short, hyper party planner was busy berating a hunky tuxedoed waiter about pomegranate seeds not floating in champagne flutes filled with hundred-pound-a-bottle champagne.

Head down, Felicity maneuvered around a bubble-gum-pink kazoo and accordion band and then scooted past the humongous pink thermometer. I thought she was history as her tripod knocked two goodie bags off their table, but she lucked out once more.

"Here comes another wave of guests." Mrs. Party clapped.

With that, Felicity did a double take at the bank of photographers, corralled near a feathery pink tunnel. I could tell what she was thinking. Conrad's cronies wouldn't excite these photographers, let alone retirement home dearies. So why were they jockeying for position with cameras aimed at the front door?

I felt a little guilty. Two years ago, Felicity and I would have endlessly chatted about tonight's details. But after Jake died, I clammed up. Then I married Conrad, the "non-chandelier swinger," as Felicity put it, and things got worse.

Tonight was only Felicity's second visit to Cranmont. *Her first?* My uncharacteristically lavish wedding, courtesy of the same crazed woman who just clapped her hands again to signal the arrival of a white-and-chrome stretch limo. With that, the kazoo and accordion band began a painfully loud rendition of "Oh When the Saints Come Marching In."

Felicity peered through her video camera but a second later her head whipped up and around it. A non-Conrad-crony had arrived. In fact, it was a gold medal Olympic sprinter wearing a coppery-pink creation on her lithesome torso and a Chelsea football star on her arm. Next, a stretch Humvee pulled up. When two gorgeous Hollywood A-listers hopped out and strolled past her, I could tell she was itching to follow.

So I texted: *Leave video rolling. Bring little camera. Meet in art gallery.*

In a blaze of pink, she took off to follow the actors past the paparazzi and through the feathery tunnel. So, I hiked up my dress to clamber halfway down the stairs. I peeked through the tethered pink helium balloons as she was squeezing into the gridlocked art gallery and wading through throngs of guests. She'd aimed her camera straight up to the top of the circular stairway above me. Slowly, she turned, scanning down and around the ballooned railings.

Her camera scanned right past me.

It stopped.

It backed up.

Good, she's seen me.

I expected a big smile, so wasn't prepared for her grimace.

Or her lens turning like it was zooming in.

Or her almost dropping her camera.

Or her looking around her camera with eyes bugging out.

It was safe to say she didn't like my dress or anything about my appearance. I needed to get down there fast to explain *and get food.* With my dress still hiked up, I made great time. But near the bottom when I pulled my hem back down I got into trouble.

Delicious smelling eggrolls were on their way past and I went for them. Mid-stride my left leg hit my dress front and I started to tip toward a well-aged rock star with surprised-looking hair.

Trying to slow down, but mostly trying not to look like a complete idiot, I wrapped one arm around tons of balloon strings and yanked. Unfortunately, I set enough balloons free to suspend a small pony *and* slowed myself down so much that a scarecrow-thin model plopped *my* egg-rolls into *her* skinny little mouth.

Grrrr.

OK. Egg rolls were out, so I chose fruit. Pomegranate seeds to be exact. They were floating in champagne, which was also technically a fruit.

It was a win-win.

Sandwiched between the walk-in humidor and a tall, thick row of Mrs. Party's palm shrubs, I scanned the crowd. Felicity was near the bar. I was about to join her when I smelled an obnoxious floral scent, wrinkled my nose, and dove behind the shrubs.

I peeked past the expanding waistline of an ex-*Dancing with the Stars* contestant and confirmed my suspicions. The scent belonged to Prunella Poppledish, the 'psycho'-bitch and WhistleBlown client who despised me just for marrying Conrad.

Prunella was glaring up at the "champagne flute" of balloons. Eyes flashed green, the color of envy. She kind of smiled, which for Prunella wasn't easy, given her too-taut face. Everything about Prunella was taut, even her voice.

"That wretched demolition American sleeps with her tools, you know." Prunella's smug, high-pitched whisper was loud enough for people on the terrace to hear.

Although, Prunella's accusation was hardly a new one. My tool obsession was widely known. For the record, I did sleep with a screwdriver once, but the story was not as interesting as it sounded. It was my bookmark. It fell out during the night. *Honest.*

Prunella kept yapping. "I am certain she requested everyone wear pink because it makes me look jaundiced."

I wish I could take credit.

The mousy man beside Prunella patted her shoulder and said, "Darling, no one would do that."

"Oh, shut up you silly man," Prunella said with such force that her plate tipped.

She was so busy abusing her escort, Prunella didn't notice her egg roll had gone AWOL.

It hit the floor and bounced to the base of my palm shrub. My mouth watered. Every tutu shook. *Ten-second rule? I was going in.*

I turned my head so far to reach it that when my arm brushed something hairy, I couldn't see what it was. Either Lady Wolverhampton forgot to shave again, or…I whipped my head around, and Conrad's bare knee brushed my nose. *Ugh.*

"My darling Samantha, what are you doing?" Conrad's quiet voice sounded good-natured enough, but as he pulled me up his grip on my upper arm actually hurt.

It might have been worse. Prunella could have seen Conrad and descended on him like a Labrador on its dinner. She'd have left drool dripping from his formal plaid kilt and black cutaway jacket. *Yuck.*

"What is that bulbous satin monstrosity in my ballroom?" Conrad pointed through the art gallery doors at a twelve-foot-high bra. I noticed that his frozen "not in front of our guests" smile held back a downright scary frown.

I followed his pointing finger to the bra, my London theater prop shop find. I noticed that it nearly touched his turn-of-the-century chandelier. *Looked smaller in the shop.*

"Lady Wolverhampton said it's the best donation pot and formal photo backdrop she's seen," I gushed. "She also said that Cranmont has attracted the largest crowd for this event ever." My turquoise eyes smiled into his. I batted my eyelashes to the swift beat of the terrace swing band. I was going to be sick.

"Largest crowd ever?" Conrad asked and a hint of a smile soothed his brow.

I nodded.

Done and dusted.

That was *until* the same Led Zeppelin guitar solo from the tunnel screeched out of the ballroom speakers. It obliterated the swing band's beat, and Conrad roared like a lion. Startled guests watched open-mouthed as he raised his fist and stomped toward the speaker controls beside his walk-in humidor.

Mere inches from impact, I caught his arm and shouted, "Zeppelin. Off."

Instantly, Led was dead.

"Bloody electronics," Conrad chortled to his guests.

Amused guests returned to food, drink, and gossip.

An *unamused* Conrad twisted his arm from my grip and hissed in my ear. "Your bloody system recognizes verbal commands in fifty languages and can be changed from China, for Christ's sake, so do something about this Lord *Zippelin* or else."

Or else what? I was used to Conrad's little tantrums, but this caustic mood change was entirely different.

He turned to leave. His kilt pleats flew out around his knees. I was so close to escaping, and then the obnoxious floral scent got stronger.

Shoot.

"Oh my. What a lovely sight," Prunella said. With eyes riveted on Conrad's kilt, she pushed a palm frond out of her way. Then she squeezed in beside Conrad like she must have squeezed into that gown. Even her neck had cleavage.

Well, if I can't escape, I might as well have fun.

"Darling, you look a little jaundiced," I said as I turned "concerned" eyes on the witch. Having said that, Prunella's true skin color was a mystery, buried beneath thick clotted foundation. "I hope you're OK," I added, using my best lady-of-the-manor imitation. A bit of modest superiority and condescension with kindness.

Right at that moment, some Royal Navy muckety-muck clapped Conrad on the shoulder. So Conrad was shaking hands with him as Prunella continued our sparring match.

"I thought the invite said no costumes." Prunella smirked at my dress with an evil "two can play this game" expression. She finished with another angry swat at a bent palm frond that was tickling her neck.

"No costumes tonight," Conrad said, turning back and giving Prunella his full attention.

"Prunella, this isn't a costume," I said. "This is the dress that Conrad handpicked for me." *Take that, you bitch.*

"Conrad, you are such a dear," Prunella said. So much smug charm oozed from her every pore that her foundation should have been making popping sounds. She tried to bat her surgically over-tightened eyelids, but that was a messy affair.

I would have thrown up, but my stomach was still empty.

"You must be the most wonderful husband in the world," Prunella added. She swatted at the intruding frond again before latching onto Conrad's arm. "Conrad, you'll have to tell me where you shop while we dance."

"Why certainly," Conrad said, looking pleased to be in her company even with the furious face she made as that same palm frond smacked her neck again.

Go figure.

"I'll be back," he said over his shoulder.

I wasn't sure if that was a threat or a promise. Either way I wasn't sticking around to find out.

"You can come out now," I said to the potted palm as Conrad and Prunella moved away.

"That was fun," Felicity said, sliding from behind her pot.

"Too true." I grinned.

"I hate that I agree with that bitch, but dear Lord, your dress," Felicity said as she tugged at the plate-sized silk rose near my neck. "There I was filming those spectacular balloons on the stairway. I'm thinking beautiful, gorgeous, perfection—until I see this matronly-looking head and shoulders poking through. Pearls. Spinster bun. That ridiculous fuchsia gown. What's happened to you?"

"Tell me about it." I grimaced. I tossed my small beaded evening bag to Felicity so I could roll up my hem again to walk.

"What's in your bag tonight?" Felicity asked, bouncing it in her hand.

"Pocketknife, several clamps, soldering wire. Oh, and duct tape. The usual stuff," I said.

"Too bad you can't fix your dress with them."

Hmm. I snatched my bag back.

"I've got to be on stage in ten minutes. We'd have to be quick. Want to help?" I called over my shoulder as I bolted for the walk-in humidor, already ripping the largest of five tutus from my hips.

"This is the Sam I know and love," Felicity said, helping pull hairpins from my bun.

CHAPTER EIGHT

Ten minutes later, I was on my way to the terrace stage to welcome everyone. Felicity followed, not for moral support but as "sag wagon" for my dress. We went a little crazy with the deconstruction. The reconstruction was kind of out-there too. While I artfully wove the bodice together with soldering wire, Felicity used bright spring-loaded clamps to secure the back. With the help of a new very long slit up the side, I was taking full strides too.

The packed ballroom looked impossible to get through, so we'd gone outside and around. Halfway to the terrace, we were rewarded with a gorgeous sight. A waiter pulling on black trousers and a crisp white tuxedo shirt.

Grinning and silently giggling, we crouched behind a shrub as he began talking to himself. Or at least I thought he was talking to himself.

"Damn these Brits and their friggin' fancy dress. Are you sure about this?" the waiter asked as he clipped on a cummerbund covered in pink satin roses with an oversized bra clasp at the back.

"Uh-huh. It's for charity," a bemused British-accented voice said. "Funny thing you doing *up* a bra clasp. Wouldn't have thought putting *on* a bra, would be in your skill set."

"Ha-ha," the waiter said as he donned formal white gloves.

"You look fabulous," the Brit laughed.

"Just let me know when she gets here," the waiter said.

"And how about the other one?" asked the Brit we still hadn't seen.

The waiter said nothing.

"My friend, if she affects your mood, ergo our working relationship, it is my business. So why risk it?" the Brit asked.

The waiter didn't answer.

"Man, this one is going to break your heart," said the Brit.

"I don't have a heart, remember? Another woman took it," the waiter said with a grimace. "Get back to work."

That was odd. From their banter, I'd assumed they were gay.

"OK, OK," said the Brit.

We followed him toward the terrace dance floor where he hoisted a pink Lucite hors d'oeuvres tray overhead. I lost sight of him as he squeezed between loud, gyrating guests.

I'd have loved to know which woman that hunk had been talking about, but as I climbed onto the stage, I focused on Lady Wolverhampton. "You look gorgeous," I said, giving her a kiss on each cheek.

"Dearie, no one's going to be looking at me," she said, eyeballing my altered dress and its new plunging neckline.

I blushed. I had a feeling her astonished expression wouldn't be the last.

"You've done the most fantastic job," I said. "Everyone's here. It's like a who's who of the world on this dance floor." I meant it too. But I was actually watching the waiter who I'd spotted making his way up Cranmont's curved terrace stairs.

"I think it's time to begin," said Lady Wolverhampton.

"You're sure you want me to do this?" I asked, pointing at the lectern. "You've worked so hard."

"They'll be tired of my voice by the end of the evening," she laughed. "You're perfect for this. You're the Demolition Queen and lady of the manor." She said "lady of the manor" *exactly* like James had.

I cleared my throat and bent to speak into the microphone, hoping the waiter would turn and look, which he did, but so did everyone else. Especially as I yelped loudly. Something had jabbed my chest and I knew, without looking, that it was soldering wire. I smiled apologetically at Mrs. Wolverhampton, casually adjusted the wire, and then said, "Ladies and gentlemen, I am Sam Albany, and I've been given the great pleasure and honor of welcoming you on behalf of the committee. We thank you so much for supporting this worthy cause."

The roar of applause was overwhelming *and* fun. As it died down, a twenty-foot-wide plasma screen flickered on behind me and lit the smiling faces in the crowd.

"You might not have noticed this in the ballroom." I joked as the donation bra filled the screen. I paused as guests laughed. "This is where you can put all your pocket money." I grinned and rubbed my hands together like a greedy merchant. More laughs. "But save your really big bucks, because you'll want to bid on auction items like this," I added as, on screen, George Clooney walked out of a sprawling ornate Italian villa.

"If you bid enough, you could vacation at my villa," said George's sexy, smiling voice. *But* his onscreen lips weren't moving. It was because the *real* George was there, moving into the spotlight beside me.

George was no Bob Vila, my home renovation hero, *but he'd do in a pinch.*

"Everyone please welcome the marvelous George Clooney," I said, applauding.

With that, he swept me into a playful hug and I felt indescribable pain. His hug had repositioned one of my clamps. Instead of creatively holding my dress together, it was chomping extra sensitive skin between my shoulder blades. I had to get out of there.

Pecking George on the cheek, I made my getaway. As I climbed the terrace steps, the pain got worse. Felicity, who could have helped, was nowhere in sight. By the time I hit the clogged ballroom doors, I almost couldn't see for the pain. I wanted to rip someone's head off. Instead, my fingers ferociously went for the only thing in reach, a pink cummerbund at the base of a broad, muscular back. They pulled hard and then let go.

Smack.

Instantly, furious gold-specked eyes crowded my face. I tried arching away but my clamp pinched harder. A new, more excruciating pain shot down my legs too. I couldn't move let alone react as the angry man leaned against me. His cummerbund pressed against my stomach.

I wanted to bolt.

Then I blinked.

The pain was gone.

I heard a clanging sound and saw my red clamp resting against the base of a martini glass on the waiter's pink tray.

He cleared his throat and I looked up. This was the waiter from outside. He flashed the most mesmerizing smile.

Furious to charming in under sixty seconds? Kind of like Conrad.

He smelled delicious.

I heard the auctioneer rapping his gavel for bids on George's villa, but with this mesmerizing, delicious man in my face, my brain was thinking, *Villa what? George who?*

"How about a martini? Owner's filthy rich so it's all top-shelf brands." He nodded conspiratorially and put his tray between us. I smelled cinnamon, apple, and boysenberry.

So he doesn't know who I am?

Martinis weren't my thing, but if martinis were what he was offering, then that's what I was drinking. Anything for another chance to ogle him.

"Start with the cinnamon one. Might warm you up," he said, staring at my chest.

With 50 percent less fabric and 100 percent less netting, every contour stood out, so to speak.

"Thanks," I said. I vaguely heard the auctioneer offer the second of three holidays at George's villa. Meanwhile, through my lashes, I studied this ruggedly handsome waiter. His slightly off-center nose hinted at violence, but something about his lips made me want to touch them. I couldn't stop staring.

Our eyes locked. The auctioneer's voice dropped away as if I was wearing industrial-strength earplugs. Not only that, I felt a shift in my chest, and it wasn't soldering wire. I stared for what felt like forever. He stared too.

Finally, the auctioneer's gavel brought me back. "The third villa holiday goes to the Wolverhamptons," the auctioneer announced as party noises roared in my ears.

The Clooney holidays were all gone and so was my cinnamon martini. I now held an apple one and the waiter was grinning at me.

"You want help getting out of your clothes?" I asked and then shook my head. "I mean cummerbund…?"

"I thought you'd never ask," he said with a laugh. His grin got maddeningly wider.

What is wrong with me? Alcohol and no food?

I hoped that was it. This was ridiculous. I silently swore off martinis.

"That cummerbund looks ridiculous," I said, to hide my embarrassment. I glared at it, but already missing his gaze, I forsook the martini ban and turned back for a boysenberry one.

Alas, he was gone.

"Nice face," Mom said, leaning her smooth oval one into my line of sight. "And here I thought you'd be happy to see me," she added, with hands on hips.

I rearranged my disappointed frown into a smile. Didn't want Mom reading me like a proverbial book.

"I've been looking for you forever…," I checked my watch and said. "How could it be ten-thirty already? You've missed so much fun." *And you show up when it was getting really interesting.* I surreptitiously inventoried the nearby groups, but my waiter was nowhere in sight.

"I'm sorry. As usual, work kept me busy," Mom said and a frown pulled down the corners of her red lips. A very serious-looking frown. Then it was gone.

"So hanging up on your biggest supporter, what was that about?" I teased her.

"Sorry. I had to take that call," Mom said, then added, "Sweetie, you look gorgeous."

"OK you're forgiven." I laughed. "Look who's talking." I leaned in to hug Mom, but she leaned away.

"Sorry, nasty cold setting in," Mom said.

"Taking your Cs?"

Mom nodded.

"I'm so happy you're finally here and we can de-brief your MedMaker launch," I said.

"It was amazing. Everything I'd hoped for," Mom said, but her smile slipped away too quickly.

There's that look again.

"Are you sure you're OK?" I asked Mom. She should be looking ecstatic.

"Sam, it's just a cold, and I'm tired. Nothing to worry about." Mom looked around the ballroom. "This is one amazing party. And all those balloons on the stairs are quite something."

Mom eyed the balloons. She wasn't full of awe like everyone else. She looked uneasy, but then said, "I have another gift for you. It's not very PC at a party, especially with so many dignitaries." She slipped something into my bag.

Looking in, I glimpsed a fluorescent-pink pocketknife and gave a little laugh.

"I know you already have every attachment there is, so this might sound odd, but this one holds everything you'll need," said Mom.

"That does sound odd. Can't imagine an attachment I don't have but I can't wait to get a good look at it. Thanks so much." I almost hugged her, but remembered not to. "I'm the one who should be bestowing gifts on you."

"You already gave me crayons," she said, smiling.

"Oh, I almost forgot I got an email from Rock—"

"Really? What did it say?" Mom urgently asked.

"That he'd tried emailing you but it kept bouncing back," I said.

"Oh. I finally got that one," she said, frowning and running a shaky hand over her throat as she coughed. "I need something to drink. In fact, we need to toast your fiftieth episode."

"We need to toast your MedMaker," I said, looking toward the bar.

I was very pleased to see my waiter watching. Of course, my face went beet red. I tried to cover by tilting my head back and pretending I was downing a shot. When he held up two murky brown shots, I enthusiastically nodded back. He turned toward the bar to get a tray. One look at his broad, muscular back and I was picturing us horizontal, his muscles flexing beneath my fingertips. *I am out of control.*

I snapped out of it as he headed our way, but not before I felt Mom watching me. She'd caught my entire act. The whole checking out the gorgeous waiter, face turning red, and shot-ordering scene. I knew this because Mom's lopsided smile said, "You're busted."

"Here you go, little ladies," the waiter drawled as he smoothly dodged a newly formed conga line. He held our shots. He paused as if trying to decide who got which one and then handed them over.

"What are these?" Mom asked.

"They're called Breast Strokes. Kahlua, vodka, and Bailey's." The waiter grinned.

"Headaches waiting to happen," I murmured.

Mom and I smiled at each other and then raised our shot glasses.

"I've loved being your mom and am the proudest one in the world."

"Loved? You going somewhere?" I frowned.

"Just commemorating our big day," Mom said, touching her shot glass to mine.

We tossed them back and then slammed the empties onto the waiter's tray.

I've had lots of shots in my life but never ever the reaction this one gave me. Instantly, a surge of adrenaline hit me. Everything seemed brighter, louder, and faster. The auctioneer's gavel boomed like Big Ben. As the conga line circled, I felt like I was inside a merry-go-round.

So it didn't seem so over-the-top when I playfully slung my arm around the waiter's neck, massaged his chest, and seductively whispered into his ear, "I want more Breast Strokes…from *you.*"

Everything was so loud. I couldn't hear what he said and the way he'd turned his head away really pissed me off.

"Pay attention when you talk to me, boy," I'd shouted so loudly that guests, even the ones snaking past in the conga line, stared.

This meant that they also witnessed my humiliation when the waiter locked me tight against his very hard body.

Well that part wasn't so bad. Mmmm.

But then he growled, "Get your own damn Breast Strokes." His hot, buzzing words rushed deep inside my ear.

The growl I understood. His lusty, sad, conflicted expression I did not.

What did I do?

Without another word, he dropped me faster than a red-hot drill bit. Thoroughly embarrassed, I yelled at his back as he broke through the conga line, "I will if I want to."

I will if I want to? How lame.

I turned back toward Mom. The woman looked madder than when I'd drilled through our antique kitchen table with my new Dremel set.

"I was only joking," I said.

Mom didn't answer; she pointed at the donation bra.

Great, another critic.

"I thought you'd love that bra—"

I stopped short. Mom's sales manager, Max, was bouncing on top of it like he was King Kong. At least I thought it was Max. Unlike today at the stockholders' meeting, he had no starched hankie, no stiff upright carriage, and no perfectly pressed anything. Instead, his mangled bow tie dangled near his cummerbund. His cheeks were so slack he almost looked his real thirtysomething age. With each bounce, his head grazed the crystal chandelier so it was swaying back and forth.

I wasn't crazy about the way the bra shuddered with each bounce.

"What are you doing?" Mom asked as I kicked off my shoes.

"Getting him down," I shouted back as the music got much louder.

I ducked beneath the arms of Prunella's escort who was dancing in the conga line. If Prunella's escort was conga-ing, then Prunella was probably still entertaining Conrad. *Excellent.* It would be better for everyone if Conrad didn't see what I was about to do.

I pulled up my gown and nimbly climbed over the three-foot high bra hooks at the back and waded through the donated cash and checks. The bra's ginormous ten foot high cups towered over me as I began climbing the bra's wooden support frame.

So focused on getting Max down, I ignored the first *crunching* sound of the bra's frame. But nearing the top, the second *crunch* was too loud to ignore. The Lord Mayor, having his photo taken in front of the bra, looked around with concern.

The flimsy prop, already way beyond capacity with Max and his gorilla bounces, couldn't handle my 130 pounds.

It all happened über fast.

I topped the bra and…

Crunch.

Crunch.

Crunch.

The bra's left side began pleating like an accordion. My body somersaulted around the shoulder strap. I landed on Max's back and threw my arms around his neck. Max was underneath like a live toboggan as my toes left the satin slope. We were airborne, flying right over the Lord Mayor. Max's Adam's apple quivered under my hands as he screamed. I wanted to scream too. His horrendous cologne was clogging my nose but our brief flight ended. We didn't stop though. We slid across the ballroom floor and finally lost speed as the crisp white buffet tablecloth brushed the top of my head. We came to rest beneath the trestle table and I rolled off Max's back as fast as I could.

"Shtupid day," Max slurred as he struggled up to sitting and hit his head on the metal table strut.

"Shtupid? What, no obscure, pretentious word like *magniloquent*?" I said aloud.

"*Je suis...*" Max began blabbing in French.

Blabbing on in French and pretending not to notice. Now that was Max. Between my pidgin-French and his odd accent, I rarely caught his drift, but I did understand the last word he said. The one recognized by schoolchildren worldwide.

"*Merde*," he said again and again and again. Then he dropped his head into his hands.

That's how he was when Mom lifted the tablecloth and stared at the two of us.

"Are you OK?" she asked.

I nodded. "That was…" I was about to say *fun*, but one look at her expression and I knew Mom was not in the mood. That and the way she grabbed Max's ear to drag him from beneath the table.

Right before the tablecloth fell back into place, I glimpsed Max's face. He really looked scared.

The party was swiftly becoming one of my all-time favorites.

CHAPTER NINE

That toboggan ride off the donation bra really raised the bar on party fun. The conga line grew exponentially to a multi-armed life force. Right before my eyes, it sucked Conrad in and spat him out with a ruffled kilt and the tight smile of a host with urgent matters to attend to.

Unfortunately, it looked like *I* was his "urgent matters," because he was headed my way and fast. As he reached me, he breathed down my neck until the conga line wound past and out of earshot.

"What in bloody hell have you done?" He angrily shook a fistful of fuchsia tutu at me. "I was so pleased when guests asked where your amazing dress came from. Then I found this in my humidor and saw this…this…" Conrad pointed at my cleavage like it was a poisonous snake. "And now I realize they should have been asking where your amazing dress *went*."

"I'm sorry. I had an allergic reaction to the netting." This fib was such a doozy I was twisting my hair into a tight ringlet.

But then a cool, smooth hand touched mine. It untangled the ringlet from my fingers. I couldn't see whose hand it was, but my stomach flickered, thinking it might be my waiter. Lips brushed across my fingertips. I was on fire imagining that spiky blond head of hair bent over my hand.

I looked down and blinked. Chandelier light reflected off a shiny bald patch encircled by sandy brown hair. I pulled my hand away as if this was some cruel joke.

Unfortunately, the bald spot was the only place this Casanova didn't have hair. It sprouted from the rest of his head like bean sprouts on a Chia Pet. Thank *gawd* his wide-sleeved tuxedo shirt covered his back and a black silk cravat filled its open neck.

He had a tragic beak-like nose that threw a shadow over his nonexistent chin. Although, I had to admit his shapely eyebrows were perfection. I was considering asking where he got them waxed when his riding boots distracted me. Boots for a black-tie affair? I was jealous. I'd have worn my steel-toed ones.

"Ms. Demolition Queen, I am Mr. Schott." His voice was reed-thin like his lips *and* like his fingers, which had the audacity to grasp my jaw and move it left, right, and back to center as if selecting a new mare.

Mrs. Party's Breast Stroke shots must have had hallucinatory powers because my insanely jealous Conrad wasn't even fazed.

"Stunning." Schott stared at my face. "You know I am a huge fan. Never miss a show."

Fan? Right.

My male fans, rarely out of blue jeans, gave me pats on the back or firm overcompensating handshakes.

However, Schott did have the whole staring at my chest thing down. And I was pretty sure it wasn't the soldering wire holding his attention.

Oftentimes, Conrad's naughty male guests would pinch my bum or linger over a second peck on the cheek, but not when their host, *Mr. Jealous*, was a foot away. For kicks, I rechecked Conrad's face. He looked positively jovial and merely jangled loose change in his pocket.

"Mr. Schott. Your philanthropy is legendary." Conrad's voice sang. He didn't even bat an eye as the Lord Mayoress, who had become an integral part of the conga line, whisked my fuchsia tutu from his hand, put it on her head, and danced away.

"Random acts of kindness, that's me." Schott laughed. "And by the way, congratulations, you newlyweds." Instead of looking at Conrad, Schott's dark eyes moved from my cleavage to the hollow at the base of my neck.

This guy had balls in spades.

"Ah, yes well my dear Samantha captivated me at last year's *Demolition Queen* party. Thank goodness I am on her network's board and received an invitation."

Shoot. Here it comes, his "how we met" story.

Conrad cleared his voice and launched in. "I would have talked with her all night, but my dear Samantha asked, 'Would you like a new drink?' When I said yes, she left and never returned. Me, the most eligible bachelor in London, deserted by a woman who demolishes walls for a living." Conrad laughed and slapped his kilt-covered thigh. "The next day, I rang and announced my intent to court her. A month later we became engaged."

Conrad smiled triumphantly. He kept smiling even as the DJ switched out his adored swing band for super-loud "Burn, Baby, Burn, Disco Inferno." Everything quivered, including his prized crystal chandelier and two hundred-year-old window glass. Even his Albany family portraits.

I *saw* him *see* all this, but *still* no reaction.

I looked back at Schott. I wondered who this weirdo was.

Sadly, my best and favorite escape line, "Would you like a new drink," was blown. So when Schott looked like he was going to grab my face again, I said, "Oh, I must go greet Senator Benedict." I waved at the crowd around the late night/breakfast buffet. Conrad and Mr. Schott didn't even notice that I was really waving at the eggs Benedict and Felicity, who was gorging herself on the chocolate truffle fountain.

About to move, I felt a tug on my hair. Schott was holding a thick golden strand of it and letting it run through his fingers.

OMG.

"I will see you soon." His low, reedy voice slithered through the "Burn, Baby, Burn" chorus.

"Not if I see you first," I said under my breath as I made a beeline for the buffet.

I had to pause as the conga line passed with such speed that the last six participants, which included a noted female member of Parliament and pillar of London's upper crust, struggled to hold on in this unlikely game of crack the whip.

"You filthy rich folks sure know how to party," Felicity shouted across the buffet. She was holding a Bloody Mary in one hand and waving a skewer loaded with marshmallow, pineapple, and cherries under the truffle fountain.

"Yes, we do this every Friday." I laughed.

We both looked up as the twenty-strong fundraising committee flew past with Mrs. Wolverhampton in the lead. In a very un-Brit-like fashion, she was excitedly bobbing the pink thermometer up and down like a drum major on speed.

"What's gotten into them?" I asked.

"You'd do that too if you raised thirty-five million pounds," Felicity said.

"Thirty-five million?" I nearly choked on my first bite of "Mr. Benedict."

Felicity stared at me. "You missed that? That was over an hour ago. Where have you been?"

I looked over my shoulder at Conrad and Schott at the very moment Prunella, Conrad's 'psycho'-bitch client, joined them.

"I've been in a bizarre parallel universe," I murmured, and just like that, the most appropriate tune began. The 1980s head-banger, "Turning Japanese."

Of course, Felicity and I had to sing along.

"I think I'm turning Japanese, I think I'm turning Japanese, I really think so."

We bobbed our heads as a flickering laser light show began and flashed across stodgy ancestral portraits. If this were a well-know wizarding film, Conrad's ancestors would be huddling in the largest frame over the mantle.

"We have our first casualty," Felicity said, pointing to the end of the buffet table where the Member of Parliament spun into the dancing crowd with dress hem flapping.

I think I'm turning Japanese…

Oblivious to her comrade's defection, the ecstatic Mrs. Wolverhampton kept up the pace. So it was not surprising that a second conga line participant, a portly BBC presenter, spun out as well. His pudgy spinning arms barely missed the Bloody Marys and Mimosas that crowded the breakfast drink bar.

I think I'm turning Japanese…

But they did hit the buffet table and toppled Mrs. Party's carefully stacked pyramid of swan-shaped napkins.

I really think so…

Spinning MPs and toppled napkins were nothing compared to what happened next. Casualties three, four, and five slammed into the still-intact, but previously weakened donation bra, so that the word *Japanese* in the song's next line punctuated a loud *thwack*. Now not only was the monumental satin bra heavily listing, its now even *higher* shoulder strap lassoed Conrad's quivering car-sized chandelier.

I'd witnessed hundreds of falling walls, but this was my first falling bra.

Mesmerizing stuff.

That was *until* I realized people were in the way.

I think I'm turning…

I tried to shout, "Timber!" but instead I blurted out the next word in the song: "Japanese!"

Bizarrely, the crowd understood. Or maybe it was the lengthening shadow from this monstrous bra. Either way, Conrad's stately festive ballroom became the set of a Godzilla film with terrified guests looking up and lips moving that didn't match the soundtrack.

I think I'm turning Japanese…

Thank goodness, everyone was clear of the fall zone as the shoulder strap wrenched the chandelier from its circular eighteenth-century plaster crown.

AND that we were clear as the bra *and* chandelier knocked into and swept along the breakfast drinks bar.

AND that we were clear when it slammed the entire mass into the buffet's chocolate fountain so that a psychedelic kaleidoscope of bing cherries, fluffy white marshmallows, and bright yellow pineapple wedges flew into the air and merged with liquid chocolate, Bloody Marys, and Mimosas to fall fully coated onto guests.

Just in case anyone was feeling a sense of calm, the sparking and leaping of the chandelier's exposed and stretched to the floor electrical wires, kept everybody moving. It started a gunk-covered guest stampede. Some slid and slipped toward the terrace doors, but the more cognizant guests, not willing to miss out on the extravagant goodie bags, squeezed through the feathery tunnel into the foyer.

Somehow, I was swept up in the latter crowd and was extruded like Play-Doh from the tunnel, spitting pink feathers. I peeled off to the left and was surprised but pleased to see red emergency lights already raking across the ceiling. While some guests rushed out the door hugging goodie bags to their chests, others stopped and surrounded two ambulance attendants who knelt down just inside the door.

At first, I assumed a guest had slipped on a Bloody Mary-marshmallow or an equally bizarre concoction, and had fallen and been trampled by shoes labeled Marc Jacobs, Louboutins, and Chanel.

But then I saw Max's stricken face with downcast eyes.

Last time I'd seen Max was at least forty-five minutes ago when Mom dragged him away by the ear.

A silent alarm began in my head.

I pushed through the rubberneckers.

As the attendants raised and locked into place the rain-slicked gurney, that silent alarm in my head became a pickax on every nerve.

The small, motionless body on the gurney was…*Mom.*

I desperately squeezed through the inner circle of onlookers in time to see the attendant tighten gurney straps across her chest.

"What happened?" My voice vibrated with fear and anger.

"That horrid man yelled at her," Lady Wolverhampton shouted and pointed at Max. Then she glared at Lord Wolverhampton, who was red-faced, soaked in orange juice, and trying to shush her up.

Meanwhile, a black-haired attendant pushed thick black glasses up the bridge of his nose and nodded at his ginger-haired colleague. They began wheeling the gurney toward the door, but I grabbed its cold bars and protectively leaned over Mom. "My mom has a cold. She's overworked. Just take her to her suite," I said.

Mom must have heard me because her eyes opened and when she smiled, I said, "There you are. You had me worried. Tell these guys you're just tired—"

"I love you," Mom said. The corners of her mouth quivered.

"I love you too," I said, relieved. "See, she's fine," I added as I looked at the black-haired attendant. Then I felt the gurney shake. I looked down as Mom's red lips contorted and a violent tremor shook her body.

"Ma'am, we've got to go," said the ginger-haired attendant and pulled the gurney bars from my clenched hands to wheel Mom out the door.

"Samantha, let the men do their job." Conrad's stern voice came from behind. He tried to grip my shoulders, but I wrenched free and raced after the gurney, down the pink steps. At the back of the ambulance, I tried to hop in, but the ginger-haired attendant blocked my way.

"You'll have to meet us there. Helicopter's too small," he said.

"Helicopter?" *That's good. She'll get there quicker.*

I shielded my eyes from the rain as the boxy white ambulance whipped around the curved, sloping drive. Gaining speed, its lights flashed across a purple Lincoln and a dark-green stretch Humvee and then blurred into one colorful stream as it raced past the remaining limos. Finally, its headlights flashed and sparkled across Cranmont's open wrought-iron gates before going dark as a tomb.

My legs felt light.

My chest felt so tight I couldn't breathe.

It telegraphed me back to that Swiss cliff watching razor-sharp rocks tear at another irreplaceable person.

CHAPTER TEN

On the rain-slicked motorway, Conrad masterfully wove his turbocharged Bentley Arnage in and out of traffic. He passed each car as if it was backing up. We reached the hospital in half the time, but nothing was fast enough for me. I was so desperate to see Mom. I leaped out before Conrad had time to stop at Battersea Hospital's emergency door entrance.

"Samantha!" Conrad bellowed.

I hiked up my dress, soldering wire and all, and ran. High heels skimmed the sidewalk's rough cement as I dodged matching brick pillars, slipped sideways through the barely open sliding glass doors, and then slammed into the hospital's speckled tan reception desk, gasping for air.

"Where's Helen Palmer?" I shouted. I didn't recognize the shrill voice that came out of me.

A startled young receptionist looked up from playing with the buttons on her hospital smock. Her eyes widened, and she dropped her chewed pencil. "Were you in an accident? Do you need medical attention?" She urgently reached for her phone as she looked me over with such wide eyes I had to look too. I was sopping wet. My gown gaped open. Silver wire stuck out in every direction.

"I want Helen Palmer. She just came in." I leaned over and frantically scanned the young woman's computer screen.

"We haven't received a Helen Palmer tonight," she said.

She gave me a very guarded look as her hand searched for something under the edge of her desk. *A panic button?*

"We've had one burn victim and one stabbing. Both men," she said, sounding like she was talking me down from a ledge.

So I was surprised as her voice turned flirty and her "panic button" hand began fluffing her hair. I assumed that the security guards had arrived to relieve her from this crazed woman (me).

That was *until* I heard…

"Any word on your mother?" Conrad's voice boomed beside me. His blazer buttons hit my wrist and felt like ice. He undid his bow tie and unbuttoned his sweaty collar.

"Young lady, could you please check your roster once again?" Conrad asked conspiratorially.

The receptionist actually smiled as she invited him to lean over her desk and check the monitor for himself.

The Conrad "cause" strikes again.

Whatever.

Anything that got me in to see Mom was good.

"I'm sorry, sir," she said and this time looked truly disappointed.

I didn't care how many cold looks I got, I wasn't leaving until I knew something. "Could you find out where the helicopter is?" I leaned over her counter again.

"Samantha, perhaps they took your mother to another hospital," said Conrad.

I noticed for the first time that Conrad sounded stressed too. It occurred to me that he was probably as worried about Mom as I was. Even so, I shook my head and glared.

"This is the only London hospital where helicopters land. Don't you know someone who could tell us where that helicopter is…?" I paused and realized *I* knew someone. MedMaker Corp's helicopter pilot, Candace. She'd flown for a *Demolition Queen*'s episode. She knew everyone.

I started dialing Candace, but my fingers froze as Conrad's no-nonsense ringtone sounded from his cutaway's breast pocket.

"Hello." His small smile reassured me, but ten seconds later he said, "*No.* How long ago?" Pause. "I will tell her. Thank you," Conrad said and I *knew.*

I knew not from Conrad's subdued tone. It wasn't how his manicured fingers hesitated before dropping the phone back into his breast pocket either. It was that look. The same one that the search and rescue pilot gave me after Jake's death.

Mom was dead.

My throat constricted. I couldn't breathe again, but I could sprint. Across the linoleum and through the sliding glass doors I raced, until outside I bent at the waist and tried to suck in air.

"Samantha, I am so very sorry. The MedMaker should have saved her life," said Conrad.

I snapped upright. "MedMaker? Mom had a MedMaker?" I screeched in that unrecognizable voice again. It made a young mother snatch up her child and detour around a pillar away from me.

"Her MedMaker worked fine for two years." Conrad's voice remained unruffled.

"Two years? The MedMaker was only approved six months ago. You knew she had an unapproved product in her body and didn't tell me? What the hell were you thinking? What if it malfunctioned and killed her?" The clenched fists at my sides wanted to punch something. I closed my eyes and tried to focus on less murderous Conrad-centric thoughts.

"Darling…"

He leaned in and nodded slowly as if addressing a child, and something snapped inside me. My eyes flew open. They flashed as if I was taking snapshots.

Flash.

My eyes searched for a nonhuman target. They locked onto the sliding door's safety decal, a circular hospital crest.

Flash.

I tilted sideways.

Flash.

I coiled my raised leg for a Tae Bo side kick. I wanted to beat the crap out of that door.

Flash.

One problem. At the precise moment my leg uncoiled, Conrad grabbed my arm.

Flash.

Instead of smashing the door to smithereens, my foot violently sliced the sliver of air closest to Conrad's left cheek.

Flash.

Flash.

Flash.

Numb, I spun to a halt and sagged against the brick pillar, not caring if it scraped every bit of skin from my bare arm.

Conrad offered his hand to help me up, but I knocked it away. I didn't want him to touch me.

A flicker of light somewhere across the dark car park drew my eyes. Deep in my head, I knew that flicker wasn't good, but I couldn't process anything except the thought that Mom was gone forever.

CHAPTER ELEVEN

It was three a.m., and I needed to be alone in Cranmont barn. There was nothing anyone could say or do that I wanted said or done. The more Conrad tried to coax me back to the manor, the more repulsed I became. Felicity begged me to stay with her, but her tiny Soho flat, usually warm and cozy, would have felt claustrophobic tonight.

I wanted to be alone.

Except, as I stared out of the barn's kitchen window at the Bentley's receding taillights, I'd never felt more alone in my entire life.

Only two people could have consoled me tonight.

They were both dead.

I tried inhaling the strong smell of damp plaster, but this time it wasn't comforting.

I dragged myself into the main room where my motion-detector halogen spots flashed on. Thanks to my one-man cleanup crew, I nearly tripped over piles of demolition debris.

It didn't matter.

Nothing mattered.

I just kept picturing Mom's scared white face and how her blood-red lips said, "I love you," before twisting in pain. And then sitting alone in the cold, sterile morgue hugging Mom's lifeless body, crying so hard I couldn't breathe, damning the heart attack that finished her off.

Devastated and furious my throat constricted. A low moan began deep inside my chest. It grew louder and louder until finally a primal war cry erupted.

I charged at the speaker wires dangling and exposed from the demolition. I clawed and yanked until a dust rain covered my head, arms and dress. I gagged and coughed but kept on pulling, ripping at the endless strands that stretched the wall's forty-foot length. I fed them through my hands even as my palms bled. I paused only to hastily wipe eyes and cheeks. I reached up to yank some more, but seeing a savage, blood-smeared face in the dark window stopped me. I stared in shock.

That savage, blood-smeared face was *me*.

I exhaled with a sob. Arms fell to my sides like cement blocks. I dragged bare feet backward. Legs clipped the coffee table's edge and I collapsed to the hard wood floor with remnants of my fuchsia gown billowing up around me before silently settling in the dust.

***

I woke suddenly to an odd buzzing sound and found myself on the couch. I felt drugged and heavy. I struggled to sit up. Bleary eyed, I blinked at the bright sunlight streaming through the barn's windows.

"What is that buzzing?" I asked, vaguely displeased that I was talking to myself.

I stared at my beaded bag from last night. It seemed to be the source.

I winced as one blood-caked hand stretched to open it. Peering in, I pushed aside duct tape, snippets of wire, and my new knife from Mom. Then I raised an eyebrow at Mom's buzzing cell phone and answered it.

"Hello?" I croaked.

"Sounds like you had a wild time last night," said a cranky male voice. "OK, I let you have a lie-in, but I couldn't wait any longer."

"Who is this?" I peered up at the Waterloo Station clock high above my desk and couldn't believe it was eight a.m.

The male voice went low and hesitant. "Who is this?"

"It's Sam." I turned on Mom's speakerphone and then dropped her phone into my lap.

"Sam? This is Rock."

Mom's ex-MedMaker Corp employee and favorite virus hunter sounded kind of casual but not quite right.

"How was your big 'do' last night?"

With that one question, the horror of last night came flooding back. A lump formed in my throat, and I sagged against the couch.

"Not so great," I said.

"I'd love to chat, but I really need to speak with your mom," Rock added impatiently.

"You can't." I drew a deep breath.

"Sam, I don't have time for games."

"She's dead," I tried but failed to hold back a sob.

There was a long pause, and I thought we'd been cut off.

"What?" Rock said in a shaky voice. "I spoke to her yesterday. How could that happen with her MedMaker?"

"Who didn't know about Mom's MedMaker?" I asked.

"I don't know what to say," Rock said, sounding as lost as I felt.

"Rock?" I croaked. My swollen throat made it hard to speak. "Did you need something?"

"Nothing," Rock stammered. "It's not important."

From his tone, I was pretty sure it was not "nothing," and it *was* important, but honestly all I could think about was Mom.

CHAPTER TWELVE

A light drizzle hit my window as James inched the limo up Gatwick's steep, slanted approach to South Terminal. James, as chauffeur, was driving as slowly as he walked. So slow that a teeny little woman struggling to pull her black overstuffed suitcase up the sidewalk passed my window.

I'd pretty much stared out this window since we left Cranmont. Partly because I couldn't watch James drive. On the M25, he steered the limo into another lane while it was occupied by a double-length lorry. The lorry had to swerve out of our way and nearly ended up straddling the guardrail. The worst thing about the near catastrophe was that James seemed oblivious.

Conrad had taken James on as a favor to some royal he knew, not long before we married. That was no reason for me or any other innocents to die. When I got back from France, I'd talk with Conrad about replacing James.

Or maybe I *wouldn't* talk to Conrad. I'd pretty much avoided doing that since the scene outside the hospital. I had thought that being stuck in this limo with him would be a problem but his phone hadn't stopped ringing.

Max rang four times in a panic. Making it the second time in three days that I'd actually felt a tiny bit sorry for him. The other big caller was Conrad's ex-wife. I knew it was her because Conrad's voice always went soft and intimate.

To tell the truth, any distractions were welcome. I'd do anything to *not* think about walking into Chateau Momo in four hours. Knowing that Mom wasn't going to be there today or ever again was killing me.

Marking things off my to-do list had helped a bit.

> 1. ~~Book flights~~
> 2. ~~Book appointment with Mom's attorney~~

~~3. Reconnect speaker wires in barn~~

It took forever to clean up the wire mess and reconnect them all. Those things went everywhere.

~~4. Rehang ballroom chandelier~~

Amazingly, the chandelier sustained only minor injuries. Apparently, the marshmallows, fondue, and mandarin oranges padded its fall.

~~5. Begin editing 50th episode footage with Felicity.~~

Felicity and I did this for hours yesterday.

~~6. Schedule *Demolition Queen*'s one-man cleanup crew to come while I'm away.~~

When I spoke with him, he apologized and explained he'd been called away on an emergency job after our filming in the barn.

7. Finish selecting 50th episode-footage.

I planned to finish *7.* while traveling or when I got back. Not a big deal in the scheme of things.

Conrad clicked his phone shut and brushed a speck of dirt off his otherwise immaculate suit. I frowned at my to-do list, hoping I looked too busy to talk.

"Samantha…"

Oh come on.

"… you still haven't explained why you must go to France. Couldn't the attorney just fax over your mother's will?" Conrad pouted. *Not the twenty-eighth in line to the throne's best look.* "But more importantly, why can't I go with you?"

I eyed him from the opposite side of the limo's broad leather backseat. He'd actually been very sweet this week, even after the heirloom chandelier debacle and the who's who guest stampede. Maybe because his precious manor was looking pretty normal. God bless the housekeeper. I think the cook helped too. Although, I did find a maraschino cherry stuck to the back of Colonel Albany's bust this morning. I popped it into my mouth before Conrad saw, hoping it was not just the tip of the proverbial iceberg.

"The French attorney insisted on reading Mom's will ASAP," I said. "And you're staying here because Max needs your help—"

Without warning, the limo jolted and tilted so sharply I had to clench the door handle to keep from sliding down the seat toward Conrad. I heard Conrad's and James's doors open and then slam shut. With some difficulty, I pushed mine open, climbed out, and saw exactly why we had tilted. James had parked us on the triple-high curb, designed to discourage exactly that.

"I'll get a trolley, madam."

"Don't worry," I said and stared at James's stooped back as he shuffled away to find one anyway. "I don't need a trolley…" My words trailed off as I noticed the crumpled silver trolley corral hanging from the limo's trunk.

Next, there were hysterical screams, screeching brakes, and honking horns coming from the slanted approach. I turned in time to see the teeny woman leap surprisingly high, onto the sidewalk railing as a long row of freed luggage trolleys (freed when the butler took out the trolley corral) impaled her suitcase and held it hostage as it barreled down the steep sidewalk with traffic wardens in hot pursuit.

"Sorry, madam, there were no trolleys available," said James.

OMG.

I stared at James's droopy lids and tranquil, empty eyes. I'd have given anything to be as out-to-lunch right then. "Don't worry, James, I can carry my things," I said.

"How about having a coffee?" Conrad asked in a soft tone.

"I'm so sorry, but I've got to get through security," I said thawing a bit. But then I realized he was on the phone with his ex again. "Get me the heck out of Dodge," I said and stormed inside, ready for some normalcy.

Fat chance.

While my "fly first class or don't bother" husband insisted I fly first class, all I cared about was Fast Track. Of course, today, Fast Track was closed. Getting stuck behind ten semi-inebriated middle-aged men on a Dublin stag weekend, didn't help. Especially with them dropping their lederhosen.

So, when the word *DELAYED* flashed beside my flight, I'd had it.

I began walking the terminal's perimeter fast. *Angry fast.* So fast, people got out of my way, fast. Shops selling clothing, sunglasses, and caviar flew by. I lost count how many times I passed the central waiting areas but stopped short as the MedMaker Corp logo flashed across their TV screens. I cut across green-checked carpet and dropped onto a molded plastic bench. The logo disappeared and a photo of Rock came up. It had been cropped from an old MedMaker team photo with him wearing his orange team bandana.

These words streamed below his headshot:

Doctors For ALL *team and world-renowned epidemiologist, Duncan Rockney, missing in Bolivia seven days. Feared dead.*

Rock was *with the missing group?*
In Bolivia?
But what was this missing seven days stuff?
Feared dead?

I fished Mom's phone from my plumber's bag and studied her call list for Rock's last call.

UNKNOWN, Sun, 8:00 a.m.

"Well, he was alive a couple days ago," I said to the TV.

But while he was presumed missing, he called Mom.

Did he tell her where he was?

Could that have been Mom's little white lie?

If so, it sure was a doozy.

Why wouldn't he tell me his reason for calling? Why not ring others?

I leaned back against the hollow plastic seat.

A creepy thought made my scalp crawl. What if he really was dead now?

There was only one way to find out.

Even though his number had come up as *UNKNOWN* before, it was in Mom's phone now. I dialed it and five rings later heard, "No viruses were harmed while making this message. Please use the same care as you leave yours."

Unusual message.

Reassuringly Rock's.

I hung up. I rubbed my forehead, trying to remember our brief conversation the morning after Mom died. How had Rock sounded?

Happy?

Sad?

Stressed.

He sounded stressed even before I told him about Mom.

What if he was in some kind of trouble and didn't want others to know that we'd spoken? If so, I shouldn't leave a message. At least, not a message that would tip anyone off that we'd previously spoken. I thought about that for a minute.

I redialed. His phone rang at the same time I heard a polite but firm voice reverberating through the terminal. "This is the final boarding call for flight number three-four-five. Samantha Albany, please report to gate eighty-seven."

Shoot.

I slung my plumber's bag over my shoulders just as Rock's phone rang a second time.

On ring three, I was barreling into the concourse labeled "Gates 55–87."

I picked up speed as Rock's message began.

"No viruses were harmed while making this message…"

I whipped around the first corner of the quarter-mile concourse, and my plumber's bag flew out perpendicular to my shoulder, almost taking out three flight attendants. *Good thing I'd had to check my tools.*

"Sorry," I shouted and waved apologetically.

Rock's message continued as I zigzagged down the concourse.

"Please use the same…"

As the gate attendant scanned my boarding pass, I mentally composed the cryptic message I'd leave.

"…care as you leave yours."

I charged down the boarding ramp just as Rock's machine beeped for me to start my message.

"Rock, I know we made tomorrow's appointment months ago, but I have to cancel…."

I said as I lunged into the plane breathing hard and waving my crumpled boarding card at a pinch-faced flight attendant. I headed for 2B while quietly continuing my message. "…I just got a hair appointment that I desperately need to keep before my stylist goes on maternity leave."

I wasn't quiet enough.

All seven of my fellow first-class passengers were staring at me. There were two or three admiring glances. But from the other expressions, I'd guess they were thinking, *You bimbo. You made us late for your hair?*

"Call me to reschedule," I whispered into my phone and sank as deeply as possible into 2B.

CHAPTER THIRTEEN

Usually I loved arriving at the Champagne airport in France, but not today. All I could think about were the bad reasons I'd previously arrived here. Dad's funeral. Hiding out after Jake's death. And now, for my meeting with Mom's attorney about her will.

I threw my plumber's bag and backpack into the trunk and then dropped into the driver's seat. "Thanks for waiting," I said to Martin.

Martin, my secret love, was a mint-condition, chromed, and deep-red 1946 Aston Martin. He always waited at Reims/Champagne airport for me.

Exiting the airport, I zoomed past one field after another and inched through small villages without noticing any of it. By the time I entered my quaint village, it was under a dusky rose-colored sky. The sight of Monsieur Tremont sitting in his boulangerie's shadowy recessed doorway comforted me. He waved the glowing tip of his self-rolled cigarette overhead. I waved back before steering Martin between massive brick pillars and down Chateau Momo's quarter-mile track.

Three years ago, Mom and I bought the then decrepit three-story country chateau. We bought its unsuccessful vineyard too. Luckily, its exquisite raspberry-infused champagne only needed a new name and packaging. We slapped acid-green *Demolition Queen* labels onto the lot, advertised it during my show, and it flew off the shelves throughout London and Europe.

The chateau's renovation took more time. Renovation wasn't Mom's thing. Unfortunately, renovation wasn't my thing either. Two long years later, I finished and celebrated by driving to Switzerland. That night, I found Jake swinging on the antler chandelier. The same chandelier I saw through the foyer's stained glass window as I stopped in the chateau's circular drive.

I dragged myself from the car. My sagging Appaloosa, Comanche, looked up from the clover then whinnied and trotted to the fence. I leaned my forehead against his neck and inhaled his coat's familiar mix of molasses-covered oats, grass, and dust. Then I looked over his forelock at Mom's home office window.

"I wish you could come in with me," I said, giving Comanche a hug and a kiss before heading toward the chateau's faded blue front door and then opening it. Like ripping off a Band-Aid, I ran straight across the foyer's slate floor, up the stairs, and into Mom's office. I settled yoga-style in her desk chair. Normally I'd spin too, but this was not a spinning kind of day.

As always, a tall, tidy stack of documents and newspaper clippings filled one side of Mom's desk. A spiral-shaped paperweight sat on top. To most people, the paperweight probably looked like a cross section of a conch shell.

To me?

A phi swirl.

To be exact it was an "equiangular spiral formed by pentagrams and golden triangles." The golden ruler. Golden number. Golden grid. Dr. Levin's golden mean gauge 1.618. All of these terms Mom had engraved on the paperweight's sides and, unfortunately, on my brain.

Her "phi spiral talk" was worse than her sex one. Her eyes lit up as she rambled on about the "amazing puzzle of science."

Even now, my eyes glazed over just thinking about it.

Although, when I was little, I ate this stuff up. I wanted to be exactly like Mom.

At age six, I painted a wooden ball puzzle to look like a soccer ball with the word "buckyball" on it. I presented it to Mom for Mother's Day and recited, "The buckyball's carbon 60 molecule's nearly spherical configuration is a truncated icosahedron like a soccer ball." I smiled, remembering how Mom beamed.

Maybe the buckyball was why Mom liked Buckeye Balls so much.

Since chemistry was Mom's passion and I idolized her, I struggled through a four-year chemistry degree at Denison University. Thank goodness for Dr. Brown, my pipe-chewing advisor, who senior year said he'd let me graduate *if* I promised to abandon chemistry *forever.*

When I finally got the courage to tell Mom, she grinned and said, "Good. Now you know something you don't want to do."

Mom's love for the "puzzle of science" always made sense. However, what never made sense was her infatuation with cheap plastic children's puzzles. Those square ones with pieces you had to slide within their frame to form a dog or a cheesy-looking Santa Claus. I think she loved them because she could actually *do* them.

I could too, when I used a screwdriver.

When Mom wasn't looking, I'd pop out the squares and arrange them to complete the picture and then force them back into place. Mom was so proud. I didn't have the heart to tell her the truth.

Just thinking of Mom made me so tired, I hugged the phi swirl and buckyball to my chest, laid my head on her broad oak desk, and that was the last thing I remembered.

***

At nine a.m. the next morning, forty-five minutes before my appointment with Mom's attorney, I was in the kitchen munching a croissant and gulping down coffee from a thermos that *le domestique* had left for me. I rarely saw her. Probably because my awkward attempts at French conversation embarrassed us both.

I grabbed the English-language newspaper she'd left for me. Then I headed out into the lavender-scented morning air to enjoy the view of grapevines stretching off into the distance beyond the endless wine caves.

In hopes of keeping my mind off Mom's will reading for a bit, I decided to read the paper while sitting on Comanche's back.

I maneuvered through the jagged barbed wire fence as I read the headline. "MedMaker Corporation's Miracle MedMaker Kills its CEO." Then I stood straight up. Unfortunately, at the time, I had one foot planted in Comanche's field and the other on the driveway. Barbed wire gashed my arm, but I didn't feel a thing. I was numb.

"Indefinite delays to the MedMaker rollout…," the article began and I shivered, even in the hot sun.

Ignoring the blood streaming down my arm, I pulled out my phone and practically sprained my thumbs, dialing Max so fast.

Two quick British phone rings later, I heard, "Max Carlisle."

"Who did this…this…?" I demanded. Comanche nudged my shoulder, and I had to push him away.

"Read on." Max's tone was frigid.

I pictured him readjusting his horn-rimmed glasses.

"Outside Battersea Hospital, Sam Albany, the CEO's daughter, was quoted as saying, 'My mom had the MedMaker, an unapproved product, in her body for two years which could have malfunctioned and killed her," I read aloud.

My memories of those minutes outside the hospital had been a bit foggy, until now. This was like a slap in the face.

"The photos are particularly lovely," Max snipped.

I flipped over the paper and cringed at the eight-by-ten photo of me mid–Tae Bo kick, still in my formal gown. With my leg lifted, I looked like a male dog about to pee. Someone had photoshopped Conrad out and added spidery cracks to the sliding glass doors. Below the photo, it said, "Ms. Demolition Queen does Demolition at Battersea Hospital. Mick Tambour."

"Of course that weasely reporter, Tambour, did this," I said.

"Your mom would roll over in her grave if she saw it," said Max.

I'd hated to admit that I was thinking the same thing. It was ten times worse hearing him say it. I felt the heat drain from my face.

"It was my fault," Max blurted.

"What was your fault? That I kicked at a window and Tambour wrote this article?" I asked as I used the sports section to wipe at the blood streaming down my arm.

"No. That your mom died. Our argument at the party pushed her beyond healthy limits. I impelled her heart attack," said Max.

"Max, we both know it would take a lot more than an argument to give my mom a heart attack." I tried to imagine how his disheveled appearance and bra-hanging antics at the breast cancer fundraiser could cause anything but laughter. "What did you argue about anyway?" I asked as I stepped up onto a tree stump.

"Why do you want to know?"

Max's defensive tone piqued my interest.

"Because you're pleading guilty to murder," I said as Comanche obediently came alongside.

I waited and waited for his answer. Was that the tinkle of paper clips I heard?

"I authorized surveillance. Borderline illegal surveillance," said Max quietly, and then he rushed on. "But as I explained to your mother, we couldn't afford another disaster like last year."

"Fair enough," I said, throwing one leg over Comanche's back and waving away the dander engulfing my jeans.

"Yes, that's bad, but *you* might have caused the death of the MedMaker," Max said and hung up.

His accusing tone rang in my ears. I fell back onto Comanche's broad rump. A fitting place after the mess I'd made.

CHAPTER FOURTEEN

Mom's attorney of forty years, a lovely French gentleman, clasped my hands. Then he solicitously offered, of all things, a black-lacquered Wake Forest University chair. Unfortunately, he was still at my side as I sat. So, he witnessed the cloud of Comanche's dander and dust escaping from my jeans. As it floated through the chair rails, he politely coughed, but his grimace said it all.

I'd meant to change. Except, that conversation with Max about him "killing" my mom and *me* "killing" Mom's MedMaker, not to mention her company, was distracting as all get-out.

The attorney settled behind his desk and I braced for the obligatory sympathetic words about Mom. I dug my fingernails into my thighs to hold back the tears. Therefore, I was surprised *and* relieved when he looked through gold-rimmed bifocals and unceremoniously began reading.

"Your mother wanted you to clear her personal effects from her Paris MedMaker lab and office right away." From across the desk, he peered at me first through his glasses, and then he tilted his head down to look at me above them.

"Yes, sir. I will today," I responded obediently.

I hadn't realized I'd been picking at a small hole in my jeans until he aimed a look of disapproval at my knee.

"Could you tell me why she wanted me to do this so soon?" I asked, while casually flattening my hand over the hole.

"Good," responded the attorney, who either didn't hear the question or chose to ignore it.

Next, he gave me a sympathetic look.

Here we go. Tears welled up on my lower lids, and a lump the size of a tangerine formed in my throat. The lump was so large, I couldn't swallow. Nor, it seemed, hear correctly because I thought he said, "Sam, you crackerjack, I think you'll be tickled pink to have Grandma's Chinese dragon."

"Pardon moi, could you repeat that line please?" I leaned forward, releasing another dusty cloud.

"Due to the confusing nature of your mother's will perhaps you should read it," he said and handed a copy to me.

> *Sam, you crackerjack, I thought you'd be tickled pink to have Grandma's Chinese dragon.*

So, I'd heard him correctly but, *Crackerjack? Tickled pink?* Mom didn't talk like that.

Plus, the Chinese dragon she mentioned, I'd bought in a London antique shop. It now sat by Cranmont's fireplace.

I read on…

> *Because of Sam's dedication to science, I was puzzled why she didn't continue her research into the effects of xenan on polyporphyrin balls and dansnurmur.*

"Unerring dedication…to science? Right." I smirked. "My senior chemistry project was with xenon not xenan. It should be polyporphyrin *rings* not *balls* and what the heck is a dansnurmur?" I asked out loud.

This made no sense. The solicitor shook his head, looking equally confused. Mom loved a good knock-knock joke, but her making light of a legal document? *It didn't fit.* I leaned forward and rested splayed fingers on the attorney's desk. "Are you sure my mom wrote this?"

He nodded. "I witnessed it."

"Her most recent will?" I raised my voice and stood. I couldn't help noticing the layer of horse dander that outlined where my bum and thighs had been.

"Oui, madam."

I stared at him. "And how did she seem? Crazy? Drunk?"

He shrunk from me like *I* was crazy and drunk. "No, madam. A little under the weather. Otherwise of sound mind and body, I assure you," he said.

"I'm sorry. All this is a little much," I said, tilting my neck left and then right to loosen the kinks before reading more.

I'm leaving Sam my Triumph Bonneville motorcycle to
*see the world because cats are **an** puzzle. Please call*
June Thorpe. Sealed with a kiss. Mother.

The solicitor avoided eye contact as I finished and put the paper down. He instead stared at the hole in my jeans that I'd unconsciously enlarged to the size of a melon.

"Do you know what my mom would do if I so much as looked at a motorcycle?"

He barely shook his head.

"She'd come back to life and kill me," I said.

He didn't respond to that but said, "Your mother wanted you to have her Matisse now." He gave a small tentative smile. Then he produced a one-foot-square brown parcel, tied with green string. He pushed it across the desk.

I swiftly cut the string with my pocketknife, ripped the paper away, and frowned at it. It was an exact replica of the line drawing she gave me as a wedding gift. The one temporarily in the guest suite. Why give me a copy of something I already own? Or was this the real one and the other the replica? It made no sense.

"OK, what else have you got?" I asked.

The attorney looked startled. It could have been the way I'd ripped into the priceless line drawing or my lack of reaction to the gift.

Probably both.

He squinted at my face as if he was afraid to look at the whole shebang and rushed on. "Your mother requested a cyber-funeral."

I slammed my hands on the desk and the poor gentleman sprang backward like a skittish racehorse.

"A cyber funeral?" I laughed a crazy kind of hyena laugh that would have scared me if I were him.

I headed for the door.

"But you need to sign these…" The attorney's feeble attempt to stop me died on his shaking lips. He probably just wanted me out of his office. At least *he* didn't reach for a panic button like at the hospital.

So when I did march back in, sign the papers, slam his Mont Blanc pen on the desk, he didn't say so much as an *au revoir* or *merci beaucoup* as I marched out again.

CHAPTER FIFTEEN

I plopped down behind Mom's desk at MedMaker Corp's Paris office with one thing in mind—eradicating all copies of her last will and testament. I didn't want people remembering her for that will. If others had read it before her multibillion-pound MedMaker launch, they'd have had her committed for sure.

Of course, once I calmed down and thought about it, it made perfect sense. *Tickled pink* and *polyporphyrin balls* were clues for a scavenger hunt. Mom probably devised the hunt to distract me in the event of her death.

I'd searched her paper files and found no will, so tried her computer. The sheer volume of MedMaker news alerts was overwhelming. I'd be embarrassed to admit it, but I was extremely happy that Rock's predicament was getting top billing over mine, the "killer" of MedMaker Corp.

Mom's folders for WhistleBlown, *Demolition Queen*, and breast cancer alerts barely had any.

Mom was a breast cancer survivor, eight years this month. Chemo had almost killed her, so conquering cancer was tops on her list. She vowed to do *anything* to help other women avoid what she'd gone through.

I thought about that for a moment.

Mom would have told me if her breast cancer had returned. Right?

I thought about that for a longer moment until a ringing phone nearly toppled me off Mom's chair. I grabbed for my cell phone first, then her desk phone, and finally *her* cell phone, the one actually ringing.

It was Rock, Mom's ex-MedMaker team member.

His call shouldn't have surprised me. That morning, I'd set up Mom's phone to ring him until he answered.

"Sam?" Rock whispered.

Rock's whispered words sounded silly, but right then I needed "silly." I pictured his pale, skinny arms inside plaid shirtsleeves and his knobby knees beneath khaki shorts.

"So are you lost, hiding, or in jail?" I whispered back.

"Those options would be a laugh riot compared to my week," Rock said. "Can you see this? I want a witness."

His tone was serious and scared as he turned on his phone's camera. On my screen, I could then see the inside walls of a small hut and a skeleton dead ahead.

"Yes, I see it," I said, not sure what the big deal was. "Rock, don't you see this stuff all the time…?" I stopped talking. An eyeball dangling from the skeleton's eye socket had swiveled to follow Rock as he and his phone crept closer. *Until*, without warning, the eyeball leaped at him.

I almost fell off my chair *again*.

The phone was aimed at Rock's head as he shielded it with pale arms. His eyes were pinched shut behind thick glasses. He was hyperventilating and shaking. The phone shook too.

Finally, Rock parted his arms a fraction. He squinted and then opened eyes wide.

He wasn't eyeball-to-eyeball. Nor pupil-to-pupil. To be exact he was eyeball-to-beetle. The corpse eyeball had been only a small, shiny beetle that was bumping through the maze of his sweaty copper arm hairs.

He pointed his phone at the beetle as it flew toward the hut's dirt wall, bounced off the now pupil-less corpse, and crawled toward another body.

Then I said, "Well, the press is having a field day—"

Rock cut me off, saying, "When I arrived, Bontero looked so idyllic. The mist from the waterfall wafted across the village. Flowering thistle trees swayed in the breeze but there were no villagers in bright, colorful clothes lazily steering donkeys across slanted green fields—"

"The press—" I began again.

"But I was staring at—"

I impatiently cut him off. "The press is having a field day saying this was all yours and MedMaker Corp's fault."

"Beneath the runner beans there was a crop of corpses," Rock said.

We both said, "What?" at the same time.

"I said the press is having a field day. They're saying this was all yours and MedMaker Corp's fault," I repeated.

"I've been too busy burying bodies to cause problems," he said, and his voice broke.

"Bodies?" I asked, pushing the phone tight against my ear.

"Yes, bodies, hundreds of them," he snapped.

He sounded angry at me, but I knew he was frightened. He paused so long I thought he'd hung up.

"They don't know," Rock finally said in a mystified tone.

"Know what?" I asked, rubbing my arms to tame my goose bumps.

"About the virus," Rock said.

"What virus?" I asked, again thinking his reaction seemed a bit excessive.

He didn't answer. This time I was sure I'd lost him. His silence gave my goose bumps goose bumps.

He finally said, "Hundreds of victims died within minutes of each other, less than an hour after complaining of stiffness. Although dead twenty-four hours, these bodies don't smell. They have no blood or skin. Bones are so brittle that hands and feet snap off. Toes spontaneously disconnect. Never seen anything like it. Odder still, strains this virulent should kill everyone, but lots survived."

"Oh, Rock, how horrific for—"

A loud, squawking walkie-talkie cut me off. I also heard an ice-cream-cone-like crunch.

"What's your count?" a harsh female voice barked.

"That's the doctor. Wait a minute, I'll see what the witch wants," Rock said.

Rock held his phone aimed at the ground, so I saw him slide his sandal aside. He must have inspected the long, curved vertebra that his sandal just snapped in two, which explained the ice-cream-cone-like crunch, because he answered with a nervous laugh, saying, "Forty-nine and a half…and a half."

"Dr. Witch" added Rock's halves and announced, "Your fifty makes a total of four hundred and ninety so far. Anything else?"

She didn't wait for him to answer and said, "List identifying items like jewelry and clothes. Label everything and keep a running count."

She was ordering Rock around like a soldier, not a volunteer giving generously of his time. I pictured her face scrunched like a bulldog.

"Well, toe tags are out," Rock joked again. "Not enough of them. That's toes, not tags."

"Any new symptoms?" Dr. Witch asked, ignoring Rock's second attempt at humor.

"Nope. Exposed areas dry and open. Still can't find any blood," Rock said. Then he added, "I was attacked by an eyeball."

"We've got to wrap this up," Dr. Witch snapped. "It'll be chaos after the quarantine of which we have two to three more weeks. Remember my no-communication rule. Don't want to spread panic."

"Two to three weeks?" asked Rock.

I could practically hear his stomach drop.

"Sorry." Dr. Witch signed off, sounding anything but sorry.

"Will do, Sergeant," said Rock.

I saw his safety mask hit the ground and his leather sandal stomp it into the dark, dusty earth.

"She doesn't want to spread panic. Panic? We're in the middle of frigging nowhere. Who the hell are we going to panic?" Rock said and then took a deep breath. "I came to do the virus thing with Gabby. Not get quarantined with pouncing eyeballs and disintegrating limbs."

"Who is this Dr. Witch?" I asked.

"She's this—"

"Actually, I don't care," I said, cutting Rock off. "I'm getting you out of there. I'll call Candace, my helicopter buddy. She knows pilots everywhere. They'll get you to an airport and have you eating a full English breakfast in no time—"

"No!" He shouted so loudly, I moved the phone away from my ear. "I can't risk spreading this virus."

"Of course, you're right," I said. "Is this why you called Mom that morning?"

"No…"

He hesitated.

"Come on, spit it out. I'd rather deal with your problems than mine. I'm sitting in front of her computer. Can I look something up for you?" I said, not liking how desperate I sounded. At least it made Rock talk.

"OK. Here goes. The night of the fundraiser, after your mom and I spoke, and I told her where I was, she supposedly sent me an e-mail but I never got it," Rock said.

So I was right, Mom did tell a white lie. Rock had told her where he and the others were even while under the no communication quarantine.

"Just a second, I'll check for it," I said. "OK, there's nothing in *Sent*, but in *Pending* there's an e-mail from Mom to you, and it says, '*Doctors For ALL* never heard of your Dr. Witch.' Then she says, 'You already know this Bolivian virus.'" I paused. "Rock, does the virus stuff mean anything to you?"

"Not a thing."

CHAPTER SIXTEEN

Boarding the Champagne-to-London flight, I was less than thrilled to see the same attendant from my London-to-Champagne flight. I handed her my boarding card, proud that this time it wasn't crumpled, wondering if she'd remember me. Let's just say that if frowning took more energy and muscles than a smile, this woman should have gotten a pound lighter right then.

She remembered me.

I shoved my tool-less plumbers bag under the seat with such force that the man in 1A peered at me between the plush navy leather seats. Normally I'd scoot over out of his line of sight, but I couldn't be bothered. A miffed man in 1A was nothing compared to the veritable bizarre-fest that was my life.

Let's see, there was:

> 1. My possible ruination of the MedMaker and MedMaker Corp because I blabbed at the hospital.
> 2. Bizarre contents of Mom's will.

Not to mention her cyber funeral request. Especially from a woman who believed funerals were an essential part of the grieving process for those left behind.

> 3. Rock's bizarre Bolivian predicament, including disappearing blood and a killer virus.

Ah, but there was more. Not ten minutes before boarding the plane, Cranmont's housekeeper had capped off the fest with a call about...

> 4. A Cranmont break-in.

The housekeeper said, "Mrs. Albany, James and I discovered that someone broke into the barn—"

She stopped abruptly and I heard a crash in the background.

"What was that?" I asked.

"Your saw, Mrs. Albany," the housekeeper said.

"Which one?" I asked, hoping it wasn't my new laser one, back-ordered for months.

"The only tool left," she said.

"What bastard would take all my tools?" I asked and angrily pounded my fist into the back of 1A. I'd forgotten 1A was inhabited. Immediately, the man peered between the seats again, looking more pleased than angry.

"Sorry." I vaguely smiled. I had revenge on my mind.

I was going to make that thief sorry he was ever born.

Brainstorming revenge, I came up with:

Giant mousetraps
Clamps
Torture racks
Handcuffs
Acid

I was on a roll.

I hadn't planned to break for dinner *but* there was chocolate mousse. My tray had barely touched down but after two quick mouthfuls, my mousse was gone.

"I'll take mine back there please," I heard Mr. 1A say to the flight attendant as he hopped into the empty aisle seat beside *me*. "Chateaubriand is meant for two, so I thought I better join you," he said.

The enthusiastic man tilted his head side to side. I half expected him to say, "Fly me."

"Afraid I won't make good company. I've had a break-in at my home among other things," I said.

I just wanted him gone. That was, *until* I noticed that his chocolate mousse was much larger than mine.

"Oh, I am terribly sorry about your break-in," he said with what sounded like heartfelt sincerity. I felt a little guilty vying for his mousse until he leaned over to pat my arm and then let his elbow linger on my thigh.

Oh, brother. You picked the wrong woman on the wrong night. I smiled sweetly.

"So did the police catch your thief?" he asked, scooting closer and taking my hand.

"Police? No. No. No. I am going to trap the bastard myself," I said, smiling as I tilted my head side to side.

He smiled along with me until my words sank in.

"Unspeakable pain awaits him." I accentuated the word *pain* by crushing his hand in mine.

His eyes expanded. He looked up and down the aisle for the flight attendant.

"Which do you think would be best…acid or clamps?" I asked in a low, serious tone.

"What for?" His voice cracked, and he pulled his hand free.

"Torture," I said, pointing at his lap.

"I-I-I don't know," he stuttered and slid his dinner tray tight against his body to cover that sensitive region.

"Excellent." I grinned. "I'll use both."

With that, he hopped up. "I've enjoyed chatting…"

He stopped talking as he disappeared into his seat, probably hoping I'd forget he was there.

No way.

I stood, peeked over his seat, and pointed at his tray.

"Are you going to eat that?" I asked. He jumped a mile as I reached for his untouched mousse. I think he'd lost his appetite anyway.

Thirty seconds later, as I was finishing off his dessert, I crossed *acid* off my list.

Clamps would do.

Always best to stick with what you know.

CHAPTER SEVENTEEN

In the last forty-eight hours, with only six hours of sleep, all I wanted to do was flash my UK passport and go home, but as I steamed down the ramp at Gatwick Airport, even UK passport holders were tapping their toes. If not for the retinal eye scanner that flashed like a beacon a couple rows away, I might have made a run for it.

Seconds later, I was through the scanner, headed to baggage claim, and had Mom to thank.

I wasn't so happy with her the day she'd insisted we arrive at the airport two hours early to register for retinal eye scanning. She was adamant, so I didn't argue.

Exiting the main airport doors, I spotted James's frail smile. Never been happier to see him. Even five minutes later, leaving the airport. I didn't give a toss that we swerved dangerously close to the airport's tall metal arch. For all I cared we could have been dragging the whole mobile phone advertisement.

I gobbled down Cook's smoked salmon blinis, threw back a flute of bubbly, and was out cold.

***

Forty-five minutes later, James held open the limo door. I slid out feeling more tired than ever, especially as I faced the barn, both dreading and dying to see my workshop. I rubbed dry, scratchy eyes and noticed that not only were the outside motion-activated lights on but so were the inside ones.

"Ms. Samantha, I took the liberty of calling the insurance company who came earlier," James said. "Yesterday, before this unfortunate incident, the main room was cleared by your, what do you call him? One-man cleanup crew? Your workshop has not been touched. You may expect the housekeeper's call any minute. She is anxious to get started."

That was the most I'd ever heard James say.

"Would madam like me to accompany her inside?" James shuffled to my side.

"You're wonderful, but I'll be fine on my own." I kissed his cool wrinkled cheek.

"You are most welcome, madam," he said. He blinked and touched a gloved hand to the spot.

I waved good-bye from the kitchen door and stepped inside. My phone immediately rang. I didn't even get to say hello. "I'm on my way," said the housekeeper.

"No, thank you. I'm fine, really. I'll clean it myself," I said firmly.

"I insist," she said.

It took three more "I'll be fines" before she finally hung up.

Next, I marched toward my desk. I was like a woman possessed so didn't notice my book, *It's Not About the Wall*, until I'd kicked it halfway across the main room.

I left it.

I had chocolate reinforcements on my mind.

"It's going to be all right," I said to myself, taking my Buckeye Ball tin from my hidden fridge. I popped one chocolaty peanut butter ball into my mouth and then looked into the workshop. I scanned the walls, the shelves, and the floor. Immediately, I knew that *no* amount of Buckeye Balls was going to make this all right. Every precious tool, lovingly collected over two decades, had vanished.

I touched the shelf where Mom's Knock 'em Dead hammer should have been. My hand came away covered in oily goo. I slid the goo between my fingers and sniffed. It was my favorite tool lubricant, WD-40. The thief had gone on a quite a squirting spree. It even dripped from the ceiling like stalactites.

I didn't need housekeeping. I needed garbage.

For the next two hours, I scrubbed, scraped, rinsed, and fielded three more calls from the housekeeper. I also tweaked my revenge plan.

Finally, at ten p.m., as the last greasy bubbles circled the old horse-washing drain, I headed into the barn's luxurious bathroom. I wrangled off oil-slicked jeans and T-shirt and then entered the pebbled shower stall. Tilting my head under its steamy jets, I blasted the goo from my hair.

I was on my fourth shampooing when my shower phone rang. Certain it was the housekeeper again, I said, "Don't worry, it's all clean now. *I'm* even clean too."

Water was smacking the hard pebble floor so loudly I couldn't hear too well, but I'd swear she whistled. The housekeeper was a bit cheeky, but she *wouldn't* whistle at me in the shower.

I turned off the water and heard another loud, flirty whistle.

"You missed a spot," said a husky male voice.

I recognized the cockney accent of my one-man cleanup crew.

"Just a minute," I said, squeezing the water from my hair.

"I said you missed a spot, but don't worry, I'll stay on the phone in case you need more guidance," he said with a laugh.

"What are you talking about? Where are you?" I asked, snatching my acid-green *Demolition Queen* robe off its hook.

"On the phone, doll."

I pictured his smile, slow and sure. "Can I call you back?" I reached for the shower phone to hang up.

"Please don't touch that—you'll kill my will to live," he said.

He sounded half-joking half-serious. I laughed along until he said, "You look frigging incredible."

"You can really see me?" I pulled my robe closed. "I'll kill more than your will if you had anything to do with this." I yanked the sash tight at my waist.

"A phone cam in the bathroom? Inspired," he laughed. "And yet I can take no credit."

"Where is it?" I demanded.

"Above the sink," he moaned, sounding almost suicidal

I glared at a pea-sized spot two feet above the mirror that must have been a camera lens.

"Explain," I shouted. "NOW."

"Not my fault. You re-connected the wires."

"True, but I didn't do this." I pointed at the camera.

"Somehow you've connected your webcam to security cameras, and may I say, praise the Lord?"

"Would you shut up," I said, thinking of much worse people who could have called. Mom's attorney, Lord Wolverhampton, Max, and that creep from the airplane. *Ugh.* My face in the mirror looked tomato red.

Well, I might be guilty of the disastrous rewiring, but I knew who was guilty of installing extra security lenses in the first place.

Conrad.

***

From day one, Conrad had wanted to beef up security. He stood in my barn and put a protective arm around me as he explained his plan, which I rejected.

"I don't need extra security cameras. No one would hit the barn with your veritable treasure trove up the hill," I said, wiggling free from his arm.

OK, so I was wrong. But the decision should have been mine.

"Darling, I do get your point," Conrad said. "I cannot imagine anyone wanting to take any of these things."

Conrad pointed at Mom's Knock 'em Dead hammer. Then he frowned at the rhinestone-studded saw and hand-painted tool belt that fans had made for me. As well as Mom's wedding gift, the beautiful Matisse line drawing that hadn't made Conrad's cut for his art gallery.

"But a deranged fan like your Mousetrap Stalker might wander into your secluded barn," he added.

"I don't want your cameras, and that's final," I said.

Clearly, my "final" word didn't impress.

Perhaps being strangled by me *would* impress Conrad.

***

"So, will you?" my one-man cleanup crew asked, still laughing.

"Will I what?" I pulled on steel-toed boots. They peeked from under my green robe as I climbed the ten-foot yellow fiberglass ladder I'd leaned against the bathroom wall.

"Keep the shower cam just for me?" he begged. "I promise not to tell a soul."

"You are so not getting your wish." I was no prude about my nudity, but I liked to decide who saw it and when.

Using a screwdriver, I attacked the plaster above the mirror and dug out the first lens. It resembled a miniature unopened tulip with a wire pigtail.

"What else can you see in my barn?" I demanded as I carried the ladder out into the main room.

"Well, it changes as you move. The system must have motion detector lenses. Very clever. Couldn't have done a better job if I tried," he said.

"Do you want to keep *your* job?" I asked.

Heavy sigh. "I can see the rear bottom edge of your hanging clock."

My ladder hit the wall. I climbed up. Thick black chains clanked as I heaved my massive Waterloo Station clock onto a rafter to my right. "Could you do me a favor?" I asked as my call waiting beeped.

"Anything, doll."

"Hang up. I've got another call coming in," I said.

"You wound me."

I grinned, picturing his fake wounded look. I was sure he had hand on heart too.

"Thanks for the, ah, help," I said.

"For the record, it is not officially help when someone forces you to do it." He laughed and hung up.

"Hello," I shouted from my perch.

"You're home already?" Felicity's voice sounded surprised.

"Yes, a couple hours ago," I grumbled as I gouged a lens from beneath the clock. Much easier when I knew what I was looking for.

"I tried ringing you in France, but never got through. You don't sound so good."

"I'm surviving," I said, cutting the dangling lens wires. "I'll be in the office tomorrow."

"That's why I'm calling. I've got a bit of a surprise for you." Felicity's hesitant voice paused. "You don't really need to come in."

I stopped digging. I was getting real tired of surprises.

"Um. The chief rang this morning to tell me, um…" Longer pause. "The board voted unanimously to put *Demolition Queen* on hold." Longest pause yet. "Sam?"

With that, I clamped my boots and hands onto the ladder's sides and slid down fast. My heavy boots banged the floor so hard that the ladder bounced. It slanted sideways. Then it crashed loudly onto the coffee table that I'd built from a Danish-barn-door and four large red plumbers wrenches for legs.

"Sam?" Felicity yelled. "Did you know I can see you?"

"I'll call you back," I shouted, marching out the door of the barn.

I was furious. I headed straight for my zip wire, hit hyper-drive, and flew toward the manor with my robe waving behind me. When I reached it, I hurdled up the stairs, raced through the den door, and nearly plowed into James. He was always lurking somewhere in my path but this time he was sweaty, red faced, and breathing heavily.

"You OK?" I asked with concern. He gulped and nodded. That's when I realized my robe was wide open. I was flashing a full frontal at this ninety-something-year-old. As I re-tied my sash it occurred to me that he'd seen more of me than Conrad had.

But so had the cleanup crew guy, ironically *because* of Conrad.

Conrad. Grrr.

With renewed anger, I dodged around the den's two full-sized sitting areas. Ashes flew from the east fireplace as I whipped past. I clocked a "new" Old Master painting over the mantel, glad to see Conrad had finally covered the old dark outline where a painting had been missing since I arrived.

"James, is Conrad in Old Mr. Albany's study?" I shouted, as it occurred to me he might not even be home.

"Yes, madam," he answered in a wobbly voice, still looking shell-shocked.

I charged up the curved stairway and entered the silk-lined hallway.

"Conrad, you f—" I stopped short.

Arms loaded with fresh towels, the housekeeper had flattened against the wall to get out of my way. Her mouth hung open too.

I nodded at her and then pushed into Old Mr. Albany's study without knocking. Even at ten p.m., Conrad was at his dark oak partner's desk. Impeccable in a charcoal gray suit, smoking a cigar, and talking on the phone.

Even though I slammed the door, Conrad enthusiastically waved me in. The words "Game Over—Resume Life" floated across his screen like he had just shut down a game of Snood.

"Prunella, I know this report is upsetting," he said, continuing his call.

Prunella? Psycho-bitch Prunella?

"But HFNC Bank will be fine. We've caught it early. WhistleBlown will fix this with very little disruption. Now, I must go. We'll speak tomorrow." He hung up and moved around his desk with arms wide. "Samantha, darling, when did you get home?"

"Who do you think you are?" I shouted.

Conrad dropped his arms. His eyes narrowed seeing the tulip-shaped security cameras in my hand.

"What good did your ridiculous cameras do? All my tools were stolen," I said, shaking the cameras in his face.

Conrad gingerly removed the lenses from my clenched fist and laid them on his desk. "Yes, you would think this twenty-thousand-pound 'bouquet' would have worked. But your stalker was very clever and cut the external wires. My dear Samantha, by Monday, security will be tighter than ever and with a seamless transition."

"How about with a lens-less transition?" I crossed my arms. I puffed air through tight lips, and wisps of blond hair flew up around my hot face.

Conrad shook his head as he lifted a manila folder from his desk.

"No facts or figures you show me will change my mind. First you invade my privacy, and now you've cancelled my show," I said, ripping the folder from his hand and shaking it under his nose.

He looked surprised at that one.

"Yes, I know what you did to *Demolition Queen*, but it's mine and all I have left." Much to my disgust, tears pricked at the corners of my eyes.

"As a member of the board, I help make decisions about all shows. And a legitimate stalker like your Mousetrap one is reason enough to put a show and its host out of harm's way," he said in a quiet, controlled voice as he eased the bent folder from my hand.

"The Mousetrap Stalker is dead. He killed himself a year ago out of sheer stupidity, remember? And this new idiot only took screwdrivers, drills, and a rhinestone-covered saw," I said.

Conrad looked at his hands. "But the Mousetrap Stalker never came to your home, or rather, your barn. Nor did he write things like this."

Conrad flicked open the thin file and handed me a piece of paper. I saw right away that it was the contents page ripped from *It's Not About the Wall*. The book I'd kicked across the barn floor? I ran a finger along its jagged edge, and then I rolled my eyes at Conrad.

"What's the big deal?" I asked.

Shaking his head, he took the page and flipped it over in my hand. Someone had scrawled diagonally across it using my favorite crayon color, wild watermelon. I read it aloud:

I am watching your show. I am watching you. I am going to have you very soon.

"I am going to have you?" I smirked. "Icky, yes, but don't you think you're overreacting?"

"The security company's handwriting profiler examined this. This intruder is much more dangerous than your Mousetrap Stalker. The profiler said it was a serial stalker with violent tendencies." Conrad rounded the desk again, staring at me with his cement-gray eyes. He kept his distance. He knew better than to try and touch me. Then he said, "The board voted unanimously—"

"The board voted unanimously? Like that's going to get you off the hook. Ha! This has your controlling, possessive self written all over it."

"Sam, in light of this letter, do you not think that it is time to stop empowering the female masses?"

"Over my dead body," I yelled as I reached the door.

Seeing Conrad blanch, I almost took it back, but I was not in a charitable mood. Let him stew for a while.

I stomped down the hall but even its thick silk lining did nothing to muffle Conrad's booming voice.

"Samantha, you come back here."

I kept on going.

CHAPTER EIGHTEEN

"Music," I shouted as I grabbed ahold of my zip wire. With that, the infinitely appropriate song, "Every Day I Love You Less and Less," began to play. I sang along loud and hard.

Cold, damp air clawed at my hair until I reached the tunnel's end where I jumped off, letting the zip wire's acsensor slam into its backstop. I snatched a large box labeled "Extra Rush" from the post basket where James always left my mail. I charged toward the barn and steamed inside.

I was still furious, but as I shook the box, I smiled. It made the loveliest metallic clatter. That meant my "Acid and Clamp Revenge Kit," *minus the acid*, had arrived.

Grabbing a heavy black combat knife, I cut open the box, and inventoried silver chains, drywall screws, relay switches, low-melting-point solder, flux, propane torch, and yellow clamps.

"I know who I'd like to use you on right now," I said, glaring out the window in the general direction of Old Mr. Albany's study.

I went to change, pulling on a t-shirt and tracksuit bottoms. On my way back to my desk, I noticed a letter stuck to the box. It was addressed to:

Mr. & Mrs. Conrad S. Albany

I rolled my eyes, regretting my name change for the umpteenth time. I opened the envelope and slid out an invite along with a gold plastic doubloon and read:

Yo Ho Ho

Mr. Horatio Ignatius Schott

requests your presence at his Pirate Fantasy Party

7th November, 8:00 p.m.

Venue: Victoria and Albert Museum

Pirate Ships for 1:00 a.m.

Using the combat knife, I pinned the card to the front of my knife collection shelf and noticed that to RSVP I needed to send back the doubloon.

A pirate party thrown by Schott at the V&A sounded fun. Even though creepy Schott would be there, I'd definitely go. I flipped the RSVP doubloon up in the air and caught it in the palm of my hand. It said *Arr* and *Narr*. Assuming *Arr* meant yes, I circled that and crossed off the *Narr*, which had to be no.

On the night, I'd definitely take some tools and a sword, but I knew one thing I wasn't taking—*Conrad.*

I stared at the invite and stared some more.

I stared so long it blurred, and my pocketknives behind it came into focus. It occurred to me how odd it was that the stalker/thief took every single tool but left my knives.

Thank goodness.

They held so many memories. Like the azure blue one that Jake gave me, saying it matched my eyes. The knife reminded me of my old self and how happy I was.

I cleared my throat. I focused on the invite again, thinking it would be a fun event to film for a *Demolition Queen* episode…

I stopped.

I couldn't film Schott's party for an episode.

There was no *Demolition Queen* to film it for.

Conrad cancelled it.

"I'm getting my show back," I shouted at the walls as if Conrad was listening. Then I slung the azure knife at the dartboard, hard. It missed by a mile and disappeared into the rafters.

"No more ugly-ass dresses or lady-of-the-manor crap," I screeched in my best glass-shattering Chinese opera voice and hurled a canary-yellow knife. This one bounced off the wooden file cabinet beside my workshop and rebounded onto my coffee table.

Out of frustration and anger, I kicked at one of the industrial spools under my desk. With that, my camouflaged fridge door popped open. The top row of full-sized *Demolition Queen* Champagne bottles beckoned me and I grabbed one.

Popping it quick, I guzzled a quarter of the bottle and mentally reviewed the five 'highlights' of my last twelve hours.

1. The break-in

2. Security camera discovery
3. Shower cam
4. Conrad confrontation
5. Stalker letter

This bizarre-fest showed no signs of letting up. I guzzled the next quarter of the bottle just for good measure.

On the other hand, all the weird stuff kept my mind off what I really didn't want to think about…*Mom*.

With that thought, I finished off the bottle and took out another. I stared at the new bottle and came up with a new distraction. *Champagne sabering*. I had no sabre to use like Silverblade, so I quickly detached one of the plumber's wrench "legs" from my coffee table. I raised it high above the bottle's neck and swung down hard.

Unlike Silverblade's flawless execution, shards of acid-green glass and 750 milliliters of raspberry-infused champagne rained down on my table, steel-toed boots, and the wood floor.

Normally, wasting champagne was sacrilege, but this was an emergency.

Unfortunately, five minutes later, the contents of bottles number two, three, four, six, and half of five pooled around my boots. Only *half* of five because I drank the first half and then tried breaking off its neck with its cork already removed.

That left only a magnum. That equaled two regular-sized bottles of champagne. It wasn't that much of an emergency. Time for a champagne-safer game.

I'd shoot the magnum's cork across the room to impale the open blade on a pocketknife.

Barely a challenge.

I gave Mom's fluorescent-pink knife first honors. I rammed one of its blades into the as-yet-untouched dartboard and opened another of its blades so it pointed at me. Then back at the dark-blue corduroy couch, I cradled the heavy, perspiring magnum in my arms. I aimed it at the open blade. I closed my eyes to toughen the challenge. The room was spinning a bit, so I steadied one leg against the couch and the other against the table.

"One, two, three," I counted and let the cork rip.

The immediate ping told me that the cork hit the knife.

The metallic thud told me the pink knife was now wedged behind my file cabinet.

"Game Over—Resume Life," I repeated the words from Conrad's Snood computer game.

"What life?" I moaned.

I pictured my brand new knife behind the file cabinet. It was the last knife I'd ever get from Mom. That thought made her anguished face float before my eyes.

"Mom…" I said and dropped to the couch. I gulped from the super-sized bottle and then cradled it between shaky knees. "Why didn't you tell me about your MedMaker?" I asked.

I felt myself sinking to that awful place I went after Jake died. The dark place that Felicity, Silverblade, and Mom had all tried to dig me out of.

Several more *huge* swigs later, I laid the empty magnum on my lopsided coffee table. As I pulled my hand away, I stared at the raised diagonal ridge on my palm. I ran one shaky finger along it like Mom had when she played fortune-teller.

"You are lucky, my dear. This extended lifeline will help you cheat death. But that prize will come at the expense of other lives," I said, repeating Mom's words.

"Mom, you were right. First Jake, then you, and now your MedMaker," I said.

My devastated tone made me even sadder. I could barely see for the tears. Never felt more powerless.

"My path of death and destruction is far and wide," I said.

"Who's next…?" I asked in my one-sided conversation.

I squinted at a tiny red pocketknife on the coffee table. I unfolded its thin blade.

"Is Rock next?" I asked.

Immediately I shouted, "NO."

Then, with one fluid motion, I drew the blade across my palm, cutting my extended lifeline in half.

A bead of red bloomed quickly. It seeped into the creases on my shaking palm but I felt nothing.

***

"Madam?"

A quiet, stiff voice sounded in my ear. I lifted my pounding head from the couch. I braced it against the heel of my hand and felt drool in the deep corduroy grooves on my cheek.

Disgusting.

My mouth burned with canker sores. Through half-closed eyes, I saw my empty Buckeye Ball tin. Although, half-eaten balls dotted the table like landmines. Obviously, I'd forgotten I'd started one and began another, several times.

I'd also forgotten about the voice from a second ago and jumped as it again called, "Madam?"

I flopped onto my back and looked up. Registering the butler's repulsed expression, heat began on my scalp and wrapped around my cheeks. I pulled a stained cashmere throw over my T-shirt and burning face, but I still saw his outline.

"Would madam like a shower?"

"No way," I snapped. "Not with shower cam."

"Very well, madam. You must come as you are."

"I'm not going anywhere, and quit looking at me." I was embarrassed that I'd spoken to James like that *and* that I'd snaked my hand out from under the blanket to grab a half-eaten Buckeye Ball.

"I regret to contradict your orders, but madam *is* coming."

With surprising strength, the nonagenarian pried the chocolate from my hand and looped shaky arms under mine. Two empty acid-green magnums rolled off the couch and one after the other, thudded to the floor.

The butler's stiff bow tie pressed against the back of my head as he marched me across the room and out under a dusky sky. He roughly pushed me into his spotless lavender-scented limo and slammed the door in my face. Stunned, I looked around. None of Cook's salmon blinis perched on silver trays this evening.

As he got in, I glared at the back of James's head and was slightly curious to see that instead of two shaky hands at ten and two on the wheel, one gloved hand dialed a cell phone while the other steered the limo out of Cranmont. He also stepped on the gas and turned the corner so fast it threw me against the black leather seat. Like a maniac, he passed everything in sight.

Thirty minutes later, he slammed on the brakes behind a brick building plastered with No Parking signs. Beyond overflowing bins, a grimy brown door burst open. The butler turned off the engine and hung his head as someone wrenched open my door.

The man who grabbed my arm was larger, slightly younger, and a lot more intimidating than my nonagenarian butler.

***

A minute later, I was inside, looking around a dim locker room.

"Shower. Now," barked the man who threw a towel at me and dropped a bag at my feet. "Downstairs in ten minutes."

"I am not in the mood," I snarled. "And it's Sunday, a day of rest."

"It's Monday," he bellowed. "Buck it up, kid."

Silverblade's tall, sinewy body receded down the dark hall and disappeared, leaving only one small patch of dim reflected light on the linoleum floor.

*If this was Monday…*I stopped to calculate…*then it had been seventy-two hours since my last shower.*

I sniffed my shirt and almost retched. Poor James had smelled that when he dragged me from the barn. *Oh geez.* He was probably sanitizing his limo at that very moment. *Could I ever face him again?*

Tossing my clothes straight into the bin, I stepped into the locker room shower and sighed. Even the sporadic lukewarm spray felt like heaven on my tight neck and shoulders. I gulped in deep breaths, trying to clear my head.

I knew what was coming. I was going to need my head as clear as I could get it.

***

Ten minutes *and* thirty seconds later, I sauntered into the gym wearing breeches, knee-high socks, T-shirt, Kevlar padding over my heart, plastic chest protector, jacket, mask, fencing glove, knee high socks that I hadn't bothered to pull up, and double-knotted fencing shoes. My footsteps echoed in the large room. It was empty but for one fencing piste, occupied by Silverblade, whose formal aggressive stance resembled an impatient general.

I rejected his handpicked foil and selected my own from a sheaf on the bench. I flexed it to gauge its stiffness and then took a lopsided stance on the piste opposite Silverblade. Against all fencer etiquette, I answered his crisp salute with a wide casual one that ended with my foil bouncing to the floor. I slowly retrieved it and donned my mask. Silverblade positioned his right leg forward, poised and ready.

"En garde." His staccato voice echoed around the gym.

I didn't even attempt to fend off his first parry, which struck my arm. "I told you I was not in the mood," I said through clenched teeth as I rested my foil on my shoulder.

"No worries. Target practice will do me good," Silverblade said, thrusting his foil hard at my chest.

"What is your problem?" I spat the words at him, rubbing my chest.

"My problem?" he asked. "My problem is you."

With the tip of his foil, he pulled up my socks.

"You're a mess, soldier," he added.

"I am not a soldier." I pushed the sock back down using the opposite foot and returned to the piste. I made two small slow thrusts at him with my foil and then turned and headed for the door.

"Well you better get ready to act like one," Silverblade roared.

I was a couple feet from the door when Silverblade's foil slapped my thigh. Massaging my throbbing leg, I swung around and angrily thrust at his chest. I missed by a lot.

"Pathetic." He laughed. Then he began an unrelenting series of jousts that worked me into a corner. Trapped but not scared, I lunged with my arm outstretched. Fully committed to the lunge, I had no defense as Silverblade flicked his foil's tip over my shoulder and soundly *thwacked* the already sensitive skin between my shoulder blades.

With that, I screeched. I leaped onto a long, low bench, and loomed over Silverblade. Nostrils flaring, I parried and riposted with all my strength. My heart pounded. Sweat dripped. I forced him toward the end of the bench, jumped off, and darted under his arm, ready for the next onslaught. It felt amazing.

Piste long forgotten, we battled past climbing ropes, basketball hoops, and exit doors. He deployed every technique, every maneuver he had ever taught me, bar one.

Then Silverblade's left shoulder dipped by two inches. That one small adjustment, told me what was coming. Silverblade's unbeatable move.

Parry, riposte, parry, riposte, flick and stab, pull back. Silverblade's balletic grace unwavered to the end.

He removed his mask and a lock of his silver hair flopped onto his forehead. He inhaled sharply through flared nostrils.

"Almost acceptable," he said, saluting and then smiling with laughing, crinkled eyes.

"OK then, teach me the rest of your unbeatable move," I said.

Silverblade crossed his chest with his foil and nodded.

CHAPTER NINETEEN

I'd barely launched through the closing doors of the Waterloo-to-Esher train when its high-pitched warning beeps sounded. The door's black rubber seals merely clipped my shoulders, but a medium-height man, with eyes and nose hidden under a floppy fishing hat, was not so lucky. One loafer slipped on the linoleum, and his thigh caught between the doors. Crouched and trapped, his mouth formed a silent scream as the train jolted and began to move toward yellow signal poles that would soon snap his leg right off.

I dropped my bag, straddled his thigh, and faced the doors. Sore, overworked hands grasped and pried apart the rubber seals so that a millisecond before the killer poles flew past, the man pulled his leg inside. I leaned my head against the cold metal door for a second. Then I looked around, but the man was gone. Without so much as a thank-you, he'd plunked himself down on the second bench along and opened his paper.

"You're welcome," I said under my breath. I glared at the brim of his fishing hat as I sat behind him. *Odd hat to wear in London.*

With everything that had gone on, I peeked around, wondering if that guy was stalking me.

Knock it off Sam.

I shook my head and dismissed my paranoid ponderings.

Then I thought about how glad I was to be taking the train home because:

    1. I loved train travel.
    2. Nearly empty trains, like this one, were perfect places to think.
    3. I never wanted to face James ever again.

As we slowed for Vauxhall Station, I flexed aching forearms. The pain was worth it. Silverblade's tough love workout did me good. Drills till two a.m. Awakened at six a.m. with a bucket of water hitting my face. Five more hours of drills.

My head was so clear. I was ready for anything.

Or so I thought.

Then I noticed thirteen missed calls from Gabby, Rock's missing-in-action virus hunting partner. Another call from her was coming in right then.

I anticipated her quiet, polite voice, so the angry male one took me by surprise.

"Where have you been?" it shouted.

"Conrad?" I asked, wrinkling my nose.

"It's Rock," snapped the male voice as the train clattered over a rough section of track.

"Rock?" I shouted back, then turned up my volume to the max to hear better. "Why are you using Gabby's phone? You found her?"

"No, I only found her phone," he said, sounding more upbeat than last time.

"Where are you?" I asked, hoping quarantine was over and he was headed back to England.

"Climbing down a cliff to Bontero falls." He kind of laughed.

"Now you're making dangerous climbs?" I asked with surprise and a frown, concerned for his safety.

"I'm about to go through some vines and stuff. It's a long way down. If blood-sucking snakes, spiders, and jungle rats pounce on me, you'll know by my screams," he said.

"Honestly, have you considered a job change?" I asked, exasperated.

First, strands of ivy inched past his phone screen so slowly a turtle would weep. Then I caught a glimpse of his black-socked-feet in brown leather sandals feeling their way down the cliff side. The views were odd. He must have hung his phone on a chain that swung from his neck.

"Why are you going down there?" I asked.

"I'm looking for more info *and* Gabby," he said.

"I thought Gabby took off for the next big virus," I said.

"Me too, but evidently before the virus hit Gabby was asking about other Bontero viruses and mentioned heading to the falls. I'm worried she fell and can't climb back up," Rock said, sounding hopeful. But then he yelped, "Something grabbed my ankle."

Next, his scrunched terror-stricken face flashed past the screen, looking like a dried-out potato. One shaking hand passed the screen too.

"Rock, don't let go with both hands…" I said but I was too late.

His other hand went past and after that sharp-looking rocks and dark vines zipped by the screen. Rock somersaulted head over feet, feet over head, howling the whole way down.

Finally I heard a *thump*. I saw the "terrifying" leafy tunnel. Rock's death-defying fall looked no more than six whole feet.

"What grabbed your ankle?" I asked.

"I think it was a snake," Rock gasped.

"Glad you're OK," I said, picturing the gnarly vine that was more likely the culprit. "See Gabby?" I asked.

"No," he said. His voice dipped. "But I see something else."

My view spun as he began crawling. One second I was looking at the falls, the next his knees, and then the tip of a grimy plastic bag that he pulled from a horizontal slit between two boulders.

"Sam, it's a rolled-up piece of paper," he said.

His phone was aimed at his chest so I couldn't see the paper but I heard him unrolling it.

"It's a word map with "VIRUS" in bold at its center," he said.

"Aim your phone at it so I can see it," I said. A second later I read:

10:30 a.m.: Hundreds ill, low-grade temperatures, achy, stiff.
Noon: Temperatures above 105°. Translucent, yellowish skin. Eyes glazed.
1:00 p.m.: Bodies everywhere. Unidentifiable. Bloodless. Desiccated.
Blood and Bontero. Bontero and blood.

"Blood and Bontero. Bontero and blood," Rock and I said in unison.

"Eww," Rock said.

"Why hide a timeline of Bontero virus symptoms?" I asked, puzzled.

"Sam, these aren't from this virus," Rock said.

"What?" I asked, balancing against my seat back to close the window and hear better.

"This is dated ten years ago," he said.

"No way." A chill ran up my spine.

"The old and new virus symptoms are identical," Rock said. I heard papers rustling and Rock continued. "There's a Bontero family tree here too. It lists every family and shows who died back then. Deaths looked pretty random." Rock paused. "Last week's was so different. If the mother died, the father didn't and vice versa. But if one parent died, all their children did too."

"So it was gene related," I said louder than I'd normally speak on a train. My ungrateful "friend" put down his newspaper.

"Exactly," Rock said. "I wonder…"

"What?" I asked.

"Gabby vaccinated the children on this trip…"

"Are you saying the vaccines could have caused this virus?" I asked.

"What now?" I asked as I heard Rock gasp.

"Gabby was adopted. Her real name was Gabrielita Lopez."

"So?" I asked, not getting the connection.

"Three guesses where from," Rock added, sounding flat and drained.

I didn't notice that the Wimbledon Station sign was already showing through the window or that the train had slowed down.

"Gabby was from Bontero?" I shouted as the train stopped. "Do you think the virus got her too?"

"Oh Lord I hope not," he said. "There's a note in the corner, it says, 'Did Dad bring it?'"

"What? She thought her dad brought that other virus ten years ago?" I asked.

"Looks like it," Rock said.

"Like father, like daughter," I said loudly, without considering someone eavesdropping. *Did I learn nothing after the hospital incident?*

"Rock, you need to snoop around Dr. Witch's hut. Get more answers," I said in a quieter tone, not expecting him to say yes.

"I already did," said Rock.

"Really?" I had a hard time believing that.

"Could have bounced a quarter on her bed. Had a gun too," said Rock.

Another person with a gun? Great. That made two. The first was Nunchuck from the cliff that night Jake died.

A one hundred percent increase.

"I found reports about the virus under her mattress," he said

"Who's she reporting to?" I asked.

"Don't know," he said.

"Then find out," I said.

"OK," said Rock, not sounding so enthusiastic as he hung up.

"Blood and Bontero. Bontero and blood," I said to myself.

CHAPTER TWENTY

A3 motorway traffic into London was always the pits. So *why* was I driving into London when I loved the train? A better question was how the heck had Conrad convinced me to join him in London this evening? Especially as I'd just come out of there yesterday morning. More importantly, I was officially still not speaking to Conrad. At least not since the whole security camera and canceling *Demolition Queen* affair.

For one thing, Conrad had sounded uncharacteristically nervous on the phone. Tonight was the Business Excellence Awards reception. The event was nominees-only, so he'd asked me to meet him at a flat he'd rented for tonight to celebrate, or be consoled.

Somehow, the Conrad "cause" won out. *Whatever.*

I decided a change of scenery might do me good. Might help make more sense of things.

At least it was a beautiful evening. My Mustang's top was down. Setting sun glinted off its chrome dash. Great tunes. *Glorious.*

That was *until* the news began. I was about to switch if off when I heard, "…in a second we'll bring you investigative newspaper reporter, Mick Tambour live from Bolivia. Tonight he's in front of the camera for this special report."

I stomped on the brakes so hard my overnight bag flew off the passenger seat and hit the dashboard. Car horns blared from behind as I maneuvered to the breakdown lane. I'd just tuned in on my computer screen when Tambour, surrounded by dense foliage, smiled smugly at the camera and then said, "I am a quarter mile outside Bontero, Bolivia, where a deadly virus holds hostage a small village and the missing *Doctors For ALL* group. Among the 'captives' is world-renowned epidemiologist, Duncan Rockney, who has agreed to talk with us."

The screen split. Tambour was on the left. On the right, a distant cliff appeared and then moved closer and closer until Rock's face came into focus.

"Hello, Rock can you hear me? You got the radio mic we dropped?" Tambour asked.

"Rock, don't talk to that creep," I shouted. The woman stuck in traffic next to my car stared suspiciously from her Porsche.

"Hello, Mr. Tambour. Nice to hear a new voice," Rock said, waving and smiling broadly.

"You're laughing?" Tambour asked. His friendly smile disappeared. He scowled under the brim of his hat. "Didn't the virus kill off more than half of the people in that close-knit community?"

Rock looked shocked. "I was only smiling because...no, no it's been a nightmare here."

"A similar virus hit Bontero ten years ago. Correct? So, did the old virus come back to finish what it started?" Tambour asked in a sinister tone.

Rock shook his head. "That couldn't—"

"After some digging, I discovered that although the symptoms for the two viruses were the same, this latest virus appeared to be gene related," Tambour added.

"How did you know that?" I leaned toward the screen. I hadn't noticed before, the type of hat he wore, a *fishing* hat. I inhaled sharply. Tambour was the ungrateful jerk on the train. "Digging, my ass. More like eavesdropping," I shouted at his sleazy face.

He must have gone straight to the airport from the train.

I felt ill as footage of Mom appeared onscreen. It was from her Savoy press conference.

"My biggest concern is the well-being of this group," she said.

With that, Tambour started in on Rock, like an attorney cross-examining a defendant. "Mrs. Helen Palmer, CEO of MedMaker Corporation, sounded very convincing at her MedMaker launch. Didn't she, Rock? And yet, you two spoke that very day, minutes before the launch. Isn't that right?"

"Uh...uh...uh..." Rock sputtered.

"So while the world frantically searched for you and your group, she knew exactly where you were," Tambour said, glaring into the camera.

I envisioned viewers everywhere backing away from Tambour's scary onscreen face.

"I was trying to help," Rock said, sounding defeated.

Tambour's eyes lit up. "Aha. So you admit that you two broke the no-communication quarantine?"

Livid, I clenched my steering wheel with white knuckles.

Rock bowed his head and rubbed the back of his neck.

"You asshole," I hissed at Tambour.

As Rock and the jungle disappeared, Tambour's obnoxious commentary paused, but he wasn't done. Next, the front of MedMaker Corp's London offices appeared with an equally unhappy-looking Max. He was fidgeting with his tie and staring at the microphone someone had shoved in his face.

"Joining us is Mr. Max Carlisle, MedMaker Corporation's sales manager. Mr. Carlisle, what about these claims that an ex-employee..." Tambour checked his notes. ".... Gabby, brought the virus to that poor village inside your drug packages? A virus which more than likely has killed her as well?"

"These allegations are preposterous," Max sputtered. "Our products are manufactured to the very highest standards using rigid safety controls. They are shipped all over the world and not once have we had a contamination problem."

"Is it possible sabotage was involved?" Tambour asked.

"Let's not jump to conclu...clusions," Max said, backing away from the microphone, but the microphone followed. "I would like to add that we are distressed and saddened by this Bolivian disaster." Max looked around like a cornered animal. "That is all I have to say. Thank you."

Max darted into the foyer and Tambour's serious face filled the entire screen again. "Yes, we've found the brave *Doctors For ALL* group, but how long will they be safe with tainted MedMaker Corporation products lying about? This discovery comes on the heels of their newly launched MedMaker killing its CEO. Things look very bad indeed for this international biotech firm. Ladies and gentlemen, we'll bring you further developments as they unfold."

I poked a finger at Tambour's onscreen face. "No one attacks my mom or her MedMaker. This is war."

I was about to pull back out into traffic, but then lifted my foot from the gas as a new thought struck me.

Tambour clearly found out about Bontero from Rock's and my conversation on the train. So why share the Mom/Rock connection but not the Rock/me one?

Why hold that tidbit back?

Was Tambour planning to reveal it later for maximum damage?

I tried but failed to ignore the uncomfortable knot in my gut as I merged into traffic and detoured toward Silverblade's morgue.

CHAPTER TWENTY-ONE

I pushed through the cold stainless steel doors into Silverblade's white-tiled basement morgue to find the man himself staring at a massive white board. He wore a psychedelic eye patch over his left eye. There was nothing wrong with his left eye, or his right, which he then switched his eye patch to. This was Silverblade's trick for getting a fresh perspective on puzzling cases. That and munching popcorn nonstop. The crunchy stuff supposedly helped him think. It must work. People were always sending him difficult cases from all over the world. Silverblade was the best.

"To what do I owe this honor?" he asked, writing one last note on the board before placing his popcorn bowl on a dissecting table.

"Here's payback for ruining my arms," I said, playfully strangling his neck and then giving him a hug.

"Sam, glad you're here." He wiped his hands on his signature tie-dyed lab coat and pushed floppy white hair away from his eyes. "I've got something for you. Eat some popcorn while I get it." He pointed at the bowl and then headed for his gleaming metal desk.

I loved popcorn but this bowl looked suspiciously like one of his organ-weighing vessels. I pictured a kidney rolling around in the bottom with unpopped kernels stuck to it and said, "No thanks. I just ate."

Silverblade looked reflective as he returned from his desk. "Here, I thought you might want your mom's MedMaker chip." He placed the flat quarter-inch square chip in my hand. "I know how proud you are…were of her." He gave me another hug.

"Thanks," I said, staring at the chip.

"It doesn't have *her* name on it, but of course I know it was hers," he said awkwardly because we both knew exactly *where* he got it.

"Not *her* name?" I asked. Puzzled, I turned it over and squinted at the tiny words on its back.

"It says Suzy Q," Silverblade said.

"Suzy Q?" I swallowed hard. Suzy Q was Mom's test subject on her MedMaker trials.

I immediately thought of Paris, when I sat at Mom's desk reflecting on mom being a breast cancer survivor. And how she'd vowed to do *anything* to help other women avoid almost dying from the chemo like she had.

What if Mom's anything *included being a MedMaker guinea pig for breast cancer?*

Chills began at the back of my neck. They traveled up and around my scalp. In that moment, the question became a certainty in my mind.

Mom had implanted herself with the MedMaker two years ago, not for heart problems, but for breast cancer. Which meant, on that night two years ago, we weren't celebrating the success of Suzy Q as a test subject for the MedMaker chip. We were celebrating the working chip that was inside Mom's body.

I sat very still and let it sink in.

Ohmygawd.

Mom was Suzy Q.

Mom was Suzy Q.

"Way to share, Mom," I said with a frown.

I felt betrayed.

Although, at the same time I understood exactly why she hadn't told me. I would have tried to talk my headstrong, intractable, stubborn-to-a-fault mom out of it.

Who did that sound like?

I pictured our last hour together at the breast cancer fundraiser when Mom slipped the fluorescent-pink knife into my purse.

This one holds everything you'll need, she'd said.

I'd laughed.

How could she give me, the Demolition Queen, a knife attachment I didn't already have?

And then her toast "I've loved being your mom. I am the proudest mom in the world." It had been so over-the-top dramatic.

Now I knew why.

Mom knew her cancer was killing her. The MedMaker launch probably kept her going.

Our last meeting at the fundraiser wasn't about gift-giving.

It was about Mom saying good-bye.

CHAPTER TWENTY-TWO

I'd needed to get my mind off the Suzy Q discovery so I'd challenged Silverblade to a fencing session in the morgue and completely lost track of time. For that reason, I was incredibly late letting myself into the ginormous suite Conrad had hired for the night.

"Conrad?" I called. He didn't answer. That was a pleasant surprise. If he wasn't there yet, he couldn't be mad at *me* for being late.

I looked around and let out an appreciative whistle. A bit trendy for Conrad's tastes, but "first class or don't bother" certainly applied. All except for a white Perspex cuckoo clock by the front door. He'd hate that.

I dropped my keys onto a round, chunky mahogany entryway table and touched a gargantuan tissue-wrapped bouquet of red roses. Daisies were my favorite. Conrad knew that too, but an Albany never bought *or* gave such a "common" flower.

I shot an admiring glance at the cream and chocolate brown bull's-eye rug beneath the table, designed by one of the latest "it" designers. I glanced across the large square living room. Twin angular orange and white flower arrangements shot up between matching chocolate brown suede couches. From the balcony, the views of Hyde Park were incredible, all lit by intermittent lanterns.

Back at the table, I tucked the roses under my arm and tried to guess which of the seven closed doors led to the kitchen *and* a vase.

The first two were guest rooms with king-size satin duvet-covered beds. The third was a coat closet with twenty perfectly aligned hardwood hangers, befitting cashmere top coats and jeweled shawls.

Door number four led to a wall of frosted-glass and eucalyptus-scented air. "I'll see you later," I said to the steam room.

Five was the dining room. A multi-tiered chandelier hung over a large round table surrounded by sixteen leather dining chairs.

Finally, the second-to-last door led into the kitchen, which had more creamy white marble and appliances than Cranmont Manor. Its walk-in pantry enveloped me with what I could only describe as opulent abundance, like a Fortnum & Mason's food hall. Balancing a bone china vase in one hand and palming a jar of thumb-sized cashews in the other, I was backing out of the pantry when I heard jangling keys, banging coat hangers, and Conrad's booming voice.

"Max, no one is out to get you," Conrad said.

I sneaked a look through the louvered kitchen door and spotted a newspaper half-in and half-out of Conrad's open briefcase. The words *MedMaker Corporation* and *Bolivia* practically screamed from the front page.

Oh, shoot.

What if Tambour already decided to drop his bombshell about me and Rock?

I could picture that headline…

Ms. Demolition Queen Knew Bolivian Team's Location and Left Them to Die

Conrad would be beyond livid.

I plastered my best "happy to see you" expression across my face, hugged the cashews, vase, and champagne to my black cashmere wrap dress, and swung through the door.

Well, if that imagined Tambour article *was* in that paper, Conrad's warm smile and appreciative glance told me he hadn't seen it yet.

I had a brief moment of doubt as Conrad turned his back and lowered his voice to continue his call. Luckily, Tambour had nothing on me when it came to eavesdropping. I caught every word.

"Listen, Max, what if I try to intercept any samples that come out of Bolivia and give you first crack at testing them? Would that make you relax?" Conrad's voice went back to normal as he looked back at me and finished his call. "My wife, the gorgeous Samantha Albany, is here, so I must now bestow all my attentions upon her. I shall see you at breakfast tomorrow morning."

Conrad shut his phone and leaned over to kiss my temple. I pushed the cashews into his hand and scooted around the table to place the roses in its center.

"They're beautiful. Thank you," I said.

"My pleasure."

"Is Max OK?" I asked from behind the roses.

"No." Conrad frowned. "Not with this whole Bolivia situation heating up. Today, I went back and scoured the MedMaker Corporation-WhistleBlown reports but didn't find any disgruntled employees who could have tainted products. If I've missed some vital clue that could have avoided this I would be beside myself …"

"You couldn't possibly blame yourself for this," I said to Conrad.

While *I*, on the other hand, *could* blame myself, at least for the PR part of the disaster.

"If possible, Max is in a worse state than before. He has rung me twenty times since the press accosted him outside his office." Conrad popped a handful of cashews into his mouth. "On a brighter note, I have organized breakfast with Max and your friend Felicity tomorrow."

"That was a nice idea." *All except for the part about Conrad and Max being there.*

Conrad shook his head. "But enough about work. Time for more important things." Conrad paused and glared at the cuckoo clock as it pinged the quarter-hour. "At the awards dinner, all I could think about was seeing you," he said, disappearing into the dining room.

Fingers crossed he didn't say 'because of the Tambour article'.

The beautiful sound of a popping champagne cork and tinkling crystal sounded promising. He emerged with two shallow, old-fashioned champagne glasses.

"I have wonderful news," Conrad said, handing me a glass. "WhistleBlown won."

I'd been so worried about my own tail, I forgot about the awards.

"Congratulations," I said and clinked Conrad's glass. "Mom would have been so happy for you."

Conrad nodded and placed a hand on my shoulder to steer me into the living room. "I need to talk to you about something."

Shoot. Here it comes.

"So what do you think?"

His excited expression completely threw me. "About…?"

"About this place," he said.

I stared at him.

"Silly me. Sorry, darling, let me back up. First, I want to apologize." Conrad sat on the suede couch nearest the balcony's sliding glass doors. He laid his phone on a square mahogany tray that spanned the entire low suede coffee table. Then he patted the down-filled cushion he was sitting on for me to join him.

This should be interesting, I thought, downing my champagne. He looked annoyed as I chose the couch opposite but he tried to hide it by casually sipping from his glass.

"I want to apologize for my abominable behavior. An explanation is long overdue. After that, I think we deserve a nice long steam to relax," he said.

I didn't think steaming was his thing, but said, "Sounds good. OK. I'm listening."

I set my empty glass on the mahogany tray. I leaned back on my couch so that the tall flower arrangement obscured his face. He grasped the vase and scooted it aside. His plastic smile *was* pretty entertaining.

"I have behaved abominably and I apologize," he said. "Not only have I been devastated by your mother's death, I have been working on a highly confidential and stressful case." He looked down at his hands and twisted his wedding band. "I'm thrilled to report that it's finally sorted."

Going to have to do a lot better than that.

Conrad stood, took one huge step, and then sat beside me. He refilled my glass. "I know that I overreacted to your newest *Demolition Queen* stalker, but it was only because I worry about you." Pause. "To rectify the situation, I convinced the governors to reinstate your show." Big smiles.

You're darn right.

"And…this London pied-à-terre is a gift to show you how very sorry I am." He proudly looked around the suite as the clock began its midnight cuckoos.

Cuckoo, cuckoo.

"The breakfast with Felicity and Max is to celebrate *Demolition Queen*," he said, glaring at the clock like before.

Cuckoo, cuckoo.

"This place is also an early anniversary gift," he said.

Cuckoo, cuckoo.

The words *anniversary gift* still hung in the air as his phone's old-fashioned ringtone sounded from the coffee table.

Cuckoo, cuckoo.

Reaching for it, his sleeve caught my refilled glass and sent it somersaulting. The glass clipped the table. It rang like a bell until the plush black rug silenced it.

Cuckoo, cuckoo.

"Bollocks!" Conrad roared.

Cuckoo, cuckoo.

With my show reinstated, wasted champagne didn't upset me tonight. "It's only champagne," I said, grabbing a napkin to mop it up.

Cuckoo, cuckoo.

Conrad launched off the couch. I looked up as he furiously punched buttons on his phone and slammed it against his ear.

Cuckoo, cuckoo.

"Prunella, I told you I have this sorted," he shouted into his phone, purple-faced. He stiffly marched toward the foyer.

Cuckoo, cuckoo.

"That is precisely why you pay me my exorbitant fees, remember?"

Cuckoo, cuckoo

Empty wooden hangers clanged in the front hall closet.

Cuckoo, cuckoo.

The twelfth *cuckoo, cuckoo* never had a chance. Conrad punched the Perspex clock so hard it crashed to the floor seconds before he slammed the door behind him.

"Happy anniversary to me," I said, toasting the *empty* room with my *empty* glass.

***

I woke with a start and checked my watch. *Already 4:20?* How could that be? I'd planned to lie down only for a second. I looked over the back of the couch and down at the floor. The barely ticking cuckoo clock also read 4:20.

What woke me?

"Conrad?" I called out, thinking he might have returned.

No answer.

Probably just a nightmare. Conrad's charming-to-crazed act in under thirty seconds was truly nightmare material. And the color of his face? *Heart attack city.*

Odd that he hadn't come back but I knew he'd return by morning. Conrad wouldn't miss a breakfast date with Max.

Now wide awake, the steam room's etched glass door beckoned me. My mood immediately lifted.

Thirty seconds later, I was naked as a jaybird and pulling open the steam room door. I passed the flat red emergency button and had the fleeting thought that it should be *inside* the steam room, but I was willing to risk it.

Scrumptious eucalyptus-scented heat engulfed me as I entered the long, narrow room. Only four blue pinpricks of light lit the space. My bare thighs tingled as I slid onto the hot half-moon shaped shelf and aligned tight shoulders with the first two lights. A hiss of steam seductively caressed my arms, legs, and shoulders. I sighed. The intense warmth brought back memories of baking on a private dock in the Maldives with Jake.

Jake.

***

The week after we met in Switzerland, I had a location-scouting trip in the Maldives and stayed in one of those awesome huts down a long dock out into the sea. *Gorgeous.* That first morning, I parted the mosquito netting on my side of a four-poster bamboo bed and leaped out onto the open ocean-facing side. Immediately, I spotted wet footprints leading from there to the opposite side of my bed. I followed them and barely peeked inside the netting when a firm, wet hand grabbed my naked body and pulled me back into bed.

"Thought you'd never wake up," said Jake.

He was grinning but he'd invaded my turf, and I was ticked off.

"I've got work to do, and I'm starving. When my feet hit the floor again, I'm out of here," I said, struggling against his arms until the cool drops of water on his chest warmed against mine.

"OK, so your feet won't hit the floor," he said as he grabbed the netting and tied my wrists to the bedpost. "Don't move," he said with a laugh and then left me like that.

Ten minutes later, he reappeared. He fed me coffee, fresh fruit, and eggs. When he finally untied me, the last thing I wanted to do was get out of bed.

We were still there when the sunset came straight through the hut. It lit Jake's stubbly face and ruffled hair as he raised his head and shoulders above me and said, "I love you."

He looked as surprised as I felt.

***

Still thinking about that amazing day, I hugged my knees to my chest and then lowered them into a lotus position. I flexed my shoulders and felt a slight loosening. Inhaling the steamy air, I held it in my lungs for four beats, exhaled, and repeated. With a slight turn of my body, I lowered my shoulders until the hot tiles pressed against my bare back and bum.

Heavy eyelids closed.

Breathing slowed.

Brain emptied.

Steam thickened.

And...light fingers brushed my closed eyes. *What?* I should have looked or done something, but I had no desire to move. I hadn't been touched like that since Jake. I held my breath. It felt so good, fingers trailing over my nose and parted lips. They left a fiery trail, snaking down my throat, between my breasts, and to my stomach. They moved to my tattoo. My hips arched off the tiles to meet the hand that traced its fine swirling lines. The touch was so delicious, so familiar. I finally peeked through half-opened eyes.

Then my eyes opened wide.

I was staring at the twin to my tattoo.

Jake's tattoo.

"Jake?" I yelped with joy.

Consciousness shifted. I grasped the edge of the shelf, swung my legs over and sat straight up. My breathing was so fast that steamy pinwheels spun away from my mouth.

First a nightmare and now a dream?

A hugely frustrating dream, albeit a delicious one.

How could my brain be so cruel?

I stood ready to go. Then I noticed that only two pinpricks of light on the wall were visible. The two in the far corner weren't lit. Odd that they'd burn out at the same time. As eyes adjusted it looked like something was covering them. My scalp tingled. I bent at the waist and peered into the darkness. A whole lot more than just my scalp tingled as I made out a man's suit sleeve with one shaky hand extending from it.

Conrad?

Had Conrad touched me when I thought it was Jake?

Talk about extreme voyeurism.

"Conrad?" I said between clenched teeth.

The hand twitched, but no answer.

Conrad would answer me...wouldn't he?

If that wasn't Conrad, then I wasn't hanging around to find out who it was.

Every nerve was on fire. I felt hugely vulnerable sitting there naked. How fast could I reach that emergency button? I looked away from the dark-suited figure to gauge the distance. Looking back, my eyes again took a second to readjust. The guy hadn't moved.

That was odd too.

Well, if he was giving me a running start, I was taking it.

I stretched my toes to the wet floor and was about to run when something struck my shoulder. My head smacked the tile wall, and I was pinned to the shelf.

"Get off me," I shouted and pushed at the heavy, damp mass of a man pressing against my naked body. I tried to kick, but he was too heavy. I punched his back. Still, he didn't get off.

In fact, he didn't *move*.

Not even an inch.

I grabbed a fistful of hair and lifted his head. His face was slack with eyes closed, but I saw right away it was Conrad.

I patted his cheeks.

"Conrad?"

Nothing.

I reached round his soggy gray shoulder and pressed fingers into his carotid artery. The pulse racing through my fingers was much stronger than the one in his neck. I locked my hands behind his back to partially lift, partially drag his 190 pounds of dead weight off the shelf.

I lowered him and his Bond Street custom-made suit into the eucalyptus-scented puddle. Boy was he going to be furious about that when he woke up.

What was he thinking waiting in a steam room in his thick suit?

How long was he in here?

Steam billowed out into the foyer as I propped open the inner and outer doors and then struck the emergency button.

Grabbing Conrad's shoulders, I dragged him out onto the bull's-eye rug. I unbuttoned his collar, patted his pasty white face, and waited for the emergency crew.

This anniversary celebration just gets better and better.

CHAPTER TWENTY-THREE

Felicity was doing a two-handed wave, to get my attention from across the crowded Wolseley restaurant. Max just glared at me, then at Felicity, and back at me. He was in good company. The stares I got from the maître d' and then the London crowd as I wove around endless tables were legendary. OK, I wasn't looking my best. Disheveled black tracksuit. Matted wet ponytail. I could have called but I couldn't have given this news over the phone.

I stumbled into the chair Max held out and Felicity joked, "Already started celebrating?"

"Nice of you to show up for your own celebration," Max said, making a big deal of checking his Rolex and thumbing his nose at my ponytail.

"You owe me big-time, leaving me with him," Felicity quietly joked as she touched my shoulder.

Her hand felt like fire on my skin, and I flinched.

"And where is Conrad?" Max asked, drumming his fingers on the table.

"You're so cold. Are you OK?" Felicity stared at me as she repositioned her headband.

"I took a long steam, and he fell toward me with his eyes closed," I said, launching right in. It didn't even sound strange. Honestly, bizarre had become my norm.

But Felicity and Max looked completely lost.

"Who fell? Whose eyes were closed?" Max asked with detached interest, sounding rather annoyed. He did offer me a glass of water, but I ignored it. Social convention didn't seem to fit right now.

"Conrad fell," I said. "He must have been waiting there a long time," this I said more to myself than to them.

"Conrad fell?" Max asked and leaned toward me.

"*Now* you're concerned?" Felicity glared at Max.

"I dragged him out. I even laughed about him wearing a business suit in the steam room," I said.

"So, where is he?" Max demanded. Silverware rattled and water glasses rocked as he nervously collected the tablecloth in his hands.

"I don't know." I shook my head.

"What *do* you know?" Max snipped.

"Max, calm down, I think she's concussed," Felicity said.

My head did hurt. It had smacked those tiles pretty hard. I reached around and felt a fist-sized lump.

"The ambulance came and they couldn't resuscitate him," I said and took a deep breath.

"They took him to the hospital?" Felicity asked.

"Conrad didn't need the hospital," I said.

"That's good news. I'll ring him," Max said, pulling out his phone.

"Not really," I said, replying to his first comment.

"So what happened?" Felicity asked.

"He's dead," I said.

I dropped Conrad's ringing phone onto the table as Max's name began blinking on its screen.

Max looked confused.

"Conrad's dead," I repeated. "The coroner said possibly a massive stroke brought on by overheating. Apparently, Conrad had been in the steam room for quite a while. Haven't a clue why."

"He can't be dead," Max said. His chair scraped loudly as he pushed away from the table and stood. He stared down at me looking furious, petrified, and hopelessly lost.

"Did Silverblade say anything else?" Felicity asked.

"What?" I asked.

"Silverblade, the coroner, did he tell you more?" Felicity asked.

"Oh. No, it wasn't Silverblade, he wasn't on duty," I said.

Max's lips moved, but he said nothing. Instead, he turned and marched out of the restaurant.

Stupefied, Felicity watched him go and then looked back at me.

I rubbed at my palm and its "killer" lifeline.

"My path of death and destruction keeps on widening," I mumbled the words so Felicity couldn't hear.

It sounded way too loco to say any louder.

CHAPTER TWENTY-FOUR

Finally back at Cranmont Manor, I sat on its sloped acreage at the front. I tried very hard to focus on the damp prickly grass, the cool dewy air, and the stars crowding a perfect blue-black sky. It didn't work. I was feeling like my own personal demolition gone wrong.

Demolition Queen was in limbo.

Rock was stranded in Bolivia, *or not.* I didn't know which.

I'd been widowed and was interring my husband's ashes tomorrow.

Mom was dead, and nothing would bring her back.

I was dealing with the situation by making everyone and everything disappear. I'd sent the butler, housekeeper, and cook away for the night. Cranmont Manor was next. Grabbing its remote controls, I turned out every single light so that Conrad's big white block on the hill vanished.

Then I turned on music. It was supposed to help but of course it didn't when I chose "Amnesia", the song from that night Jake and I met.

When you hit me on the head with your beer bottle,

That first line made me picture Jake swinging from the chandelier. It was like a sledgehammer to my stomach.

Something in my chemistry changed.
And though I've already decided to forgive you,
My friends think I'm permanently deranged.

I hope that it's only amnesia,
Believe me, I'm sick but not insane.

The insane bit felt a little too close to home.

Yeah, I hope that it's only amnesia—

The song abruptly stopped and surprise, surprise. Led Zeppelin screamed from the speakers. I glared at the mansion and angrily pushed the CANCEL button.

Zeppelin stopped.

That was good.

What wasn't good was that a basement light, near the old kitchen, blinked on and then quickly off, like someone had turned it on by mistake.

I hopped to my bare feet. A sense of excitement skittered across my shoulders as I raced toward the manor to find out who was here. I was already up and inside the moonlit foyer, gasping for breath, when it occurred to me that this was could be a pretty stupid thing to do.

Of course, that didn't stop me. The Pousette Dart Band song still blaring outside urged me on.

Believe me, I'm sick but not insane.

I tiptoed into the pitch-black art gallery and inched toward the den door. I couldn't see a thing. I held my hands out in front so I wouldn't smack face-first into a column. It helped. I was moving much faster, so when my bare foot hit a cold wet spot, I slipped. I had to hug a column so I wouldn't go down.

Still hugging, I swung my pointed toe in an arc along the floor. It skimmed another wet spot nearer the wall. I crouched and repeated the arc. Then I crept my fingers forward until they hit a damp, sturdy lump. My fingers recoiled.

What was that?

Cleaning supplies left by the housekeeper when I shooed her out? Or moldy maraschino cherries and pineapples from the fundraiser?

Even in pitch-black, I squeezed my eyes shut to concentrate. My fingers touched the lump again and felt thick round strings. They followed the strings down until mud slipped under my fingers.

OK. We have mud.

I felt rounded leather and a rubber sole.

We have a shoe.

I felt a second rounded section of leather and another rubber sole.

Make that two shoes.

Heels were snug against the wall. I crawled closer to pick them up, except I couldn't.

They were too heavy.

Why would shoes be too heavy to pick up?

Because something's in them?

That thought sank in double quick. The hairs on the back of my neck stood up.

But before I could move away from the shoes-with-something-in-them, they hopped from my grasp. Something pushed at the back of my neck and a gust of air hit my face.

I scrambled to my feet as the shoes-with-something-in-them pounded toward the back of the manor. Slipping and sliding, I lost time fending off curtains and dark columns. Finally, I raced through the moonlit ballroom and out the open terrace doors. Doors that should have been highly alarmed and very secure.

I leaned out over the railing and scanned the field beyond the terrace. I looked to the far right and then left toward my barn.

The moon's reflection looked so bright and harsh on the barn's copper weather vane.

Why?

Because that wasn't a reflection *or* the moon. The roof's motion-activated security lights had turned on.

The *indoor* motion-activated lights were on too. I saw a dark figure move inside.

"Watch out. Here I come," I growled through gritted teeth.

I catapulted off the stairs and raced diagonally across the field. I felt like our old family dog. He used to catapult off our back stairs and race across our fields when chasing foxes.

I reached the barn and ran in the open kitchen door with a sense of dread. A well-founded sense of dread. For like our dog who never caught his fox, I hadn't caught my thief.

No one was there.

Neither were my knives.

CHAPTER TWENTY-FIVE

I heard Felicity before I saw her at the kitchen door. She was saying, "Sam's here in the barn. Could you please bring down the black dress and shoes I laid out on her bed? Dark tights too," Felicity added, probably noticing the scratches and oil stains on my calves and shins.

"Sam, what are you doing...?" Felicity's words trailed off. "Sam. No!" she screamed.

I turned in time to see her tripping over the propane torch, wood scraps, and chains spread at my feet with a wide-eyed terrified look.

"You scared me to death," she then said, glaring at the four chains that ran from my neck up into the rafters. She also looked puzzled and incredibly peeved. "I thought you'd hung..."

My friends, they don't look at me the same.

I grinned, which only made her more steamed up. But a grin was all I could manage. My mouth was busy holding the ends of the four chains.

I nodded toward a nut and bolt on my desk, just out of my reach. When Felicity handed it to me, I slipped it through a link on each of the chains and screwed on the bolt, then let the chains dangle.

"Perfect timing," I said, flexing my jaw.

"What is all this?" Felicity pointed at a wall-mounted cleat and small black box that had wires running between them.

"It's a booby trap to catch my stalker. That bastard came back last night and stole all my knives," I said.

"Booby trap?" The color drained from Felicity's face.

I shoved a desk stool in her direction. She didn't look so good.

She sat as I wiped greasy hands on my rolled-up coveralls and then grabbed the rafter chain. Pulling hand over hand, I raised the joined chains. Along with them went a white bedsheet and two bags of drywall screws. I kept pulling until all of it disappeared into the rafters.

"I'm so annoyed at myself for not setting this up earlier," I said, wrapping the single chain around the cleat to secure it.

Felicity peered uncertainly into the dark rafters. Lowering her gaze, she stared at the blue *Demolition Queen* hats intermittently hung along the wall's top edge. I'd hung them the night before to cover what looked like more hidden cameras.

"This is a bit out there, even for you," Felicity said, looking back at me. She pulled a piece of newspaper from her pocket, looked like she might hand it to me, and then pushed it back in. "You're scaring me," she said.

"I'd be more scared for that stalker when he comes back." I grinned.

I must have resembled something scary like Jack Nicholson's grin in *The Shining* because Felicity had never looked more alarmed.

My friends, they don't look at me the same.

"Surely he won't return." Felicity's voice rose in panic.

"Lots to come back for." I pulled open a file drawer stuffed with my second-string knives.

Felicity looked toward the door as tires crunched on gravel, and then said, "Well, right now it's time to get you ready for Conrad's service." She hopped up, grabbed my shoulders, and tried to turn me toward the shower.

Why were people always grabbing my shoulders?

"First, you've got to see this," I said, scooting from Felicity's grasp.

I slid a sawhorse in front of my desk, clamped a male-shaped cardboard cutout to it, and handed Felicity my phone.

"OK. Now point my phone at that black box on the wall and press star, hash symbol, hash symbol, star and then hit enter," I said.

Felicity obediently entered the code. *Swoosh.* The white sheet dropped over the cutout. A split second later, two screw-filled canvas bags swung down from the rafters and, *bam*, smashed into the sheet.

"Perfect," I said, whipping the sheet off the mangled, screw-riddled cutout like a matador.

Felicity looked horrified. She also looked startled as the housekeeper bustled in with an armload of my clothes I'd just heard her request on the phone.

"Time to get your arse in gear, my dear," said the housekeeper. She took no notice of Felicity's expression nor of the mangled board. She didn't even bat an eye when removing the fan belt holding my hair back or at the handful of drywall screws that fell out. "Time for a wee shower," she said, grabbing my shirt.

"I'll take a shower, but there's no way I'm taking off my clothes," I said, yanking my shirt hem away from the housekeeper.

That she noticed. They both stared at me like I was possessed.

My friends, they don't look at me the same.

CHAPTER TWENTY-SIX

I scrubbed at my legs, long and hard, but I needn't have bothered, and not just because of my black tights. Only me and a very strange minister were there to inter Conrad's ashes in the remote Albany family graveyard on Cranmont Manor grounds.

The sermon was brief, impersonal, and *flawed*. The minister said "Steven" as Conrad's middle name instead of Simon, his real one. Plus, his tall black cap tilted rakishly, and he read Corinthians 13, words more suited to a wedding than a funeral.

For propriety's sake, I was about to invite the odd man to Conrad's wake, when he abruptly turned, folded into his Ford Fiesta, and drove away without another word.

I decided that if anyone asked, I'd describe the service as "fitting" and leave it at that.

Relieved it was over, I strolled back toward Cranmont Manor. As I reached the tower, I looked up at its top where that stone was missing. Evidently, before the tower was condemned, guests who stood up there could see Windsor Palace and St. Paul's Cathedral twenty miles away. I'd have given anything to play hooky up there today. Sadly, I didn't have a choice.

I peeked around the side of the tower to check out Conrad's wake. It was in full swing. Conrad would have loved it. His favorite Vivaldi concerto played. His manor looked positively regal. Huge flower arrangements like bookends framed each terrace door, and many of the who's who fundraiser guests spilled out onto the terrace. Plus, there'd be no towering bra crowding his ballroom, and no plasma screens covering his art.

"Here goes nothing," I said, pushing away from the tower.

I'd walked a mere six feet when the earth shook under my feet. I swung around to see a massive square stone had sunk into the earth where I'd stood seconds ago. I looked way up and spotted a second gaping hole in the tower's top, like a missing tooth in a child's smile.

If I hadn't headed for the wake, I'd have been history.

A reminder from the grave to stay away?

OK Conrad. I get it.

The near miss didn't scare me. It did make me move a little faster. I marched across the bridge above the ravine and over the section of lawn, still matted from the fundraiser dance floor. I even marched up the terrace stairs, into the ballroom. No one rushed over to see if I was OK, so I assumed no one saw my near demise.

To my left, Max was acting all lord-of-the-manor-ish, smoking a cigar, and entertaining Conrad's cronies. So I turned right.

I skirted the chandelier drop zone, *just in case*, and entered the path of a bent ninetyish-looking woman waving a hankie at me. I was about to say hello when she pounced.

"Your husband screwed me out of a croquet trophy," she said through shriveled pink lips.

I opened my mouth and then shut it, not sure how to respond.

"That son-of-a-dog sent my croquet ball under the prickly holly hedge to win," she said, her shaky voice rising.

"It is very sportswoman-like of you to pay your respects." I forced a smile.

"Bollocks to that. I came for my trophy."

I stifled a laugh as the woman opened her upholstered handbag and pointed to a cavity where it was meant to go.

"Unfortunately, I am not sure where the trophy is, but if you leave your details in the guest register, I promise to send it to you," I said.

She had a rigid look like she wasn't going anywhere without it, until a waiter slid his tray of hors d'oeuvres under her nose. Her eyes lit up, and right in front of me, she started filling up the trophy spot with king prawns. She was struggling to snap her bag's metal clasp as I escaped to the foyer.

It was a strange crowd. A couple of women near a triple-thick bank of flowers stopped talking. Some of Conrad's cronies snickered like schoolboys behind the Albany busts. The old muckety-muck in full Royal Navy uniform actually pointed at me. Their looks weren't exactly grieving-widow material. Not that I felt like a grieving widow.

I felt horrible that Conrad was dead, but in a detached sort of way as if it was not my death to mourn. I felt pretty darn guilty about that too.

This was so darned uncomfortable. I'd have loved to take one giant "Mother May I" sidestep into the bank of funeral flowers. Unfortunately,

I was in the military-trained sights of the Royal Navy muckety-muck. He was headed my way with open arms.

"Hello, I'm Colonel Benjamin at your service day *or night*," he said, winking to emphasize *night*. His medals clanked as he leaned in and kissed my cheek.

Was the old fart making a pass at me?

"Thank you so much for coming." I repeated my standard line in a very neutral tone even as I felt a little pinch on my bum. With that, he turned and gave a thumbs-up to his friends and left.

I wasn't taking any chances of his friends lining up for the same. I said a silent, *Mother, may I?* and took one giant sidestep between bushels of lilies, freesia, and birds of paradise. One more step and I heard, "Ow."

I looked down. I was standing on Felicity's high-heeled black suede shoe.

"What are you doing behind here?" I asked as Felicity brushed lily dust from my black dress. I brushed her cashmere cardigan right back, even though it was spotless.

"That old geezer was making a pass at you. Got the evidence right here." Felicity patted her camera.

"I know. Weird or what—?" I didn't finish because I heard an outraged female voice say, "That American gold digger was married less than a year. She probably got Cranmont and everything else."

That made me smile but Felicity puffed up like a mama bear ready to protect her young. I grabbed her arm, shook my head, and whispered, "Everyone's thinking it. I'm sure Conrad's ex will get most of his stuff anyway."

"Oh, I don't think he'd leave her anything. Not from what she said," Felicity said with a frown.

"What? Where is she?" I eagerly peeked between the greenery.

"Gone. Only came to see Cranmont one last time. Hated the guy, hadn't seen him in years." Felicity nodded.

"Years? He talked to her all the time." I gave Felicity a skeptical look.

"It would be impossible to fake that level of hostility." Felicity's red hair bounced as she shook her head.

I thought about that. "Maybe it was Prunella he spoke to in that soft voice. Never occurred to me that they might be sleeping together."

"Tight-assed Prunella with the brown helmet for hair?" Felicity snorted. "I don't think so."

As if on cue, Prunella's perfume beat out the acres of flowers surrounding me. It went right up my nose.

"That tart. I'm ever so glad that Sam's been exposed for what she truly is," Prunella said.

I looked at Felicity, expecting her to be halfway through the flowers. Instead, she pushed the bit of newspaper, from earlier, deep into her pocket.

"Felicity, do me a favor?" I whispered. "Would you get footage of guests leaving?"

I knew she'd say yes. I leaned over, hugged her, and dipped my hand into her pocket. So that as she exited the flowers, I was reading the article she'd been trying to hide.

Sam Albany Frolics with Unknown Male on Eve of Husband's Wake

Of course there was a photo with Cranmont Manor as backdrop. I was running through the field with an "unknown male" in black. We were even holding hands.

I scrunched Tambour's paper with both hands. *What is that guy's problem?*

Thinking about the "unknown male" reminded me, that last night, I'd felt his boots right about where I was standing now. I quickly dropped to the floor and inspected every smudge and every partial until I found a full print of both boots near the lilies. One boot was missing a chunk near its toe. An easy identifier if I saw it again.

I took a quick photo. I sat back to make sure it was good and then frowned. *It* was fine, but like an apparition, a pair of small white bucks were aligned with the footprints. I almost dropped my phone as I heard the station chief's jovial voice come from above.

"This was the last place I thought I'd find you. I'm so glad Felicity was coming out from behind these flowers." He paused to take my arm and pull me up. "I hate to be indelicate, but the board is very eager to gear up *Demolition Queen* ASAP."

Interesting. Conrad was barely gone, and pound signs spun behind the chief's fluttering eyelashes.

"Now, Samantha—"

I held one finger to my lips and shushed the chief as more of Prunella's scent hit me.

"I can't believe Conrad is gone," Prunella wailed.

The chief cleared his throat. "I have a stupendous idea. How does a *Demolition Queen* relaunch and fiftieth episode party sound?" he asked. He still wasn't quiet enough for me.

I shook my head and muttered, "No party please—"

"I want to speak with Sam," wailed Prunella, in a pleading, tearful voice.

I couldn't imagine what Prunella had to say to me, but I wasn't interested. To my horror, the chief snaked his short, tweedy arm through the flowers and began to wave. I was snapping lilies left, right, and center to grab it back before Prunella saw it, or worse, saw me.

I urgently whispered to the chief, "Actually, a party would be fine. Something small, intimate. Wait a couple months, OK?"

That kept him quiet.

Meanwhile, "lord-of-the-manor" Max exited the humidor, saw Prunella in floods of tears, and came to her aid. While she was distracted, I said a quick good-bye to the chief and sprinted upstairs. I thought I'd be alone but turning the corner in the silk-lined hallway, I ran right into a distinguished-looking sixtyish gentleman.

"Oh my heavens. Terribly sorry to intrude. I hope you don't mind that I made my way up here. I am Conrad's cousin from his *father's* side." His twinkling eyes were the same gray as Conrad's.

His emphasis on "father's side" was comical. I wouldn't have wanted anyone assuming I was from witchy Wilhelmina's side either.

"Played outstanding games of Sardines up here," Conrad's cousin said.

"Sardines?" I gave him a blank stare.

"One person hides and everyone else searches?" He chuckled and continued. "Once you find the hidden person, you hide with them. By the end, you're all packed into a very small space. Hence Sardines." He smiled and pressed his arms tight at his sides.

I smiled too.

"Conrad and I usually won. We snuck from floor to floor on the dumbwaiter, or we'd climb up the outside of the tower and then in through the third-floor window." He pointed out the hall window at Cranmont Tower.

"Sounds like great fun," I said with eyes lingering on the tower. "And your favorite hiding place was…?" I looked back at Conrad's cousin, hoping to hear about secret passageways.

"Expert Sardine players never give away their secrets. Although, we did rig the dumbwaiter to squirt water at passengers. That was quite amusing," he laughed.

I laughed with him.

"Conrad never talked about his childhood," I said.

"When we were young, we were more like brothers. Had lots of fun. Got into even more trouble. Being kept apart from the age of eighteen is probably why we're still alive today," he said, and then his face turned bright red, realizing what he'd said.

I shook my head and gave him a comforting smile.

"I used to visit every weekend until the fire," he said.

"Fire?"

"Well, he wouldn't talk about that, would he?" His gray eyes clouded over. "We were smoking in the barn, that day it caught fire. Flames were everywhere. Auntie Wil's favorite horse, Winchester's Grand Day, died." He wrung his hands and shook his head. "That was the last time I saw Conrad."

CHAPTER TWENTY-SEVEN

Walking along bustling London streets was one of my favorite things to do. So today as usual, I left Waterloo train station on foot headed for Conrad's solicitors. My mind was skipping from one recent event to another and back again. There'd been too many thefts. Too many clues. Too many deaths.

Too many everythings.

What was I missing?

For starters, I was missing a loo. All of sudden I needed one badly. Public loos in central London weren't easy to find. Although, Conrad's private clubs were. Could have bought another chateau with his membership fees.

I was extremely grateful for his cigar club as I nipped into its dark oak-paneled lobby. Right up until I ran into the most unlikely group sitting by a round, copper-topped coffee table, relaxing in tall wing-backed chairs.

"How lovely. Look, dear, it's Samantha," Lady Wolverhampton said as she rested her smoldering cigar in a crystal ashtray next to another cigar and pushed out of her chair.

I loved the woman, but now I'd be crossing my legs for the next ten minutes.

"Yes, I can see that, *my love*." Lord Wolverhampton sounded exasperated, per usual.

He rested his cigar on the ashtray too. I was wondering who that third cigar belonged to as I heard, "Samantha, my dear. What a lovely coincidence." With that, Schott emerged from the third chair, the one with its back to me.

Are you kidding me?

Of all the ridiculously overpriced cigar clubs in all the towns, in all the world, I walk into his.

"I'm so glad to see you out and about," Lady Wolverhampton said, patting my shoulder.

Kisses went all around. Being so close to Schott, I put my hands and chin on high alert.

"We were just telling Mr. Schott how very much we are looking forward to his Pirate Fantasy Party," said Lady Wolverhampton.

"Haven't been to the V&A for donkey's years. Not since that school trip we took together, I believe." Lord Wolverhampton chuckled and puffed on his cigar.

"You all went to school together?" I asked, fascinated. Schott's petite frame made him look so much younger.

Lord Wolverhampton nodded to me and then asked Schott, "What's the occasion for your party?"

I was glad he asked. I'd been wondering the same thing.

"You've all entertained me so graciously. This is your compensation," Schott said with a friendly nod at Lord Wolverhampton.

"You know, I think I'll brush off my admiral uniform for the party. A little *Pirates of Penzance* perhaps," Lord Wolverhampton said, looking more animated than I'd ever seen him.

"There's a very real possibility that I might not be able to attend and I am gutted." Lady Wolverhampton's pout accentuated her double chin. "My dear little doggie is scheduled for surgery." She looked up with tears in her eyes.

"That's unthinkable," Schott said. "I must send you a special treat."

"How very kind." Lady Wolverhampton smiled.

"If you can't make my party you must come round for dinner. All of you," Schott said.

"We'd be delighted." Lady Wolverhampton nodded enthusiastically. Then she looked at me with eyebrows raised, as if prompting a child to say "thank you."

They all looked at me.

"Yes, I'd be delighted too," I said, already concocting excuses to get out of dinner with creepy Schott.

"It's official." Lord Wolverhampton piped up to seal the deal.

"Wonderful," Schott said, tapping a new fat unlit cigar on the arm of Lady Wolverhampton's wing chair. "Don't you just love private clubs?" He winked as he lit his cigar.

Lord Wolverhampton waved his own cigar in agreement.

As Schott moved away, I followed. He was headed in the general direction of the loos. He was whispering something too. It sounded like

"Sodding prick." Odd. *I must have got that wrong.* I racked my brain for words that rhymed. Best I came up with was "plodding thick" and "lauding brick."

I then realized he was whispering into his phone. Schott *had* to whisper, for although killer tobacco sticks were accepted here, cell phones were not.

Next, he impatiently whispered, "So, how long *will* it take?"

It sounded more like a middle-of-argument question possibly interrupted by running into the Wolverhamptons.

Interesting.

CHAPTER TWENTY-EIGHT

Having weirded out Mom's French solicitor, I was on my best behavior and smiled broadly at Conrad's. All I wanted to hear during this will reading was that Conrad hadn't saddled me with Cranmont Manor.

"I, Conrad Simon Albany, being of sound mind and body, do hereby—" Midsentence, the solicitor stopped and scratched at a tuft of black hair peeking from under his white powdered wig. "This is most unusual," he sputtered. Red blotches appeared high on his puffy cheeks.

He studied the papers and then peeled off a small Post-it note, which, unfortunately, I couldn't read.

"Most unprofessional. I do apologize for any inconvenience," he said, tapping his pince-nez glasses on the back of his hand.

With that, he lumbered out of his squeaky swivel chair and left the room. Of course, he took the darned will *and* Post-it note with him.

For forty-five very long minutes, I busied myself with e-mails from all kinds of people and then came across one from Conrad's accountant. I'd lost count of the messages I'd left for that man. I needed to know what bills were due, etc. After reading his e-mail, I understood why he'd avoided me.

> *Dear Mrs. Albany,*
> *Below, I have included Cranmont's balances for your perusal.*

There were lots of numbers, but two jumped off the page at me.

For starters, the £10 million withdrawal the day after Conrad died. I had no idea Conrad had £10 million pounds in the bank.

Who keeps £10 million in a regular old bank?

Then there was the bottom line…£0.

No money?

The accountant's e-mail continued…

Hours after Mr. Albany died, an unauthorized £10 million withdrawal was made.

No shit, Sherlock.

The bank is investigating and will be in contact.

With kindest regards,
Weber & Weber Accountants

Weber & Weber must have praised the Lord for e-mail that day. Giving this news to me in person would have been *no* picnic.

This was bad. This was very, very bad. I was mentally exploring my options as Conrad's solicitor reappeared. With a grumpy smile, he plopped down behind his desk. He scratched at that tuft of black hair again and shouted, "Well get in here. I'm due in court soon," he said, yanking a new clump of papers from his assistant. He skimmed them.

"It appears that Mr. Albany filed an addendum with my partner, of which I was not made aware," he said. With that, the solicitor folded the addendum *and* the will that he'd begun reading to me before spotting the Post-it note. "The proper will reading is scheduled to take place in a year's time," he said and scratched his head so his wig rode way up.

"So nothing happens with the Cranmont estate for a year?" I asked in a high-pitched tone that sounded whiny even to me. *How was I going to support a behemoth like Cranmont?* It would gobble up my savings and inheritance in no time.

The assistant and solicitor eyed me suspiciously.

"Geez, the bastard's controlling even from the grave." *Did I say that out loud?*

I looked up and studied their disgusted expressions.

I guess so.

"Thank you very much for your time." I popped out of my chair, reached over, and tugged the solicitor's curls back into place. I couldn't resist.

CHAPTER TWENTY-NINE

No way was I waiting an entire year to find out the contents of Conrad's will. There had to be a copy of it at his WhistleBlown office. With that decided, I took off, like a satnav set on "shortest *and* fastest route." Picnickers looked up from their brie and pâté as I sped through St. James Park in blue jeans and steel-toed boots. I passed runners, kids on scooters, even Great Danes. Soon I hit the thick Trafalgar Square traffic. I dodged and wove between cyclists, taxis, and vans and then leaped out the other side. I reached WhistleBlown's front doors and its reception in record time.

Nearing Conrad's secretary of twenty years, I couldn't help thinking, *That's what a grieving widow should look like.*

Red eyes, puffy nose, drooping mouth. The prim middle-aged woman sniffled and pulled a crocheted hankie from the sleeve of her billowing Laura Ashley dress. She looked up at me with surprise as if she wondered how I could even walk, so full of grief.

"How are you?" she asked tentatively and offered me tissues.

"I'm holding up," I said with eyes as moist as I could muster. "I know this must be overwhelming for you, but I came to collect personal effects and documents." I dabbed at my eyes and inched into Conrad's office.

I was only two steps inside when she said, "Conrad's posthumous commendation for his HFNC Bank work came today."

I rearranged my impatient expression, backed up, and leaned against the heavy mahogany door to listen.

"HFNC Bank was one of those accounts where Conrad's brilliance shone through. He was brilliant at predicting exactly when their whistleblowing reports would pour in *and* the severity of them. Many reports meant disgruntled employees *and* dishonest companies." The secretary repeated these words as if they were the company slogan. "HFNC's upper management was to blame with this one. They called in WhistleBlown as a preemptive strike to cover their arses. That

Prunella..." I loved how Conrad's secretary said *Prunella* like it was a dirty word. "...brought WhistleBlown in as an independent third party to 'discover' wrongdoing. Then she attempted to manipulate the investigation to look guilt-free. Conrad felt horrible about turning her in."

I could see from the secretary's small satisfied smile that she was not so broke up about it.

Then why did Prunella cry hysterically at his wake?

"Wow. Conrad sure was lucky to have you," I said. She blushed, as I'd hoped, so I felt OK about escaping into Conrad's office.

I inhaled its leather-and-cologne-scented air. I then headed straight for what I called Conrad's "ego wall," crowded with trophies and meet-and-greet photos. First things first, I grabbed the croquet trophy. Didn't want any more nonagenarian ambushings.

With the trophy safe in my plumber's bag, I stepped back and noticed for the first time that this was also a shrine to Cranmont. Of all the paintings and photos of Cranmont crowding the wall, my favorite was an aerial one. Conrad had told me it was taken by miniature remote-controlled blimp. In the photo, there was no scaffolding around Cranmont Tower so I could see how flat and wide open its roof was.

Next, I spotted his monogrammed laptop on his mahogany desk. If I had no luck finding his will in the aluminum drawers behind his desk chair, I was going to take his laptop with me to check out later.

I pulled open the drawer and found files labeled: *Expenses, Employee Benefits, HFNC Bank,* and *MedMaker Corporation.* Nothing looked personal enough to hold Conrad's will. For kicks, I flipped through Prunella's HFNC file. I then rifled through MedMaker Corp's, which was inches fatter but basically the same stuff.

But then, I spotted a sheet of MedMaker stationery, marked *Highly Confidential.* It was from Max, addressed to Mom. It had a printout of a PowerPoint presentation attached too. I laid it in my lap as I read the brief letter.

> *Attention: Helen Palmer – Private and Confidential*
> *Subject: Viability of Converting the MedMaker to Weapon-Grade Gene-Tech*
>
> *It is my strong recommendation that we adapt MedMaker gene technology to produce marketable bioweapons. I wish to discuss this at your earliest convenience.*

I couldn't believe what I was reading.

I studied Max's PowerPoint printout. It listed potential customers, bioweapon advantages, and pricing in the millions, etc. etc. *Geez.*

Had Mom given Conrad this copy? Did Max knew that Conrad knew? It sure explains that look Conrad gave Max at the launch. It also supported my suspicions about Max.

"Sam?" the secretary's wobbly voice called from the door.

I shoved Max's letter and printout under my thigh before spinning in Conrad's leather desk chair to face her.

"May we speak?" she asked. Not waiting for my answer, she rolled her desk chair right on in. I tensed, noticing the small triangle of letterhead peeking from under my thigh. No worries. Her wide floral dress covered it as she scooted so closed our thighs touched. Then she closed moist, sparkling eyes and shivered.

Awkward. I braced myself for an incredibly embarrassing divulgence.

"Conrad was a virile, attractive, and powerful man," she said.

Here it comes.

"He was privy to passels of sensitive corporate information," she said, twisting her hankie into a tight ball.

OK, so not exactly where I thought she was going with that.

She pressed her shoulder to mine. "Conrad rescued so many companies."

Now I was really lost.

"But he also exposed slews of bad people and made lots of enemies." She said this so quietly it didn't qualify as a whisper. "At your Mum's company alone, he put someone in prison for theft. Another fled the country."

And yet another named Max wanted to convert the MedMaker tech to bioweapons.

I pictured the letter plastered to my, by then, very sweaty thigh.

"I think…" she paused and looked toward the door.

I didn't know why, but I looked too.

As I turned back, she mouthed the words slow and exaggerated, like a child telling secrets in class.

"I think Conrad was murdered."

Murdered? I doubted that. The coroner on duty that day said he died of a heart attack brought on by heat stroke.

Could Conrad's secretary be right? Did someone he blew the whistle on take revenge? If so, which client? Which company? An employee of a recent conquest, like…*MedMaker Corp?*

CHAPTER THIRTY

The next day, I hit MedMaker's London offices at the crack of dawn. I had a backup plan in case I ran into trouble. It was triple-wrapped inside my plumber's bag.

I wasn't that worried. I figured I could just say, "I am here to pick up my mom's personal stuff."

Of course, by "stuff," I meant *secret shit*. As in, more info on Max's bioweapon plans and stolen funds. Especially stolen funds because last night I scoured Cranmont's zeroed-out financial records and the WhistleBlown accounts I'd taken from Conrad's offices. In them I'd found that on the same day Cranmont's account was emptied someone had hit WhistleBlown too. To the tune of £20 million. I also found another statement from six months earlier with an additional £10 million withdrawal. "*Max?*" was scrawled beside it.

I wasn't sure if it meant, "Ask Max about it" or "Max stole it." I was hoping to find that out too.

I got in the front door of MedMaker Corp very easily. Mom's company pass still worked there. For the high security labs, I waited until the cleaner opened the door and followed him in. I donned a lab coat and safety glasses so that when he turned around and noticed me, I looked official. I stared intently into one of the labs, taking notes on what I saw. *Two flat-bottom Pyrex beakers. Each contains three inches of liquid. One blood-red. One pink-ish.*

Luckily, the cleaner moved along, because I'd run out of stuff to write.

Finally, at Mom's lab/office door, I paused as a small light above it changed from green to red. I hoped it wasn't some new mega-security measure of Max's.

Pushing that thought aside, I entered. I quickly peered through the window into her adjoining contamination lab to make sure no one was in there. Then I sat at her French country desk and felt like I'd come home.

Having said that, things looked a bit different. Someone had pushed her stuff aside. Drawers were empty except for a MedMaker team photo that I hadn't seen in ages. Everyone wore orange bandanas and lab goggles and had lips puckered into fish-faces. *A keeper.* I eased it into my bag beside my backup plan.

I checked Mom's company emails next. Lots had accumulated since Paris. I searched for and finally found one from Gabby about two hundred e-mails down. It was sent from her phone two days before Mom's MedMaker launch and had arrived the day after I visited the Paris office. I wondered where, how, and why it got hung up.

I hesitantly opened it. I liked believing Gabby was still somewhere happily hunting viruses. Her e-mail could blow that belief out of the water.

There was no message, just a video attachment. I started it up. I saw the falls where Rock had landed but I had to swiftly stop the video. Loud pounding footsteps headed my way. I'd barely hidden myself in the triangular wedge behind Mom's door before a Max, a real lab tech, and MedMaker Corp's PR manager entered.

"Bloody Helen," said Max. His face was a furious red. "Why the hell would she secretly communicate with Rock in Bolivia? And did Gabby transport lethal viruses?"

Max pointed at Mom's contamination lab window and I noticed a sealed hazmat bucket, sitting on a shiny steel table.

"Begin testing our vaccine packages inside ASAP as well as the slides on Helen's desk. Report your findings only to me," Max said to the lab tech who was yawning.

Could those be the Bolivian samples?

Like a thunderbolt, I remembered the whispered conversation between Conrad and Max that night Conrad died. "*Listen, Max, I'll try to intercept the samples and give you first crack at testing them.*"

"And bloody Conrad gets a posthumous award for his HFNC work. Christ. Next, the man will be canonized," Max whined.

Odd. Max had seemed so upset at the restaurant about Conrad dying.

I thought about that for a second.

Max was so upset because he *hadn't* received the Bolivian samples yet.

So how did Max get the samples? Is Rock back from Bolivia? Did he bring them? If so, where is he?

"If those *bloody* samples test positive for *bloody* virus cells, not one *bloody* bit of *bloody* PR you pull out of your *bloody* arse is going to help one *bloody* bit," Max shouted.

Wow. That was a lot of bloodys.

"*Merde, merde, merde…*" Max added.

I knew Max had left because his "*merdes*" got quieter and quieter as he stormed down the hall.

Emerging alone, I pressed my nose to the glass. It was inconceivable that the normal-looking hazmat bucket could finish off Mom's MedMaker let alone the whole company.

Frustration and anger boiled up inside me. I didn't give a toss about Max, but Mom's baby was not going down in flames. I had to do something.

New plan.

The slides and bucket were going with me. Rock had said those Bolivian deaths were gene-related so I wasn't bothered about transporting the samples and slides to Silverblade's for him to test.

I'd pull a switcheroo by replacing the Bolivian boxes and slides with fresh ones. Heck, the HazMat bucket was sealed so no one would know the difference. *I hoped.*

Using Mom's joystick and robotic arms, it was a cinch switching them out and then moving them through the contamination lab's pass-through drawer.

To make room for the bucket in my plumber's bag, I ended up holding my backup plan. Not an easy thing to do. It was a large wobbly balloon full of bolts and WD-40, the tool lubricant.

I almost dropped it when I heard someone right outside Mom's door say, "Security told me that these camera feeds were whacked."

From behind Mom's office door, I saw two stick-thin security guards wearing navy-blue uniforms. I nicknamed them Twig One and Twig Two because together the pair wouldn't have made one of me.

"It's definitely not recording," Twig One said, peering up at the camera above Mom's office door.

"I'll tell maintenance," said Twig Two.

The Twigs turned left and moved out of sight. I thought they were gone, so I emerged and turned right. Barely out of Mom's lab, I heard, "Excuse me, miss. What were you doing in Mrs. Palmer's lab?"

Unfortunately, uniforms gave me temporary dementia. Even ill-fitting rented ones like theirs. Once, I was stopped for speeding, eyed the police officer's uniform, and said, "Hello, Ociffer."

Ociffer? Geez. At least, a winning smile got me off.

As I faced Twig One and Twig Two, my mouth felt like cotton. My mind raced. About to deliver my prepared line, it occurred to me how I'd upped the stakes, i.e., illegally smuggling out the HazMat bucket.

Just here to pick up stuff, I repeated in my head and then eyed those darn navy-blue uniforms again. So instead, I said, "Just cheer to cock up stiffs." *Ugh.*

Twig One and Twig Two looked at each other and then at me.

I tried the same smile that had gotten me out of that ticket, but the Twigs looked immune to smiles and possibly the charms of women.

No way was I getting caught with the Bolivian slides and HazMat bucket.

While they simultaneously fumbled for rubber walkie-talkies, I ran down the long hall, headed straight for the door at the end, marked "Incinerator."

Twig One and Twig Two were now after me. It was backup plan time.

My large red balloon wobbled in my hands as I held it up and then slung it at the floor a foot in front of the Twigs' shoes. It burst on impact and sent a rolling, oily, bolt-filled tidal wave in their direction.

Understanding dawned in the Twigs' eyes. They tried to reverse but couldn't stop sliding right toward me. Three feet from impact, I opened the incinerator door and stepped inside. I'd barely locked it when Twig One and then Twig Two, or it could have been Twig Two and then Twig One, smashed into it.

There was only one way out for me now. Six floors straight down of inky-black incinerator. At least this incinerator was outlawed years ago. So I wouldn't burn up at the bottom. That was unless Max had begun illegal burning in Central London.

Even with that inkling of doubt, I hit the release button for the sixth-floor hatch. It dropped away with a *swoosh* of air and I leaped. After what seemed like forever, my boots hit the fifth-floor hatch with a hollow metal ping.

I did the same again and again, but on the third floor as my feet hit that hatch, I heard knocking. If that was the Twigs, I didn't dare stop. I scrambled for the next release button, jumped, and landed. And realized I was sweating like a hotdog in a microwave.

A small alarm went off in my head.

What if Max *was* illegally incinerating waste?

Shoot. Shoot. And double shoot.

To top it off, this last hatch had no ledge. Once its V-shaped chamber opened, I could drop into a HazMat inferno. My only choices were roast or get caught.

That "caught" headline would be a doozy…

*Sam Albany Tampers with Evidence to Cover-up MedMaker
Virus Contamination*

New knocking began. It sounded like the entire security goon squad was trying to get in. "Roasting it is," I said, punching the release button. I braced for an inferno, but as I dropped, cool air rushed up my pant legs. I then landed in a bare incinerator receptacle with soot condensing on my sweaty arms.

I looked up through the closing hatch and saw air ducts belching out hot, sooty boiler air.

I checked my watch. The whole drop had lasted all of three minutes. Twigs One and Two were probably still slipping around in the WD-40 upstairs.

Nice.

Thanks, Mom.

I wiped soot from my face and hands and then wove into the heaving lunchtime crowd. I headed for the morgue, dying to share my new find with Silverblade.

CHAPTER THIRTY-ONE

All hyped up after the great incinerator escape, I pushed so hard against the swinging doors into Silverblade's morgue they hit the microwave and knocked over a Styrofoam cup full of coffee.

I didn't stop to wipe up the mess, instead I shouted, "Guess what I have?"

Silverblade took one look at the bright yellow bucket with stripy red tape and raised an eyebrow. "Do I really want to know?" he asked, placing his popcorn bowl by the microwave.

"*Yes.* I have Bolivian virus samples," I said, in my hyperexcited voice.

"What do you propose we do with them?" he asked.

"Test them. See if they're contaminated with the gene-coded Bontero virus."

He flipped up his red-fleece eye patch and said, "OK. I could do that, but first, about John Doe. He had a—"

"Not him again," I said, impatiently tapping my foot.

"Wait, I'll show you." Silverblade began shuffling through papers on his desk.

"I've got something else for you too," I said, talking to Silverblade's back as I projected the Bolivian slides onto his white board.

"Oh, I'll find it in a second," Silverblade said as he looked up. Then he flipped down his red eye-patch to cover his right eye and studied his white board.

I expected him to be fascinated by the Bolivian slides. Instead, he looked confused. He was silent so long I jumped when he finally spoke.

"You remember my particularly unusual John Doe? The one that made me late for filming your fiftieth episode?"

I nodded.

"Well…" Silverblade paused as if maybe he shouldn't be telling me this. "John Doe was pulled from the Thames. Authorities are very anxious to discover his identity. They won't leave me alone," he said, taking a photo from his desk. "Highest level security too." Silverblade absentmindedly shifted his eye patch back to the left eye. At the same time, he pushed a disgusting photo of a corpse with purplish/brown mottled skin under my nose. The corpse had an odd cloverleaf-shaped birthmark on his cheek.

"I'll take two eye patches please," I joked, shielding my eyes from Silverblade's photo.

"For someone who spills so much of her own blood without flinching you sure…"

I rolled my eyes. "About the photo," I said, pointing at it to keep him on track.

"Oh. Yes. It's the weirdest thing I've ever seen. That man's Caucasian." Silverblade touched the photo, leaving a buttery smear.

"You're kidding me." I reexamined the corpse's dark skin with fascination. "So what's this got to do with Rock's Bolivian slide?" I pointed at the image I'd projected onto Silverblade's screen.

"Bolivian slide?" Silverblade raised his bushy eyebrows and half-laughed. He pointed at the projected slides and then back at his photo. "Those are my slides from this guy."

"Uh-uh," I said as the hairs on my arms stood up.

Silverblade eyed me with suspicion. I could almost see his fencer's brain calculating the probability of a trap.

"They're from one of the Bolivian virus victims. They came with the bucket. No blood samples though. Blood left the bodies and disappeared."

I thought for sure that tidbit would shock Silverblade, so I was disappointed as he knowingly smiled.

"My chap too." Silverblade's puzzled voice eerily echoed off the tiled walls. "Veins, capillaries, and organs were clean as a whistle. But for this man, instead of leaving the body, his blood collected beneath the skin and mottled it." He paused. "On a hunch, I placed some of his blood cells into a solvent with a seven-point-four pH. Fascinating stuff. I wonder if the Bolivian cells would act the same," Silverblade said.

I didn't know what to expect. He hadn't explained what the others had done. So I watched closely as he placed the Bolivian samples inside a sealed hood and used miniature robotic arms to add a solution to each. Then he set a timer for ten minutes and went back to his desk.

"Aha. This is what I wanted to show you. John Doe had this," Silverblade said, picking up a small plastic bag.

John Doe's flat quarter-inch square cream-colored chip looked exactly like Mom's MedMaker chip. That didn't thrill me. It meant a second person had had an implanted chip *and* had died.

Could the MedMaker really be faulty?

Moving back to the hood, Silverblade cleared his throat and said, "OK, just a bit ago the Bolivian cells were in their normal inactive state. Right?"

I nodded.

"But now..." He motioned for me to have a look through the microscope.

"They're moving," I said with awe as the cells scooted around the Pyrex dish. "How? They were dead," I said as they began swirling.

He nodded. "Get this, before you arrived I introduced foreign cells into the John Doe dish and the new cells began swirling like the rest," Silverblade said.

"Introduced foreign cells to what?" Rock's whispered words came through Silverblade's speakers and then Rock's face he appeared on Silverblade's wall-mounted screen. His red frizzy hair looked as wild as the tangled vines outside the window behind him. I recognized the surroundings. Sadly, he was still in Bolivia.

"I'm back in the doctor's hut, like you suggested. I found her report," said Rock, calm as could be, tapping his checked shirt pocket.

Where did old scaredy-cat Rock go?

"Rock, we have Bolivian samples and Silverblade is running experiments on them," I said.

"How did he get those?" Rock wasn't whispering anymore. He sounded incredulous.

"Somehow they got to MedMaker Corp. Could Dr. Witch have gotten them out?" I asked.

"I heard a helicopter two days ago and thought I imagined it," Rock said as his shoulders slumped.

Silverblade impatiently piped up. "The cells went into solution and are acting like they're programmed and swirling as if on reconnaissance —"

"Swirling? Programmed?" Rock repeated. "What an idiot," he shouted so forcefully that the leaves around his head even shook.

"What did you call me?" Silverblade huffed and moved his red eye patch again.

"No. Not you," Rock said, patting his chest. "I'm the idiot. I can't believe I didn't think of this before. Those Bolivian cells sound like a combination of Helen's MedMaker technology combined with PWT that's been programmed it to resemble a virus. *The* virus from ten years ago to be exact."

"PWT?" Silverblade asked, looking between Rock and then my puzzled face.

Silverblade wrote down PWT.

Over the years, with all my snooping at MedMaker Corp, I never saw PWT written on anything.

"What's PWT?" I asked.

"It means *programmed without target*. Brilliant for quick MedMaker setups. It can self-sample and self-program its own MedMaker using trace amounts of someone's DNA. There's a built-in self-sampling limit of one person. Helen considered using it for a while."

"Rock, could someone remove that limit?" I asked, hoping he'd say no.

"Yes. That's why Helen dropped the PWT project," Rock said.

"Because it could be used for bioweapons?" I asked, thinking of Max's bioweapon memo. Again, I hoped he'd say no.

"Exactly," Rock said.

I stared at my hand, the one I'd used to carry the Bolivian hazmat bucket. I'd quadruple bagged it, but I had a very bad feeling about this.

"Silverblade, what foreign cells did you feed it?" Rock asked.

"Blood," said Silverblade and pointed at his chest then said, "Mine."

Immediately, Rock asked, "Sam, may I to talk to you *in private*?"

I really really didn't like his quick, tense tone.

Silverblade had caught that too. It was unnerving to watch my mentor's face go as white as his corpse-covering sheets.

About to pat Silverblade's shoulder, my hand hovered over it and then pulled back just in case.

I picked up the phone, and Rock's face disappeared from the screen.

"Is Silverblade exhibiting any symptoms?" Rock asked.

"Like what?" I asked, but wasn't really so keen to find out, as my "bucket" hand had begun to itch.

"Stage one, victims complain that their mouths taste sour. In this phase, smart cells are charging to designated areas in your body to set up communications. Stage two, you're ravenously hungry because cells are rapidly multiplying—"

"Could you please use words other than *you* and *your*?" I asked.

"OK. In stage three, *you*…sorry I mean *the victim*, is extremely tired. Stage four, they are achy and feverish like they have the flu. It can take days for some. For the Bontero villagers this all happened within hours."

"What can I do for him?" I whispered to Rock as Silverblade fidgeted with his dissecting blades.

"Just watch him for symptoms. He's probably fine." Rock paused far too long and then asked, "You're not related, are you?"

"Of course not," I said, trying to remember the exact color of Silverblade's eyes.

Even if I wanted to check his eyes, I couldn't. He'd donned a second eye patch so both eyes were covered. Also, he was stuffing popcorn in his mouth like there was no tomorrow.

Not good.

"Rock, it's time to get you out of Bontero. Candace, MedMaker Corp's helicopter pilot, has identified a rendezvous point near the cliffs. She's arranged for a chopper to be there in the next four-to-six hours," I said.

"I'm ready," said Rock, excitedly.

"I'll message you later…" My words trailed off as Silverblade made a horrible face and spit out his popcorn.

Symptom one: Mouth tastes sour.

Shoot.

Shoot.

Double shoot.

CHAPTER THIRTY-TWO

Well after midnight, I finally drove through Cranmont's massive wrought iron gates and pulled up to my dark barn. I was exhausted. I'd spent three excruciating hours on Silverblade "symptom watch."

I felt like an idiot.

When Silverblade made that horrible face and spit out his popcorn, I assumed it was Rock's *stage one*, mouth tasting sour. I thought MedMaker smart cells were attacking Silverblade's body.

Wrong.

If I'd just let Silverblade hear my conversation with Rock, Silverblade could have said he spit out his popcorn because it tasted like rubbish because it was soaked with coffee. Coffee *I'd* spilled.

Geez.

Sitting here in the dark, with eerie, elongated shadows falling across my dashboard, I did another not-so-smart thing. I finally watched Gabby's video. The one I'd found in Mom's emails and started to watch right before Max appeared.

So I again saw the falls and the boulder. But then a petite hand appeared, wrapped in a blood-soaked MedMaker team bandana. That gave me the heebie-jeebies.

As the video continued, instead of the bandana getting bloodier it got *less* and *less* bloody. I checked the timer thinking that the video was going backward. *Nope.*

Then I flinched as Gabby's other hand darted across the screen and urgently ripped the bandana away. I expected a gross bloody wound. So her dry bloodless one with feathered edges was more unsettling.

Then it got weird.

Gabby flexed her hand once and then twice. I involuntarily flexed my own hand too but immediately stopped. Because the third time she did it, her knuckles ripped through the skin like it was tissue paper. Tendons, muscles, and vessels popped like dusty old rubber bands. Bones snapped like breadsticks. Then her phone tumbled to the ground. Nestled in decomposing leaves, it filmed bare, bleeding feet.

Repulsed yet fascinated, I pulled my screen even closer as the blood, like minute red bugs, streamed from her toes in orderly spirals, like on reconnaissance.

Like Mom's phi swirl.

Like John Doe's blood in Silverblade's morgue.

If bioweapons killed Gabby, and if Max made those bioweapons, ergo, Max killed sweet Gabby.

I thought about that. Max *was* a greedy, overly competitive social snob and possibly a thief, but was he a murderer?

I couldn't see it.

I reached to turn off my Mustang, and another thought struck. Before Mom died, she must have figured out that someone hijacked her MedMaker technology.

Therefore, Mom would have devised a plan to stop them.

What form would Mom's plan take?

A hunt with clues, of course.

And where would I find those clues?

Her will *and* her gift, the inlaid box.

I stomped a work boot on the gas. Driveway pebbles flew and hair whipped my face as I sped around the triangle. Reaching the manor, I slammed on the brakes, hopped over the car door, and hit the broad front steps running. I raced through the foyer and art gallery, up three flights of circular stairs, and straight into the linen closet. Frantically feeling around under the stack of duvets, I reached in further and further. I was up to my shoulders in duvets when my knuckles rapped Mom's inlaid box.

"How did I forget you?" I asked the box. I was backing out of the closet while studying the words *an eye for an eye* in its border as my phone rang.

It was Max.

His spin on the MedMaker intruder could be quite entertaining, so I answered it.

"Hi Max" I said, as I put him on speakerphone.

"There were no viruses in those Bolivian samples." Max's excited voice bounced off the walls. "I mean the independent lab tests showed no viruses and no contamination," he added in a more subdued, guilty-ish tone.

The guilty tone reminded me that my own list of felonies had grown. Tampering with evidence in an international investigation being the newest addition.

Oh well.

"I thought you should know that someone broke in at our offices," said Max.

"That's horrible." I raised my voice, trying to sound shocked *and* concerned.

"Nothing important went missing, but security guards…"

That would be Twig One and Twig Two.

"…chased someone out of your mom's office. Rather strange," said Max.

"Did they catch him?" I asked, in a puzzled anxious tone. Saying "him" was a nice touch too.

"Unfortunately not. Oddly, none of the security cameras caught the culprit either."

"That *is* odd," I said as I kicked the closet door shut. I heard a sliding sound in the guest suite so went to investigate. Mom's painting had tilted again.

"The guards said the thief was huge and used an advanced biochemical compound to circumvent their progress," Max continued.

That would be WD-40.

"Really?" I asked and covered my mouth to muffle my laugh.

While Max babbled, I stared at Mom's painting trying to decide if I should take it back to the barn along with the box. And then I saw something in Mom's latest line and swirl additions. It made my heart beat a little faster. The swirls were made up of itsy bitsy words. Some of the same ones from Mom's will and box.

Sealed With A Kiss
Chinese Dragon
Cats are an Puzzle
Call June Thorpe
An eye for an eye
Tickled Pink
Dansnurmur
lMd

lMd was new. That settled it. The painting was definitely coming to the barn with me.

So now as I started downstairs, I was carrying Mom's painting and box plus my phone when Max said, "You and your film crew can't do your demolition thingy in MedMaker Corp's annex next week."

"What?" I almost missed a step.

"No more non-employees allowed on premises," said Max.

"That decrepit annex isn't even attached to your main building. And it's being completely demolished in six months. What does it matter?" I asked, as I stomped downstairs.

"My decision is final. Film your demolition show elsewhere," Max snipped and hung up.

Grrr.

We'll just see about that. I thought, as I hit the foyer and my long legs sped me into the den, right past the Chinese dragon at the east fireplace.

Chinese dragon.

Mom mentioned it in her will and her painting.

Perfect time to kickoff Mom's hunt.

I backed up and excitedly knelt beside the hand-carved dragon. I ran a hand down each leg, and reached up inside its hollow belly. Finally, I looked between curved incisors and down its long tongue. At the very back was a thin, bright-yellow plastic something. I fished it out and was less than thrilled to see it was one of Mom's cheap plastic children's puzzles. It was a cat one from look of the fluffy-looking tail and pointed ear images on some of its fifteen tiles.

Mom's attached Post-it note said:

You have three minutes to solve this.

Love, Mom.

Three minutes? Fat chance, I thought to myself but I still sat cross-legged on the den floor and thumbs went to work. They furiously pushed the squares around the plastic frame but sadly, at the three-minute mark, the cat's nose was in its butt.

I hoped that wasn't a sign of how the rest of my clue hunt would go.

CHAPTER THIRTY-THREE

In my barn's workshop ten minutes later, I tossed the stupid puzzle onto my workbench and then carefully rested the inlaid box and Mom's painting beside it.

Should have brought the Matisse too. I stopped to think. *Did I see the Matisse? Hmm.*

I swung open my empty tool pegboards and centered Mom's MedMaker fish-face team photo on the empty white wall behind. I looked from face to face at lab goggles and puckered fish-face lips all underlined by the bright orange bandanas around each neck. Mom, tall and elegant in the center was easy to pick out. Gabby and Rock's freckles and red hair were a dead giveaway. *Gabby.* I frowned remembering her video.

Max was in the photo too and so were three men I didn't know. I was pretty sure they hadn't been scientists on the project.

I was puzzling over who they were when I noticed that one had a birthmark. A *cloverleaf* birthmark, on his cheek just like John Doe's.

"What the heck did you do to end up in Silverblade's morgue?" I asked his fish-face.

This was huge. Huge.

Would Mom's clues shed some light on it?

If so, where to start?

I decided, I'd write each of Mom's clues on its own three-by-five card along with related thoughts or info and then tack them up in columns beside the fish-face photo.

Fifteen minutes later, I stepped back. It was beginning to look like clue central.

Unfortunately, except for *Chinese Dragon,* I pretty much had "no clue" written by the rest.

People were dying.

Others might too.

And I had *no clue.*

Great. I thought as I studied my work.

> *An eye for an eye*—no clue.
> *Sealed With A Kiss*—no clue.
> *Dansnurmur*—no clue. Or a red herring? (Mom always threw one in.)
> ~~*Chinese Dragon*~~ ~~(cat puzzle inside.)~~
> *Call June Thorpe*—(Strange. Mom's Aussie friend, June, died from a shark attack two years ago.)
> *Cats are an Puzzle*—(Mom never made mistakes. This typo "an" has to mean something.)
> *Polyporphyrin Balls*—("Balls" should be "Rings.") Other than that, no clue.
> *Xenan*—no clue.
> *Tickled Pink*—no clue.
> *lMd*—no clue

Ugh.

"Could you have made this more confusing?" I asked, directing my question at Mom's fish-face photo. "Mom, I kind of get it," I said with a hint of a smile. "Each clue is supposed to look innocent all by itself." I paused. "The problem is they look kind of innocent together too."

It felt good to talk to Mom. I could even hear her standard response.

You can do this. I know you can.

"You're right Mom," I said, tapping the picture frame.

With that, the frame fell. So did six of my three-by-five cards. They fluttered to the worktop like falling leaves.

Oh come on.

I was gathering them together to re-pin to the wall. But then the *lMd* clue card made my fingers stop gathering. I snatched it up. I kept it the wrong way around like it had landed, so it read *PWT*.

PWT stood for *Programmed without Target*. The bad-ass stuff that Rock described to me and Silverblade.

Whoever typed Mom's will used an underlined *l* for Mom's upside-down *T*.

lMd = PWT.

Yeah! I'd deciphered another clue.

That is, if finding that plastic puzzle in a dragon's mouth counted as my first solved clue.

Weak at best.

OK, so was PWT important because Mom discovered it had been used in Bolivia? Or was there another reason? *No clue.*

I smoothed wisps of hair behind my ears and stared at all my index cards.

I crossed my arms and stared at the rest of the clues. *Which could I investigate right now?* Starting from the bottom, I read and rejected each clue until I reached *Call June Thorpe.* Seemed kind of morbid for Mom to include her dearly departed friend. Although, it did pique my interest.

I quickly located June's cell and home numbers in Mom's phone and rang them. They'd been reassigned as I'd expected. Then I stared at June's odd fax number: 97 64 19 - 19 64 97.

Didn't look like a phone number. More like a combination to a safe. Now *that* was interesting.

The only safe I knew was the one in Mom's office. Sadly, it was almost midnight so I'd have to leave that clue until tomorrow.

I scanned my cards once more and focused on *Sealed With A Kiss.*

I plucked its three-by-five card from the board. This one was odd because Mom would never sign a letter *Sealed With A Kiss.* Not now anyway. I do remember seeing it in her high school yearbook, abbreviated as SWAK.

Hmm.

S
W
A
K

I wrote the letters down the three-by-five card's side and tried thinking what else those letters could stand for.

Save Whales And Kingfishers?
Small White Apples Kill?
Something With A Kick?

I could have used *Something With A Kick* right about then.

"S...W...A...K." I repeated the letters, again and again. Then I smacked my palms on my workbench as I realized what it was. *Geez.* I'd been as dense as Rock when he didn't recognize MedMaker technology.

I quickly scratched out the *S.*

Then I wrote a new *S* beside the *W* to make *SW* and then added "iss" behind it.

Beside the *A* I wrote "rmy."

Finally, I printed "nife" beside the *K* to form…

Swiss Army Knife

This was awesome. Not only had I solved *this* Mom clue, but I was suddenly confident about another. Its pushpin went flying as I ripped the *Tickled Pink* clue card from the wall. I folded it between the words *Tickled* and *Pink* and then aligned *Pink* with *Swiss Army Knife*. As in, the *Pink Swiss Army Knife* Mom gave me.

Yeah!

I knew right where it was too.

Excitement surged through me as I emerged from my workshop. Even so, I casually strolled to my desk. I glanced first at the clock, then at my coffee table, and finally at my desk's camouflaged fridge door. I tapped the door with my steel-toed boot. When it popped opened, I leaned in to grab bottled water and to peek to the right. I had a perfect view of the narrow space behind my dark wood file cabinet.

"Good to see you," I whispered to the glowing pink knife, still wedged between the cabinet and wall *and* still piercing the champagne cork.

"This one holds everything you'll need," Mom had said when she gave me this last knife at the breast cancer fundraiser.

Now if I could only figure out what I needed.

CHAPTER THIRTY-FOUR

By six a.m., all my clue work had scrambled my brain. I needed a break. Felicity's and my "get back to work" meeting at our central London Soho studios couldn't have come at a better time.

Ah, Soho. Great to be back. Seemed like forever but it had been less than two weeks since Conrad's stop order on *Demolition Queen*.

Of course I brought Mom's clues with me. *An eye for an eye, Dansnurmur, Cats are an Puzzle, Polyporphyrin Balls,* and *Xenan*. I had them on a cheat sheet in my pocket. No rest for the weary.

I breezed through the front door carrying the LBD (little black dress) Felicity had asked me to bring for a "photo shoot." *Ha-ha*. She was rubbish at lying. She and the chief were up to something so I had a trick up my sleeve too.

"Boy, I've missed this," I said, entering Felicity's office and nestling into a wheelbarrow chair.

"Hi," she said, while staring at a wall calendar with X's, circles, and highlighted sections.

"What you working on?" I asked.

"It'll be crazy getting back on track. I'd canceled so many things. Fitting in that extra day filming at MedMaker Corp. has proven tricky."

"No worries about that."

"What?" Felicity asked, turning so swiftly her multilayered poodle skirt fanned out.

"MedMaker offices are officially off limits," I said. "*But* we have a new opportunity. A Pirate Fantasy Party at the Victoria and Albert Museum. Fancy dress. Silverblade's team will be swashbuckling, and there's a treasure hunt."

"When?" she asked.

"Next week," I said, pulling out Mrs. Party's email showing her approval that had arrived an hour ago.

"What?" Felicity said, sounding a bit peeved.

"Now about my photo shoot," I said, watching her reaction.

The way she turned back to her board and avoided eye contact told me what I needed to know, and *I was pissed.* Not because she wouldn't look at me. I was pissed because I knew *why* she wouldn't look at me.

"Felicity!"

"OK. OK. I'm sorry. The chief told me not to tell you that he'd already scheduled the relaunch party and so soon. He wanted to surprise you. He and Mrs. Party have worked so hard."

The way she nervously played with the folds of her skirt, I knew she expected me to erupt.

"What time does the party finish?" I casually asked. "I could take a later flight to France."

This was that thing up my sleeve.

"You're going to France?" she asked with surprise.

"I need a break. The vineyard will be perfect," I said. I also studied my nails to avoid her eagle eye because I had no intention of going to France or anywhere else. I just wanted her and anyone listening to *think* I was going to France.

"I'm so glad you're OK about the party." She flopped into her chair with relief. "I thought it would be a welcome distraction for you."

"*You* helped the chief?" I asked. Anger was back in my voice.

"Your fan club arranged a tool drive like Toys for Tots to replace your stolen tools," she said sheepishly.

I liked that.

But I was still glaring at Felicity when I heard, "Delivery for Sam Albany."

Felicity was out the door like a shot, reappearing with a tall white vase of pink fist-sized peonies. She beat me to the pale pink card perched between pointy green leaves.

"Welcome Back and Good Luck. Pull the ribbon," Felicity read. "Go ahead."

I smiled at her through the leaves as I gently tugged on the wet ribbon. I pulled some more, and droplets of blood-red water dripped down the vase's sides. They pooled on Felicity's white Formica table like blood around a victim's body at a crime scene.

Something clanked inside the vase, and a tight knot formed in my stomach.

I pulled up the last of the ribbon and frowned at Mom's Knock 'em Dead hammer, the one stolen from my workshop. The word *Dead* had been circled using a wild watermelon crayon. The blood-red plastic card attached had a note written in black waterproof marker.

Felicity had seen none of this from behind the broad bouquet.

"So who's it from?" she asked excitedly.

"No name," I said, easing the hammer back into the vase.

"Oooh. A secret admirer." Felicity teased.

"Yeah, good times." I pocketed the red card, but I could still "see" its words.

Now that you are alone, I will be back.

Obviously, my stalker sent it.

Great.

I'd kind of forgotten about him.

CHAPTER THIRTY-FIVE

A couple hours earlier, I had a chat with the chief about tonight's *Demolition Queen* relaunch party. I stressed that the focus should be on my cast and crew, *not* me. I asked that he help me blend into the background. Grudgingly, he agreed.

Now, I exited my taxi, stood opposite an "abandoned" warehouse, and could tell from the sounds of the Saints singing "Demolition Girl" inside that the relaunch party was going strong without me.

Good.

I tucked my bulky evening bag under my arm. I scanned the narrow cobbled lane and smoothed my LBD. As I did, I hit the pink pocketknife strapped to my inner thigh, and a thrill snaked through my body. Tonight, I'd find out if someone was after this knife *and* if so, who. I had a fail-safe plan. With fans, board members, crew, and waiters present, what could possibly go wrong?

My only problem now was trekking across this bumpy forty-foot-wide lane to reach the party. I had caved to Felicity's pleas and worn some stilettos left over from filming our 50th episode.

Temporary insanity, that's what it was.

I wondered how long one could claim *temporary* insanity. I hoped I had a little more time.

With that, I took one shaky step and grabbed the light pole for balance, wishing for my steel-toed boots.

"You need rescuing, little lady?"

The condescending drawl came from behind.

"No," I said and stubbornly pushed away from the light pole.

"Don't want to ruin those gawd-awful shoes," the waiter wearing the *Demolition Queen* hardhat said with a laugh.

"What's wrong with my shoes?" I snapped and pointed my toes toward the flattest-looking pebbles to start out again. Then I yelped as the man grabbed my bag, scooped me up in his arms, and silently trudged across the road.

I wriggled sideways and tried to grab my bag, but he held it out of reach. As I was about to demand he put me down, his intense hazel-colored eyes drank in my turquoise ones. My pulse raced so fast I forgot what I was going to say. Especially as he crushed me against his hard chest like he was saving me from stampeding wildebeests.

I *really, really* liked his steely arms around my body. So when he unceremoniously dropped me by the warehouse door, my body *and me* felt totally abandoned. I covered with a deep frowning glare as he bounced my bag in his hand. Then, as if he'd figured out what was in there, he gave me a cynical smirk and tossed it my way. Bending way over to catch it, I tried to think of an equally cynical response. But as I uncurled, I realized it was wasted time. He wasn't even there.

"Jerk," I shouted. As the door slammed in my face, but I couldn't help watching his broad torso until it disappeared inside a half-demolished tunnel.

Sam, that was like the third waiter you've lusted after in two weeks.

What's your deal?

Pull yourself together.

Very important stuff at stake right now.

Rock in particular.

Earlier, I'd rung Candace, MedMaker Corp's helicopter pilot. Evidently, the pilot she sent to Bolivia should have reached and rescued Rock yesterday. Then Rock was supposed to board a plane today and be home tomorrow. *But* Candace has heard nothing from her helicopter contact. No one knows where any of them are.

There's got to be a simple explanation. I told myself.

To stay focused on tonight's plan, I had to believe Rock was fine.

CHAPTER THIRTY-SIX

Inside the warehouse, I marched across a faux-painted plaster chunk entryway and into a tunnel, erected for this event. From its shadows, I cased the joint. To the right were two soaring white fluted columns that diagonally bisected the vaulted gallery. Strung between them was a twenty-foot wide *Demolition Queen* sign. Construction, architectural, and tool-themed artwork covered every wall. I'd bet Mrs. Party single-handedly located them in the gallery's overflowing loft and dragged them down its rickety metal stairs.

I spotted Felicity who was setting up her tripod by the nearest column. I'd almost reached her when poppers exploded and balloons dropped from the ceiling. On the far wall, a thirty-foot banner unfurled to the floor. It was of *me* wearing a formal black gown, slamming a sledgehammer into a stone wall. A large bubble of words emerged from my lips saying, "Demolition Queen Is Making a Breakthrough."

"So much for a low profile," I said under my breath as fans surrounded me.

When I finally reached Felicity thirty minutes later, she was *very* busy filming the biceps of a waiter balancing a full tray of Get Hammered rum cocktails.

"Remind me to send Mrs. Party a thank-you note," Felicity said.

I focused on Felicity's subject. I realized it was *my* waiter from outside at the same moment Mrs. Party poked a rolled-up tool belt into his ribs. It made me cringe.

Oddly, he recoiled as if it were a gun poking him, not a tool belt. He slowly put down his tray and sized up her "weapon." He actually looked relieved which was odd. Mrs. Party rarely had that affect on people.

"You are supposed to be wearing this," Mrs. Party said, stretching the belt wide like she'd put it on him herself.

"I got it, thanks," my waiter said as, thankfully, another tool-belt offender caught her eye and she was off.

"We should apologize for her behavior," Felicity said and nudged my side.

"Yes, we should," I said, happy for any excuse.

That was until I heard him angrily say, "Wow. Thanks for warning me about the mean catering woman."

He'd said it like it was our fault. He didn't even make eye contact.

Then he asked, "A little jumpy aren't you? Too many Red Bulls and Snickers?"

I was about to tell him I didn't drink Red Bull but that I'd never turn down a Snickers. That was, until he added, "That's fan-bloody-tastic."

With that, I hooked my arm through Felicity's and dragged her away.

"That was beyond odd." Felicity frowned as we reached the gallery's central-most bar between the two columns. "Which reminds me, what was with that message you left me? *I'm bringing the pink knife. It's safer with me.* What did that mean—?"

Felicity stopped short. She raised her camera and said something I couldn't make out. Her tone was not happy and I think she said a word and then "alert", as if she was warning me about something.

"What did you say?" I looked around. Tambour's slicked-back hair was blocking my view. Therefore, I was able to fill in her blank all on my own. *Jerk, arsehole, creep.* Too many to choose from.

"Samantha Albany, the grieving widow. You didn't waste any time, did you?" His right hand slung his black tuxedo jacket over his shoulder in the most affected manner possible. He extended his *left* hand to shake.

"Excuse me?" I ignored his hand. I was contemplating the ways I could flatten his Bolivian-tanned nose.

"Looks like the sympathy vote is working for you," he said, scanning the packed room.

OK. That's it.

I pulled my fist back, but before I could punch him, an entire tray of Get Hammered cocktails spilled down his black open-necked tuxedo shirt.

"Terribly sorry, old chap," the hazel-eyed waiter said as he dabbed at a stream of the green liquid dripping from Tambour's nose.

Tambour ripped the towel from the waiter's hand but directed his furious words at me.

"I wish you'd hit me. Attacking a reporter makes interesting news," he said. "Although, nothing like the spectacle you're making of yourself already." He pointed at the thirty-foot banner of me before knocking into the waiter's shoulder as he left.

"Why the heck did you do that?" I glared at the waiter.

He immediately grabbed at his ear and shouted, "Damn it, if you yell in my ear one more time, I'm going to…"

"I didn't yell in your ear," I shouted at his retreating back at the same time I spotted Schott slinking through the tunnel. "Oh great. Who invited him?" I mumbled to myself.

"He called personally and asked for an invite," the station chief said, looking tweedy even in a tux.

"Said he was a huge fan. Dishy…right?" the chief added.

No.

"Now Sam, I'm concerned," the chief said.

What now?

"I noticed a few gaps in your lineup, so I'm throwing an idea out there," he said with a mischievous smile.

Expecting him to request a walk-on part for Fluffy, his German shepherd, I said, "I'm listening."

An idiot move.

"Have you thought about performance art?" The chief leaned back on the heels of his white bucks and tapped the toes together. "My favorite was when I was a serving platter."

"What?" I asked a little shocked, having assumed that raising prized begonias was his most lively pastime.

"It's all rather exciting. They lay salami, hummus, and slices of cheese…" As he said *cheese*, he exposed all his teeth. *Disturbing.* But not as disturbing as his next words. "…on my naked body."

Before I could stop myself, I pictured the chief's flabby white form surrounded by cold cuts.

"I'll think about that one." I grimaced and looked around for my drink-spilling waiter, who was of course nowhere in sight when I really needed him. "May I get you a new drink?" I asked the chief.

"I'd love another," he said, shaking the green-tinged ice in his empty Get Hammered glass.

"When you return, I'll describe cleanup with Fluffy," he said, winking twice.

OMG.

Well, I was right about the dog.

It was no consolation.

As I moved to the bar, Pink Floyd's "Another Brick in the Wall" blasted from eight-foot speakers and a waiter, *not my waiter*, shouted in my ear. "You have a phone call in the office."

I would have preferred at least one moment to absorb the party atmosphere, but I entered the office he directed me into not ten feet away.

The song's bass was vibrating so strongly that my pink knife pulsed between my sweaty thighs.

"Is there a quieter place to take the call?" I shouted.

Then I noticed there wasn't even a phone. I turned around but the waiter was gone and had shut the door. I pulled at its sturdy brass doorknob. It didn't budge and there was no lock to pick. Moreover, the hinges were on the outside, so no pins to pull. My cell phone had no signal and of course yelling would be a waste of time.

My fail-safe plan wasn't feeling so fail-safe after all.

Luckily, as the Foo Fighter song "Break Out" began to play next, I got an idea. It made my shoulders go all tight and tingly.

I climbed onto the desk, pulled up my dress hem, and unstrapped my knife. Rapping my knuckles against the wall, I determined it was thin quarter-inch plasterboard. *Good.* I located the wall studs, stabbed my knife's jagged blade into the plasterboard, and quickly cut a large rectangle. One quick punch dropped it into the wall's empty stud cavity. I did the same to the outside wall. I'd planned to ease that plasterboard into the wall cavity too, climb out, and slip away. Except, as I finished cutting and tried to grip the bottom edge of the thicker and heavier rectangle, it began to fall...*outward.*

Shoot.

Not only did it rip through the thirty-foot-high "Breakthrough" banner. It somersaulted onto the crowded dance floor. With that, startled dancers jumped aside and stared at me through the hole. So that as I vaulted through the wall *and* banner, with my pink knife held high, a spotlight lit me up bright and shiny. Not a soul in the room could have missed me.

And the crowd went wild.

The chief waved at me.

Mick Tambour nudged his photographer to take more incriminating photos.

The repulsive Schott cracked his knuckles.

I felt like a "sitting duck" and the "elephant in the room."

A sitting elephant.

Well, this sitting elephant was making a move.

I stuck my knife in my bra and crouched so fast my knees slammed the floor. I got a fix on the chief's white bucks, Tambour's tasseled loafers, and Schott's riding boots and then scrambled in the opposite direction. Headed for the loft stairs, I hit people's knees left and right. I worried that the trail of hopping people would give my direction away. But as I reached the back wall and the rickety metal loft stairs, it was more likely the angry voice above me that would get everyone's attention.

"I have a bone to pick with you."

I looked up to where the voice came from. It was Iris, Conrad's croquet adversary and king prawn snatcher from the wake. She was blocking my path.

Shoot. Did I forget to have that trophy sent?

"Why didn't you tell me who you were?" Iris demanded. "Didn't recognize you without your coverall. I never miss an episode," she said, handing a tool belt and pen down to me.

Right.

I quickly autographed it and handed it back. She strapped it on over her peach-colored pants suit and I was about to crawl away.

"I bought my own jackhammer because of you," she said.

This I had to hear.

"What do you use it for?"

"Oh heavens, I don't use it," Iris exclaimed. "I dine out on it." She nodded. "Look at me. When I mention my jackhammer, people take notice."

I laughed as she jiggled away to a disco version of "If I Had a Hammer" and then looked around. All unfriendly shoes were accounted for but much much closer. I grabbed hold of the stair rail, pulled myself up, and got a shock. The waiter's maddening yet oh-so-riveting hazel eyes stared into mine.

Calling all medics. Brain freeze in lust central.

"I'll take my *thank-you* now," the waiter said, grinning down at me with hands on tool belt.

I couldn't help admiring how good he looked in leather. Especially how the tool belt gaped open in front, perfectly framing the bulging zipper of his jeans. It took me a second to respond.

"What thank-you?" I snipped.

"For saving you from hitting that journalist," the waiter said.

"You expect a thank-you for that? That creep deserved a good smack," I said.

Speaking of creep, I peeked around the waiter's broad shoulders. They were so broad, it took a second. *Geez.* The chief, now fifteen feet away, waved at me. Tambour had only about thirty more people to squeeze past. I was out of time.

"You have a good point." The waiter nodded. "OK. Will you thank me if I help you escape those guys?" His back was to them as he pointed over his shoulder.

"What is it with you and thank you?" *And how did you know about those guys?* I peeked again and saw Schott was queuing up right behind the chief. "It's a deal," I said.

As one of my all-time favorite songs started up, "Brick House" by the Commodores, the waiter said something I couldn't hear. I shook my head and moved closer to his lips. *Poor me.*

"And my thank-you?" he shouted.

I was so close and he was so loud that his words vibrated tantalizingly deep inside my ear with a direct line to my crotch.

"Oh yeah, thanks," I said and rubbed my chin in case I was drooling.

"Pitiful," he said, standing his ground.

With Chief and Co. nearly there, I said, "I am forever indebted to you." My words dripped with sarcasm.

The waiter rolled his eyes, tilted his brown head toward the rickety stairs, and grudgingly led the way. Muscular thighs and a tight bum pumped upstairs inches from my dilated pupils.

I'm in love.

As we neared the top and had to duck under thick taut wire that anchored the closest column to the loft wall, I noticed that he was wearing my favorite brand of work boots.

We're made for each other.

"Tell me something I don't know," he snapped and held his ear like last time.

"If you're asking for another thank-you, forget it," I shouted. Even so, I grabbed his hand. I didn't want to get left behind. That skin-on-skin contact sent electricity bolting through my arm. My legs went weak. I faltered.

"What's wrong now?" he asked impatiently.

I kicked off my "gawd-awful" shoes as if they were to blame. His I-told-you-so grin said it all.

Reaching the top, I peered over the loft's waist-high wall. I saw masses of head tops including Chief's, Tambour's, and Schott's. Not that I cared as the waiter and I dodged row after row of bubble-wrapped frames. I especially didn't care as we stopped in the shadows of the "Making a Breakthrough" banner.

Secluded.

I liked it.

I liked it right up until he held his ear again and yelled, "Stay out of this."

"You're the one who brought me up here," I said, glaring at him.

He didn't notice my glare. He was openly staring at my breasts. Not an admiring stare, like I was used to. It was a laughing one.

I looked down and saw a flash of metal. *My tape measure.*

"New kind of underwire," I joked, and pushed it back into my bra.

"Mind your own damn business," the waiter shouted.

"Stop yelling at me." Electricity or no electricity, I'd had enough.

Except, next thing I knew he'd ripped off his *Demolition Queen* hardhat, thrown it aside, and angled me into deep tango dip. We were eye to eye. He pulled me tight against his chest. One hand worked up and down my back as if checking if it was OK. Electricity charged through my body. I couldn't breathe. I closed my eyes, imagining a deep kiss. I even heard a little voice saying, "Kiss her. Kiss her."

Was he talking to himself? A little weird, but hey.

I opened my eyes with a soft, sensual gaze. I searched his face, expecting a similar expression. So imagine my shock at the cynical, mocking one staring me down. I felt like a moron.

What came next was worse.

"Give me the knife," the gorgeous waiter said, extending his open palm toward me.

"I see. Your back rub *wasn't* foreplay," I said. *So much for lust and romance.*

My shoulders dropped. I stared at the floor. That's when I saw it. A chunk was missing from the toe of his boot, exactly like the footprint in Cranmont's art gallery.

"You're my stalker?" I sighed. "It was your idea to lock me in the office, wasn't it," I said and half-turned in the direction of the office. As I did, I snuck my knife from my bra, slipped it behind my back, and flipped open its corkscrew.

"Come on." He flexed his fingers to speed me up. "You were locked in to avoid a confrontation like this." His stern, remorseless eyes darted from my face to the rickety stairs and back.

"Oh." I nodded. "Or did you mean like this?" I shouted as I stabbed and then twisted the corkscrew into his palm.

"Dammit," he roared just as the song "Brick House" ended.

That's when I heard a hyper-tinny voice from an ear bud, dangling from his collar.

"Man, I warned you. I said, get the knife and get out of there," said the unidentified voice.

"Someone's been talking in your ear all this time? Who are you?" I asked.

I looked over the wall to make sure someone clocked that I was up here with him. I was shocked to see hundreds of guests peering back as they stood sandwiched in between and around the columns. Felicity even had her camera trained on me.

They think this is a Demolition Queen *stunt.*

I looked back at the waiter who was untwisting the corkscrew. As he closed the knife he lost his grip and dropped it.

And I caught it.

"Felicity," I shouted and tossed it in her direction.

Unfortunately, my adrenaline-fueled toss was more like a missile launch. The knife flew so hard and so high, it cracked a skylight and dropped, spinning, twenty feet away onto the first column.

Give me a break.

I eyeballed the eighty feet of taut wire running from the loft wall to the closest column. Then I wrapped my hands in bubble wrap and swung my stockinged feet over the wall. I lunged for that wire and my hands latched on. Bubble wrap popped like, *well*, bubble wrap.

"Damn it, Sam," the waiter yelled behind me.

I clambered along the wire with my dress flapping around scissor-kicking legs. Of course, Tambour and his photographer were looking straight up and snapping away.

Oh come on. What are we, second graders?

"Sam!" shouted Felicity. She also pointed at the waiter who had already bounded down the loft stairs, grabbed a ladder, and was headed for the column with my knife on top it.

Oh, no you don't, buddy.

I held on to the wire with one hand. Then I extracted the tape measure from my bra with the other and flung it at the column. Like a stone skipping across a lake, it bounced twice on the column top and hit the knife. With that, the knife flew off the column and began to drop. The heavy tape measure followed.

What happened next was a thing of beauty. First the knife and then the tape measure hit Tambour's head and he went down. Like in a cartoon, his black jacket hung midair for a split second then dropped onto his motionless body.

I couldn't have written it better.

Although, my excitement evaporated as my wire violently shook. I looked back at the loft where it was fraying and popping. This was surreal.

Scrambling like mad, I reached the nearest fluted column an instant before the wire broke free. *That was the good news.*

The bad news was that with no wire anchoring my column to the loft, nothing held it up. More bad news. It was also tethered to the second column. Next thing I knew, I was straddling and gripping the first column's as it tilted toward the second *equally unstable* column.

Several shouts from the crowd included, "Ride 'em cowgirl" and "You go girl."

That was before my column, like a dog in heat, mounted the second one and catapulted me through the air. Guests scattered as Mrs. Party began waving her arms like a rookie cop on America's first roundabout.

Then I hit the wall, literally. I didn't fall to the floor. I just hung there staring past my toes at ripped artwork and broken glass eight feet down as well as the radial arm saw-cum-cocktail bar to my left.

"Pretty as a picture," I heard the waiter laughingly say and I realized I was hanging from a picture hook.

"Wish I could stay, but I got what I came for," he said and waved my pink knife at me. Then he leaped over a ripped painting of a sledgehammer, picked his way through a sea of smashed up columns, and jogged into the tunnel, out of sight.

A cough came from somewhere up high and I looked up. Fans were lining the loft's half wall. Iris and thirty others crowded the stairs. Even the chief watched expectantly from the top of a speaker.

Time for my finale.

I wrapped a foot around the upright pole on the radial arm saw and rolled the whole thing toward me. I stood on its flat top and unhooked myself from the wall and then paused to watch a bloody-nosed Tambour limp past, dragging his sticky, dusty jacket. I grinned from ear to ear.

So there I was straddling the upright saw and grinning a moronic grin when Tambour's photographer got the shot. But could it beat that view up my dress? A real toss-up.

The show must go on. Hugging the saw's upright, I pushed away from the wall. I rode it rolling and crunching through the debris as I shouted, "*Demolition Queen* has returned." The crowd went wild, *again*.

Felicity was right. This *had* been a welcome distraction *and fun*.

Although, nowhere near the fun to have seen my waiter's expression when he discovered that knife he so cleverly stole was a decoy.

I'd have given anything to see that.

CHAPTER THIRTY-SEVEN

I was still smiling about the decoy knife as my taxi barreled down the dark A3 motorway. Halfway to Cranmont, that smile widened as I noticed a missed call from Rock and his message that began with, "The helicopter…"

Those first two words filled me with a sense of calm.

The next two? Not so much.

"…never showed," said Rock and my euphoria sank through the taxi's dull green carpet.

"I've been holed up in the woods hoping I'd either got the day wrong or there was a minor delay. Thirty-six hours later, my snacks have run out. I'm headed back to the village for a map and more food…who the…oh shoot," Rock exclaimed. I heard rustling noises along with his fast, panicked breathing. I pictured him stumbling through the woods.

My heart started racing. *What was going on?*

Rock grunted.

"What's happening?" I anxiously asked, forgetting that this was a recording.

Next, I heard faster, heavier breathing and more rustling.

"Get him," someone shouted.

I think Rock and his phone got body slammed, because there was a thud and then Rock screamed, "Shit, my shoulder."

I gripped the taxi's door handle so hard my bones hurt.

There was lots of rustling, and then a female voice gave one-word commands like a doctor in surgery.

"Blindfold."

More rustling.

"Rope."

Even more rustling.

"Lift."

Rock grunted. He also screamed loud and hard. Then he stopped. Either he'd run out of breath, passed out from the pain, and/or was too scared to make a noise. I assumed it was all of the above. So when I heard a soothing female say, "You dislocated your shoulder," I thought I'd heard wrong. I couldn't press my ear any tighter to the phone.

"Doctor, is that you?" Rock panted.

Rock's Dr. Witch?

"Yes, sorry to scare you. The fatigues and face paint were necessary and we couldn't risk you reaching the village and getting yourself killed," said Dr. Witch.

"Killed?" said Rock. I could hear him swallow.

I also heard what sounded like a helicopter.

"An insurgent group rushed the village and tried to capture my Special Forces team. We were in Bontero to find out who planted the killer virus," said Dr. Witch.

Her Special Forces line fit with what Rock had said about her gun and bouncing a coin on her bed.

"Who planted it?" asked Rock.

His tone sounded guarded. Was he worried he or Gabby would be blamed?

"Rock, we believe someone is plotting more murders with bioweapons. We need your help," Dr. Witch said.

The message ended. It sounded like he was in safe hands.

I was glad I could relax about Rock. I had a waiter/stalker/knife thief to catch.

Tonight was a triumph. Well, aside from the warehouse owner banning me and Mrs. Party for life.

I'd nailed Mom's *Sealed With A Kiss* and *Tickled Pink* clues. That was too cool. I felt superb about progressing the hunt. But as I climbed from the taxi outside Cranmont's gates, a niggling thought stole my joy.

If the bad guys had already known about the *pink* knife, then during the break in, shouldn't they have only taken pink knives?

That would mean that tonight, I stupidly gave up valuable information.

I told them that the knife was pink. *Not too smart.*

I shook my head.

I knew one thing for sure. My plan was working. My thief/stalker would be lured back for the *real* pink knife very soon. Then I'd catch him *and* extract information.

My booby trap and my "Revenge Kit" were ready and waiting.

CHAPTER THIRTY-EIGHT

As I jogged toward the barn's kitchen door, I frowned. I could *feel* the Led Zeppelin music blasting away inside. Thank *gawd* I didn't jog into the kitchen and shout, "Music off."

I wasn't alone.

A tall man stood at my desk, arching backward for an air guitar solo, plucking long fingers at the black T-shirt over his taut stomach. He had Conrad's laptop and my second-string knives spread out before him. *The nerve.*

I watched from the door, thinking, *You are not going to know what hit you.*

Even so, being new to the whole torture/interrogation game, I was nervous. Not only did my shoulders go tight and tingly, my palms got sweaty. I had to wipe them on my jeans twice before I furiously pulled out my phone. The "guitarist" was mid-pluck when I punched *##*.

First, my weighted sheets dropped over his head and shoulders. Then two ten-pound boxes of drywall screws swung in from the sides. They punched his temples dead center, and burst on contact. Sharp black screws swarmed like horse flies at the beach. The sheet even went black with them.

He staggered away from the desk and passed my coffee table, but didn't fall.

This was one tough bastard.

The last thing I needed was a *furious* tough bastard coming after me. I was looking around for a dull instrument to finish the job, when he fell, stiff and fast, like the statue of an exiled leader.

Bam.

He hit my table.

Bam.

He hit the floor, laid flat out. Boots extended from under the sheet. One had a chunk missing. *Bingo.*

I pushed my phone into my bra and stood over him to admire the contours of the sheet on his broad, muscular chest. That was *until* I noticed how his broad muscular chest *wasn't* moving.

Shoot. Shoot. Shoot.

My knees hit the floor. I urgently cleared away screws and then lowered my head to listen for a heartbeat. His earthy masculine scent stirred me up inside. I almost forgot what I was listening for. That was, until, his peanut-buttery-chocolate *breathe* hit my face.

I was furious.

Stealing my knives was enough reason for revenge. But eating my Buckeye Balls? I'd show no mercy.

I whipped my "Revenge Kit" from under my desk. I lined up its propane torch and sparker. Then I pulled out my low-melting-point solder. Frying the guy's wrists with superheated wire was not part of tonight's interrogation plan.

With more focus than I'd felt all night, I stretched his heavy arms overhead. His biceps hugged his ears as I wrapped wires around his wrists. I threaded them through the coffee table's old doorknob hole three times, sparked my torch, and soldered the whole shebang in seconds.

I wiped sweaty hands again. I unzipped his fly and then blinked at a layer of plastic that encased his lower abdomen. It ended an inch above his private parts. Lifting his thick black T-shirt, I saw that the plastic reached to his neck.

Armor?

"Boy, are you going to wish it went all the way down, buster."

It took a minute to get his trousers halfway down his muscular thighs, but it was worth it. I sat back to admire my handiwork, well actually the view. Tight black T-shirt. Brawny arms stretched overhead. White formfitting boxers and tan muscular thighs.

Like an S&M Ralph Lauren ad. Mmmm.

Sam! I gave myself a mental slap.

This revenge and answers stuff made the sweat practically pool in my palms. I had to wipe them two more times before picking up my largest spring-loaded clamp. I opened its jaws and scooted close. My knees touched his hip. I held the clamp over his boxers, ready to apply the torture instrument, and then sat back again.

"I can't do this. What was I thinking?" I shook my head.

To be honest, I was more relieved than disappointed.

However, as I stood, my still sweaty fingers let the clamp slip and it swan-dived onto his boxers and clamped shut on impact.

Laughing and gasping, I fell to my knees and reached for the clamp. But the second I touched its release button, long, firm jean-clad calves shot up around my shoulders.

Next thing I knew, he'd trapped my face in the vee of his pulled-down jeans. I couldn't see a thing. His legs also trapped my arms at my sides so I couldn't reach my knife.

What to do? What to do?

Tighten the damn clamp.

I wriggled one arm free and snaked fingers between my neck and his steely inner thigh.

If…only…my…fingers…could…just…reach…the…clamp…*YES.*

My fingers squeezed it and instantly his legs straightened.

I was free.

I somersaulted away and swayed dizzily above him. I should have tied him up first thing. Instead, I stumbled to my file cabinet and grabbed my *real* pink knife from behind it. I removed the champagne cork, closed its blade, and stuffed it into my bra for a quick getaway, if necessary.

Then I rushed into my workshop but as I reached for the rope I felt something prick my arm.

"Hey, that hurt," I said in an indignant tone.

Although, I wondered if whoever did that even heard me. My voice sounded so very faraway.

Everything went into slow motion.

I felt so relaxed.

I was only vaguely annoyed as a man tied me up with my own ropes and threw me over his shoulder. My head dangled upside down near his black leather belt and I laughed as he opened my fridge door. Even as he pulled out my Buckeye Ball tin, everything seemed just *dandy.*

"JJ, you're here because?" the man carrying me asked.

I was pretty sure I wasn't JJ so I didn't answer.

"She's good at this tie-me-up tie-me-down stuff. Good thing I cut you lose when I did."

That must have been JJ talking.

I felt panicked and asked myself, *They know I'm here?* I knew it was a stupid question but couldn't think why. *Then* I remembered that they had to know I was there because one of them was carrying me. That made me giggle.

Then cool air brushed my face and neck. There was a bit of shuffling and someone not so gently folded me into the backseat of a very small car and then nothing.

CHAPTER THIRTY-NINE

I merrily pressed *##* on my phone. I grinned too. The sheet dropped over my thief's shoulders. Drywall screws swung in to hit him and then *crash* he hit the floor.

Before I'd even pressed *###* again I heard a second crash. It came way too quickly and didn't sound like a body or even screws hitting a wood floor.

Come to think of it, the other one hadn't either.

They'd sounded more like waves. As in, waves *crashing* on a beach.

My ecstatic grin dissolved. Eyes flew open, and I looked around. I was not in my barn happily springing booby-traps. I was lying on a hard, dusty wood floor. I was also looking sixteen feet up at a round, sea-sprayed window covered in a maze of spider webs that rivaled the old Cranmont kitchen.

Between each crashing wave came a rousing drunken chorus. The few words I made out sounded Scandinavian. That could explain my slight seasick-feeling. I'd been on a ferry ride.

It would have riled me up more except I felt incredibly well rested. Superb, in fact, better than I'd felt in weeks.

Pushing the slight nausea from my mind, I tried to remember what had happened in the barn. Let's see, I was about to interrogate my waiter/stalker/thief. I went for rope. Then I was tied up. The rest was a blur.

So, what was I doing on a dusty floor in Scandinavia?

Why kidnap me?

Why not just take my pink knife?

Because they wanted me as their sex slave?

Ha-ha. That sounded as ridiculous in my head as if I'd said it out loud.

I sniffed the air and followed a delicious scent to a tray that held fish chowder, fresh buttered bread, and a Snickers bar. My captors couldn't be all bad. *Super rats wouldn't share their chocolate.*

Starving, I reached for the Snickers bar with my left hand, but as I did, my right hand lifted toward the ceiling. It killed my wrists too. *What was going on?* I stared at my wrists. Each had a rusty gulag-style shackle attached to a chain. The chain looped over a monstrous beam high up near the window.

I was in shock.

"What kind of paranoid monster would do this?" I thought for a second and then grinned.

Someone who, say, had his balls clamped?

I felt around in my bra. Not that it was that big, but it took a second to find my phone. It was sandwiched between my ribs and underwire. But my knife was gone.

So, I had a phone. Big deal. It had no signal. Wait there's a signal…nope… it's gone again…wait…no…*shoot.*

Even if my phone had a dependable signal, who would I call? Felicity? *I don't think so.* What would I say? Someone has me chained up somewhere in Scandinavia? *Nope.*

Sure, someone could track my phone and come crashing in, but they could get themselves killed too.

If I rang Silverblade, he'd just accuse me of avoiding boot camp again.

I was on my own.

The way I saw it, I had three options. Break these grisly chains. Break off the shackles. Knock down the monstrous beam above me.

Whatever I did, I had to be quiet. These floors couldn't have had any insulation. I heard everything, even chairs scraping the floor downstairs.

Either way, I needed tools.

The orangey setting sunlight wasn't enough for me to search the sparse room so I turned on my phone light. There was a dark-green door with a shiny new bolt. An overstuffed chair. A stack of waxy-looking boxes labeled: "Records," "Cassettes," and "Sewing Machine." And a mini-mig welder box which was empty.

I decided that the sewing machine box was my best bet for tools. I stood and took small quiet steps toward it until my arms were stretched overhead and shackles bit into my wrists. *Ow. Ow. Ow.* I reached my toe a little further and hooked the box. I dragged it back and excitedly opened it but only steel bobbins and a miniature screwdriver were inside. *Bummer.*

I whisked my phone's light across the door wall again to see if I missed anything. Same green door, same shiny bolt and same overstuffed chair. But then my light glinted off something I'd missed. It was small, shiny, and fluorescent pink. *My knife!* Must have fallen out when they carried me in.

It was much farther away than the sewing box. I'd need more range. I quickly unlaced my shoes thinking two laces tied end-to-end might be enough. I attached one end to my ankle and the other to a boot.

Time to go fishing.

I quietly stretched the leg with the tied-on shoelace as far as possible in the knife's direction. Next, I *cast* the boot like a hook on a fishing rod and it hit the knife spot-on. Sadly, it did *no* hooking. Instead, the knife shot away from me, under the overstuffed chair.

Oh, give me a break.

OK. Next up? Try to break these rusty chains.

Standing beneath the beam, I began turning. I'd barely made one turn when I heard another chair scrape the floor below as if someone was coming to investigate the noise.

Well, I'm not stopping until he's on the stairs.

My wrists already hurt like heck, but I was twisting my little heart out when I heard a boot on the stairs.

I'm not giving up until he's halfway up.

My wrists were bleeding. Steps got louder and louder, but still I twisted.

I'm not giving up until he's at the door.

Blood was dripping down my arms as I heard floorboards squeak *outside the door.*

I'm not giving up until he unlocks that door.

As a key rattled in the lock, I lifted my feet to spin and untwist the chains.

The door began to open. A small wedge of hallway light slowly grew. Bleeding, dizzy, and about to throw up, I dove to the floor. I closed my eyes a split second before the light hit my eyelids.

Through eyelashes, I watched hiking boots approach and then stop inches from my face. A well-built man knelt beside me. I studied the contours of his face beneath his tight ski mask. Hazel-colored eyes looked out.

Yep, it was my waiter from the relaunch party.

Eyeing me, he knelt. "Resting like a viper," he said in a cynical tone.

Those amazing eyes scanned the length of my body. He didn't even touch me, so that sex slave thing was definitely wrong. Well, he did gently pull two drywall screws from my hair. Then he ran his fingers through it, just like Schott had at the fundraiser.

He stood to go, but something made him turn back. Maybe he wanted to double-check my chains. Maybe muscle memory from his recent "clamping" made him wary.

Whatever it was, he yanked the chains. With that, shackles bit into my wrists so hard that I flinched and moaned. He kneeled, inspected my bloody wrists, and then looked up at the gnawed beam where my spinning had left rusty marks. He shook his head and actually laughed.

You snake.

I wasn't cursing him minutes later when he gently took my left wrist, cleaned off the crusted blood, and bandaged it. *With my shackles still on, of course.*

He silently did the same to my right wrist. It was Zen-like right up till my emergency foghorn ringtone shattered the silence.

With that, he roughly rolled me sideways, ripped my phone from my back pocket, and chucked it through the open door. I heard Felicity's voice saying, "Sam, are you there?" as my phone hit a step. She was cut off as it hit another. The only noise after that was of my phone hitting many many steps on the way down.

"JJ, your frisking job sucked," my stalker/thief shouted as he stomped out. "She had her phone. Anyone could have picked up that signal and be headed this way."

I was glad to hear he was worried about someone coming to find me.

"The boss will not be happy. We better come up with something soon," JJ said.

The boss? Who was that?

Then I thought about Felicity and how odd it was that her call got through. I also thought about others who might have tried to ring. Like Rock. What if he returned and couldn't reach me? What if Rock, Felicity, and/or Silverblade rang *le domestique* at the vineyard, where I was "supposed" to be? She'd tell them I was *not* there and *not* expected.

Not so great.

Next, I heard my thief/stalker say, "I've got no reception here. I'll go ring the boss and be back as quick as I can." He slammed the door and a motorcycle started up then took off.

So it was just me and JJ.

Time to get back to work.

On account of the chains not breaking, the beam had to go. More specifically, the four screws holding the beam hangers had to be unscrewed using only the metal sewing machine bobbin and miniature screwdriver. I'd then jump up and down on the beam. Just as it came loose, I'd have to slide the chain off *before* the beam hit the floor.

Easy peasy.

I grabbed the chain, backed up, and dragged it along the beam. Stopping under the window, I reached arms up high as I could and gripped chain on either side of the beam. Holding on extra tight, I walked my feet up the wall, like Spiderman only not so graceful. I awkwardly threw one leg over the beam and struggled upright to straddle it. Looking out the window through spider webs, I could just make out the drunken singing crowd dancing around a beach bonfire.

Wasting not a second, I wedged the bobbin into the first screw's slot and pushed the screwdriver through its center. Amazingly, those first three screws came out like a charm and I rested them by my thigh. I had the fourth screw three-quarters of the way out when I felt a thud.

What was that?

The screws by my thigh even bounced. They slowly rolled in a lopsided arc toward the beam's edge as the door and its frame burst inward. A man in a black ski mask, JJ I assumed, lay unconscious across the threshold.

Oh, that's what that thud was.

Stepping over him was a scary-looking thug. He was huge like Mr. Nunchuck from that Swiss cliff but reminded me more of the weird minister at Conrad's internment. He held a black semiautomatic handgun too.

Really?

Another gun?

Oh, that's just great.

It got worse. One of my screws was about to roll right off the beam. If I reached for it, my chains would rattle and this gun-for-hire would look up.

But if the screw dropped, he'd look up too.

Either way I was screwed.

Pulling the sexy female card was usually not my thing, but it would be heaps better than getting shot. I quickly pulled down my T-shirt's neckline to expose about a thousand inches of cleavage. I also flung my arms wide and said, "Oh, thank goodness you're here. Please, please, please help me down." I sounded like a Southern belle after too many sweet iced teas.

Come to think of it, I might get screwed this way too.

Incredibly, the thug walked beneath the beam, shoved his gun in his waistband, and lifted his arms. I might have been the slightest bit comforted if he weren't saying, "Yeah, baby. Come to papa."

Him thrusting his hips out wasn't so great either.

Even with his gun temporarily out of the equation, I wasn't taking his help.

Instead, I bounced on the beam to free it. As it started to give way, it dawned on me that the thug was still underneath. Understanding dawned in his eyes too, but his lust-filled brain was too slow. I heard a scream, a crunch, and then silence. *He wouldn't be coming after me.*

With his body acting as "temporary beam support," I whipped the chain free from the beam's end and leaped onto the stack of boxes. I didn't look back.

I *did* look toward the door as I heard a noise downstairs. Either the waiter was back or the thug had a friend.

Moving into high gear, I found the mig welder behind its empty box and fired up its 10,000 °F flame. It sliced through my chains in seconds. All was good except now I had a pigtail of glowing hot chain attached to each shackle. Like two tigers by the tails.

I was extra careful as I reached over to shut-off the welder. I'd almost touched the valve when the hair at the back of my head hurt, *a lot.* Someone was yanking my hair. That bent me backward with such force that the unextinguished torch went flying. It must have hit the waxy boxes because instantly I saw a triangle of fire in that corner.

The idiot yanked again and this time my arms flew up. As the red-hot chains did too, a bloodcurdling scream erupted behind me. I pulled my arms back down and a second, louder scream followed. I looked up horrified to see a hissing, bubbling *orange* cheek. One chain had crisscrossed an existing jagged scar to form an X near the open screaming mouth of…*Nunchuck.*

OMG.

His body rocked forward and then went backward, tripping over the smoldering acetylene tank. That tank was worse than a ticking time bomb. It could go off at any moment.

Somehow, smoke was already billowing up the stairs. If I didn't get out now, I'd be done for. I ran for the door, grabbed my knife, hurdled over my masked captor, and then pondered his unconscious form.

JJ didn't try to kill me.

JJ shared his chocolate too.

I couldn't just leave him there.

Fuzzy logic sorted, I grabbed his ankles and dragged what felt like three sacks of concrete down the stairs. Flames were already running along the ground-floor ceiling like a gas oven broiler so I moved double-quick. Still dragging him, I'd nearly reached the screened porch door when I spotted my plumber's bag on the kitchen table. A low rumble sounded from upstairs but I still lurched through the smoky haze. Wheezing and coughing, I swept Mom's and my phones into the bag along with euros, explosives, disguises, tools, my empty Buckeye Ball tin, and drugs which I assumed were the knock-out ones that worked so well on me. Conrad's monogrammed laptop was nowhere in sight.

Gasping for breath, I threw my bag *and* JJ over my shoulders. Then I ran out the front door, across the sandy driveway, and past a MINI. Finally, I threw us both behind the nearest sand dune and barely put my arms over Jimmy's and my head when the house went *kaboom.* A fiery ball shot up into the sky. Bits of shingles, glass, and wood hit my legs, back, and arms.

Not exactly the clean getaway I'd pictured.

Still in the shadow of the dune, I rolled onto the cool sand and glimpsed the inferno that *had been* a house. I also saw one of the beach partiers racing to the top of a dune. One of them must have called the fire department because sirens started up in the distance.

I realized my hand still lay protectively on the Jimmy's head. Saving someone's life kind of changed things. I wondered, *Would he return the favor?*

I felt for his pulse. Slow and steady. Dilated pupils. Possible concussion. Minor open wounds. The emergency crew could handle it.

Sirens were getting closer.

I had to get going...but first...

I flicked open my knife, slipped its blade beneath his ski mask, and slit it open. Blood oozed onto my fingers as I peeled back the cut edges and looked expectantly at his face. His slim cheeks, pink slack mouth, and curly brown hair didn't look familiar. Maybe because of all the blood. I wiped it from his face and neck. I finished with his ear and sat back stunned.

I may not have known the face, but I knew this stitched-up earlobe.

It belonged to James, Conrad's "decrepit" butler/chauffeur.

JJ a nickname for James.

My first reaction was beyond angry. "Harmless, decrepit old" James had seen me naked on numerous occasions. He also scared the bejeezus out of me with his lurking and his driving when really he was this twentysomething *JJ.*

I was so confused.

On the other hand, I couldn't help but be a bit amused. *How in the world had James kept up the nonagenarian act all that time? And why?*

"So James you had a wild side after all, didn't you?" I said, sinking deeper into the shadows as a fire truck bounced into the drive.

I decided to stay until the emergency crew noticed JJ's body. But I was still there ten minutes later when the crew had him sit up and hold a pack to his head. He looked perfectly normal except for the soot smudges on his face.

I was particularly glad I'd stayed, when the deep throttle of a motorcycle approached. Grinning from ear to ear, my waiter/stalker/thief whipped into the driveway with a 1961 Triumph Bonneville between his thighs.

No bike ever looked so good.

"Kurt," JJ shouted.

Finally, I had the real name for my waiter/stalker/thief.

Kurt.

Kurt hopped off his motorcycle and jogged toward JJ, saying, "What happened? I leave you for two hours and this…" He sounded like he was joking. As if this kind of thing happened every day. "The boss wanted to send some backup, but I convinced him to call off the dogs—"

"Oh, he sent them all right, and we had a little difference of opinion," said JJ, rubbing his head.

Boy, if that was a difference of opinion between colleagues, I didn't want to see a real argument.

"Where'd they go?" asked Kurt, looking around.

"Don't know. I was out cold," JJ said.

"Did our prisoner, Sam, do this?" Kurt asked, pointing at what was left of the house.

Thanks a lot.

"Where is she?" Kurt looked around again as two firefighters emerged through swirling smoke. They were carrying a body bag. I cringed thinking about their colleague, possibly two being inside it.

JJ just stared.

When they found out I killed their men, they were going to come looking for me.

Sam, scram.

With the flaming house at my back, I spotted lights from the island ferry way down the beach and took off. Minutes later, I reached the dock and leaped onto the ferry just before it pushed away.

As I stood watching the shoreline to make sure no one followed, I overheard a truck driver speaking French behind me. What transpired after that was not a pretty story. I wasn't proud of it either.

I needed a ride to France, so first I tried talking to the Frenchmen.

It went something like this.

"*Bon…*" I only said 'bon' because that's all I could remember of *bonjour.* Then I patted my chest and said, "Sam."

"*Bonjour*," the man said. He gave me a grumpy frown and mumbled "Francois."

"*Ou et votre aller?*" I asked, trying to find out where he was going.

He didn't do that annoying French thing of pretending not to understand. He didn't have to.

Instead, Francois frowned again and climbed up into his truck.

That's when I spotted a shuffling, bent James-look-alike approaching. What can I say? I panicked. I leaped up into the passenger seat. Francois looked so shocked I was afraid he was going to shout. So I used the knockout drugs on him. I must have used a lot more than my captors used on me. In seconds, he was stretched out cold on the passenger seat beside me.

After the James-look-alike-who-really-*wasn't*-James shuffled past, I studied Francois's satnav and confirmed that I wouldn't be taking him too far out of his way.

That part I felt good about.

What I didn't feel so good about was not knowing whether Francois was going to wake up, *ever.*

CHAPTER FORTY

If I hadn't got all that sleep while kidnapped, I'd have been done for. Being on the run was exhausting. I'd driven nonstop until well inside the German border and now parked at the far end of a motorway rest stop.

I needed to re-group.

I took off my disguise of brown beret, fake sideburns, and bushy mustache. I also checked Francois's pulse for the millionth time before trying to remove my shackles again. One after the other I discarded useless tools onto Francois's disgusting brown shag carpet. My knife's file was the only tool left. As I began sawing, I couldn't help thinking about James, my bent, shuffling butler. That "sweetie" used to bring me champagne in the bathtub. "Solicitous my ass," I said aloud. He probably rigged up shower cam too. What had he been up to?

Those thoughts stirred me up so much, I didn't notice my nail file had worked until a shackle rattled to the floor. With renewed energy, I sawed off the other so fast and with such force, my knife split in two.

"Hello there," I said to the memory card that landed in my lap. "Are you what everyone's been looking for?" I asked.

As I held it to the light, I saw a small Ford enter the car park and head straight for me. The huge shoulders of the man inside reminded me of the barbecued Nunchuck. *Could it be?*

I quickly stuffed my hair back inside Francois's beret, slapped my facial hair back on, and slumped behind the steering wheel.

He parked and then blew smoke out his window. His upturned face had the unmistakable fake orange tan and the new oozing injury on his cheek that crisscrossed the old.

Shoot. Shoot and double shoot.

At least he couldn't see me way up in Francois's truck. His phone was ringing too. I took a quick look and saw him hesitate like he didn't want to answer it. When he finally did, he held it away from his ear as if his caller was yelling.

"We lost Fred," said Nunchuck.

So the minister's name was Fred. *Amen.*

The caller was definitely yelling because I heard some of what he said.

"Like I give a toss about Fred. Were you successful in Denmark?" the caller asked.

"Not exactly. I swear that Ms. Demolition Queen is some kind of agent," Nunchuck said.

Me? Why thank you.

"She was in Denmark?"

"Yes, she *was* in Denmark, but now she's dead like Fred," Nunchuck said. "Hey, that rhymes."

He must have forgotten his new injury because he grinned, and then he yelped.

"That will make things simpler," the caller said.

He sure sounded happy about my "demise." That didn't feel too nice.

"Don't worry. I'm getting the knife back," Nunchuck hesitantly added and then held the phone away as if bracing for an angry response.

None came.

Nunchuck blew out a big puff of smoke and I gathered from his expression that no response was lots worse.

"I put a tracker on their MINI," he said quietly. After that, I think the caller hung up because Nunchuck relaxed back in his seat.

A tracker on the MINI meant he was following JJ's car. *Interesting.*

I started the truck. Then nonchalantly as I could, while wearing a mustache and driving a stolen vehicle, I ground the worn gears into first and gave it a little gas. Of course, the truck backfired so long and so loud that every head in the car park popped up, including Nunchuck's.

But as I left, I wasn't being followed. *Not yet anyway.*

All of a sudden, I remembered my memory card find.

"Better make a copy," I said aloud. "*J'ai besoin un l'ordinateur magasin.*" I added and paused. "Seriously? You can't remember '*bonjour*' but '*I need a computer store*' just rolls off the tongue." I rolled my eyes.

I probably should have been more concerned that I was talking to myself.

CHAPTER FORTY-ONE

After 908 of the longest miles I'd ever driven, I threw my plumber's bag behind the driver's seat of my ever-loyal Aston Martin. "Thanks for waiting," I said to Martin. He'd waited for me at Reims/Champagne Airport tonight even when I arrived, not by plane or truck, but on *foot*.

I'd driven the ramshackle truck from the top of Denmark to Germany. I then carried on into France. I was less than two miles from the airport when I had to ditch the truck and walk, all because Francois was beginning to wake up, *praise the Lord*.

Of course, before ditching, I copied his address so I could send him a big fat *untraceable* check when I got home.

Now, anxious to reach the vineyard, Martin and I tore out of the sleepy airport. We were halfway around a slow-moving ramshackle truck when I realized it was *Francois's* slow-moving ramshackle truck. I spotted his face and droopy mustache in the driver's side window and immediately slammed on the brakes to move in behind him. I whipped off his beret, checked that my stuck-on sideburns and mustache were still in place, and pulled a baseball cap down low on my brow. This time when I zipped around him, I waved. I noticed in my rearview mirror that Francois gave a friendly wave back.

See the "rest" did him good too.

From then on, I practically wore out my rearview mirror checking for bad guys. Blurry vineyards and farms whizzed past, but no Francois, no police cars, no Kurt, no Nunchuck, and no JJ. Even thirty minutes later as the last pinky glow left the sky.

Martin and I crawled through my teeny village of Cousteau alone. Having said that, Monsieur Tremont *was* in his dusky recessed doorway. He waved the glowing tip of his self-rolled cigarette overhead more enthusiastically than usual. I smiled and waved back enthusiastically too.

I was still smiling as I entered the circular bit of my chateau's driveway. I passed its magnificent oak front door and drove beneath the low, broad poplar tree lit with miniature lights. I rounded the lavender-ringed island and then concealed Martin in a vine-covered tractor shed.

The feeling of calm from coming home was so nice, but it didn't last long. The same deep-throttling motorcycle from the Danish beach house passed the shed, circled the island, and then skidded to a stop under the poplar, spraying pebbles over my beautiful lavender. The driver hopped off and headed for the chateau's front door. Crouching, I ran commando style and only saw the back of his navy-blue baseball cap as *le domestique* let him in. But I knew it was Kurt, my waiter/stalker/thief.

How did he find my chateau?

Was there a tracker in something I took from the beach house?

More importantly, what was he up to?

When next, lights popped on in the den, I squeezed in behind broad, prickly holly bushes and scooted to the den window, but I was too late. *Le domestique* was already lying unconscious at his feet.

No. NO. NO.

"Mess with me, but don't mess with my people," I snarled under my breath. Pushing holly branches aside, I raced back to the shed, brainstorming a diversion.

I saw rakes, tractor parts, and two red petrol cans. Petrol cans. *Bingo.* The first can was empty, but the second was full as a tick. I lugged the heavy red can to Kurt's bike and put it down. I checked the bike's saddlebags. Thank goodness. Conrad's monogrammed laptop, Kurt's phone, and his gun were inside. I unclipped the bags and took the lot.

Next, I liberally doused the bike's worn leather seat, handlebars, and tires and then retreated to the chateau's front left corner. I knew the best and only way to light it, and I wasn't pleased.

I had to shoot it.

Just touching Kurt's cold, heavy gun made my hand shake. This felt so wrong on so many levels, but I had to get him out of the house and save *le domestique*.

Think of this gun as a cordless drill, I said to myself as I pulled the trigger.

Only one problem. Cordless drills don't have kickback.

I missed the bike by *a lot.* The wayward bullet sliced through and broke off a heavy poplar branch. Although, the branch *didn't* crash to the ground. Instead, it hung on the string of miniature lights. Its weight stretched and strained the wire until finally the wire snapped. Sparks flew and *POW.* Like a magic act, the leather scat disappeared in a puff of smoke. I jumped back as a smoldering side view mirror landed at my feet and a black tire, bubbling like a burnt marshmallow, rolled past.

My ears were still ringing as Kurt raced from the manor. Oddly, he was talking on a cell phone. He didn't even look at his bike before he ran up the drive out of sight.

Bravo, Sam.

***

Freshly showered, I exited the chateau an hour later and began to plan my next move. Kurt never returned, so I was patting myself on the back as well.

If nothing else, I was becoming an expert at expecting the unexpected.

With that in mind, I'd decided to hide a GPS tracker tag in Kurt's phone. I'd purchased it from the pet store beside *l'ordinateur magasin*, when I stopped the truck to copy Mom's memory card. Having that tracker in Kurt's phone would be invaluable. That is *if* he returned and *took* his phone. All part of my expect the unexpected plan.

I was celebrating a little by lounging in my most favorite spot, beside a billowing white marquee, overlooking the vineyards and curved stucco wine caves. Sadly, the view was about to disappear in the night, but the stars twinkling at me through high tree branches were making up for it.

Right after Kurt disappeared, *le domestique* regained consciousness. It was so strange. She seemed much more concerned about me than herself. Kept doing things for me. For example while I showered, she built the beautiful bonfire I was sitting before. She used the poplar branch remains from out front. I knew it was that branch from the bits of red leather bike seat stuck to it, which made me smile.

Now I frowned, hearing her crunch down the gravel path *again*. All her pampering and super-speedy French were wearing me out. Although this time the baguettes, olive tapenade, assorted cheeses, and red wine were welcome.

Once she'd placed them on the low boulder wall I expected her to scurry away. Instead, she dabbed her eyes with the corner of her floral apron and repeated the sentence she'd already said over and over. I nodded with a sympathetic expression, but like before all I understood was *l'homme* and *mort*.

The man and *dead.*

"*Il a pleurén,*" *le domestique* added with a deep frown.

I shook my head and held up my hands. "*Non comprende,*" I said, pretty sure I'd used French *and* Spanish. Or was that Italian?

The woman tapped fingertips down her cheeks to simulate falling tears.

"The man cried?"

"*Oui, madam.*" She nodded quickly and blew her nose.

Now *that* was new info. *Hmmm.*

"*Bonne nuit,*" she said.

If that meant she was leaving, I was happy.

I waved good-bye and then faced the fire. I barely sank back into the lounge chair when I heard crunching gravel again.

"Unless you've brought me something tall, dark, and handsome, go home to bed," I joked, knowing she couldn't understand me.

"Will tallish, blond, and handsome, in a rugged, used sort of way, do?"

The perfect English response in a deep Danish accent made me sit up fast. Even so, I was too late. Rough ropes clamped my shoulders to the chair, and I heard a laugh.

Kurt circled my chair. His exposed shins came into view, and I kicked at them, missing by a mile.

"Haven't you already inflicted enough pain on my body? Not to mention my beach house and bike?" He raised his hands in mock surrender. Then he effortlessly flipped a bulky tree branch onto the fire.

In the firelight, I finally got a great view of Kurt. His chiseled, freshly shaven face and damp blond hair, sticking from under his baseball cap, were oh-so-appealing. Even so, I returned his glare with a smirking laugh.

"Thanks for the shower and shirt," he said, tugging at its collar.

It was my turn to glare. He was wearing the white polo button-down shirt I'd "borrowed" from Jake's chalet.

"You showered here?" I asked, wondering how I'd missed that.

OK, so I celebrated a little early.

"Nice wine cellar, by the way," he said, holding up two flutes and an unopened bottle of *Demolition Queen* Grand Reserve. "How about a toast?"

"Super idea," I said. "We have so many things to toast, like these." I wiggled my bandaged wrists out to the side for him to see. "We could start with kidnapping, or how about ball clamping?" I eyed the upside-down V in his pants. "Shall we toast motorcycle bonfires perhaps?" I pointed one lose finger at the scrap of red leather on the branch by the bonfire.

Ignoring my obvious enjoyment, he continued, "How about those words in your barn? What were they? Oh yes, *Demolition Queen* and *Carpe momo*—seize the moment. Right?"

I looked away from his piercing gaze.

"Seems appropriate," he continued. He popped the cork, which soared into the inky black space beyond the fire. "No?" He paused. "OK, how about we toast your successful escape?" He tapped the filled glasses together and then sipped from his before holding the other to my lips.

I sipped. *It was a curse.* I couldn't resist champagne or looking directly into his incredible eyes. I silently damned my tingling crotch. "You are a sick, sick woman," I said under my breath.

"Men four times your size never got the best of Fred," said Kurt.

"Good friend of yours?" I asked. My tone was icy, but my eyes were melting.

Kurt straddled a lounge chair opposite me and grinned, staring at me for a full minute. It made me squirm in my seat.

"This whole picture is beautiful," he said. "You sitting there tied up, that seductively waving marquee behind you. Mmmm." He gulped his champagne. "Do you know that every cop from that Danish island to Champagne was looking for you? '*A rough, masculine-looking woman*' was how you were described." His eye roved over my tan cheeks and then my long-sleeved white T-shirt. I was very aware of the taut ropes tied above and below my breasts as his eyes lingered there. He followed my blond hair almost to my waist. "An accurate description," he said. Then he laughed, stood, and walked toward me.

"Would you like to hear my description of you?" I asked, hoping it might slow him down.

"Nope." He took off his cap and curled its bill. A piece of paper fluttered to the ground before he pushed the cap into his back pocket. He didn't seem to notice, and I paid no attention. I was too busy planning my escape.

As Kurt untied the ropes around me, I pulled my feet in. I prepared to run, but he was ready. He caught me by the shoulders and backed me into the marquee's corner post. It was like a spike through my body. *A nice spike.* One that put every nerve on sensual alert. His lips brushed against my ear, and his hot breath plunged inside. It took my breath away.

"So how about it?" he asked.

"What?" I wheezed, gasping for breath.

"A truce?"

I thought about that. "No way, buster. You kidnapped me…" I lost my train of thought as he lightly brushed my forearm. It tingled, even through my sleeve. I inhaled and smelled the chateau's lavender shampoo in his damp wisps of hair. Out the corner of my eye, I saw him stare down my arm as if he were searching for an answer. Next, his hand followed, sliding down and down until he touched my hand. Bare skin touching bare skin was almost too much. I wanted to say something but couldn't think of anything that wouldn't come out scrambled.

So I watched as he tilted his head and then pressed his hand into mine, opening it palm side up. He slid his hand away, and I saw a hand beneath it. It looked like mine. It even had my extended lifeline with the new scar at the midway point, but it didn't feel like my hand. It was numb and tingly.

"Where are we right at this very moment?" he asked in a hoarse voice as he ran a finger along my lifeline. He tilted his head again to rub his cheek against mine.

My tongue was so dry it felt like a hairdryer had worked it over. I couldn't speak if I wanted to. I needed a break. I looked away for a second, but all I saw was the erotic rippling of our shadows on the white marquee. I looked back, surprised to see him still staring at my palm.

"Well, if you had died, like I told your housekeeper…"

Was that a tear on his cheek?

Could le domestique have been right?

Why would this guy care if I died?

Why was he telling my housekeeper?

"…we, you and I, would be here." He pressed the tip of his finger into the end of my extended lifeline.

When did he and I become a we?

Is there such a thing as reverse Stockholm syndrome?

"But we're here," Kurt said.

His forefinger skimmed my midway cut. I tried to pull my hand back, but he held tight.

"I told her you were dead," he said and gently held my head between his hands and stared into my eyes.

Not sure where he was going with this, I decided to let him finish. I had time.

Next, he scooped all my hair from my neck, inhaled, and said, "You smell exactly the same."

The same as what? I asked myself, but I didn't really care.

At that moment, I didn't even care that he'd kidnapped me. I thrust my lips at his. We connected with force. His tongue flicked the underside of my tongue and ran along the inside of my lips. Lightning seared my crotch, flipped-flopped my stomach, and slammed the center of my chest. I held him away, stared at his face, and tried to catch my breath.

He opened his eyes and looked at me. He was out of breath too but looked desperate for another kiss.

I angled in and kissed him again, this time deep and slow. I pressed tight against his body. I felt his heaving chest and bulging trousers. I knew what I wanted.

I backed him up until his calves hit the lounge chair. I gave his chest a little shove. He willingly dropped onto the chair and looked up with parted swollen lips. He had a surprised but happy look, like a puppy that got a stroke *and* a treat. His grin widened as I straddled the chair and sank onto his upper thighs. His chest rose and fell under my hands. I stared at him. I saw something else deep in his gorgeous eyes.

What was that look?

Conflicted? Afraid?

Who cared? I tucked my hair behind my ears and began to unbutton his shirt. He pushed my hands away, and I sat back. Out of the corner of my eye, I saw the paper that had fallen from his hat before we kissed. I must have kicked it and turned it over because I could now see it was a photo. I could see what the photo was of too.

Suddenly, I was unsure of everything.

Everything.

I made a snap decision.

Probably not a good one.

I leaned toward Kurt and ripped open the perfect white button-down shirt and buttons went flying. Flickering orange firelight glowed on his bandaged midsection and muscular chest.

Leaning back on his elbows, Kurt tilted his head to the right and watched my fingers trace the edges of his bandages and then dip inside his waistband. I felt his abdomen flinch under my fingers, but my eyes were glued to his as I slowly unzipped his jeans. I slid my thighs further down his and began to lower my head.

His head fell back in anticipation.

He even moaned with pleasure *until* a second later. That's when he screamed in agony because I'd ripped off his bandages.

His head whipped up.

He glared at me with the same wild-eyed glare he gave me in his own Swiss chalet.

He glared at me because I'd exposed "wounds" that weren't wounds, but scars.

Scars I knew really, really well *because* I'd inflicted them in that Swiss bar when I pulled him from the antler chandelier.

The coup de grâce was his tattoo...*the mirror image of mine.*

I hauled my knee back as far as I could and then slammed it into his nuts.

"How's that for seizing the moment, you bastard?" I screeched.

CHAPTER FORTY-TWO

"You bastard," I screeched again as I leaped off Kurt's writhing, contorted body and stared down at him. The bonfire's orangey-red glow made him look like he was burning in hell.

Extremely fitting.

I would have slammed his nuts again, but I was too shocked.

From the dew-covered grass, I scooped up the damp photo that had slipped from Kurt's cap. The exact photo taped to the back of my framed cover of *It's Not About the Wall.* Wrapped sarong style in a blanket, I stood beside a bare-chested Jake, whose tattoo swirled above his jeans.

"When I think of the hours I wasted trying not to look at this photo. Just touching it made me sick," I said. I sure didn't want to look at Kurt right then, so I circled the bonfire. "That kiss...*your* kiss got me thinking. This photo clinched it."

I stopped beside him and stared. Ghost-like images of Jake's face superimposed on Kurt's.

Jake-Kurt.

Kurt-Jake.

Kake-Jurt?

"How did I not at least recognize your body?" I asked.

In our year together, I'd admired it from every single angle, clothed and naked. It was a bit more muscular now, but the framework was the same.

"Dammit, Sammers, give me a break," Kurt said.

"That's not going to happen," I said.

Kurt moaned as he sat up. "I've imagined our reunion a million times, and not once did I have this particular sensation in my balls." He took a swig from the champagne bottle and then nestled it between his thighs.

"Where's your other face? I liked it better," I said.

With that, champagne spurted from Kurt's mouth like a fountain. As it sizzled on the hot logs, he said, "Thanks a lot."

Who was I trying to kid? If possible, he was even better looking than before.

"The old one had to go," he said matter-of-factly as he scooted to the end of the chaise lounge. He shook the unburnt end of the poplar branch. Sparks and thick smoke trailed up through the tall pines. "I thought for sure I'd blown it that day you were in the shower. Can't believe you didn't recognize my whistle."

My eyes widened. "You're my one-man cleanup crew too?" I sidestepped the smoke that shifted my way.

"At your service," he said, flexing his biceps.

"Was this some kind of sick joke to you?" I asked.

Smoke swirled around me as I lurched at his lounge chair to hit him. He was quick and grabbed my wrists so I was stuck inches from his face as I shouted, "I was there. I watched your body bash against those rocks." I wrenched my wrists free to beat at his chest. "I was there," I repeated and my voice cracked. I felt tears brimming on my eyelashes. "I watched the blood drain from your body. I couldn't move." I paused to catch my breath. "Did you come to your own funeral too? Did you have a good laugh when I cried so hard I almost passed out?" I wiped my wet cheeks with quick, angry strokes.

Kurt struggled to his feet to limp after me.

"Don't you dare touch me." I spat the words at him and started around the fire again.

Another thought stopped me in my tracks. Disbelief and hatred choked me. I could barely get the next words out. "You watched me mourn my own mom and you did nothing," I said.

He massaged his chest. His faced softened. I waited for comforting words.

"I was busy with work," he said with a shrug.

His offhand comment completely threw me. "What kind of work? Being a suicidal extreme sportsman wasn't enough?" I crossed my arms and eyed him through the smoke.

"That was my back story," he said.

"Back story? Who has a back story? What are you MI6 or something? " I asked.

"Let's just say, the wrong people figured out who I was, so I had to 'kill' Jake," he said and shrugged again.

I gasped. "That was you with Nunchuck on the mountain watching Jake, or rather your hang glider?" I asked. "You almost got me killed," I added angrily.

"You shouldn't have followed me, for Pete's sake," Kurt shouted. "JJ flew the glider, disguised as me. He faked the crash and dripped fake blood from his boots."

My turquoise eyes shot daggers at him.

"This whole kidnap thing was your fault," he said defensively and waved his arms in wide circles. "I wouldn't have needed to get you safely out of Cranmont if you'd been here at the vineyard like you said you'd be." He pointed his finger at the ground.

"And you knew I was at Cranmont because?" I stared at him with narrowed eyes and hands on hips. He looked away, uncomfortable.

I preferred that. Then I could think straight.

"Aha." I inhaled sharply and pointed at him again. "The Led Zeppelin song at Cranmont was you signaling JJ."

With that, Kurt sat heavily on the chaise but that tipped the champagne bottle and cold champagne spilled. It seeped into his jeans so that he jumped back up again.

"Yes I know about James or JJ. Who did you think pulled him out of your burning house?" Pause. "You two were masters of disguise, and yet you forgot to cover a scarred earlobe?" I paused. "So were you his sidekick?" I asked, knowing he wasn't.

"He's my sidekick." Kurt bristled.

"OK. So let me get this straight. You were protecting me, and yet, under your so-called protection…" I held up my hand and ticked each point off on a different finger. "I've been robbed, attacked, and almost burned to death." I continued. "May I say for the record that I am not impressed?"

"You could do a lot worse." He shook his head.

"Well from here on, I'll try that," I said.

"You?" Kurt laughed. "You're your own worst enemy. Defiant, headstrong, intractable, pigheaded, and fearless to a fault. You love being unpredictable just to prove me wrong."

"Gee, don't hold back," I said and kicked at the unburnt end of the large branch. "To think I mourned for you, married Conrad, and got stuck with Cranmont because of you and your back story."

While he thought about that one, I asked, "So what should I call you? Jake or Kurt?" I didn't give him a chance to answer. "Actually, how about asshole?"

With one giant step, Kurt was beside me, squeezing my upper arm. "You don't get it, do you? This is so supremely dangerous."

I was about to kick the log again but his exasperated voice got my attention. "Stay out, and tell Rock to stay out too."

I froze. "You know about Rock?"

"Sam, everyone knows about Rock. They're not bothered right now, but if you two keep it up, he'll get killed and so will you."

Did he know Rock was helping the good guys?

"If you know so much then tell me where Rock is," I said to gauge his reaction, but then a phone pinged. I was extremely pleased to see him pull out his phone. The one I'd put the tracker chip in. *Excellent.* Must have found the phone when he was inside showering.

"Got to go," he said after reading a text.

"Oh no you don't." I grabbed the tail of his shirt, and it occurred to me that it was really *his* shirt. "I'm not done with you."

"Come to think of it, I'm not done with you either," he said, aiming a gun at me.

I gasped. I was looking down the barrel of *the gun* I'd confiscated from his motorcycle.

Now I could add, "Looking down the barrel of a gun" to my gun-related hate list.

I took a quick step back, uncomfortable with how at ease Kurt/Jake looked pointing that thing at me. In all those moments when I'd felt right inside his head, as if I knew him better than anyone, I'd never have guessed he could do this.

"Why a gun?" I asked.

"Drywall screws and clamps don't work for us mere mortals." He shook his head. He also held out his hand exactly like he had in the loft at the *Demolition Queen* relaunch. "I still need that memory card."

This time I didn't have a corkscrew. I did have a burning log. I swiftly kicked it into the air. Kurt was dodging it as I leaped over the low boulder wall and hit the dark mounded earth running. With just enough moonlight to see, I raced between grapevines as gunshots whistled overhead.

Amazing the motivational power of bullets. I moved faster than I thought possible, but I didn't duck into the arched one-hundred-meter wine cave. I circled back to the trees near the fire so I could listen.

"Why didn't you answer my text?" JJ demanded.

"I was kind of busy," said Kurt.

"You know what makes me the maddest?" asked JJ. He glared at Kurt through the spokes of one of the motorcycle's twisted, charred wheels.

"This was the quickest death of a Bonneville motorcycle ever?" Kurt joked.

I didn't get the joke, but it must be a regular occurrence because JJ didn't laugh.

"Next time you're on your own with the fan club," he said and rolled the wheel onto the grass where it fell over.

"This one was not my fault," Kurt said, pointing at the dead wheel. Then he handed over Conrad's laptop and tossed JJ something small, flat, and square.

I felt my bra but already knew he'd stolen the memory card from it.

"To tell you the truth, I'm angrier about Sam," said JJ as he turned his black Kangol hat backward and then opened Conrad's laptop.

"I know. She shouldn't have done that," Kurt said, chucking the useless motorcycle wheel onto the fire.

"I mean *you* and Sam. You should have told me you were in love with her," JJ said, offended.

"Ancient history," said Kurt, giving his best cut-the-crap look.

"Not from what I saw." JJ touched his chest and smiled. "You make a cute couple."

"She's a pain in the ass. A means to an end. I'd have kissed you to get that memory card," Kurt said.

"Yeah, right. You certainly bring out the worst in her. She's not like that at home," JJ said as he began typing on the keyboard.

"You're blaming me for her behavior?" Kurt asked.

"Perhaps if you didn't shoot at her," said JJ.

Pretty funny. They fought like an old married couple.

"So, got any *helpful* advice?" Kurt asked.

"Yes." JJ rubbed his chin as if he was really giving it some thought. "Next time, wear a cup," he chuckled.

"Ha-ha." Kurt said, and then knocked off Jimmy's backward Kangol hat.

JJ caught his hat, put it back on, and then said, "The card should have unlocked all the MedMaker and WhistleBlown files, but I'm getting nowhere." He turned the screen for Kurt to see.

I could just make out its blinking words. *Access Denied.*

"But from the last 'saved' dates, I can see these were all accessed in the last week," JJ said.

"Dammit, Sam," Kurt said and looked over his shoulder toward the wine cave.

Like I'd be cowering in there.

"I'm not so sure it was Sam," said JJ.

"Well, I know of only two other people who could have accessed them. And I'm really hoping it wasn't either one," Kurt said.

I couldn't hear the names, or if he actually said any, because he and JJ headed for the car. I didn't fancy getting shot at again so I stayed put.

The MINI's taillights were still glowing like two cigarettes, at the end of the drive when my phone rang and I answered, "Hello?"

"So I said to myself, why would she put the memory card somewhere, such as, in her bra, that I'd think to look?" He chuckled. "Was it because she didn't know it was me, *someone* who knew she kept important things in her bra?"

I pictured his cocky smile and wanted to wipe it right off his gorgeous face.

"Or, I asked myself, was that memory card in her bra an inferior copy? And, yes, I do know you well enough to know that you would make a copy."

"Ah, but people change." I forced a laugh. "What if I had two fake copies?"

"Unlikely."

I liked that Kurt didn't sound quite so cocky.

"And did you consider I could have been playing you the entire time?" I asked.

He didn't respond.

"What's so important about those files anyway?" I asked.

When I realized he'd hung up on me, I shouted, "You bastard," for the third time that night.

CHAPTER FORTY-THREE

Two days later, my body sat in my convertible Mustang, waiting for the light to turn green in London's Trafalgar Square. My head was still in the Champagne region of France, furious, exhilarated, and murderous.

It was in shock too. I couldn't stop saying, "*Ohmygawd.* Jake's alive."

Kurt-Jake.

Jake-Kurt.

Two images of him and me kept playing in my head. It was like those 3-D cards you tilted side to side. First, I was strangling him. Then I was on top kissing the heck out of him.

Geez.

"*Ohmygawd.* Jake's alive," I repeated as I secured my hair with my doubled-up fan belt, removed it, and then redid it over and over again.

Hiding Mom's real memory card in my bra should have worked just fine. But if Kurt kept showing up I'd have to be more resourceful. Prior knowledge and his *very* capable hands put me at risk. I inhaled sharply thinking about Kurt's *very* capable hands, and smiled in spite of myself.

"There's no way I'm staying out of this," I said to an imaginary Kurt.

The bigger question was, what was *this*? It sure wasn't just about a pink knife or memory cards. How did Kurt and JJ know those files were in my knife before I did? I was way behind. I felt as if I was planning a demolition for a wall that had already been knocked down.

The car behind me tooted and I noticed that the light had turned green. About to move on, my phone rang. It was Silverblade. I veered into the empty lane to take his call.

Without a hello or anything, he asked, "Remember John Doe and his MedMaker chip?"

We kept calling him John Doe even though we knew who he was.

"How could I forget—?"

"I've discovered that its material when exposed to a laser first…"

Silverblade's chemistry lesson faded to a background buzz as I felt a jolt and heard a loud long scraping sound. I looked up. A towering double-decker bus was pushing me toward the curb. Meanwhile, my chrome side-view mirror was removing a wavy line of red bus paint. It hung in there right up until it hit a framed deodorant ad and then snapped off to become chrome dust under the huge bus tire.

That's when I caught a fleeting glimpse of the driver in *his* side-view mirror and blinked. It was *Nunchuck* staring back with bloodshot Cruella De Vil eyes.

Meanwhile, Silverblade droned on like elevator music. "...it polymerizes and no longer dissolves, making it the perfect photo-resist for..."

I was bracing myself as Nunchuck slammed on the brakes and backed up for more.

Shoot.

"...that means John Doe's chip was photolithic. The process involves..." Silverblade continued.

I heard Nunchuck gun his engines. I stepped on the gas but I was too late. His bus shoved my Mustang against the double-high cement curb. My metal hubcaps were screaming.

I was preoccupied, to say the least, but something that Silverblade said caught my attention.

"...C60 or carbon 60. Named after Buckminster Fuller. It's got a funny name..." Silverblade paused.

"Buckminsterfullerene or buckyballs," I said as my hazy biochemistry memories kicked in.

With that, Nunchuck leaned out his window and swung his monstrous arm at me. He missed and snapped off my Mustang's antenna, which I caught. Not that it was worth anything now.

"Buckyballs. Well done, Samantha!" Silverblade exclaimed.

Nunchuck angled his bus out sharply like he was going to ram me into oblivion. I swiftly stood with one foot on the gas. I stretched to steady my other foot on my rolled-down window.

Silverblade continued, "I've got two more things to tell you. I received another body today."

While my right hand steered, my left clenched the jagged antenna in a fencing salute. So that as the bus pulled alongside, I lunged at Nunchuck's arm. I missed and instead skewered the bus's vent. Thick black smoke immediately billowed out.

I'd just shouted, "Take that. Ha," when I noticed another passing bus. Its two levels of passengers were eyeing me with varying degrees of alarm. An older woman had put her window down and had her umbrella at the ready, presumably for a counterattack. Tons of phones were pressed against the windows probably filming the sordid event, sure to go viral in a matter of moments.

Sirens had begun and were getting closer fast.

I pictured the headline:

Crazy Demolition Widow Attacks Trafalgar Square Bus with Antenna

Tambour would have to start paying me for making his job so easy.

Silverblade cleared his throat. "As I was saying, this new body had a patch with very similar properties to John Doe's MedMaker chip. I nearly missed it though. Very difficult to see on his body. This corpse is some old Royal Navy chap, Colonel Benjamin. Poor man, his fingers are mangled with rheumatoid arthritis."

Colonel Benjamin from Conrad's wake?

"Well they worked just fine last week," I said, remembering that pinch he gave my bum.

"What?" asked Silverblade.

I cleared my throat. "That's horrible that he's dead. So, he had a chip?" I asked.

"No, he had a patch that worked like a chip," Silverblade said, exasperated. "That's what I've been trying to tell you."

I didn't know about any MedMaker patch but this was the third person with a MedMaker product *and* before it had been officially distributed.

Mom, John Doe, and now the colonel.

"Any chance you could keep this MedMaker stuff quiet for a while?" I asked.

"It's going to cost you," Silverblade said.

"OK, how much?" I asked with a laugh.

"Another day in the gym. You need practice," he said.

"I've *been* practicing…sort of," I added with a small laugh as I watched Nunchuck's smoking bus tear out of Trafalgar Square, with my mangled antenna still protruding from it.

Of course, I wasn't laughing a minute later when the police, Tambour, *and* his photographer showed up.

CHAPTER FORTY-FOUR

An hour after nearly buying a one-way ticket to oblivion, I stood in Mom's London office. Something didn't fit about that bus debacle. Surely, if Nunchuck had wanted me dead I'd *be* dead. It seemed more like Nunchuck was trying to scare me off just like Kurt. Or, at least put me out of action for a while.

I did wonder how Nunchuck found out I was alive, but then figured Kurt had told him.

Either way, between the kidnap and bus stuff, I was way behind on clue-solving. Keen to catch up, I rushed to Mom's desk. I didn't care about Max's mandate that non-employees weren't welcome at MedMaker Corp. This would always be Mom's place. Evidently, Mom's favorite security guard felt the same way. When I arrived, he spotted me and waved me on in.

I had high hopes of making important discoveries. Perhaps stuff I didn't want Max to see. So first things first, I dumped everything from my plumber's bag onto Mom's French country desk. The plaster-dusted pile would revolt fastidious Max so much he wouldn't stick around.

The main reason I was her was to prove that the *Call June Thorpe* number, 97 64 19 - 19 64 97, was the combination to Mom's square black safe. With only my phone screen to light the way, I knelt before the safe and spun its dial, ninety-seven right, sixty-four left, and nineteen right.

Click.

It unlocked, *and* without using the second half, 19 64 97.

It *worked.* It *worked.* It *worked.*

I'd solved another one of Mom's clues. How cool was that?

I scooted closer, swung its thick door open, and eagerly peeked inside. I expected an epiphany and a huge leap in the clue hunt. So the small flashlight sitting all by itself on the safe's shelf made my shoulders sag.

I sat back on my heels and clicked the flashlight on and off, on and off. It wasn't very bright. Kind of useless really. But I kept clicking on and off, wondering if Max had beat me to Mom's stuff. I honestly didn't know.

Then, I studied the other half of the June Thorpe number, 19 64 97. I scooted close again. I felt for a second combination dial but didn't find one. I ran a thumbnail around the door edge until it caught on a small ridge. I grabbed my pocketknife from Mom's desk. I was going to try and pry the door open, but before I could, I heard the sound of metal sliding against metal. My eyes widened as another combination dial poked out of the door's *inside* surface.

Very cool, Mom.

"Samantha!"

I recognized Max's surprised snarl instantly. I didn't want him seeing the safe's secret dial so I swung around with my phone's halogen light aimed at his eyes.

"What are you doing in here?" he snapped. He tilted left to avoid my light.

I moved the light left, but then he went right much quicker than I expected.

"How'd you get that safe open?" Max's angry voice sounded eerily like Conrad's angry voice. From his tone, Max definitely *hadn't* been in Mom's safe.

"Mom's will said her insurance papers would be here," I replied, not answering his question.

With that, Max flipped on the overhead lights. Before I could shut the door, he squeezed between me and the safe. I was looking at the back of his knees and then his butt as he knelt.

I held my breath, waiting for him to say something about the second dial. Puzzled that he hadn't, I peered around his legs.

The dial had vanished.

"At least I found her flashlight," I said.

Max turned up his nose at my find but then oddly changed his tune. "How about we celebrate with a spot of tea?" he asked.

"Ah, sure. I'll just tidy up in here." I pointed to the dusty pile on Mom's desk.

As planned, Max eyed the chisels, hairbrush, wall anchors, mascara, and extra pocketknives with disdain and *presto,* he was gone.

With Max out of the way, I scooted close and heard the same scraping sound. The dial reappeared, and I quickly used the second half of the combination. Nineteen right, sixty-four left, and ninety-seven right, and *click.* The two-inch-thick door split open.

*My mom is…*was *so brilliant.*

With the door split open, I saw a felt-lined tray. Nestled inside was Mom's MedMaker controller #01. A one-inch round metal disc with ridges was there too.

I shut the second door and slid the disc into my pocket. While I leaned over to put the controller and knife on the desk, the second dial vanished. I wondered why it had appeared for me in the first place.

Did Mom's safe have some kind of DNA breathalyzer? I breathed on it and felt silly as nothing happened.

Next, I took Mom's controller from the desk, thinking maybe it and me near each other had made the difference. That didn't work either, but all of a sudden, I *knew* what would.

This one holds everything you'll need, Mom had said at the fundraiser about my pink pocketknife.

I grabbed it again, held it near the safe, and the dial materialized once more. I did it a couple more times just for fun but then remembered Max was waiting. Having tea with him was about the last thing I wanted to do, but I quickly stowed Mom's #01 controller in my bag's side pocket. The same pocket where her MedMaker chip had been since Silverblade gave it to me. I chucked everything else from the desk into the main pouch.

I kept Mom's flashlight out to play with in case I got bored. I was clicking it on and off as I got ready to leave her office and a curious thing happened. Masses of purple fingerprints lit up on Mom's desk. It was a cross between connect-the-dots and a Rorschach test. *Hmm.* I studied my new flashlight with interest.

I was still clicking as I headed into Max's office.

Never been in before, probably because I never wanted to. Max was obviously nervous today from the looks of the long paperclip chain snaking across his desk.

I reluctantly plopped into a black, deeply slanted leather chair and immediately recognized it. I also recognized the desk, rug, and Max's desk chair. Everything was just like Conrad's even his glass humidor with Conrad's favorite Cherokee cigars inside. Heck he even had a photo of Cranmont Manor, with him and Conrad shaking hands on the broad front steps.

Clothes, cigars, friends, and furnishings? I wondered if Conrad ever noticed what a major suck-up Max truly was.

The only difference was their colognes. Conrad's was subtle and classic while Max's was disco-fever-like and recently reapplied from the smell of it. *Gag me.*

Max laid down his tortoiseshell glasses, the ones he rarely went without. As he began fishing through his drawer I tried them on, curious to see just how blind he was. As a non-eyeglass-wearer, I expected major eye strain, but I blinked. His glasses held nothing but plain glass.

"My life is a nightmare," Max moaned, which confirmed my suspicions that he hadn't invited me in for a celebratory anything.

"First your mother dies," Max continued.

He said this as if she'd planned it or something. I didn't like where this conversation was headed.

"Then the MedMaker debacle and this Bolivia business." Max put on his glasses and dramatically swooped to the window. "Your mum had a hand in both," he said, with his back to me.

I started to flip him the bird, but he must have seen my reflection because he turned with a suspicious look.

"And now I uncovered the truth," Max said, looking at the window again.

To keep my hands out of trouble, I clicked Mom's flashlight on and off. With that, fingerprints and spots glowed purple all over Max's desk and especially around his cologne bottle.

Did Max's cologne leave those spots on Mom's desk? If so when did he leave them? After or before she died?

What Max said next, made me forget my cologne/spot correlation. It couldn't have surprised me more than if he'd begun spouting the advantages of hammer drills versus conventional drills.

"Conrad set up WhistleBlown not to help companies but to bring them down. He stole from his clients," Max said with a snort.

"What?" I asked, struggling to the front edge of the angled seat. "Conrad was controlling and jealous but not a thief."

Max shook his head so hard his glasses slid down to rest on the bags under his eyes. "Think about the brilliance of his WhistleBlown setup. He gained client confidence and then collected every shred of information about weaknesses and illegal activities. He learned the rest from his own illegal surveillance and wireless computer siphoning. After that, he controlled all of us like puppets. He even used blackmail.

"I had this place swept. Bugs were everywhere." Max eyed his desk, his walls, and rug as if not entirely sure all were gone. "Conrad played one group off the other. No one knew who to trust except..." Max held up a finger to emphasize his point, "...the exalted son-in-law, Conrad

Albany, whistleblowing extraordinaire." Max blinked rapidly. He was on a roll and began pacing. "In the meantime, Conrad robbed us blind. Someone he blamed for the mess fled to Jamaica."

My ears perked up. "Someone went to Jamaica?" That was news.

"Before Conrad founded WhistleBlown, he interviewed hundreds of corporate criminals to understand their thought processes and techniques."

"Who went to Jamaica?" I asked. I impatiently clicked the flashlight at him, trying to get his attention. Still pacing, he didn't notice the black light effect.

"When your husband, an expert in his field, came to the rescue we didn't suspect him. We unwittingly welcomed the enemy in with open arms and paid huge sums to have him bugger us," Max said as he unconsciously added four paperclips to his chain.

"If your mother *and* Conrad were alive, she'd kill him. To think, Helen pounced on me for the semi-questionable activities I arranged to *protect* the company."

"How long ago did he flee to Jamaica?" I asked, raising my voice and impatiently tapping my bag.

"What?" Max turned his annoyed glance.

"Who went to Jamaica?" I asked.

"One of our investors," Max said. He also pointed at his copy of the MedMaker team fish-face photo, specifically at the man with the birthmark.

"Investors?" I asked.

But that's John Doe with the cloverleaf birthmark in Silverblade's morgue. He was an investor?

"Why are you so interested in Jamaica?" he glared at me.

Not wanting to answer that, I asked, "How many companies did Conrad do this to?"

As I was finally with the program, Max enthusiastically answered, "Three that I've identified so far. From what I can tell, Conrad chose them based on two vital elements. One, upper managers ripe for blackmail. The second was companies with something worth stealing like information, money, and/or technology, i.e. our MedMaker technology." Max added a few more paperclips to his chain. "At HFNC Bank he trumped up charges of internal 'wrongdoing' against poor Prunella."

I wrinkled my nose, picturing "poor" Prunella's surgically tightened everything. I just couldn't wrangle pity for that woman.

"And the blackmail here?" I asked, watching Max's reaction.

"What about it?" Max snapped.

"Who did Conrad blackmail at MedMaker Corporation?" I asked.

Was it you, Max?

Developing bioweapons would make perfect blackmail material.

"That man is in jail," Max said and then abandoned the paperclips to tug his eyebrows so hard he winced.

Right.

Max wasn't done.

"And you know what else? I think this horrid reporter, Tambour, was on Conrad's payroll. I think Conrad broke the story about your mom's MedMaker to keep suspicions off himself."

"I don't believe that," I said.

I wasn't so sure I didn't believe it, but I wasn't just going along with Max. "Except, Conrad isn't paying Tambour anymore, and he's still at it."

Max shrugged. "Tambour knew things your mom and I only told Conrad. Tambour also knew things we didn't tell Conrad or anyone else. I'm positive Conrad's bugs collected that information." He looked around the room again. "Tambour's story put twenty thousand MedMakers on hold. The man is singlehandedly killing it," Max said, pounding the desk with his fist.

Probably not the time to check for a purple fist mark.

"I wish we could prove that your mom's MedMaker didn't malfunction," Max moaned as he pulled off his glasses again.

This time without glasses, he looked diminished, younger, like a lost little kid. His tight, anguished face didn't look like the face of an evil rogue.

"So what can we do?" I asked, believing his story a bit more.

"If only we had your mom's chip and controller then we could access her numbers for the day she died," said Max.

I reached into my bag's side pocket. My fingers even closed on Mom's chip and controller as I said, "I've got her chip and—"

"You do?" Max asked. He looked like a poker player about to lurch for his winnings.

Sure, he was desperate to clear this mess up. I was too. However, something in his overeager eyes gave me second thoughts. Conrad's business dealings might have been dirty, but there was no way Max was squeaky clean.

"Darn it. Must be in my other bag," I said, releasing the chip and controller, then twirling strands of my hair with my fingers.

Maybe Mom's chip could prove that Max had developed bioweapons beyond the memo stage. I decided that I'd hold onto it for now and do more investigating of my own.

"Tomorrow?" I innocently asked.

"That would be fine." He turned back to the window, but not before I saw his mouth silently form the word *bugger*.

CHAPTER FORTY-FIVE

If what Max said about Conrad was true, then my husband was a liar, a thief, and possibly a murderer to boot. That meant Conrad had a back story just like Kurt. The irony was not lost on me.

I was kicking myself all the way back to Cranmont for *never* snooping through Conrad's Cranmont desk. Me and not snooping? What was that about? Probably had to do with my unwillingness to face the sum total of my own stupidity, i.e., marrying Conrad in the first place.

Standing at Old Mr. Albany's study door, I was itching to make up for lost time but first, I had to shake the housekeeper.

"Do you think James will be back tomorrow?" she asked, pulling at her crisp white apron, patting her cheeks, and pressing down her frizzy brown hair.

"Your guess is as good as mine," I said, impatiently scratching my thumbnail on the doorknob.

Wouldn't she just faint if I told her about our dear butler's real identity?

Or would she?

I focused on her face. If Kurt was Jake and James was JJ, who's to say she was really a housekeeper, let alone a woman?

"You've got something on your cheek," I said.

Her startled eyes went cross-eyed watching my finger rub an imaginary spot on her round, weathered face.

"Got it," I said, relieved to feel warm *real* skin move beneath my thumb.

She smiled appreciatively.

"If I hear from James, I'll let you know ASAP," I said.

Don't hold your breath.

"Thank you, ma'am," she said, dipping into a small curtsy.

"Now, I must locate some important papers," I said, giving her my downcast grieving-widow eyes.

"Of course, mum." She backed away from the door as I went on inside.

I sniffed the air, surprised at how strong the cigar scent was weeks after Conrad's death. My long legs got me to his desk chair in two steps. Sitting, I ran a hand across the desk's worn wooden ridges and then pulled open the middle drawer. Only fountain pens, pencils, and small jars of India ink rattled in their leather dividers. The next two drawers held envelopes and stamps.

Disappointing.

Then I pulled open the bottom drawer. "Well I'll be damned," I said, smiling down at a copy of a birth certificate.

Theodore Maximillian Tuloitte.
Place of birth: New Orleans
Mother: Maxine Tuloitte
Father: Unidentified

Max's mother tongue was *Creole* French. That sure explained his non-*France* French.

There was more. The birth certificate was paper-clipped, *very fitting*, to a Louisiana State University diploma. That meant Max's whole Eton and Cambridge pretentious prick act was just that, an act.

That also meant that when Max copied Conrad's attire, furniture, and choice of smokes, he wasn't sucking up. Copying Conrad was the only way he could pull off his British gent masquerade. No wonder he reminded me of someone. He was a Conrad clone.

Talk about your blackmail material. I whistled.

If possible, I thought even less of Max now. His Conrad-as-corporate-thief-story wasn't quite as convincing either.

Sour grapes, perhaps?

"OK, Max, let's see where you and your cologne have been." I flashed Mom's black light across the desktop and the open desk drawers. Whoa. Mom's office had nothing on this place.

I twisted toward the wall to see what else he'd touched. The Albany antlers were dot-free but not the framed hunt scene above the overstuffed chair. Two crescents of purple fingerprints hugged its bottom corners.

Cool.

A tinge of excitement tickled my shoulders as I climbed onto the chair. I lined fingertips up with the purple crescents and tilted the painting. With that, a muffled click sounded inside the wall, a narrow floor-to-ceiling section rotated inward, and an overhead light turned on.

I wrinkled my nose as an even stronger cigar-scented draft of air smacked my faced. It was like Max had just been there.

Interesting find, but that was nothing. This floor's dumbwaiter was in here. Its beveled glass doors were wide-open too, like an invitation to ride. Plus there were fifteen screens, which flickered to life beside it. Each one showed a different area of Cranmont. The foyer, terrace, and art gallery. The den too, where the housekeeper was dusting. My barn showed as well, with my Mustang parked outside. That all made sense.

What didn't make sense was seeing Mom's office on the next screen. My nostrils flared, just thinking about Conrad spying on Mom.

Then I thought for a minute.

Maybe Conrad watched Mom's office to keep tabs on Max.

Although, from what I'd just learned he was more likely, keeping tabs on Max *and* spying on Mom.

I'd never seen the next screen's brick-walled room or its extra-long snooker table.

The very last screen showed a crude-looking lab with dark, flaking, water-stained walls, cracking linoleum floor, *and* two flat-bottom Pyrex beakers, one blood-red and one pink-ish. My hackles went right up. Those beakers looked just like the ones I took notes about at MedMaker Corp. I backed up the footage for clues as to how they got there and lo and behold, there was Nunchuck. Couldn't have picked a more fitting place for him. His cheek had only the one red scar that my plumbers wrench had caused on that Swiss mountain. Not the *X* formed by my red-hot chain. That meant this footage was from before Denmark.

He guiltily looked over his Naugahyde-covered shoulder toward the door, like he wasn't supposed to be there and/or doing what he was about to do. He scooted close to the beakers. He put his gold gun on the worktop.

I was intrigued. He knew exactly what to do. He picked up a small black controller, shaped just like Mom's MedMakcr oncs. Then he pressed a button and the beaker's blood-red liquid came to life. It churned as if hundreds of tiny sharks were fighting for prey. He quickly pushed another button and the red surface went dead calm.

Next, he bent his head to look through a microscope. It was a projection microscope so I saw what he saw but projected onto a grimy-looking whiteboard. Hundreds of pale pink forms floated like minute ghosts. Each had two black, lifeless beady "eyes."

"Do you want to play?" Nunchuck asked the "ghosts" in a sinister tone. He pushed a new button, and immediately they swam toward the beaker's sides. He adjusted his microscope to follow some. Like vodka fumes on a shot glass, they formed wiggly columns that flowed up and up. *Unlike* vodka, these columns climbed the four-inch sides in nothing flat. As they neared the top in seconds, Nunchuck stabbed at the OFF button but missed. Beads of sweat broke out on his forehead. His single red scar violently twitched like it was going to jump off his face.

Several of the "ghosts" were teetering at the beaker's top as an angry voice shouted, "What are you doing in here?"

Nunchuck didn't look up. He stabbed at the OFF button again and again until finally his fist hit the mark and ghost cells slid back down the beaker's sides. It had taken so long to turn them off, I briefly wondered if any had slid down on the *outside* of the beaker.

"Oh, hello screw-up," Nunchuck finally said. He stood and towered over a toothpick-thin man wearing a lab coat. "The boss isn't going to find out about my little visit here, is he? If he does, I'll convince him Bolivia was all your fault. I mean, what didn't you understand about killing one nosy-assed woman?" Nunchuck's voice hummed low and dangerous. He picked up his gun and waved it at the lab tech. "That Gabby was supposed to wander into the jungle, contract a deadly Bolivian virus, and die. End of story. Instead, you wiped out an entire sodding village."

"B-B-Bolivia was my first go. We all knew there could be complications," the lab tech said. Then with new bravado he added, "You know, Bolivia could just as easily happen right here to you."

"You're threatening me? I can't believe…" Nunchuck trailed off.

The lab tech was staring at Nunchuck's gun not with fear but fascination.

Nunchuck looked down and frowned as a circle of blood moved from the gun up his wrist and onto his cuff.

"Bloody hell," he said angrily. Grabbing a sponge, he scrubbed at the spot.

Anger swiftly turned to surprise as the blood shape-shifted into more of a swirling tropical storm shape.

This was the YouTube video Silverblade showed me in my barn. Except, this one had sound.

Knowing this was real was a bit unsettling.

On the other hand, knowing it was Nunchuck made it sort of fun. *Wish I had popcorn.*

Bloody tentacles swirled right up his sleeve to his shoulder. Like before, Nunchuck ripped open his shirtfront like a Superman wannabe. He tried to pull the whole thing off, but his still-buttoned cuffs held tight. Barebacked and bare-armed, he bent at the waist with his shirt dangling from his wrists. I particularly enjoyed him hopping around like a gorilla *and* how he blubbered, "Get it off me," as the bloody tentacles started back toward his cuff. He stomped at his shirt, trying to free his wrists, and then screamed when the lab tech drove his scalpel into the sleeve to cut off the cuff. Finally, Nunchuck ripped off the shirt and threw it onto the counter.

Except for shirt shifting on the counter and jumping into the sink all by itself, which was disturbing, I gave the video a ten out of ten for pure entertainment value.

It had also answered my question about ghost cells sliding down *outside* the beaker.

What it didn't answer was how, if the blood was controlled by pressing buttons, could it swirl up Nunchuck's arm outside the beaker with *no* button pressing? Had converting Mom's MedMaker technology to bioweapons do this? *I sure hope not.*

The Nunchuck "show" had been so freakish, I had to think for a second why my heart felt so heavy. Then I remembered that the 'nosy-assed woman' they'd killed with MedMaker bioweapons was Gabby.

Did they kill Gabby because she'd discovered their secret? Did she know that they'd hijacked and converted the MedMaker technology to bioweapons and planned to test it in Bontero? Or was she close to finding out?

They'd killed her in the village she'd been adopted from. Was that just a coincidence?

How much had Mom found out before she died? I had no clue.

I was about to cue up more footage, curious to see what else was here, when it occurred to me that Max probably watched all of these. I bet he could access them from work too. If so, that explained how he "discovered" me in Mom's office. Except, then he'd have known I found Mom's #01 controller. Could he be playing with me to see if I fessed up?

What also occurred to me was that Conrad used to watch this stuff too. Probably why he had been rarely in his office when I looked for him.

Next, I fast-forwarded the Breast Cancer Fundraiser footage to when Mom arrived. She kissed a couple people in Cranmont's foyer then glanced at her watch and rushed toward the stairs. I watched other screens that showed other parts of the stairs. Oddly, a bit of footage came up with no balloons on railings. Mom never appeared on the stairs or the guest suite landing. Not even when the balloons came back.

Next, I searched and searched for footage of Kurt when he was caught in my booby-trap. Sadly, I found none.

Of course, my shower scene was there. Every inch of me was in plain sight *including* my tattoo.

Conrad's wake was next. I had just begun counting how many times Max went up and down Cranmont's stairs that day, when the doorknob to Old Mr. Albany's study rattled. I checked the den screen. The housekeeper was still dusting, so it wasn't her at the door.

I didn't want anyone to know I'd found this compartment so I pushed the wall shut with me inside.

I eyed the dumbwaiter and jumped in. I pushed its worn *TF* button, *top floor I presumed.* I didn't expect anything to happen so was pleasantly surprised as the bottom horizontal door slid up and the top one slid down to "kiss" it. They closed slow and silent so when the dumbwaiter took off like a shot, I wasn't prepared. My butt hit the black leather bench and I was struggling to stand as I zipped past a thirty-inch gap between floors, labeled STORAGE. I saw no stored things but spied the orange water pipe that Conrad's cousin said they'd rigged to squirt water at passengers. I heard a rattle and looked down at the air vent as a rather pathetic squirt of water came out.

Reaching the top floor, a puff of black powder flared from the door edges as they opened. I pushed aside a black smudged curtain, entered a sea of duvets and Egyptian cotton sheets, and realized I was in the upstairs linen closet. *Wow.*

It made sense. Conrad's cousin said they'd snuck into the dumbwaiter without Wilhelmina knowing. So where was their secret passageway? I pushed aside stacks of fluffy white bath towels and guest-sized shampoos to find a panel under the lowest shelf. Sliding it aside, I crawled around fake logs and out through a fireplace. I was standing in the one Cranmont room I'd *never* seen—Conrad's nursery.

I pulled sooty hair into an imaginary ponytail as I studied the nursery. Its twin sleigh beds and life-size rocking horse were nursery-like, but it wasn't warm, cozy, and inviting like a nursery should be. This dark room made me uncomfortable. Especially as I lifted the horse's wooden chin and its eight-foot runners creaked and groaned on the coffee-colored floorboards.

I unlocked the door to the landing thinking that might help, but it made a loud click that echoed across the bare wood floor and abruptly died as if something supernatural had stopped it.

I crossed the room and opened its broad double doors to the balcony. Cool, refreshing air did help a bit. I walked out to the waist-high stone wall. I noticed guide wires that lead all the way from this roof, across the ravine, and to the top of Cranmont Tower. From there they disappeared inside all that scaffolding.

Conrad's cousin said they'd climbed up the outside of the tower. I wondered if they ever went by wire to the tower. I stared down into the dark ravine and decided that only a crazy person would do that.

Back inside, I tapped my boot against a tall steel Albany-crested trunk and admired the crossed wall-mounted swords above it.

Boy, would I stomp Silverblade's butt with those.

I smiled and flicked a finger at their thick gold tassels and noticed the frolicking horse wallpaper behind them. I wondered if Conrad liked horses before the fire or if wicked Wilhelmina had picked that wallpaper to taunt Conrad after the accident.

Sam, get a grip. No one could be that cruel.

Focusing on the sleigh beds, I pictured Conrad and his cousin lying there, plotting their next marauder-filled day.

And then it dawned on me that whoever had turned the doorknob to Old Mr. Albany's study could be watching me up here right now. I didn't like that thought.

I was about to go when a huge framed portrait between the beds caught my eye. The frame was about the size of the empty faint brown rectangle that used to be over the east fireplace. The portrait was of a beautiful mahogany-colored thoroughbred with majestic peaked ears and flared nostrils. Its engraved nameplate said, "Winchester's Grand Day."

Where have I heard that name?

I gasped. Eyes darted back up at the horse. Conrad's cousin told me that Winchester's Grand Day died in that barn fire.

Had wicked Wilhelmina put it in here to punish Conrad for his sins? Was I wrong? *Could* someone be that cruel? Or had Conrad locked it in here to forget that horrible day?

"Madam?"

No other word or voice could have made me look toward the open nursery door quicker. *We're talking whiplash.*

In his first Cranmont appearance since France, JJ bowed like it was the most natural thing in the world.

"Boy, you're good," I said, studying his butler posture and worn face.

"Madam, Mr. Max Carlisle is here to see you," JJ said.

I glared at his innocent blank gaze and said, "Oh, cut the madam crap, will you—"

"Oh mum, isn't it wonderful? James is back," the housekeeper said from the landing door. She was beaming.

"Yes, it is." I plastered a smile on my face.

"Could you please tell Max that I will be right down?" I asked her, figuring I was safe enough to be alone with JJ since she'd seen us together.

But it was JJ who answered first. "Yes, madam," as if I'd asked *him*.

He bowed and shuffled out the door behind the housekeeper. His coattails had just disappeared when my phone *barked*. The bark was the special ringtone for my old family vet.

"Hi there. So it's working OK?" I asked.

"Yes, it's giving off a very strong signal," she said.

"Thanks for the great news," I said, hanging up.

The vet was talking about the dog GPS tracker tag I'd put in Kurt's phone in France. With everything else going on, I'd forgotten all about it until this morning when I asked her to check its signal.

On my phone call with the vet I'd purposely not said *what* was working, because knowing JJ, I suspected he'd not gone far. Confirmed as I looked up and his coattails left the doorway *again*. Oddly, as I left the nursery he was not on the broad, chandelier-lit landing or curving staircase.

I still had my hand on the nursery doorknob when I felt that same mechanical vibration the dumbwaiter had made when I rode upstairs. Although, it felt much stronger up here. Could that vibration have been what made Mom's paintings in the guest room tilt so much? If so, then someone had used the dumbwaiter a lot. And since Conrad, the housekeeper, and I thought it was out of order, it had to be JJ, Kurt, or Max sneaking around, spying on us.

I practically jumped out of my skin as the nursery door opened and JJ stood there, hunched and crooked.

"How'd you do that?" I asked, with hands on hips.

"I know not of what madam speaks," he said.

"So saving your life counts for nothing?" I asked, standing close to his stitched earlobe.

"Yes, madam. I am dreadfully appreciative." He nodded stiffly.

"OK, if you want to play it that way," I snarled. I also swatted at his perfect bow tie.

Not a glint of a smile.

"As Mr. Carlisle still awaits your arrival in the den, I suggest madam changes," he said, giving my jeans and T-shirt that repulsed glare he did so well.

CHAPTER FORTY-SIX

Ten minutes later, I'd changed and was sizing up Max from the art gallery door. He had an arm casually draped on the den's east fireplace mantle, directly below where the portrait of Winchester's Grand Day used to hang. He looked way too at home. Having said that, his right hand gave his true mood away. It had a circular assault thing going from glasses, to eyebrow, to paperclip chain, and back to glasses.

"Max? Aren't you the eager beaver?" I said extra loud to see his reaction. I was rewarded as three eyebrow hairs fluttered to the carpet. "So, what brought you all the way out here this early?"

I know exactly why you're here, I thought as I walked toward him.

Max's broad smile surprised me. So did the way he firmly clamped his hands on my upper arms, pulled me to him, and kissed each cheek. From the look of his still-puckered lips, he planned a centrally located kiss too.

I said a silent *hallelujah* as JJ rolled in with a rattling tea trolley. With that, Max cleared his throat and moved away, saying, "I had a meeting in Weybridge, so thought I would save you the trip into my office. Tea please," he said without being asked. Then he snagged one of Cook's mini–Victoria sponge cakes.

James placed a silver-rimmed china cup on its saucer and poured Max's tea so achingly slow that Max finally ripped the cup and saucer from his hand.

"Coffee for me please, JJ," I said, biting my lip to suppress a smile.

"Samantha, I am certain Conrad would not approve of how informally you address the help," Max said as he sat on the couch nearest the fireplace and pulled perfectly polished wingtips in close to the couch's fringed skirt.

"Yes, well sometimes the help need a little reminder of who they really are," I said.

"James, finish pouring Ms. Samantha's coffee and then leave us," Max said.

James stiffened and stopped pouring.

"That will be all, James," I said, flashing a small evil smile and easing the half-filled cup from his clenched hands.

"With Conrad gone, why keep him?" Max asked and nodded at JJ's back.

"I've asked myself that a lot lately," I said loud enough for JJ to hear as he did his best and slowest shuffling-exit act yet.

I'd keep him around because for me it had to do with that whole, "Keep your friends close and your enemies closer" thing.

"So you're here because?" I asked innocently. I wanted Max to work for it.

"Two things really. I assume you will be going to WhistleBlown at some point to collect Conrad's personal effects, so I have a favor to ask. Could you please collect a folder marked 'MedMaker Corporation Accounts'? Particularly, one dated a year ago this month. I worry that without Conrad there to protect our interests, the security of our documents may be at risk."

"Makes sense." I shrugged.

"Now the other reason," Max said, putting down his cup and saucer with the same eager look from yesterday.

"Oh, that's right. Mom's chip," I said through clenched, barely smiling lips. I pulled a MedMaker chip from my pocket and dropped it into his outstretched hand. "Here you go."

Max whipped off his glasses and turned it over. His quick smile disappeared.

This was kind of fun.

"This is not Helen's ch-ch-chip," Max stammered.

His crestfallen expression almost made me sorry for the creep.

Max stood so quickly that his china and silver quivered on the coffee table. "It's a sodding prototype."

I knew that already. Its label said "Prototype" when I peeled it off this morning.

"I'm so sorry." I paused. "Max, how can you be so certain that Mom's MedMaker malfunctioned?"

He didn't answer. Instead, he looked at me funny. I couldn't read him, especially as he began pacing the den's length so fast his starched trouser legs snapped like popguns. His glasses bounced on his nose too. Back and forth he went until fifty-paces away, at the west fireplace, he stopped and eyed me. At least, I thought he was eyeing me. Hard to tell with his glasses at that angle.

I'd lost interest as he started another "lap" in my direction. So, I was studying the deckled edge of the new frame above the fireplace when *whoosh*. Victoria sponge breath hit my face, and then came lips. I was so off guard, I didn't get my arms and hands between me and Max until the wet, repulsive damage was done.

"What was that?" I pushed him away and wiped the back of my hand across my lips.

"I've known for so long that you wanted me," Max panted.

"Are you insane?" I glared at him.

"I saw you behind those flowers at Conrad's wake when I ushered Prunella out of the foyer. I know jealousy when I see it."

"What are you on about? Try hatred and relief. I can't stand that woman," I said.

Bright red patches formed on Max's cheeks. His frown was so deep its lines extended beneath his chin. Then he blurted out, "There was no malfunction. That arsehole killed…"

He glared at me as if I'd made him say whatever that was.

"What?" I asked and leaned toward him.

"That arsehole killed the MedMaker," he said and then raced from the room. *Forget popguns.* If his legs were matches, they'd be on fire.

He'd said "arsehole." The problem was I didn't know which arsehole he was talking about. Hard to pick just one.

The first that came to mind, the one I couldn't stop thinking about, *dammit*, was…*Kurt*.

That settled it. My next break-in would be at Kurt's place. Unfortunately, I had Schott's dinner to go to before I could.

Having said that, I was glad I hadn't sent my regrets to Schott. It was time to find out how he fit into all of this.

CHAPTER FORTY-SEVEN

On my way to Schott's townhouse, I stopped in at Mrs. Party's office. I'd wanted to check up on the hyper woman. The stampede at the breast cancer fundraiser had been bad enough. After the column incident at the *Demolition Queen* launch party I'd been a little worried.

"Samantha, so nice of you to stop by," Mrs. Party said and then kissed each of my cheeks. Her eyes were guarded like she was worried I'd knock something over. *Fair enough.* I handed her a bouquet of lilies, which in the scheme of things seemed overwhelmingly unimpressive, so I also blurted out, "I'm so very sorry for wrecking my, *your* parties—"

"Darling, everything is just fine," she said and waved away my apology. I expected that reaction. She'd want to keep me happy. I could influence too many of her clientele.

OK, so my parties were disaster-filled. At least they were memorable.

"What exciting event are you working on?" I asked, knowing it would be Schott's.

"We're assembling the last-minute pirate party packs," she said, leading me into the conference room. There were six young men and women furiously packing pirate paraphernalia into individually labeled black glossy boxes. At the head of a long table, two of them assembled the four-inch-square boxes. The next two put cards in, similar to the save-the-date one I got weeks ago.

Yo Ho Ho

It's Almost Here...

Schott's Pirate Fantasy Party

7th November, 8:00 p.m.

Venue: Victoria and Albert Museum

Carriages for 1:00 a.m.

The next two workers added an eye patch, hoop earring, mustache, and booking form for Silverblade's swashbuckling lessons.

"Oh, the trials I had convincing the V&A to allow Silverblade's swordplay on the balcony. Paid thousands to secure the Chihuly chandelier away from Schott's gangplank," she moaned.

"Silverblade's excited," I said. I didn't know whether he was or not. She just seemed to need the encouragement.

It seemed to help. She smiled and continued. "The event should be very entertaining. Schott had me order in baby crocodiles for a 'pit' beneath the gangplank. Rooms have special names like *Blind Man's Bluff* and *Pirates Cave.* There's a stripy tented Grog Bar in the center of the foyer and the waiters will be dressed as shipwrecked sailors in ragged white button-down shirts and shorts."

"It does sound fun," I said, picking up a miniature brown rum bottle.

"Everyone gets one of those. There's a treasure map inside. Although, I'm skeptical." She *tsk*'d. "Could you really see the Wolverhamptons hunt for anything themselves, let alone climb all those stairs?"

Realizing she was talking to one of their best friends, she turned bright red and rushed on. "If I remember correctly, your map leads to the ceramics room at the top of the V&A named, *Dead Men Tell No Lies.* Oh, I probably shouldn't have told you that." She looked even more flustered but that still didn't stop her. "I had no idea Mr. Schott had so many prestigious acquaintances," she said, waving at stacks of labels. I leaned over to study the accompanying list. It was very similar to the sociopolitical power base from the fundraiser but with twice the people.

Mrs. Party and I reached the end of the assembly line where the last two workers sprinkled a generous scoop of glittering pirate hat and dagger-shaped confetti over the box's contents.

"I had everything counted out for these boxes and then Mr. Schott makes late additions to the party." Mrs. Party said as she waved two sheets of calligraphied address labels past my face. I didn't get to read them. But as she slid the offensive labels back into the pile, at least I helped myself to a Pirate Party 'Staff Pass.'

"Of course, I didn't complain to Mr. Schott about the extra labels. Wouldn't want to ruffle his feathers." Mrs. Party said, and then looked up with a grimace. "He's a little bit scary. Absolute nightmare to work with. Right now, he's in North London inspecting my coconut shell signage," she said with a pout.

I tried to picture Schott inspecting coconuts and failed.

As this visit was all about making nice, I didn't tell her my next stop was Schott's Eaton Square townhouse.

CHAPTER FORTY-EIGHT

At the open front door of Schott's townhouse, I gave his stiff formal butler the once-over. His mug appeared to be authentically butler-ish, but so had James's.

"Mr. Schott is not expected for another twenty minutes," he said.

I knew that.

It was precisely why I arrived early.

This was my chance to give Schott a closer look. He'd become so central to the group so quickly. His pirate party was causing such a stir. Yes, he went to school with the Wolverhamptons but I'd never heard of him before Conrad introduced him so glowingly at the breast cancer fundraiser. Then the chief fawned over him at my relaunch party. Mrs. Party's comment about Schott being a bit scary was interesting too.

Entering the lounge behind the butler, I was already casing the joint and quickly spied Schott's study through double doors to the left. *Perfect.*

"May I get you a drink?" the butler asked.

I should have said, "No, thank you." That way, he wouldn't have a reason to return, but I couldn't help myself.

"I'd kill for champagne," I said.

As soon as he left, I darted into the study. First, I pushed aside Schott's heavy, silk-lined curtains. I wanted a clearer view of posh Eaton Square, in case his limo pulled up early.

Next, I sat behind his clear glass desk. I was surprised to see one of Mrs. Party's shiny black invite boxes. Seemed silly for Schott to get one for his own party. I pulled it toward me. I wanted to see if he'd received a V&A treasure map. I peeled back the box's gold-embossed skull-and-crossbones seal and pulled out his miniature rum bottle. With that, glittering pirate hats and dagger-shaped confetti sifted down onto Schott's desk. *Shoot.* Wedging my fingernail against the bottle's cork, I popped it off. Out slid a tattered sepia-colored V&A treasure map. It had an *X* in the top left corner, the V&A's top floor and ceramics room.

Same as my map. We'd be there together? *Not if I could help it.*

His map was already tattered, what was one more tear? I quickly ripped off his *X* and shoved it into my pocket. I was deciding where to send Schott when headlights flashed across the wall.

Damn. He was early, and I wasn't even supposed to be here yet.

I was gathering confetti like a crazy person when the front door slammed. I dumped it into the box and smoothed the seal back into place. Schott was marching down the hall as I realized I'd left the bottle *and* map on the desk. With mere seconds to spare, I grabbed them. I jumped behind the curtain right before Schott swanned in, speaking on the phone.

"Lunch at the palace was as expected," said Schott.

I felt pretty safe behind that curtain and would have been too but then the butler entered. I saw his reflection in a mirror diagonally across the room. He had *my* champagne on a silver tray and was looking around with a puzzled expression. I held my breath, sure he was about to ask where I'd gone. But I was saved as Schott took the champagne and dismissed the butler with a curt nod and *no* thank you.

Not very nice.

Schott continued his call by saying, "You're so kind. Yes, I do try to commit 'random acts of kindness' wherever possible." He paused to listen. "Yes, it is rather a lot of gold to have at the V&A, but I've increased security tenfold," Schott said. "Thank you ever so much."

Gold? Gold what?

He frowned as the doorbell rang and a dog barked.

"Sir, the Wolverhamptons have arrived," the butler announced at the study door.

"They brought their sodding dog?" Schott cursed before stomping out of the study.

Random acts or no random acts, that wasn't very nice either.

That settled it, I'd put several floors between us. I *X*'d his treasure map to send him to the V&A's British Galleries on the second floor. If I remembered correctly, there was even a prominent dog portrait there.

I swiftly shoved Schott's map into its bottle and bottle into box. I almost dropped the lot when I spotted a familiar photo behind Schott's desk.

Mom's MedMaker team fish-face photo.

I took a closer look and there, second from the left, was Schott. I hadn't recognized him before because in the photo his hair was long and wavy. Plus the lab goggles hid his distinctive eyebrows.

So was Schott a MedMaker investor too? *Was that one of his random acts of kindness?*

"Investing" sure hadn't worked out well for John Doe.

What if Schott was in grave danger? Throwing a massive party right now wasn't so smart.

I heard Schott and Lord Wolverhampton talking in the hallway, so streaked into the lounge right as Lady Wolverhampton entered, flapping Tinker Bell wings.

"Sam, so lovely to see you," she said as she kissed my cheeks and Tiger, her darling poodle, pawed my arm.

Over her shoulder, I could see Schott's surprised expression.

"Samantha, how lovely. When did you arrive?" Schott asked.

"Been here for ages. Got the time wrong," I said, surreptitiously removing confetti from my dress, then sprinkling it into Lord Wolverhampton's pocket as I greeted him.

"Love the fairy wings," I said to Lady Wolverhampton.

"I decided if I couldn't go to the party because of Tiger's surgery, I'd wear them here," she said.

"And I'm so glad you did," said Schott. "Samantha, are you coming to my party?" Schott asked, with a hopeful expression.

"Yes. In fact, I sent my RSVP doubloon ages ago." *Or had I?*

"Sam, you should see what our kind host sent to me because I can't go to his party. A *real* gold doubloon," said Lady Wolverhampton.

Real gold doubloon? Was that the gold he mentioned on the phone? Would everyone get one? Geez.

"Thank you once again for the very special treat," she said to Schott.

"I wish I could do more. I get to be Captain Hook commandeering my party, and you will be nowhere in sight. Such a pity," Schott said.

He used such a sincere tone and looked truly frightened by Lady Wolverhampton's poodle that I was disgusted by my petty behavior, sending him to the gallery with a dog portrait.

Especially as his life might be in danger.

Way to go, Sam.

CHAPTER FORTY-NINE

At ten p.m., after Schott plied me with enough champagne for four, I toddled over to the King's Road address that the vet had given me for Kurt. She'd tracked both the tag inside the decoy knife Kurt stole at my relaunch party and the one I'd slipped into Kurt's phone in France.

I knew I was taking a chance assuming Kurt lived in this apartment building, that had a wild looking safari-themed bar in its lobby, but it was all I had.

So I waited outside, and I waited and I waited and I waited. When Kurt finally emerged I was a touch hung over but I followed anyway and not just because he was looking ruggedly gorgeous in black jeans and a black polo shirt. I hoped to find out what he was up to.

I kept at least five people between me and him as I shadowed him straight into Victoria Station. He moved quickly toward the Gatwick Airport shuttle trains and darted on through the ticket stile. Buying a ticket slowed me down so I was minutes behind when I boarded the first-class car and spotted the most unlikely pair facing each other in the first two rows. Kurt had his back to me. Nunchuck in his cheap, crinkly Naugahyde coat was facing my way. Luckily, his ugly orange mug was already lowered in discussion with Kurt.

I ducked into the small luggage compartment by the door and folded my legs in tight, behind a hard-sided suitcase. Pressing against the crack in the glass divider, I was able to hear them. I was eyeing the horrible *X* on Nunchuck's cheek as coincidentally Kurt joked about it.

"Sued that surgeon of yours yet?" Kurt asked in his calm Danish-accented voice.

Nunchuck just growled and then said, "That was another tidy little MedMaker death."

Another MedMaker death?

"Wait, you've been hounding me for the codes to make it work, and you already had them?" Kurt asked, grabbing Nunchuck's lapels.

Kurt's been looking for codes to kill people with the MedMaker bioweapons?

"No. I was complimenting *you* on the colonel's death. It was about time too," said Nunchuck, pushing Kurt's hands away.

Colonel Benjamin? Silverblade's muckety-muck in the Royal Navy? If these two didn't do it, then how did they know Colonel Benjamin had a MedMaker patch? Silverblade promised he wouldn't tell.

I heard the crinkle of Nunchuck's Naugahyde as he leaned close to Kurt's face. It reminded me of Nunchuck's cigarette/coffee breath. My gag reflex was strong.

"As we both know the codes can't be reconstructed without a MedMaker team member. So the boss was delighted, thinking you had the codes and had performed another successful MedMaker demonstration like Bolivia," said Nunchuck.

The same Bolivian MedMaker demonstration he'd mentioned in the video with the lab tech.

"Not me," Kurt said. "Why kill the colonel?"

"Maybe he was running out of money or about to blow the whistle," Nunchuck said.

Running out of money? Had Colonel Benjamin been an investor too?

"Maybe a competitor is trying to make the MedMaker look like total rubbish and ruin the company," said Kurt.

He had a point there.

"Or you're lying and sold the code to someone else. A fatal mistake," Nunchuck said.

I heard another crinkle and saw Nunchuck mime a shot to Kurt's head. Good thing he didn't have his gold gun.

"I know how much the soiree means to our client," said Kurt. He calmly looked sideways and tossed a cashew between taut, unsmiling lips. "That and I know how little my life means to you," Kurt added and looked back at Nunchuck. "I'll get the code. Don't worry your pretty little head about it."

Soiree? What soiree?

And what was that about a code?

For whatever reason, I thought of Schott and his impressive guest list. It made me think of the buyer in Max's PowerPoint. His list had sounded super long and impressive too.

What if that buyer's list included Schott and all his party guests?

"One more thing. This Sam woman is digging around too much. She's hot, but—"

"As if we'd need to worry about her," said Kurt with a laugh.

I'll show you.

"Nothing is going to stop us," said Nunchuck.

"Relax. The boss promised it would go as planned. I've got it under control," said Kurt.

The train beeped like its doors were getting ready to close. Kurt hopped up, sped past the luggage compartment, and was off the train before I could even untangle my legs from the suitcase.

I was headed to Gatwick Airport with Nunchuck.

That was great.

Just great.

CHAPTER FIFTY

My calves were killing me. My whole body was stiff. Hiding in the luggage compartment to and from Gatwick Airport did it. Luckily, the time spent wasn't wasted. Well, at least the time I was *awake*. I'd dozed off but the nap energized me. I came up with the most the ingenious plan to sneak into Kurt's apartment.

First, I called Kurt to lure him to the champagne bar at Harrods. I'd promised to give him the code Nunchuck had threatened him for. Of course, I didn't have the code but Kurt didn't know that. He also didn't know that I wouldn't be at Harrods.

Instead, I was in the safari bar among the pre-theater crowd at Kurt's building. I was about to get someone to help me break into his apartment. That someone just didn't know it yet.

But everyone sure knew I was in the bar as my phone loudly *barked*. In such a hurry to get out of earshot, I bumped into a Land Rover seat-cum-couch and caught my dress on a lethal elephant-tusk-turned-coatrack. I was limping toward a cheetah-print bar stool as my phone barked again.

"Hi there. Did the dog tag get to its destination?" I asked as I reached the far end of the bar.

"Yes. It's at Harrods," said our old family vet.

"That's fantastic news. Thanks so much. Talk to you soon," I said, grinning into the vine-shrouded mirror behind the bar.

I was here.

Kurt was there.

It was all going to plan.

But then I frowned at my reflection. The bodice of my little black dress was beyond dangerously low. In such a hurry when I bought it earlier, I must have put the darn thing on backward. Although, the pith-helmeted bartender didn't seem to mind. He smiled broadly and handed me a flute of *Demolition Queen* bubbly.

I almost had the sweet nectar to my lips when something knocked into my chair. As half of my champagne dripped down my arm, I turned on my cheetah chair with an annoyed frown. I felt super rotten as I realized an elderly wheelchair-bound woman had backed into me.

"Terribly sorry, my dear. It's a bit tricky in here. Brakes keep sticking." The woman shook a full head of white curls and then waved one liver-spotted hand with bright red fingernails.

"Oh no, it was my fault. I'm blocking your way." I smiled. I scooted in and noticed the woman check her delicate gold watch. Then she looked around as if expecting someone.

I pictured Kurt doing the same thing at Harrods and grinned. As I toasted myself in the mirror, I spotted a man and woman who would unknowingly get me upstairs. Gulping what was left of my champagne, I slid off my stool and was about to follow.

"Yoo-hoo." The old woman waved her phone at me. "Terribly sorry to trouble you again. However, it appears that I've been stood up." Her proper British tone dripped with disappointment.

What sort of creep would stand up a lovely old woman like this?

I looked up and frowned as my couple disappeared behind the closing lift doors.

"Would you mind horribly pushing me to the lift?" she asked.

"I'd be happy to. I'd even get you to your flat," I said.

The woman's spotted hands clasped mine as if her prayers had been answered.

What sort of creep uses an old woman to sneak upstairs? That would be me.

That thought made me picture what would probably be Tambour's favorite headline ever:

Sam Albany Kidnaps Elderly Invalid to Break into King's Road Flat

Feeling way beyond guilty, I steered the wheelchair into the bamboo-lined lift. As penance, I ignored my barking phone in the lift and again as we reached her tenth-floor flat. I didn't even check it as it pinged with a text. I was too busy pushing open the heavy spring-loaded apartment door.

I looked into the cave-dark flat and hesitated. Something told me not to go inside. That was *until* the old woman said, "Heavens, you couldn't even see an old black Lab in there."

Picturing a cute little Lab, I pushed her on in, asking, "Where's the light switch?"

When the lights popped on without my help, I looked around and found that my helpless liver-spotted woman wasn't sitting in her wheelchair anymore. She was glaring *down* at me like an angry linebacker *or* nonagenarian croquet player. *Geez.*

At first, her lips moved as if she wanted to say something but she looked too worked up to spit it out. She finally shouted, "What the hell are you doing here?"

The very familiar deep male voice vibrated in my chest. "Kurt?" I eyed his cracking foundation and old lady dress, and still my crotch went warm and moist.

"What the hell are *you* doing here?" I shouted to counteract my physical reaction. "You're supposed to be at the Harrods Champagne Bar."

"You have James to thank," said Kurt.

"I'll do that next time I see the rat," I said.

"He said your phone was in the barn. You never go anywhere without a phone. So I figured you left it at home, because you didn't want it to be traced. Which meant you weren't really going to meet me at Harrods. You were going to be somewhere you didn't want me to be." Kurt snatched my bag and pulled out tonight's temp phone.

"So James came back to Cranmont just to keep tabs on me?" I snarled.

Kurt didn't answer. Instead, he read the text I'd ignored at the apartment's door. "The dog tag has reached the King's Road flat." Kurt's drop earrings rattled as he shook the phone in my face. He looked angrier than I'd ever seen him. "You're frigging kidding me. You tailed me with a damned dog GPS tracker?" He pulled out his own phone.

I stomped the floor. Now I'd have to find another way to track him.

"You did this in France, didn't you?" he asked. Then he half-laughed and ran fingers through his hair. "I swear I'm losing it."

"You so deserved that," I said as he extracted the tiny tracker from his phone. "You took *my* Mom's memory card."

"So Harrods was just a wild goose chase, and you don't have a code for me," Kurt said, dropping the tag on the floor and crushing it under his heel.

"Exactly," I said. I didn't want him asking how I knew about the code, so I looked around saying, "By the way, this is not a very safe 'safe' house."

"It *was* until you got here." Kurt kicked off his black high-heeled shoes, unzipped his dress, and dropped it to the floor. "Sam, if you are going to play at this spy stuff, at least follow some basic rules."

My eyes couldn't help lingering on his tan, muscular calves before he rolled down the legs of his jeans.

"For starters, know your surroundings. Before entering a building, check exits and know where all doors lead." He paused. "Watch your back. Have an alternate plan. And wear something inconspicuous." He smirked at my dress.

I blinked and looked down at my dress. "Black is inconspicuous."

"Black cargo trousers. Black T-shirts. Those are inconspicuous. Not that dress, for Pete's sake." Kurt's eyes lingered on my cleavage.

"OK. OK. Anything else?" I asked, smiling to myself.

He tilted his head, took a deep breath, and ran his hand through his hair again, saying, "Honestly, doesn't anything scare you?"

"Yes." I paused. "You in those dentures."

Kurt spat out his fake teeth. They bounced along the glass table as my phone pinged again, and I snatched it back from Kurt.

"Let me guess. Felicity's in the hallway about to break down my door with her tripod."

"Nope. The vet was worried about the dog GPS tracker's signal dying," I turned my grinning face away as I texted her back and then said, "If you'd just clued me in on everything that night in my barn…"

"You mean as the blood was rushing to my semi-crushed balls? Not bloody likely," he said.

He grabbed my upper arm. He pulled me into the bedroom. His expression looked detached, but his thumb drew small searing circles that felt like a blowtorch on my arm. His warm breath hit my bare shoulder and those darned flipping 3-D images were back in my head.

Jake-Kurt.

Kurt-Jake.

Him touching me felt so good. I was craving more but all too quickly, he let go and stomped toward the bathroom, pulling off fake red fingernails as he went.

"I'm warning you. Don't touch a thing," he said over his shoulder.

His taut bare bum disappeared into the shower, and for a split second, I considered following, but this would probably be my only chance to search his sparse bedroom.

Regrettably, I spotted the touristy Maldives wallet on his nightstand and lost the plot.

***

I pictured that four-poster bamboo bed in my Maldives hut. Jake's firm, wet hand grabbing my naked body and then pulling me back into bed. Struggling against his arms until the cool drops of water on his chest warmed against mine. Jake tying me up with mosquito netting and staying in bed until the sunset lit the bed. Jake's stubbly face and ruffled hair above mc as hc said, "I love you."

Mm, mm, mm.

***

"I told you not to touch anything," Kurt said, pulling the wallet from my hands. He then dropped it back onto the nightstand and headed into his walk-in closet.

Making up for lost time, I opened his nightstand drawer and grabbed every piece of paper that I saw. I quickly stuffed them into my pockets and then strolled into the closet as spoilsport Kurt was putting on his underwear *under* a towel.

"I'm not leaving until I know what you know," I said, grabbing a top hat from a shelf.

"You mean until you get yourself killed?" Kurt said and then pulled on black jeans before taking the hat from me and putting it back.

"If that's what it takes," I said as I began flipping through his coats and jackets. Finally, at the end of the rack, I felt an envelope in the pocket of a tuxedo jacket. Kurt was pulling on a black cashmere sweater so I slipped the envelope into the front of my trousers.

"You mean that, don't you?" he asked, looking at me through the sweater's V-neck.

I nodded. I also stared so long and so hard, Kurt looked away first.

Ha.

"OK, here's a little something to think about. Why was your Matisse stolen but not Conrad's prized art collection?" he asked.

So my Matisse *was* gone.

"Art? What a pathetic attempt to change the subject," I said.

"*Because*, every piece of Conrad's art was fake. He arranged to have those screens cover them at the fundraiser so no one would notice. He'd already sold them all."

"You're making that up. Conrad wouldn't part with his collection," I said.

Kurt nodded. "Uh huh. Someone I do odd jobs for put pressure on him." Kurt pursed his lips like he regretted telling me. "The boss needed cash so searched out people like Conrad with something to lose. One of my odd jobs was keeping tabs on Conrad *and* you. Once, you came home early and I hid under your workbench for an hour." He paused. "At least I had snacks."

"That's where all my Buckeye Balls went?" I frowned.

He gave me a disbelieving look. "You find that more upsetting than your 'dead' boyfriend extorting money from your new husband? Not to mention that your life *was* and *is* in danger."

"OK, I'll bite. Why was, or rather, *is* my life in danger?" I asked.

"If Conrad refused to fund my boss's project, the man was going to kill you. So Conrad sold his art, cancelled your show, and beefed up surveillance all to protect you." Kurt pointed at me. "When Conrad ran out of funds, the boss told me to get rid of him."

That made me wonder if John Doe and Colonel Benjamin had been coerced into investing, run out of funds, and got killed off just like Conrad?

More importantly, was Schott next?

"Lucky for you, Conrad worried more about your safety than what you thought of him," said Kurt.

"You're not going to scare me off," I said, getting right up in his face.

With that, Kurt grabbed my shoulders and shoved me hard. I was deep into scratchy wool suits and dress slacks when he yanked me out so fast my head snapped back as if punched. Kurt's black holes for eyes were so close they blurred into one. His fingers felt like vise grips on my arms.

"I killed Conrad," he shouted.

I blinked.

"Did you hear me?" he shook me again. "I killed Conrad."

Breathing heavily, he released me and stepped back. I tried to regain balance by grabbing at capes and coats, but they came off in my hands. Hangers clanged loudly around my skull, so I wasn't completely sure what he said, but I thought it was, "Rock and Schott are definitely next."

CHAPTER FIFTY-ONE

Kurt had come back to his closet a couple minutes later and manhandled me out of his apartment. That was fine by me. In that short time I'd found a floor plan with rooms circled in red so I wanted to get back home ASAP. I needed to re-group again and study my new clues.

I hightailed it to Vauxhall Station and had just stepped onto the train headed for home when Rock's name flashed onto my ringing phone.

"Thank goodness, you're alive," I said as I answered it. After what Kurt had said at his flat, I thought for sure Rock was already history.

"Yep. I'm fine and I'm back," he said.

"Back where, in London?"

"Yes," he said, sounding bouncy, happy. "I'm working on a top-secret project with Dr. Witch. She's actually a good guy. I've been sequestered for the project. Don't have a clue where."

"Wish I could see you," I said.

"Me too. I'd also love to go home. But a few more weeks of dirty underwear is a small price to pay for international security."

"Ah yes, well, they'll inscribe that on your key to the city," I joked.

"Duncan Rockney, Terrorist Annihilator and Savior to the People."

"OK, let's not get carried away." I laughed.

"The lab I'm in is the pits. Can't be good for all this expensive equipment. A far cry from MedMaker labs." Rock paused, and I heard a clanging sound. "Looks like I have another assignment. They've been coming fast and furious." He paused a couple seconds and then said, "It's a golf club. I'll need to take samples from it. I'd love to see that terrorist scum's face when he searches for his favorite driver." Pause. "Sam, there's actually a label on here. Maybe I can tell you who he is…"

Rock's words tapered off as if reading the label. Then I heard another clanging sound, like the club hitting a hard worktop.

"Bloody hell. Oh shit…" Rock said.

"Rock?"

CHAPTER FIFTY-TWO

After Rock hung up so abruptly, and with all those expletives, I thought the absolute worst. If he hadn't texted me right away to say he'd just cut his finger and was OK, I'd have been useless tonight, and I needed my best clue-solving concentration.

I was getting closer. I could feel it.

Mom's clues and Kurt's activities were so intertwined it was scary. That I'd missed that fact earlier was hugely disturbing.

Better late than never.

Back in Cranmont barn, I decided to ramp up the clue-solving by sorting clues into two columns, *Clueless* and *What I Know*.

At least, that's what I was about to do when I heard the barn door open. I exited the workshop in time to see Felicity with arm extended out the door, shaking rain from a vibrant orange umbrella. Rain drumming on my Mustang's soft-top was almost deafening until she closed the door.

"That was fast," I said, hugging Felicity.

"One state-of-the-art micro-cam," Felicity said. She bowed and presented the grape-sized camera in the palm of one hand.

"Thank you so much." I hugged her again and tried to lead her back to the door, but she was having none of it.

"So why do you need my camera?" She crossed her arms and eyed me suspiciously.

"Don't worry, I'm not trying to take your job," I joked as I clipped the camera to the bill of a black baseball cap. I wanted to check its weight.

"I'm not worried about that," she said and squinted at me as if she was considering telling me what she *was* worried about. "Are you up for some relaunch party scene selection?" Felicity asked, waving the disc under my nose.

I pointed over my shoulder at the workshop and said, "I'm doing…"

"Yes. What have you been doing?" Felicity asked, edging her orange suede stilettos toward "clue central."

"Actually, maybe I could manage a few minutes on scene selection," I said, guiding her to my desk. *I wouldn't mind seeing Kurt's hand getting screwed again.* I started the footage at quadruple speed. The yellow hardhats worn by waiters bounced through the crowd like popcorn kernels in a hot pan. We'd just reached the part with Kurt dragging me up the rickety loft stairs when Felicity hit the pause button.

"See this waiter with the hazel eyes, the angle of his shoulders and curve of his thighs. Doesn't he remind you of our one-man cleanup crew?" Felicity's bright eyes were on me. "You remember that waiter, right? He stole your knife. Waitered at the breast cancer fundraiser. He had gold eyes that night. He worked Conrad's wake too. I even thought his thighs were not unlike Jake's," she added quietly to herself.

I couldn't believe it. Felicity recognized Jake/Kurt when I hadn't?

It certainly explained my sudden hankering for multiple waiters. I wasn't a letch after all.

I knew Felicity was looking at me, but I couldn't help the gamut of emotions that ran across my face. Feigned disinterest, surprise, and annoyance. Of course, it didn't help that the sight of Kurt's taut thighs, even his recorded thighs, sent my fingers to my lips as if I was bloody Pavlov's dog.

"Is this guy what you've been 'doing' in your spare time?" Felicity asked with a playful tone.

It was awful; my face turned red.

Felicity pointed at me. "You're in love."

"Was. Was in love," I snapped, immediately regretting it.

"That was quick."

It had been torture not telling anyone. I immediately twisted my right side toward Felicity and lifted my shirt.

Felicity's eyes widened. She touched the purple and orange bruise blooming beside the swirling tentacles of my tattoo.

"He gave you a bruise?"

"No." I shook my head. "I found the person who gave me my tattoo." I pulled my shirt back down, thoroughly annoyed about my hasty decision to share.

"You are in love with a woman?" Felicity asked.

I rolled my eyes.

"I distinctly remembered you saying that a woman gave you that tattoo because she bragged about a piercing through her…" Felicity's grossed-out expression went blank, and then her eyes lit up and bugged out. "No."

I grimaced and nodded.

"Jake? Jake's alive? That *was* Jake?" Felicity lurched at the screen and pressed her finger against his thigh.

"He didn't die in that hang gliding accident. He needed a new face after that." *More or less the truth.* "He had amnesia," I added, worried I'd gone too far. Felicity knew I went to a funeral. I needn't have worried because she zeroed in on my wrists next.

"Did he do that to you too?" Felicity asked, outraged.

I looked at my wrists with a blank stare. I wasn't faking it. So much had happened it took me a second to remember how I got those injuries.

Oh yes, shackles.

"More my fault than his," I said, putting my injured wrists behind my back. "Can I ask you a question? Do you think I'm my own worst enemy?" I interrupted myself. "Actually, don't answer that."

"You're defending him?" Felicity stumbled to her feet and stared down at me with her mother-bear fierceness. "The first time around almost killed you, and now he's turned violent." She pointed at my waist and wrists. "Please tell me you're not getting back together."

"No need to worry about that. He's not interested in me."

He's just interested in codes that I may or may not have.

I pictured that kiss he used to distract me and steal my memory card. And then last night he couldn't care less about me being there. The old Jake would have carried me into the shower and stripped me naked. Oh yes, and he confessed to killing my husband.

"Felicity, the man faked his own death to get away from me the first time."

"If you're saying Jake left you then that's a crock." Felicity shook her head and red tendrils fanned out.

I leaned back to put some distance between me and 'medusa' and was pinned against my cement desk.

"You would have dumped him in your own little way." Felicity and her tendrils stared at me.

I felt outnumbered, so I nodded.

"Sam, do not go back to him," said Felicity.

"Don't worry, I'm waiting—"

"Oh yes, because you're so good at waiting," Felicity said, shaking angry tendrils at me again.

"It's none of your business," I snapped.

Felicity looked near tears.

I pulled my hair back, let it drop, and said, "I'm sorry. Don't worry." I hugged her and this time she let me walk her to the door.

"What are you going to do about Jake?" Felicity quietly asked.

"Nothing," I said.

Nothing in the next ten minutes, that is.

I closed the door behind her, and not a second later, I heard that yelp I'd been waiting for. I ran back to my computer in time to see a furious and in pain Kurt on screen. Watching it wasn't as fun as I'd expected.

When party footage ran out, Conrad's wake footage began. Max was coming down Cranmont's sweeping stairs, swaggering as if he owned the place. What was he up to? Probably spying on people from behind Old Mr. Albany's study wall.

Could it be true what Kurt said?

Could Kurt have killed Conrad?

And were others next?

I focused on the video one last time as 'Kurt the waiter' skirted past me with his tray of prawn packets. I gritted my teeth, thinking about the good laugh he'd probably had fooling me.

"Well it's my turn now," I said, adding my newest discoveries from Kurt's to the top of my *Clueless* and *What I Know* lists. To help empty my brain, I also added my stream-of-consciousness notes.

Clueless

"Sam" envelope = Sam was written on the envelope I found in Kurt's tuxedo jacket. Inside was a photo of Mom and me at Yankee Stadium. Why did he have it? Where did he get it?

MedMaker Corp floor plan = Mom's office, Max's office, and various labs were circled in red. On the back was the Annex floor plan with 'To be demolished' written across it. Very odd.

Mom's inlaid gift box = Inlaid picture of a princess holding a chisel and map. No secret compartments. No clue.

An eye for an eye = Still no clue.

Dansnurmur = Red herring? A made-up word? It ticks me off every time I look at it. Broken into smaller parts, it's sort of French, but not. "Dans" could mean "in." "Mur" could mean "wall," but that's as far as I get.

Xenan = No clue.

Cats are an Puzzle = I still think Mom's "an" was intentional, so it stays that way.

Mom's MedMaker chip = Can't get any of Mom's numbers off it.

Metal disc from Mom's safe = No clue.

Polyporphyrin balls = Could mean polyporphyrin ring, or could mean "balls," as in buckyballs or Buckeye Balls.

Plastic kid's puzzle = Can't form its cat picture. Maybe it's not a cat.

What I Know

"I killed Conrad" = Kurt sounded so serious, but I didn't believe him. Another attempt to scare me off? Probably.

Sealed With A Kiss = Swiss Army Knife

Tickled Pink = 'Pink' color of Swiss Army Knife

Chinese Dragon = Hiding place for kids' plastic puzzle.

Buckeye Balls = Really buckyballs. "The buckyball's carbon 60 molecular nearly spherical configuration was a truncated icosahedron like soccer balls." Mom's, John Doe's, and Colonel Benjamin's chips and patches were made from it. Were there more? How about Conrad? Silverblade said he almost missed the patch on Colonel Benjamin. Did that other coroner miss it on Conrad before cremation?

Call June Thorpe = 97 64 19 - 19 64 97 fax number was combination to Mom's safe and secret compartment.

lMd = Upside down PWT. Programmed Without Target. PWT was combined with MedMaker technology for Gabby's murder.

Max = Max snooped and spied with Cranmont screens. I'm pretty sure that he converted Mom's MedMaker to biotech weapons, demonstrated it in Bolivia, and sold it to the highest bidder.

While my *What I Know* list looked marginally better than before, *Clueless* was really getting me down. I was especially frustrated with the *Mom's MedMaker* clue. I needed to know exactly why she died. Her MedMaker numbers could tell me. Once again, I put Mom's MedMaker chip next to the blue palm-sized #01 controller and placed it beside Mom's laptop. But no numbers appeared. No iron, potassium, or white blood cell counts filled her computer screen as they had that night she showed off her "*Suzy Q*" trial.

Think, Sam.

What exactly did Mom do that night to make it work? I did remember her pretending to use magic. She waved her hand over the right hand side of her computer and said "abracadabra" then the numbers appeared.

"Mom, I need more help here." I slumped over the controller with head in hands. The overhead light was shining between my wrists. It lit the blue controller's side and the word engraved there, *June*.

I blinked. *June*? Why just June? Why not the entire date? *Or* did this *June* stand for Mom's *Call June Thorpe* clue? The clue that got me into Mom's safe and the clue that got me the small metal disc.

My stomach rumbled with excitement as I fished out the disc and blew off pocket lint. Leaving off the "Abracadabra," I waved it over the computer, and just like that, numbers filled the screen, and so did the name *Suzy Q*.

Even though I already knew Mom was *Suzy Q*, reading "*Suzy Q*", gave me a jolt.

I looked back at the numbers, wishing I'd paid more attention when Mom explained them that night. I did remember that when a patient's numbers went outside optimal ranges, the MedMaker should automatically alert their doctor. These instances should also be noted under *Adjustments and Overrides*.

I studied Mom's numbers and compared them to the ideal ranges. Hers were crazy, all over the place, especially her white blood count.

I checked *Adjustments and Overrides*. No alerts had been sent.

Reading further, I saw why.

Mom had programmed an override with controller #01 so it would block alerts to her regular doctor. Instead, they went to her oncologist. That made sense.

What didn't make sense was at the time of her impending heart attack at the fundraiser when Mom's controller #01 ordered appropriate corrections, no alerts were sent to *any* doctor.

Then I saw that a *different* controller, controller #01A, overrode the override. It blocked all alerts.

So why was there a second controller, #01A?

Where was it?

I thought about where I hadn't looked yet but that I should. An obvious choice came to mind. With all the PowerPoint stuff and evidence stacking up against him, he was now a prime suspect.

I was headed to Max' place.

CHAPTER FIFTY-THREE

I checked my watch. *8:30 p.m.* I'd been in place across the road from Max's building for thirty minutes already. Through the building's plate glass window, I'd been watching several officious-looking men and women file into a ground-floor lounge.

I knew they were there for the building's annual association meeting because Max's secretary told all earlier. "He's attending his first meeting at his new digs. Agenda items include: decorating the foyer with three-hundred-pound-per-roll wallpaper and increasing annual dues by ten thousand pounds," she whispered in awe.

At first I was impressed that Max had found time to search for a new place, but that changed when I learned the address. Evidently, last week, Max bought and moved into a flat in the same building where Conrad had bought my "anniversary" flat.

Finally, Max joined the others and shook hands all around so I darted across the street. I also kept an eye out for Kurt. I definitely didn't need him following me inside.

Five minutes later, I dropped my new high-tech lock-pickers into my black cargo pants and entered Max's new flat. I didn't need my flashlight. Every single light was already on.

"Nice energy conservation, bud," I said aloud as I turned off three of five living room lights. The fourth I extinguished by tapping a foot pedal, and I noticed the round multi-ringed bull's-eye rug under my boot. My eyes swiftly traveled up the legs of the chunky wood entryway table, took in the colossal flower arrangements, and then I stomped my boot. I didn't need my fancy new lock-pickers after all. I already had the keys. Not only was it Conrad's building, it was Conrad's flat. How could I not have recognized it?

At least I knew my way around.

First stop? The guest room. I'd noticed right away that Max had made it into his home office. He'd marked his territory too. The scent of cologne was overpowering.

I sat at his blue writing desk before a tall Venetian vase. The reddish liquid inside detracted a bit from the clear handblown glass, but it was a beauty.

Propped against it was Max's pirate party invite, personally signed by Schott. I flicked it aside, and instantaneously the vase's liquid went clear, except for one quivering mass of red on the opposite side. I tapped the glass again and jumped back as the mass charged my face with such ferocity that the vase rocked.

My heart was beating like mad but I tentatively ran a hand up and down the glass. The red mass inside hungrily followed like those ghost cells that swirled up Nunchuck's arm.

I pulled my hand away, glad to see that this vase had a secure top. Although it wasn't completely comforting. Like in the lab, this blood had moved and reacted to my presence *without* a controller.

Anxious to see what other sinister things Max kept here, I opened his side drawer. I found the longest paperclip chain ever and tidy folders labeled: *Bills, Receipts*, and *Homeowners*.

About to close the drawer, a familiar scent wafted up. I sniffed, leaned forward, and spied a honking big box of Conrad's Cherokee cigars. *A self-awarded party favor from Conrad's wake?* Or from a more recent visit behind the wall in Old Mr. Albany's study?

I had one hand on the box ready to confiscate it when I heard a click, like a cocking gun. It came from the foyer. I tiptoed to the door, peeked around its expensive molding, and almost screamed as the Perspex cuckoo clock *cuckooed* right in my ear. I had to laugh. Other than a slight bend in the minute hand, which had caused the click, no one would ever know Conrad had smashed it to smithereens.

Back at the desk, my diligence paid off in a folder marked *Confidential MedMaker Corporation*. Inside was an exact copy of the file Max had begged me to retrieve for him from WhistleBlown. That made Max a disturbingly good liar.

I found the same PowerPoint document from Conrad's files too, but with an attached memory card marked *Sales Meeting*. I pushed it into my bag to watch later and opened the shallow middle desk drawer. Like Conrad's desk, mechanical pencils, fountain pens, and a knobby handled letter opener were slotted into a black leather Smythson drawer divider.

Everything was in its proper place *except* a bit of green and yellowy-orange cardboard that peeked from beside the divider. I tugged at it. Up popped a box of crayons like Mom and I gave each other for good luck. However, this set wasn't brand new. Rolled wax clung to one crayon's worn tip. I knew the name without reading it. Wild Watermelon. The color my stalker used to write his note on my contents page from *It's Not About the Wall*. It was also used to circle the word *Dead* on Mom's Knock 'em Dead hammer in the peony flower arrangement.

Max using crayons was far-fetched enough, but Max being my stalker was really out there.

Still, he did write the letter proposing the conversion of Mom's life-saving MedMaker to bioweapons. And his purple fingerprints were all over Mom's office *and* Conrad's study. The evidence *seemed* convincing.

And there was more. I clicked the mouse pad on Max's laptop to start a video.

***

The camera that filmed this was inside a lab I didn't recognize. A lab tech walked into view wearing a full-body biohazard suit. He filled a shiny bright vial with clear liquid and capped it. I noticed that someone was standing outside the lab window beside the controls for the lab's robotic arms. I spotted the Naugahyde coat before the man inside it.

Nunchuck.

The lab tech was about to place the vial into a tray when Nunchuck swung the robotic fingers around and tapped the lab tech's shoulder. The poor man jumped a mile. So did the vial, right out of his gloved hands. He frantically stretched, clawed, and finally caught it, shouting, "What the hell were you thinking? If I die, you're out of luck."

Nunchuck just chuckled and then pointed the robotic fingers at the tray of vials. "Have you finished all two hundred PWT vials as ordered?"

PWT?

The PWT that Rock talked about? The PWT in Mom's clues? The same one mentioned in Nunchuck's swirling blood video?

Two hundred vials of programmed without target?

This was so not good.

The tech pulled off his helmet, nodded and said, "Time to talk compensation."

"The boss wants me to inspect the merchandise first," said Nunchuck.

"Like you'd know the difference," the tech smirked. He reached for a vial but the robot fingers beat him to it and he frowned.

"So this is what made the blood crawl up my arm?" asked Nunchuck.

"No. This is a hundred times worse," the tech said.

Nunchuck raised the vial over the tech's head.

"Don't do that," the tech said, as sweat popped out on his forehead.

I was clenching my seat just watching.

"So this will program itself on contact with any DNA?" Nunchuck asked in a sinister tone.

"I demand that you put it down," the tech said. He frantically tried to grab the vial and his suit gaped open at the neck.

My stomach felt queasy. My mind galloped ahead to where this was going. I pushed away from the screen but couldn't stay away. I looked back as the robot fingers squeezed so hard that the glass vial shattered.

Shards of glass flew.

PWT glistened on the lab tech's neck.

His eyes widened, but he didn't struggle or scream. He reached for a stool, missed, and crashed to the floor.

As the tech's biohazard suit deflated and conformed to his skinny, twitching body, Nunchuck sneered, "You said put it down."

***

I pushed the laptop away and stayed away.

Did Max sit here and watch this for fun?

I didn't need more proof of Max's guilt.

But *if* I *did,* I got it as I spotted a blue controller nestled beside the laptop.

Controller #01A. The one that had ordered lethal overrides on Mom's MedMaker.

I grabbed it up. I also flinched as I heard keys hit the chunky mahogany foyer table.

Shoot.

Shoot.

Double shoot.

I dropped the controller into my plumber's bag and peeked around the door again. All lights were back on, and the kitchen door was swishing in and out.

I had what I'd come for.

Time to get out.

I was two feet from the wide front door when the kitchen one swung open. If Max hadn't been backing out, I'd have been done for.

With no time to spare, I flew under the foyer table. I scooted as close to the bull's-eye as possible as Max's perfectly buffed wingtips dashed past. I had a clear view as he entered the guest suite, propped the invite against the vase again, and grabbed a file.

Worried that he'd see me when he exited, I scooted another four inches around the table's center support and hit something soft, yielding, and warm. I looked over my shoulder, hoping it was a cat, but human eyes glared back at me.

"Like a moth to a flame. You can't stay away from me, can you?" Kurt whispered.

We both watched Max's shoes approach, stop, change direction, and enter the master bedroom.

"Like a moth to a flame? Nah. More like not being able stop picking a scab," I hissed back. "And for the record, I didn't follow you."

"I'm actually glad you're here," Kurt said.

"This should be rare." I rolled my eyes.

"No bullshit now," he urgently whispered. "When you accessed Conrad's laptop in France, what files did you remove?"

"I didn't even try to get into his computer," I said, looking Kurt straight in the eye and *not* pulling back my hair or anything.

Of course I tried. Conrad's Snood icon popped up and kept asking me for an encrypted code, which didn't seem very *game*-like. That was as far as I got.

Kurt tilted his head back and silently snapped his fingers.

I wasn't sure what that look meant, but I didn't like it. "What?" I asked.

"I just remembered my dry cleaning." He grinned.

His grin made my blood boil.

"OK, another question. Did your mom give you an alphanumeric?" he asked.

This time I didn't have to pretend or avoid touching my hair. I didn't have a clue what he was talking about.

"Work with me here," he urged. "A series of letters and numbers, possibly ten to sixteen in all."

"And if she did, I would give it to you because…?"

Max cleared his throat and we both looked toward the bedroom. But as Max headed into his closet, *I* leaped from under the table. I felt Kurt's fingers clutch at my shirt but I was already in motion and slipped from his grip. I pulled open the heavy front door, backed out into the hall, and silently closed it.

Then I faced the door, smiled, and waited so that seconds later when Max exited, clutching two bottles of champagne and his thick *Homeowner's* folder, he ran right into me.

"Samantha, whatever are you doing at my abode?" Max asked suspiciously.

I peeked around his shoulder expecting to see Kurt's dark mass still lurking beneath the foyer table, but he was gone.

Shoot. Where did he go?

"I thought these would cheer you up." I waved the confidential reports from Conrad's office under his nose. I'd copied everything, except for the confidential report on Max's bioweapon plans. *That,* I kept.

"How wonderful you are." His arms were full, so he kicked the door open for me. "Would you mind putting them on the table?"

As I did I saw Kurt's head dart back behind the couch.

"Thank you very much," Max said.

I pulled his door shut and he became incredibly friendly. He leaned over to peck my cheek at the very instant I realized my plumber's bag was wide open. If I didn't do something, he'd see Mom's controller #01A and the Wild Watermelon crayon I'd snatched.

Believe me, I would have paid big bucks to avoid doing what I did next. *Especially* after watching that lab tech video. On top of that, JJ was probably spying through the hall's security cameras and Kurt through the peephole, but I had no other options.

I smiled directly at that peephole as I grabbed Max's lapels, pressed him against the door, and kissed him square on the mouth. Max's arms flailed at his sides like Roger Rabbit's when Jessica Rabbit kissed him. I would have laughed but I was too grossed out.

Instead, I closed my bag and stepped back so fast, Max was clutching at air. I started jogging down the hall. "Bye," I called out right before I turned the corner and saw Max leaning against the door. He was hugging his Moet Chandon magnums to his chest and had a dreamy look in his eyes.

The guy didn't know what hit him. I laughed to myself.

I imagined Kurt's reaction would go something like, "Welcome to the club."

Ha!

CHAPTER FIFTY-FOUR

By midnight I was back at Cranmont barn. Not caring if the pope saw me naked, I ran into the bathroom, stripped, and showered. From that one kiss of Max's slimy lips, his cologne had melded to my skin like duct tape to paper. My arms, face, and lips were on fire from scrubbing so hard.

Wrapping up tight in my robe, I paused to think about that little kiss. I'm a great kisser and all, but Max's reaction was way over-the-top. Would a stalking, murdering mastermind react like that to a little kiss? Or was kissing Conrad's wife the last jewel in his proverbial "Conrad crown"?

Having said that, the evidence I found was convincing. Too convincing. Too easy. Too obvious, like that Wild Watermelon crayon. It felt like another lame attempt of Kurt's to keep me off the case.

I sprinted barefoot across the rough barn floor and into my workshop. As overhead lights flashed on. I had an eerie feeling that someone had been in here. And I was right. A beautiful new Japanese rasp waited on my workbench. Felicity must have dropped it off. As I hung it on my pegboard I noticed its plum-shaped handle was sticky.

I was rubbing my hand on my robe as I thought about what I still didn't know as in, *Who was behind all of this?*

I faced Mom's fish-face photo and asked, "Mom, who's guilty?" I paused. "If I say the guilty party's name will you give me a sign?" I paused again. "OK. Is it Max? Conrad? Nunchuck? Kurt? JJ? All of them?"

My rumbling stomach was the only sign I got so I decided to try listening to Max's "Sales Meeting" for clues. The quality was rubbish as if the microphone had been hidden. I had to turn the volume way up. I didn't recognize the voices but there seemed to be a buyer and a seller.

***

"The product has had very little testing," the seller said. The buyer must have waved that concern aside because the seller then said, "Good. Now, you have two options. My lab tech produces a gene-coded patch or a chip. The chip must be implanted into the victim so while not impossible, it's a little trickier." He paused. "The advantage of the patch is that it can be placed on an inanimate object which becomes the 'carrier' and passes the killing sequence to your soon-to-be victim. Alternately, use a live carrier who unknowingly will deliver the killing sequence to the victim. It's like a wasp carrying poison into its own nest." Pause. "Having said that, we're not certain whether carriers survive—"

"Why on earth would that bother me?" the buyer interrupted.

"Ah. Well at least this killing method is untraceable," the buyer laughed.

"I already have my hit list," the seller said.

I heard paper crinkle and assumed he was presenting his list.

"My goodness that's a lot. Excellent choices though," said the seller as if the buyer had chosen an unmatched vintage of wine. "Now, to make your deadline we must move quickly and collect DNA samples from each victim."

***

With that, the tape ended and I thought for a minute.

Who was selling to whom?

Max to Nunchuck's boss?

Or was Conrad the seller?

Conrad had always railed on about the "evil doings" of others. Was this a case of "He doth protest too much"?

When I spoke to Max, he said that Conrad had instigated the very corporate problems that his company WhistleBlown, supposedly "found" and "fixed." But, those offenses were corporate theft and espionage *not* murder.

What Kurt had said about Conrad selling his beloved paintings to protect me didn't quite fit either. *Unless* Conrad had committed the crimes Max said he did. And then realized too late that it put me in danger.

My head was spinning.

Think, Sam. Think.

During my break-in at Max's, Kurt was anxious to find an alphanumeric. He'd said *Ten to sixteen letters and numbers.*

What was that about?

The "code" Kurt and Nunchuck discussed on the train?

Would it activate the murders?

Mom had entrusted me with the alphanumeric. That meant it had to be for *stopping* the murders.

Could it do both?

Boy, would I be ticked off if that alphanumeric had been staring at me all along.

I trotted out my *Clueless* and *What I Know* lists once again. This time, to see which had letters and numbers.

June Thorpe's fax number had *only* numbers, no letters.

Carbon 60 (C60) was too short.

How about the stupid plastic kid's puzzle? I shook it and its fifteen tiles went clickety-clack. I reread Mom's Post-it note, "*You have three minutes to solve this puzzle.*" For some reason, I decided to take her challenge again. Like last time, my thumbs furiously pushed squares around the three-by-three-inch frame. *Also* like last time, the cat's nose ended up in its butt.

My eyes darted to my clue board.

*Cats are **an** Puzzle.*

Could that "*an*" stand for *a*lpha*n*umeric? Would the completed puzzle reveal the code?

Only one way to find out.

"Don't look, Mom," I said. I unfolded my pink pocketknife's screwdriver and dug its tip under the tiles until they bulged and went *pop*. All fifteen tiles flew into the air and then landed on my worktop. I flipped, aligned, and scooted them until I had a completed cat. *A plain old tabby cat.* I frowned.

Lives may have been depending on me and I had nothing.

I was the biggest failure ever.

Why, Mom? Why did you entrust me with your secrets?

I'm no master puzzler like you.

I'm no puzzler, full stop.

My insides hurt.

My eyes stung.

My nose got all stuffy.

I stepped back and threw in the towel, or rather my knife. It bounced on the worktop. It smacked the tiles. Several flipped like tiddlywinks and I spotted a very faint "BB" on one's back.

I looked closer and another said "49."

After that, I couldn't flip those other tiles over fast enough. Every one of them had letters, numbers, and/or symbols. I never would have seen them if I *hadn't* popped out the tiles.

"Mom, you knew all along that I used a screwdriver to solve your puzzles?" I laughed at Mom's fish-face photo. It felt great to laugh at a *Mom* joke.

I flipped all fifteen tiles right side up next and then pieced the smiling cat back together. I covered its cute face with a wide strip of purple duct tape and flipped it once more. Starting from the top row, reading left to right, I copied the letters, numbers, and symbols onto a three-by-five card:

K2W49MUEP>>>XXQ8U01BB57LF88

Feeling particularly paranoid, I also wrote it upside-down in permanent marker on my side just above my hip. I was finishing the 88 when I heard my mini-fridge door open, champagne bottles rattle, and the door slam shut.

"Yoo-hoo. You decent?" a nonchalant voice called from the main room.

I rolled my eyes. I also pulled down my shirt and hid the puzzle along with its three-by-five card behind Mom's fish-face photo. Finally, I rearranged my expression into what I hoped was a bland but ticked off one.

Kurt leaned against the doorframe with rolled-up cuffs, crisp white shirt, and a relaxed expression. A passerby might think this was a social call.

He was holding my Buckeye Ball tin, the one I'd retrieved from Denmark.

"Glad you re-filled this," he said. I barely controlled myself as he popped the largest Buckeye Ball into his mouth.

"Cook did it and not for you," I said, grabbing my tin back as he moved to the workbench. "To what do I owe this honor?" I asked as I noticed his boots had left a trail of dark, clumped dirt like from the tunnel's turning circle.

"James worried that you were a little too quiet over here. Thought I'd better take a look," he said, swinging my board open with one chocolaty finger. "An eye for an eye? Tickled pink? Riveting stuff. Is this the secret clue stash you use to wreak havoc on my life?" he asked, gently tugging the fan belt that held back my damp hair.

"Yes, that's me, always thinking of ways to ruin your life." I smacked his hand away.

"Listen, I need your help," he said, smiling a smile that under different circumstances would have gotten him anything he wanted.

"You're asking for my help? After you killed my husband?"

"OK, I made that up," Kurt said, shaking his head.

"Yes, I actually knew that. You're not that good a liar," I said.

"Not that good a liar? Except for the extreme sports stuff and faking my death?" Kurt asked.

I shrugged. He tried for my BB tin, but I slid it further down my workbench.

"Are you here about that alphanumeric?" I asked.

His eager expression reminded me of Max's when I'd almost produced Mom's MedMaker chip.

"Well, I don't have it," I said, facing my pegboard. I pushed loose hands into my pockets to prevent them twisting my hair.

"You sure?" He bent down past my shoulder to study my face.

I held the relaxed and "truthful" expression I'd practiced in the mirror for twenty minutes last night.

"Right. Glad to see you're up to nothing." Kurt smirked and headed for the door. He again tried swiping my BB tin, but I body-blocked him.

He shrugged and left.

"Good riddance," I shouted.

An uncomfortable feeling made me look around. He'd left a little too eagerly.

It wasn't until a half hour later that I realized my three-by-five alphanumeric card, which I'd hidden behind Mom's photo, had been visible from where he'd been standing.

Oh shoot.

CHAPTER FIFTY-FIVE

Outside and after six o'clock, MedMaker Corp's London forecourt was pretty much what I'd expected—dead quiet. *Inside* was an entirely different story. Where last week's rent-a-cop read outdated issues of *Auto Week*, tonight four muscle-bound goons paced the black granite floor.

Max didn't mess around.

The goon squad was only one reason I planned to enter through the empty annex.

After Kurt left the barn, I'd attacked Mom's clues like a woman possessed. "Xenan" was first because it had bothered the heck out of me from the start.

Xenin was a peptide hormone. Xenon an odorless noble gas. But there was no such thing as Xenan.

However, when I rearranged its letters Xenan bother me no more.

It spelled…

Wait for it…

Ta-da.

Annex.

Talk about your entry-level puzzle. Good thing Mom couldn't see how long that one took me. Time aside, I was over the moon.

After that, I was on a roll.

Inside Mom's June Thorpe listing, I found a file identifying all MedMaker Corp and Cranmont surveillance cameras *plus* their override codes. My brilliant Mom knew someone was watching so probably manipulated video feeds everywhere she went.

That had to be why the video cameras went from green to red during my break-in at MedMaker labs. Mom must have programmed my knife with those override codes to make the cameras stop recording when I went near them.

It was almost time to go inside. Using one of my signature fan belts, I pulled my hair into a ponytail and threaded it through the back of my black baseball cap. Didn't want to leave my cap or anything with my DNA on it inside the annex.

Next, I took the costume I'd wear to Schott's pirate party right after this break-in and put it under a nearby shrub.

Sadly, my bulky plumber's bag hadn't made the cut tonight. I felt like I was missing an appendage but I had to travel light for the annex. In my shirt pocket was my pink knife that held "everything." In my back jean pocket, I had a screwdriver for making a very important hole. I also had a fiber optic scope for looking through that hole. Last but not least, Felicity's micro-cam. I'd be filming *Demolition Queen* footage against Max's orders. I loved that. *Ha.*

I pushed RECORD on the camera, held it at arm's length and scanned my all-black Kurt-inspired outfit. Next, I aimed it at the annex for a focus test and got more than just focused. I caught a man in black. He snuck through the shadows then dove into the annex airshaft.

This time I recognized the body.

Kurt.

Already excited about pissing-off Max, the possibility of pissing-off Kurt was a bonus. But I didn't dare go in the way he did. Kurt knew me too well. He might catch me in the act before I even saw anything.

Instead, I darted across the street and sidled up to the annex door. I clipped the micro-cam onto my cap's bill and tilted my chin down to film my fingers on the security keyboard. I entered Mom's alarm shutoff code. The screen blinked "00:30:00." *Thirty minutes until alarm-city.*

I was nervous about Mom's annex pass still working here but I hadn't even pulled it out when the door spontaneously buzzed and popped open. I hesitantly peeked inside. No one stood in the dim stairwell. Not even a stray goon.

My pink knife must have opened the door. *Thank you, Mom.*

But three measly steps inside, I had a problem. My boots on the painted gray floor produced the most horrendous squeak. The goons hadn't seen me coming, but they'd sure as heck hear me. I swiftly pulled off both boots, and with that, a flat quarter-inch disc popped out and spun silently on the shiny gray floor.

"You son of a bitch, you tagged me?" I angrily whispered, imagining what Kurt would say… "*Let me get this straight. You're angry because I did exactly what you already did to me?*"

I was picturing his cut-the-crap-stare as I threw the tracker down the hall in the opposite direction. It made me grin as I silently sank into the bowels of the annex.

But my next challenge, the retinal scanner, sobered me up quick.

"An eye for an eye," I whispered. I leaned toward its almond-shaped lenses and prayed that Mom had taken care of this obstacle too.

Please.

Please.

Please.

I held my breath so long the veins in my eyeballs pulsed *until* the door clicked and opened.

Yes!

"Well done, you," I whispered to Mom, knowing that somehow she'd switched my Gatwick Airport retinal eye scan with her MedMaker Corp one.

Having already lost five minutes, I made a beeline for a closet labeled "Storage," because it backed up to the one circled in red on Kurt's map. I pushed inside the stuffy nine-by-nine-foot room. My socks slipped on its smooth gray cement as I moved to the closet's back wall.

I tilted my hat-cam toward the base of two stacks of bulging mildewed boxes and then followed them to the ceiling. I wedged myself into the shoulder-width space between them and was thankful they were there. They kept my feet from slipping. They'd also steady my arms and hands, vital for my next task.

That task would be kind of like the game Operation where when its metal tweezers touch the game's sides, it buzzes. My version would be a bit different. If I touched my screwdriver too fast or at the wrong angle to these insides-for-mush bricks, the entire wall would crash down on me.

I checked my watch. *Eight minutes gone.*

I flexed my tight neck. I lifted and dropped tense shoulders several times and then exhaled. I picked up my screwdriver. I didn't want it slipping so I wiped sweaty hands on my jeans once, twice, and a third time.

I wiped sweat from the screwdriver too and then went for it.

Pushing the horizontal screwdriver into the brick's outer shell, I felt no resistance, no impact, as if it hadn't made contact at all. But my mark, three and one-half inches up the screwdriver's shaft, was already touching brick. Next, I pulled it back out in such achingly slow motion, my timer ran down to 00:15:00.

My sweaty upper lip tasted salty. My hands were like little palm-sized showers. Beads of perspiration covered the fiber optic scope that I pulled from my bra.

Hesitant *and* excited to see what I'd see, I inched the scope's ladybug-sized head through the new hole. And there it was *the* crude lab with dark, flaking water-stained walls and cracking linoleum. The one from the video where Nunchuck played with the blood-filled beakers.

Suddenly, a hairy limb filled my scope. It took everything I had not to jump. I zoomed out on hairy man legs. Zooming out further, I saw every inch of them, standing on a counter. A fluorescent light blocked the head and shoulders, but below the light, I saw the hem of a brick-red-tinged lab coat, khaki shorts, skinny freckled knees, disgusting striped socks, and brown sandals.

Definitely not Kurt.

The man crouched, hopped down, and I almost dropped my scope.

Rock.

Whoa.

Had he been in the MedMaker annex all along without knowing it?

Was this Max's secretly bioweapon lab?

Had Conrad found it the day I was down here planning my demolition? The same day the wall fell on me?

Come to think of it, that wall falling on me was probably no accident. *I'd bet I was about to discover Max's secret too.*

My first instinct was to knock down this wall, grab Rock, and get the heck out of there. And I would have too, except, he wasn't alone *or* safe. Nunchuck stood pressing his gold gun to Rock's freckled temple. He was also speaking to someone I couldn't see.

I carefully shifted my scope and saw one thin, shapely eyebrow. *Schott?*

They've got him too.

I zoomed out to see the rest of him. He was already dressed in his Captain Hook getup wearing a black hat that held enough plumes to hide a rhinoceros.

Schott was a pain, but I wouldn't wish this on him.

Bizarrely, I thought of poor Mrs. Party. Another of her events would be wrecked not by me but by the host not showing.

Although, that might be my fault too.

Maybe I could have done something to prevent this.

Maybe I still can.

I watched Schott for a minute. He didn't look stressed *or* kidnapped. On the contrary, he smiled and kind of bounced.

What was I missing?

It didn't take long to find out.

"It was so much trouble collecting these," Schott said, patting a box overflowing with the plastic gold RSVP doubloons. "And soon all my party guests will be headed away on holiday in France, Spain, and Italy. I've decided it would be so dreadfully anticlimactic not to see them die."

Die?

Everyone?

What is he talking about?

Here I thought he was being targeted but it looked like he was the target-er.

Is Schott the Boss?

"I want them all to die tonight from a deadly flu. All except one or two. They'll have fatal heart attacks," Schott said and dramatically bowed.

Is he talking about killing off London's entire sociopolitical power base?

"You can't do that," shouted Rock.

"I'm the customer and I hear we're always right," Schott said with a laugh. *Pure evil.*

"Rock finished your doubloons but they won't work without the codes," said Nunchuck.

"Then Rock's no good to us," Kurt said, walking into view.

I was horrified. With those few words Kurt might have sentenced Rock to death.

"Ah, you're just in time," Schott said, bobbing his plumes toward Kurt and then signaling Nunchuck to put his gold gun back to Rock's temple.

"W-w-wait…" Rock stuttered in a tight, squeaky voice. "I helped develop the MedMaker. I can recreate those missing codes."

What?

I wanted to jump through the wall and smack him.

Schott nodded at Rock to continue.

"When the polyporphyrin ring detaches from its current receptor, it can move on to the next one and be rendered inactive," Rock babbled.

He was stalling.

"Or it could morph into a new kind of killer," Rock continued. "One that kills other DNA patterns altogether. Entire ethnic populations could die. Everyone related to Adam and Eve…"

The word "Eve" was still on Rock's trembling lips when the lab door flung open.

All this time, I'd thought I was so clever, that no one would guess I was here. I didn't consider the brick dust I'd produce or how it might fly around if the room's air pressure changed, like when that door swiftly opened.

"I know Ms. *Demolition Queen* has a thing for walls, but that better not be her," Schott said. He was waving away swirling dust and scanning the general vicinity of me and my scope.

I wanted to step back, but the scope would drop and the wall would crumble.

Nightmare.

"You don't need to worry about Sam. I have her thoroughly confused. Plus, I retrieved the alphanumeric from her barn," Kurt bragged. He held up his phone which I presumed showed a photo of my three-by-five alphanumeric card.

Talk about wanting to smack someone.

Right then, a new hand and wrist appeared from behind the half-open door. Like a frog's tongue capturing a fly, it grabbed Kurt's phone with a flash of gold and then disappeared.

Hand and wrist was all I saw, but Rock's open mouth and wide eyes told me he saw the whole enchilada and was more than a little surprised.

Was that the Boss?

"I told you I'd deliver the alphanumeric," said Kurt. He nodded to the person behind the door.

"You've been holding out on me?" Schott asked angrily. His hooked nose even flattened.

"No," Kurt said with a nonchalant air. "I just stole it from Sam's barn. She had it all along and didn't know it." He laughed.

Yeah, yeah. Rub it in.

"So, we're sorted for tonight?" Schott asked as the good news sank in. His plumes bobbed happily in the dusty air. "The doubloons will work? My dear old classmates will die?"

Kurt nodded first to Schott and then toward the shadows.

So Schott's real gold doubloons will hold the killer patches.

"Pity, Ms. Samantha will miss the party after all her help." Schott laughed.

Just try to keep me away, I was thinking, *until* Schott's true meaning slammed home. He thought I'd be dead before the party.

Angry beyond belief *and* slightly concerned for my health, I forgot for a split second what I was doing. My scope see-sawed only a fraction, but it was enough. Dust sifted to the floor on my side of the wall. The same must have happened on the other side, because Nunchuck squinted at the hole.

"It's only a little bug," he said.

With that, he pulled back his plate-sized hand and swung. Like an apparition, his dusty hand appeared through the wall, inches from my face.

Without that bit of wall between us, I saw his shocked bulging eyes stare at his "magical" hand in the swirling dust. Then I heard rumbling overhead. I didn't need to look up. I knew that sound far too well.

I grabbed my scope and spun. My feet churned on the dusty floor as if I was the Road Runner. With a surge of adrenaline, I Tae-Bo-kicked off the stacks of boxes. That kick propelled me toward the door with the added bonus that the heavy boxes tipped toward the lab. As I burst into the hall I heard yelps, wrenching metal, shattering glass, and Schott screeching, "Get up, you idiot."

The alarm was blaring as I raced down the hall, grabbed my boots, and flew headfirst through the round steel vent. Reaching the dewy pavement, I felt warm evening air. I also felt loose strands of hair hit my face. I reached for my fan belt, already knowing it was gone, left inside like a calling card.

Amateur move.

A bruised ego was the least of my worries. I pictured that wrist reaching in for the alphanumeric.

I knew what had flashed.

It was a cufflink.

A Cambridge crested cufflink.

Max's Cambridge crested cufflink.

CHAPTER FIFTY-SIX

After ten blocks of full out sprinting, I finally stopped beside a bus shelter. My reflection in its glass wall was way beyond scary. My hair looked like a jumbled, dusty red Amy Winehouse beehive. My clothes were worse. No taxi driver was going to let me in his car, let alone take me to the V&A.

I was about to slip behind the shelter to change when a passing car slowed and a blinding flash of light came from the passenger window. I knew without a doubt that it had been Tambour's blasted photographer.

So what else is new?

I quickly put on billowing pirate pantaloons, black satin bustier, blousy open white top, black cuffed suede boots, and then a wide leather belt. So when I stepped to the curb *Voila!* Brakes squealed as two taxis practically collided to pick me up.

I chose the fastest looking one and hopped in. Speed could be vitally important tonight.

"So, pretty lady, where shall I take you?" the winner asked as we pulled away from the curb.

"The V&A please and fast," I answered, thinking about what Schott had said. His soon-to-be guests/victims weren't patched yet. That would happen at the V&A and I might have an idea how to prevent it. An idea Silverblade could confirm.

I quickly texted him: *Do patches, like John Doe's, adhere only to clean, dry surfaces?*

Silverblade was on the ball tonight and immediately responded: *Yes.*

OK then.

New plan.

I'd buy an industrial-size can of WD-40 and convince the V&A doorman to re-polish the revolving door handles with WD-40 after every use. That thin layer of lubricant would prevent Schott's patches from sticking to guests' hands so they couldn't kill them.

At least I hoped so.

"Do you know where the nearest open hardware store is?" I asked the driver.

He nodded, made three quick turns, and pulled up before a window full of chains, saws, and drills. I leaped out and urgently steamed into the shop. Heading straight for the Paints/Oil section I spotted a buzz-cut clerk stocking shelves. He frantically backed out of my way as I grabbed the WD-40. Then he sped to the till way ahead of me. He didn't even look at me until I got my change. And then it hit me. I knew that buzz cut. I'd twirled a crowbar above it not that long ago.

Ha!

***

Back in the cab, I rang Candace to sort out a helicopter ride I was pretty sure I'd need later.

Into my already full bustier, I squeezed the cat puzzle, several plastic tools, and a blue controller labeled *Max Tuloitte*. I had to retie the bustier's long satin strings at the bottom to keep the whole thing from bursting open.

I sat back and the full shock of what I'd heard in the annex finally hit me.

Schott wasn't just killing off the class bully or Miss Perfect who'd turned him down for prom. He was wiping out the whole friggin' upper crust. Kurt, Nunchuck, Max, and those killer gold doubloons were doing the dirty work.

Mass murder at the V&A tonight.

Ohmygawd.

I pictured the who's who in London's crowd at the V&A. They'd be decked out for Schott's fancy dress theme with plastic swords, glittering wands, feathered headdresses, and press-on facial hair. All would be clutching a treasure map too, blissfully unaware of the impending doom.

I'd be so tempted to yell, "Don't touch anything sticky or you die." But who would listen? Thanks to that sleazeball Tambour, this crowd thought I was a common hussy and antennae-wielding weirdo. Tonight's online Tambour photo by the bus stop sealed the deal. Let's just say the reflection I saw in the bus stop's glass didn't do my appearance justice. I looked like a total whack-job.

Hussy whack-job it was then.

I could live with that.

What I couldn't live with was Schott killing my friends and acquaintances.

Even if I *could* convince the crowd to miss Schott's party of the year, I wouldn't. Schott might panic and kill everyone off before I figured out how to use Mom's alphanumeric to shut him down.

So while the guests followed their treasure maps, I'd…

1. Avoid Schott
2. Grill Max
3. Pay back Kurt for stealing my alphanumeric
4. Use Mom's alphanumeric to stop them all

I was pretty confident that my impromptu annex demolition would have delayed Schott's arrival at the V&A but I rang Mrs. Party just to make sure.

She picked up on the first ring. "Hello? Sam? Please tell me he's still coming," Mrs. Party said in a more-hyper-than-usual voice.

"What? Who?" I asked as I pictured her darting around the V&A foyer among the parrots that I heard squawking in the background.

"Silverblade's swashbuckling lessons are oversubscribed, so where is he? I spent a small fortune anchoring that Chihuly chandelier out of the way," she said.

I'd forgotten about that. The exquisite thirty-five-foot Chihuly chandelier normally hung straight down from the soaring domed ceiling. I'd sure miss the shimmering sparkling light sent out by its hundreds of green and blue spiraling barbs.

"Silverblade's fine," I said. At least I thought so. "Is Schott there yet?"

"My heavens no." Her shrill voice made my ears ring. "He'll grandly arrive and open the party for eight p.m."

"Excellent. OK, question number two—."

"You got your earring and eye patch right?" Mrs. Party's panicked voice went up an octave.

"Yes, I'm even wearing them *and* my moustache," I said, twirling it. "Why?"

"We ran out. Those extra labels were to blame," she said.

I'd forgotten about the extra labels. *Names from Max's and Schott's personal hit lists.*

"And the maps?" I shouted over the squawking parrots. The taxi driver stared at me in the rearview mirror when he should have been watching the pedestrians crossing in front of Buckingham Palace.

"Everyone must have his or her map to enter," she said in a mechanical voice as if she'd repeated it a million times. Then she screamed, "Not on the grog bar! Those go by the pirate prison!" Her voice was like a bullhorn to the ear.

"But do we keep our maps all night?" I asked.

"Yes, dear," she said and then shouted at one of her minions "Those belong by the crocodiles." Then she was back, "Sam, once you've found your real gold doubloon you may check it. Your map becomes your ticket to collect it as you leave. There might be another surprise too." Mrs. Party's voice tinkled.

"Yeah, death," I said under my breath as I hung up.

CHAPTER FIFTY-SEVEN

"OK, pretty lady, here we are," said the taxi driver, pulling to the curb opposite the Victoria and Albert Museum.

"Remember, I might be in there for ten minutes or several hours but when I come out I'll look for you right here," I said before hopping out.

Our deal was that I'd pay him double to wait. Minutes lost hailing a taxi later could be disastrous.

Hugging the can of WD-40 to my bustier, I sprinted across bustling Cromwell Road and then crouched between the very hot hood of a Rolls Royce and the sloping, seductive trunk of a Bentley. Excited passengers were bouncing out of them like school kids out for Christmas holidays. They joined hundreds of excited guests who queued beneath a forty-foot "Beware of Pirates" banner that flapped above the V&A's two-story arched stone entrance.

I flipped down my black eye patch and swaggered right past Tambour and the other paparazzi. If I'd known facial hair and an eye patch fooled Tambour so easily, I'd have started wearing those months ago.

I flashed my 'borrowed' *Party Staff* badge to get past the bouncer. Then I spun on through the revolving door. It took me a second to realize that the man wearing weathered canvas trainers, ragged shirt, and jagged cropped trousers was the doorman.

"Mrs. Party wants the revolving door handles polished after *every* use," I said to him before I thrust my can of WD-40 and my black T-shirt from the annex into his hands.

He hopped right to his polishing like a man who didn't fancy Mrs. Party yelling at him.

Perfect.

As planned, the cat puzzle and plastic tools in my bustier didn't make a peep as I passed right through the metal detectors.

Approaching one of the Tinker Bells fluttering behind the welcome table, I said, "Hi. My name is Samantha Albany and I forgot my map."

"Not a problem," said Tinker Bell. She pulled out a treasure map labeled *Samantha Albany*, identical to last week's map.

Hmm. Schott certainly covered all his bases especially as he'd thought I'd be dead by now.

Ticktock.

Ticktock

I heard the *ticktock* and knew it had to be Schott. I looked through the V&A's glass doors and saw a stretch "Hook-mobile" with a three-foot-long silver-hook hood ornament bump up onto the curb.

Ticktock.

Ticktock.

A deafening roar went up from the crowd as Schott stepped out, wearing an upgraded Captain Hook costume. He'd attached a stuffed parrot to his shoulder and was waving a very real-looking sword.

Right before he bounded inside, I hid behind the grog bar's palm trees. I was peeking from between them when the doorman repolished the door handle Schott had just used. I couldn't help smiling as Schott slapped him on the back for a job well done. *If you only knew.*

No one seemed to care that Schott set off the metal detector with his sword and sinister-looking dagger. *It's his party. He'll kill if he wants to.*

Schott returned the dagger to his belt and fondled its hilt as he and his stuffed parrot surveyed the broad foyer. He nodded as if he was carrying out an inventorying. Central grog bar with frayed red-and-white striped awning. *Nod.* Pirate prison. *Nod.* Signage pointing to "Blind Man's Bluff." *Nod.* His smile widened as his eyes landed on the pit of crocodiles, albeit baby ones. *Nod. Nod.* Then he looked up at the Indian princess walking the gangplank twenty feet above the crocodile pit. *Nod. Nod. Nod.*

Even though human sacrifice now *seemed* Schott's style, I noticed glistening guide wires were attached to the Indian princess's waist. I also noticed a swashbuckling crew up near her on the mezzanine level. They were gracefully swinging shiny swords in broad arcs. Silverblade wasn't with them. It made me a little nervous, not for Mrs. Party's sake but for mine. He was my *only* ally tonight.

"Here we go, everybody," Mrs. Party trilled. Her voice shot up into the soaring eighty-foot-high foyer. Her "shipwrecked" waiters stood at attention in one long line, holding trays packed with full champagne glasses.

With that, the doorman released the revolving door. Like a tsunami, the crowd of laughing guests with flashing swords and fluttering wings rolled inside. I was worried the doorman couldn't keep up but he ran that WD-40 soaked cloth over every single handle.

Schott stood clapping and beaming like a little boy. He greeted each and every pirate, fairy, and Indian princess. I imagined him ticking off each of their names on an invisible hit list.

Lord Wolverhampton appeared at Schott's side. Straining buttons were working overtime on the admiral uniform he'd stuffed himself into. I wasn't happy to see Lady Wolverhampton with him. Her darling puppy's surgery must have been rescheduled. Now she'd be in danger too.

More guests surrounded Schott and all I could see were the plumes on his hat. When a very tall member of Parliament blocked out the plumes altogether, I had to scramble over rum kegs to get a better view. Rounding the "Grog Bar" sign, my damn pantaloons caught on its scratchy coconut shell letters. I had to pull so hard to free them that the entire tent shook.

Glass shattered too. I peered around and saw two surprised guests, looking at their empty hands and then the floor like their glasses had spontaneously slipped.

I had the sinking feeling my WD-40 might be responsible. *Oh well.*

My view improved as I hopped onto a crate of coconuts, but not the aesthetics. I was nose-to-cage with a stinky, very nervous-looking parrot who squawked, "Welcome to Schott's pirate party. Welcome to Schott's pirate party. Welcome to Schott's pirate party."

On a scale of one to ten, Prunella's floral perfume being a fourteen, this was definitely an eight.

I tilted my chin up to reach fresh air and was hugely relieved to spot Silverblade, balanced on the balcony railing. He was opposite his swashbuckling crew and the Indian princess's gangplank.

"*Grog bar.*" I typed and sent. Silverblade's phone must have been on loud *and* vibrate because he immediately checked it, looked down from his high up perch to search me out, and then saluted.

I was so psyched to make contact. I saluted in response. I'd completely forgotten I was incognito, and instantly heard Schott at my back.

"Ms. Samantha," he said, sounding surprised and annoyed.

I liked the annoyed part.

With that, the parrot squawked again, "Welcome to Schott's pirate party. Welcome to Schott's pirate party. Welcome to Schott's pirate party."

There I was nose-to-*beaks* with the real parrot's beak, Schott's beak *and* his stuffed bird's beak.

Schott slid his small black-booted foot out in front, and then bent at the waist. You'd think I'd have learned to keep my limbs close to my body. What could I say? I was a bit distracted. Schott's thin fingers clasped mine. His drooping moustache scratched my hand and his wet lips left a slimy snail-like trail across my knuckles.

It took everything in me to force an innocent "happy to be here" smile. I could tell from the twitch in Schott's squinting eyes that he was faking "happy" too.

"I'm so very pleased you've made it to my party," he said, releasing my hand to fondle his dagger. He also frowned at the parrot who repeated, "Welcome to Schott's pirate party. Welcome to Schott's pirate party. Welcome to Schott's pirate party."

"Right," I said as I pushed my map into my waistband so I could wipe my knuckles on my black pants.

"You have your map. Very good." His mouth smiled, but his eyes did not as he extracted his dagger.

"Ah, Captain Hook, you wouldn't kill me here in this crowd would you?" I teased.

"Who would notice you slumped behind all these coconuts?" He chuckled as he surveyed the mass of laughing, drinking, and dancing guests. "Not a soul, I suspect."

He had a point there. "At least not until the last parrot sings," I joked and twirled the parrot cage.

"Welcome to Schott's pirate party. Welcome to Schott's pirate party. Welcome to Schott's pirate party."

"Oh, shut up, you stupid bird," Schott shouted and stomped his suede boot on the granite floor, *hard*.

I enjoyed how his eyes widened in pain.

However, I didn't enjoy the way he slid his cold, heavy, and *real*-feeling dagger, across the mounds of my bustier-enhanced cleavage, as he said, "Always wanted to be a pirate. All that pillaging and raping." His black pinholes for eyes stared at me like a raving lunatic. He dragged the knife back in the other direction then he lowered it to my waist and drew it back, ready to drive it into my stomach.

What the…?

This possibility hadn't crossed my mind. Me slumped dead behind the coconuts long before the rest of this crowd slumped dead somewhere else.

Would he really do it?

Right before Schott plunged his knife into me, time stood still. I missed nothing. Not the parrot fluttering. Not two more glasses breaking. Not the lights going out in the gift shop at the rear of the foyer. Not even how the Prime Minister waved his hand above the heads of the other guests to get Schott's attention.

I was terrified. Not about the stab. I'd inflicted much worse wounds on myself with various tools over the years. I was terrified that I'd blown the chance to stop this lunatic and save all these people.

Still the knife came.

I flinched as its blade disappeared in the folds of my billowing blouse. I bent as the knife's hilt hit my stomach. I grabbed at it even though I felt no sharp pain.

Then Schott laughed.

I hit mental rewind. My eyes had fooled my ears. I'd heard that spring compress behind Schott's fake dagger blade but blocked it out. My stomach was fine, but Schott's intent was clear.

I pushed the fake blade aside and hissed in his ear, "I'm going to stop you."

Nice, Sam, real subtle.

"You're going to stop me raping and pillaging?" Schott's black eyes narrowed and froze on mine. "Too late, my dear," he said. His tight, evil smile made his hooked nose curl in so far it practically touched his lips.

Schott slithered away and was back to playing delighted host. He was already schmoozing another of his soon-to-be victims, the Lord Mayor of London.

CHAPTER FIFTY-EIGHT

That fake stabbing by Schott had made me ravenous. Very odd. I rubbed my stomach as hunger pangs sent it into spasms. My energy felt zapped too. I needed food and lots of it. I swiftly devoured one chicken, red pepper, and pineapple shish kebab. I was starting another as Mrs. Party appeared under my raised elbow.

She didn't look happy to see me. Let's face it, her odds of a successful party were greatly diminished with me around.

"Sam, I need your help keeping *people* away from the Chihuly chandelier tonight."

She'd said *people* but her eyes were talking to me.

I was about to say "Sure," when two more glasses shattered.

"Dear oh dear. Everyone's got the dropsies tonight." Her cackle sounded more like a cry for help.

Next thing I knew she grabbed my glass. She was tipping my champagne into a paper cup when she looked up and gasped. I had the sinking feeling that my WD-40 hadn't been enough. I looked up too, expecting to see dead bodies dropping from the balcony. So I was big time relieved that she'd actually gasped at Silverblade who was faux sparring with the Chihuly chandelier. I looked down to reassure Mrs. Party, but she was gone.

So was Schott.

Shoot.

This was a disaster. He could be anywhere.

Should I follow my map to the fifth-floor ceramics room? Would I find him there in the highest, most secluded floor of the V&A? The room he'd renamed tonight as *Dead Men Tell No Lies.*

Well if I was going, I needed to go soon because Felicity was easing her wide Vera Wang fairy wings through the revolving door. No way was I explaining to her what I was up to.

I just needed one more shish kebab.

I was gnawing on it when I heard Felicity's pouting voice say, "I don't get a treasure map."

"No big deal. Mine only leads to the plate room," I mumbled around my mouthful of chicken. "Nice camera," I said to change the subject. I pointed at the micro-cam on her shoulder.

"Brand new. I've programmed in your phone number already so you can ring me and see what my camera is seeing." She paused to watch me wolf down two skewers of monkfish, then said, "So about tonight's footage. I'm going to film Schott's introduction, Silverblade's crew, and these squawking parrots. If I have questions I'll ring you…" Felicity stopped to stare at the three coconut shrimp I popped into my mouth. "What is with you?"

"I missed breakfast and lunch," I said as I inventoried my empty glass and skewer lineup with growing concern.

"You? The woman whose stomach I tell time by?" Felicity gave me a queer look.

"Don't you need to go film something?" I said more sharply than I meant to.

"Right. OK. See you later," she said and angrily twirled the parrot cage as she left.

She'd made the cage rock so hard that the parrot paused between each line, like a punctuation mark between my thoughts.

Why am I so ravenous?

"Welcome to Schott's pirate party."

Ravenously hungry? I blanched.

"Welcome to Schott's pirate party."

Ravenously hungry is Rock's symptom for stage two.

"Welcome to Schott's pirate party."

I was racking my brain to remember stage three symptoms when something wrapped tight around my neck and pulled me sideways. I couldn't shout. I couldn't even breathe. I could only see the heels of my black boots dragging over the threshold into the west wing. Was this how my life would end. Would I die in this dark V&A corner by a sarcophagus never to be heard from again?

NO.

I was about to spin and deliver my signature Tae Bo kick to the groin, but then I sniffed the air and, believe it or not, was happy to smell the scent that made fourteen on my smelliest scale.

"I hated you," Prunella, the psycho-bitch, slurred in my ear.

I ducked under her loosened arm and did a double-take. Prunella's left moccasin was missing. Her feathered headdress dipped low over one mascara-smeared eye. Brown spikes of hair stuck out in every direction.

"I loved Conrad. He promised to destroy my HFNC passcodes but someone drained my accounts. He got a posthumous citation and I got the sack," Prunella said. Then she hiccupped with such force her headdress dropped over both eyes.

I anxiously listened for more but midsentence she slumped across the sarcophagus and began snoring. As snoring was *not* a symptom on Rock's list, I was pretty sure she wasn't dying. At least not yet.

"Can you help me?" I called to a man in frayed shorts and a white button-down shirt who I thought was a waiter.

"Get your own bloody drink," he shouted.

Something gold flashed at his wrist as he waved me away and continued through the crowd.

A gold cufflink.

"Max!" I yelled.

He hesitated but didn't stop. He rushed through the foyer's archway leading to the auxiliary gift shop.

"Sorry, Prunella," I said, patting her back before taking off after Max.

Surprisingly, he hadn't gone far. I could see him through the gift shop's glass walls, facing rows of posters, mugs, and coffee table books.

Was this a trap?

I pulled the MedMaker controller from my bustier before silently pushing open the shop's glass doors. I crept up behind Max. I pushed the controller into his back like a gun and jumped then turned. His eyebrows arched in surprise. I'd expected that but not the resigned and guilty look that followed.

"You've been implanted so if I push this button you die," I said as he stared at the controller. "Now, I want answers. Talk," I said.

With my thumb hovering over the controller's activation button, I maneuvered deeper into the shop so I could watch for Kurt, Nunchuck, or Schott coming to his rescue.

"Sam, there's no future for us," he said.

"What?" *Are you kidding me?*

"I'm a fraud. I was born in Louisiana. There was no Eton or Cambridge," he said in his strong American-Southern accent. It was like watching an English-speaking film dubbed in a foreign language.

"Tell me something I don't know," I said, shaking the controller at him. "Describe your bioweapon plan."

I thought that would send his fingers to his eyebrow, but he just leaned against a waist-high stack of books and said, "Your mother allocated all financial and personnel resources to the MedMaker. If the MedMaker didn't fly, then we'd all go down with it." He angrily pounded the books with his fist. "She wouldn't even consider more profitable alternatives for her technology. I wanted to save the day. So I had Rock start developing MedMaker weapons. Oh, he didn't know they were weapons. But it was the right thing to do—"

I held up a hand as a loud voice said, "Ladies and gentlemen." Realizing it was not Schott but Mrs. Party addressing the foyer crowd, I signaled Max to continue.

"I used Helen's miscellaneous marketing account to fund the project," Max explained matter-of-factly.

"And some of Conrad's?" I added. Max nodded the smallest nod I'd ever seen.

"Once the weapons were ready, if Helen still wasn't on board, I planned to kill the project. Especially when she hinted that I might become her successor one day. Imagine a Louisiana swamp boy like me running an international multibillion-pound company. I wasn't going to risk missing out on that, so I shut down the project. Or at least I tried to. That's when Conrad swooped in as WhistleBlown."

"Right." I waved the controller again. "You're going to try and pin this on your buddy Conrad after you sold the weapons to Schott, the highest bidder?"

"No!" He raised his hands in surrender. "Conrad hijacked it all. He wasn't my buddy." Max spat the words at me. "He was my keeper. Conrad discovered my annex bioweapon lab and my misappropriation of funds. I thought I was done for. To tell you the truth, I was relieved.

"But then Conrad 'suggested' that I continue the project. He would finger some poor sod for the missing funds. If I didn't go along with him, he'd tell Helen what I'd been up to. After that, Conrad kept the project going with his own money."

So, Kurt wasn't lying about Conrad selling his art.

He just lied about Conrad's reason for doing it.

"Boy, was Conrad furious that day he found you in the annex. He was sure you'd found his lab."

Hearing shuffling feet and excited voices, I cocked an ear toward the foyer. This time Schott was speaking. "Ladies and gentlemen, may I have your attention please? The treasure hunt will begin very soon. So get your maps ready to find *your* gold doubloon."

I turned on Max and said, "You liar. Your little project killed my mom, and it's going to kill hundreds tonight. I saw you in the annex earlier. I know your plans." Max gave me an odd look, but I kept talking. "You're not going to get away with…" I stopped. Over Max's shoulder, I saw two Tinker Bells flit upstairs carrying boxes.

Max twisted around to watch. He pulled up to full height and looked back at me. Next thing I knew he'd tipped over two greeting card racks to block my path. I bounded over them as he ran out the thick glass doors, but I was too late. He'd already shut and locked the doors behind him.

"Sorry, Sam," he said through the small gap between the doors. He actually looked sorry.

"Max, if you don't open these doors, I'm going to press this." My thumb hovered over the controller's activation button again and I said, "It will kill you."

"Sam, that would make you as bad as me."

His haunted, tortured expression threw me for a second.

Next Max took off, upstairs with the fairies. Then Schott began speaking again.

"I've been *dying* to get you all together." Schott's emphasis on "dying" was unmistakable. "I'd like to take a moment to remember those who couldn't be with us tonight," said Schott.

I looked around, trying to figure out how I'd escape. This shop's ten-foot glass walls had no ceiling. I'd be heard if I shouted but Schott could still prematurely "pull the trigger."

Instead, I pushed a six-foot-high stack of coffee table books against the glass wall. I was going over.

Schott continued. "Most of you probably still remember our V&A school trip many, many years ago. What you might not have remembered was that you all locked me in a closet on the fourth floor, *overnight*."

Was that the travesty Schott thought worthy of mass murder? Geez.

I pushed a four-foot stack of books against the six-foot stack.

"Tonight I put all that behind me. Tonight you hunt. Hunt or be hunted." Schott chuckled.

I pictured his slimy, smirking lips.

"It's all about fun, my friends," Schott continued. "So, study the *X* on your map and follow it to your designated pirate locale. Once there, you'll find your very own gold doubloon."

A gold doubloon that holds a patch of death that hopefully won't stick to your WD-40-coated hands.

I pushed a two-foot stack of books against the four-foot and six-foot ones and then backed up. I paused to hear Schott's final instructions.

"Let have lots of noise as you hunt. Every time you meet another guest, I want pirates to shout, 'Arrr.' Fairies say, 'Oooh' and Indian princesses, 'Ahh.' OK, pirates, give me your best Arrr."

While the Pirates obediently chanted, "Arrr," I charged at my stacks of books. I leaped up two, four, six feet, and then vaulted. As planned, my right leg flew over the glass wall. Torso and left leg were meant to follow. Except, my bustier caught on the wall's glass edge. My body ground to a halt. The half-inch glass, *albeit polished*, was gouging into my breastbone, stomach, and groin. To lessen the pain, I slowly shifted toward the outside.

Unfortunately, this small shift caused a *large* shift of the wall. I looked down, realizing what had appeared to be sturdy walls were merely glass partitions on metal supports. They weren't designed for extra weight, *especially* moving weight. Whichever direction I ended up going, this wall would not survive.

"Fairies you try now," Schott called to the crowd.

I inched my left leg over the top to the outer side of the wall as Schott's fairies all went, "Oooh." The rigid glass bit into my fingertips as I clung on and flattened my boots against the glass.

"Now Indian princesses."

"Ahh," went the Indian princesses.

"Very good," Schott exclaimed.

I bent my knees.

"When this skull and crossbones flag hits the floor, you begin your hunt. Remember, lots of noise," Schott said.

Two seconds later, the sounds of "Arrr," "Oooh," and "Ahh," were deafening *and* perfectly timed.

One, two, and three. My feet pushed off the wall. I flew backward and landed firmly on my boots. The heavy glass wall was not so lucky. As predicted, it fell inward, shattering paperweights, commemorative mugs, and *itself*.

I raced past the foyer where the crowd had already parted like the Red Sea. Angel wings, paper cups, and mustaches lay trampled in its center. I got a fleeting glimpse of Prunella who now had a pirate hat stuffed under her head. She actually looked peaceful.

The tail end of one crowd was disappearing into the main gift shop. Another wound between statues and columns. I ran upstairs trailing behind excited treasure hunters who peeled off left and right toward *Pirate's Cave* and *Blood Lagoon*.

At the landing, I caught sight of Max's wingtips. They were already two floors up. I kept going, hit the third floor, and almost knocked over Lord Wolverhampton at the door to *Pirate's Peg Leg*.

"Found your coin yet?" I yelled.

"No," he said with a harrumph.

"Good," I shouted and he gave me a puzzled look as I headed up toward the fourth floor. There the thinned-out crowd raced into a room marked *Daggers, Dungeons and Lost Doubloons*.

Still no Max.

CHAPTER FIFTY-NINE

Arrr's, Ooh's, and Ahh's echoed below as I climbed the final flight toward *Dead Men Tell No Lies*. Noises from below faded as I stepped inside the long, dim ceramics room all alone. Row after row of five-foot-high glass cases stretched before me like bookshelves in deserted library stacks. The case's thin oak rectangular frames on stilts didn't look sturdy enough for all this antique glass and ceramics.

I'd expected a 'welcome' party but there was no Max, Schott, Kurt, or Nunchuck.

"So why send me here?" I whispered as I slid my black-cuffed boots down the worn center aisle. My wide pantaloons rustled and the floor creaked. I passed plates, figurines, and pots without seeing them. I held up my map to study its squiggly *X*. Lowering it, I saw the same *X*, enlarged, cut out, and taped onto the last case in the row, *dead ahead*. Intrigued, I moved closer to look through the top V-shaped portion of the *X*. I admired the curved person-sized tureen inside the case.

I dropped to my knees to peer through the bottom of the *X*. I squinted at the blue-tinged appendage and gold ornament extending from the tureen. Then I switched my eye patch to the opposite eye like Silverblade would have done for a fresh perspective.

I looked again.

Then I saw what it really was. I lurched away so hard that my head cracked the glass on the case behind. Gulping for air, I closed my eyes and scrambled to my feet. "No," I said, staring at Max's shirt cuff, gold Cambridge cufflink, and *blue* oxygen-starved hand that extended from the tureen.

My eyes darted left and right. I bent and reached under the case. With a puzzled expression, I popped up and counted to confirm that this was the fifth case from the end. I dropped to my knees and inspected the splintered section of wood where I'd duct-taped my black pocketknife to it the day I received my original treasure map.

My ears were on high alert, so a nearby shuffling was an explosion of sound. I couldn't get up fast enough. I scratched my chest trying to pull out my plastic knife as I stared at the black hiking boots not a foot away.

"Searching for this?" asked a deep voice and I looked up at Kurt who was wearing the same black outfit from the annex. He was leaning against the *X*'d case and casually flipping my black pocketknife in his hand. Behind him was an open door. One I hadn't noticed on my reconnaissance trip.

"I must say a mustache really suits you. Almost didn't recognize you," he said, staring into my eyes as I stood.

"Do I detect professional jealousy?" I asked as he peered at my upper lip.

"Nope." He laughed and ripped my moustache off.

Rubbing my lip, my eyes trailed back to Max's arm. "How could you kill Max?"

"Can't take credit," Kurt said. "He was like that when I got here." Kurt paused. "Sam, have I taught you nothing about appropriate spy attire? This outfit is trouble," said Kurt as he curled fingers around my bustier's lacy top and rubbed his thumb against my breast.

I pushed his hand away and asked, "You're saying Schott killed Max? My money is on you." I waved my map at him.

"When I *X*'d that map, I remembered thinking she'll love being sent somewhere to work alone. Tell me, did your shoulders get all tight and tingly?" Kurt asked.

"You sent me here?" I asked, pushing my shoulders down.

He nodded. "I know you too well. It's been your biggest disadvantage." Kurt grinned. "I know when you lie and even know when you lie about lying."

I'd have rolled my eyes but a revolting sour milk taste filled my mouth. I wrinkled my nose and sucked at my tongue to get the taste off. Then I stood stock still, remembering this was Rock's symptom numero uno. My symptoms were going backward. Backward or forward, this was not good.

How did this happen? I gasped. That sticky-handled tool on my workbench.

The horrible taste intensified and I must have looked like I was dying, because Kurt lurched at me and grabbed my jawbone. His lips moved in toward mine, mouth-to-mouth resuscitation style.

Oh, what the heck. I puckered up.

Kurt merely licked my lips and then pursed his as if tasting wine. "Dammit, Sam, I warned you to leave this alone," he shouted.

"You have the nerve to *shout* at me?" I shouted back.

With that, he flicked open my black knife. He poked my fingertip and squeezed drops of my blood onto the blade. I watched as my blood immediately formed perfect equiangular spirals. Just like the ones in Silverblade's morgue.

Golden number. Invisible pentagrams. Golden triangles. Mom's phi swirl.

"Those are MedMaker bioweapon cells," Kurt said to my unasked question. "Soon they'll go gangrenous green and then coal black as they get ready to kill you."

"You did this to me," I said.

He gave his best cut-the-crap stare and laughed. "It's not like I didn't—"

"Warn me? Yeah, I got it," I said, about to punch that grin off his face. Instead, an uncomfortable feeling made me grab my chest.

"What is it?" Kurt's expression went serious again.

"A weird twitching right here," I said, pressing a spot at the base of my bra.

Kurt swiftly pressed his warm ear to the spot. I stared down at his spiky blond hair.

Here I was dying *and* with a cold-blooded murderer pressing his ear to my chest. So what did I do? I inhaled his earthy scent. Of course that kicked-off a very nice glowing sensation in my pantaloons.

"I love Morse code," Kurt said, grinning up from between my breasts.

"What are you on about?" I frowned.

Still in listening position, Kurt pulled out his cell phone and turned up the volume. It played the same rhythm twitching on my chest.

"You could have heard it on your phone?" I asked, abruptly stepping back.

"Oh come on, you do the math." He grinned as he pointed to my chest, then his phone and back at my chest.

"You bugged my bra?"

"And that surprises you because?" he asked, still grinning.

I heard an "Arrr" somewhere not far from the ceramics room. With that, Kurt killed the lights. Exit signs glowed green in his eyes as he whispered, "I have things to do, and you're in the way. Move along."

He pushed me through the small door and up narrow, musty stairs. We emerged into a greenhouse-type room where broken ceramic pots lined the shelves. I headed straight for a screen that showed a 3-D V&A floor plan with hundreds of red blinking dots everywhere.

"Each red dot shows the exact location of our guests and their maps. Here's you." He pointed at a dot on the top floor.

"Who aren't you implanting?" I asked, studying the dots.

"No one, it appears." He smiled.

I stared at Kurt. "How could I have been so wrong about you?"

"Pays the rent," he joked and flipped a doubloon in the air. "Schott was about to put 'programmed without target' patches on these—"

"I've seen its work," I said and shivered, picturing the lab tech's body shriveling inside his anticontamination suit.

"I convinced him that Rock was trustworthy enough to make the DNA-coded patches properly *without* PWT," said Kurt.

"How long until we die?" I asked, pointing at the screen.

"You were supposed to be dead by now." He shook his head like my *not* being dead was slightly annoying. "Just over two hours for the rest. Schott wants everyone to enjoy the party before they die."

"Oh, so Schott really *is* a random-acts-of-kindness kind of guy," I said.

"Yeh, I guess so." Kurt laughed.

"So exactly how much time was that? I want to synchronize my watch," I said nonchalantly, setting my timer.

"Two hours and seven minutes. But that's not necessary." Kurt pointed at my watch. "You'll be watching from right here," he added and unceremoniously shoved me to the floor by the radiator. He slapped a handcuff on one wrist, threaded the other cuff around the radiator's copper pipe, and then clamped my other wrist.

"Reminds me of a wonderful holiday in Denmark," I said with a smirk.

"Now, I've got to deliver these bad boys. Tootles." He zipped up his backpack, but not before I saw piles of miniature blue controllers inside.

"Don't leave me here," I yelled as he clipped the handcuff key to a shelf way over by the door and then headed downstairs.

Then I grinned.

I couldn't believe my luck. Cuffed to a radiator? *What was he thinking?*

I swiftly turned off its water supply and then eased it an inch off its wall hanger. Next I tilted it to the floor, to crease its pipes. Then I pushed it back up against the wall and back to the floor two more times. Droplets of water began seeping from the creases.

Not to worry. *Couldn't be more than three buckets of water in this baby.*

Two more ups and downs of the radiator and it thudded to the floor.

I grabbed those keys in a flash but as I unlocked my handcuffs, I noticed water gurgling up from the severed pipes. I was about to double-check the shutoff valve when I heard raised voices.

"I'll take them," I heard as I tiptoed downstairs to the ceramics room. I reached the shadowy doorway as Nunchuck pulled at Kurt's backpack.

"No, I can handle it," Kurt said, yanking it away.

"Schott told *me* to take them to the tower," Nunchuck said, then hauled off and punched Kurt.

With that, the backpack flew in my direction. It splashed at my feet.

Splashed? I looked down at a growing puddle. *Oh shit.*

The radiator shutoff valve was definitely faulty.

Oh well. While they wrestled, I grabbed Kurt's backpack.

I knew I'd be leaving a trail of wet footprints as I snuck from the room so I had to be fast. As I bounded down three flights of stone stairs the Arrr's, Ooh's, and Ahh's grew louder and louder but I still heard *and* felt Kurt and Nunchuck pounding the stairs not far behind.

I tore down another flight. I hit the landing. I darted to the right, and then skidded to a stop. Straight ahead, an enraged Schott burst out of the British Galleries. I ducked into the shallow alcove beside the stairs and peeked out in time to see Schott angrily trying to prop up his parrot. "I was at the bloody British Galleries, like on my map, you idiot," he shouted into his phone.

Flattening against the alcove wall, I waited for him to pass. *And* I waited. Guessing he'd headed downstairs, I inched my head around the pillar and my heart practically stopped. I was beak-to-beak with Schott and his parrot again.

Schott blinked wide, round eyes as if he was seeing things.

Like maybe, I shouldn't be there because he'd hoped I'd *finally* died.

"Yeah, I know," I said to Schott.

Through Schott's phone, I heard Nunchuck's grunts, I assumed from running hard in this direction. With that, I ripped the fake parrot from Schott's shoulder, smashed it into Schott's beak, and headed for the next flight of stairs.

"Sam is with me!" shouted Schott.

He was still shouting as I hit the next floor and sped past the metalware exhibit, where a flash of pink fairy netting and a frayed pair of shorts caught my eye. My face reddened as I realized the fairy was granting the shipwrecked waiter a very *big* wish.

Reaching the last flight, I thought I'd beat Nunchuck, Kurt, and Captain Hook but Nunchuck's orange face appeared and headed up the stairs fast.

Give me a break.

I backtracked, rounded a corner, and nearly collided with the last guest in a long queue waiting for swashbuckling lessons. The rowdy crowd was merrily chanting, "Arrr and Ooh and Ahh, Oh My," to the cadence of "Lions and Tigers and Bears, Oh My," still unaware that the gold doubloons in their hot little hands were killers.

No one gave me a second glance as I ducked beside the queue. Scurrying toward the stone railing, I was jabbed by a wand and tripped by a curly slipper but acquired a gold plastic sword right before I peered through the railing at Silverblade. He was across the mezzanine's open expanse once again faux jousting with the tethered green and blue Chihuly chandelier.

"I'll look over here," Nunchuck shouted from somewhere near the end of the queue.

Damn.

Still looking through the railing, I watched the Indian princess turn on her gangplank and got a far-out idea. I sized up her guide wires and the pulley system attached to her. Then I texted Silverblade, "Me Indian princess."

Mid-joust, Silverblade stopped. He read his phone and as he looked toward the gangplank, I hopped up. I also chopped the air with my new plastic sword before pointing at the Chihuly chandelier beside him.

"I see her," Nunchuck shouted, much nearer than last time.

The stunt that followed was perfection, as if Silverblade and I had practiced a gazillion times.

First, I commandeered the Indian princess's pulley controls, and ratcheted her kicking and screaming from her gangplank. I left her dangling over the queue, *still kicking and screaming*, and took her place on the gangplank.

Meanwhile, in one fluid movement, Silverblade lunged for and grabbed onto the chandelier's metal frame. He flicked his sword clean through its tethers and began riding the green and blue Chihuly through the air, thirty-five feet above the foyer. The crowd's "Arrr and Ooh and Ahh, Oh My" became one collective "*Whoa.*"

He was headed straight for me, gaining speed with every second.

"Back of the queue, matey," one outraged guest shouted.

Assuming the queue-cutter was Nunchuck, Kurt, and/or Schott pushing toward me, I almost looked over my shoulder. Good thing I didn't.

"Sam, duck," Silverblade shouted.

I flattened on the rough plank a split second before Silverblade and the huge tinkling chandelier whooshed overhead. My eyes followed. I was psyched I got to see Silverblade let go and slam feet-first into Nunchuck's stomach.

Watching Nunchuck fly into the queue was priceless. His puckered scar looked like a furious red rubber centipede.

It was so fun to watch, I almost missed my ride but I leaped up just as the empty chandelier began swinging back. More by centrifugal force than by design, my arms and legs wrapped around it like a monkey climbing a banana tree.

Gangplank and queue receded. I was swinging high above the foyer. I looked down and Mrs. Party stared back up with a look of terror and indescribable fury.

"*Ohhh,*" went the queue's newest cheer as I swung away.

I noticed that Mrs. Party, who was still looking up, was scrambling for the stairs and that the cheering had stopped. I didn't understand why, *until* I looked back. The queue crowd was fleeing a river of water now gushing around their ankles, flowing between the balcony railings, and showering the foyer like a waterfall.

It was as if someone had turned on the taps.

Or cut the pipes of a radiator three stories up. Geez.

No time to worry about that. Me and the Chihuly were swinging back toward the furious red faces of Kurt, Nunchuck, and Schott. Which I had to say were nowhere near as scary as Mrs. Party's.

I'd just cleared the crocodile den and was directly over the grog bar when I let go. Down and down I dropped. I hit the bar's striped tent feet first. I didn't bounce like in the movies. Instead, my feet ripped through the canvas. Drink stirrers and paper umbrellas flew up around me as I clawed through the shredded, still collapsing tent.

In such a hurry to get out, I tripped and didn't see the dessert trolley in front of me until I'd planted both hands on its sticky, chocolaty desserts. So I was a bit surprised when the desserts said, "Hello, Sam."

Prone, naked, and chocolaty, the chief waved from his performance art trolley. His black German shepherd stood at attention, wearing a jaunty pirate hat.

"Hello, Chief," was the only pleasantry I had time for *and* could stomach. Shielding my eyes from his chocolate doughnut holder, I ran for the revolving door. Its brass handle was mere inches from my grasp when the sound of tinkling glass twitched in my ears. I looked over my shoulder at green and blue Chihuly spirals splashing like raindrops onto the hard wet floor and cringed.

Almost worse than that, I witnessed the chief jiggle from his dessert trolley, slipping and sliding for cover under the gift shop portico.

Meanwhile, I powered into the revolving door only to see JJ's puzzled face stare back at me through the glass, as if I'd risen from the dead.

I was tired of getting that look.

Avoiding the slippery brass handle, I shoved the door hard. James tried to shove back, but his hand slipped, and I kept pushing. I only let up when his section of the revolving door was inside and mine was out. Of course, Tambour's photographer was right there flashing away. It gave me an inspired idea. I grabbed his packed camera bag and hooked it onto the revolving door handle. So, as JJ gave the door one excessively hard shove, the camera bag made one satisfying *crunch*.

Boy, did I smile.

It didn't last long.

I got a sick feeling in the pit of my stomach as the ground shuddered under my black boots.

I watched flabbergasted as JJ and Kurt leaped behind a column seconds before a tidal wave of green and blue glass threw itself against the front windows. I didn't wait to see if the windows held. I ran the gauntlet of flashing cameras, microphones, and umbrellas and then hopped into my waiting taxi.

"MedMaker Headquarters." I said. The driver only stared at my chocolaty bustier. "It's an emergency," I shouted to get him moving.

"Candace. Here I come," I said, into my phone as we sped down Cromwell Road.

A crackling sound came from Kurt's backpack. I looked inside at a blinking walkie-talkie.

"Man, she dropped a chandelier on us." I heard the smile in JJ's voice. "Kind of romantic.. Isn't that how you two met?"

"She's got the controllers," Kurt roared, clearly not amused.

I heard tinkling glass in the background. This time it was comforting. It meant that Kurt and JJ were still wading through the Chihuly mess inside the V&A.

But I found no comfort in Kurt's next comment.

"I think she's headed for the tower."

The timer on my watch didn't thrill me either. *01:48:19.*

CHAPTER SIXTY

A lightning bolt cut straight across the path of MedMaker Corp's helicopter. A gust of wind threw us left. Another slammed us down and then pushed up with a violent jerk. Cool-as-a-cucumber Candace steered us onward. Our destination was the tower at Cranmont Manor, only thirteen miles from the V&A chaos.

Thinking about that chaos, I pulled out my phone to watch the feed from Felicity's Bluetooth head-cam. She wouldn't even know I was 'there'.

Felicity was just finishing an interview in the British Galleries and heading downstairs. I wasn't so sure I wanted to watch as I recognized the woman weaving toward her.

"Mrs. Party, everyone loved your treasure hunt," said Felicity. "I've got great footage too." Felicity paused. "Are you OK?"

Mrs. Party's eyes looked wet and glazed, like two peeled grapes. She opened her mouth to speak and closed it without saying a word.

That was a new one.

"I'm ruined," she finally squeaked and pointed up.

"Come now, it can't be that bad—" Felicity stopped talking as she followed Mrs. Party's finger with her camera to the dome of the foyer.

"Sam swung through the air like Tarzan. Had a sword between her teeth," Mrs. Party cried.

"What did she swing on?" asked Felicity in a disbelieving and puzzled tone.

"The Chihuly," Mrs. Party sobbed.

Seeing the frayed wires gently swaying in the dome's peak made me sick to my stomach.

"Someone pulled a radiator off the wall too and started a flood," Mrs. Party said.

As she ranted on I heard a series of loud hiccups and burps.

Felicity must have heard them too. She swung her camera around to Lord and Lady Wolverhampton who were bumping downstairs on their bums. I noticed that the gold buttons on Lord Wolverhampton's uniform had lost the battle. Both were clutching empty scotch bottles and giggling like schoolchildren. That was *until* Lady Wolverhampton's mouth opened so far her double chin quadrupled.

Felicity turned her camera to the foyer, where Lady Wolverhampton had looked.

Hysteria reigned.

Uprooted palm trees formed a teepee around the collapsed, waterlogged grog bar. There was a dive-bombing toucan. I wasn't sure where it had come from but waiters frantically swatted it from the buffet. The traumatized parrot, trying to balance on a floating keg, had self-edited his "Welcome to Schott's pirate party" line and now said "Welcome to *Shoot's penis* party."

Funny though, guests were partying harder than ever. They waded and splashed as if this was all part of Schott's party plan. Mustaches, pirate hats, and plastic skeletons drifted past their waists. Many had thrown caution to the wind by tossing their paper cups and grabbing up *glass* glasses again. These still intermittently slipped from guest's hands but instead of smashing onto the granite floor, they sunk below the waterline with a *glug, glug.*

Meanwhile, several pirates were performing a hilarious water ballet near the gift shop and inebriated Tinker Bells were doing cannonballs off the gangplank.

Good news. The water seemed to have stopped rising.

Even better, the chief had covered up, albeit with a stiff tapestry gift shop robe. One that flopped open each time he tried to reassemble his now floating chocolate trolley.

The best news was that so far everyone looked fine. No symptoms had hit yet.

I sure hoped it was because of the WD-40.

***

"Here we are," Candace said, pointing at rain-shrouded Cranmont Manor.

"You are the best," I said, repositioning my hand on the helicopter's curved door handle.

Candace had made great time. I was sure we'd beat the others to Cranmont, but would it give me enough time to stop this whole thing?

I wiped the steamed-up side window for a better view of Cranmont Tower. The uneven rain seemed to be the heaviest there. The helicopter's headlight scanned the scaffolding at the top. Then it highlighted the small arched window halfway down before shining on the tower's single wooden entry door. Honestly, it reminded me of a prison break scene. All that was missing were armed guards searching for escaped convicts.

It was all about the tower.

Hidden in plain sight.

Brilliant.

Who knew?

Evidently Schott and Conrad did.

The fact that Kurt and Nunchuck were told to bring the controllers here had to mean command central was here too.

So much made sense now, like seeing tower lights from Mom's guest suite.

Not to mention, Conrad's hissy fit when I wanted to renovate the tower. And that boulder nearly squashing me at Conrad's wake. Those were about keeping me out.

If I had renovated the tower, I would have discovered computers and whatever else Conrad had kept hidden at the top. The fact that I stayed out in the first place was more proof of my mental imbalance at the time I married Conrad. If I'd been sane, nothing would have stopped me.

From the co-pilot's seat, I pointed at the open grassy area beside the tower. "Can you land there?"

"Might be tricky," Candace said, trying to maneuver into place. We were still ten feet off the ground as the copter violently bucked twice.

"Just hold it here," I said, wrenching open the door and leaning out into the wet, choppy air. Boy, it felt good. "I owe you one," I shouted.

As the helicopter dipped again, I leaped out. A cyclone of rain soaked me through as I dropped into wind-bent grass. My blousy shirt and pantaloons alternately clung and then whipped against my arms and legs. I couldn't see Candace through her rain-smeared pilot window, but I gave her a thumbs-up and then raced for cover under the trees.

Candace's helicopter was barely out of earshot when I pushed aside a mound of pine needles and unearthed my plumber's bag to do a quick inventory of tonight's tools.

> **Duct tape**—should never leave home without it.
>
> **Explosives and detonator**—courtesy of Kurt's beach house.
>
> **Mini hydraulic jack**—for the tightest of spots.

My tunnel's zip wire acsensor—not sure I'd need this one, but packing it felt right.

Mini bottle of Demolition Queen champagne—for if I got thirsty.

Last, but not least...the hammer returned to me in the flower arrangement at *Demolition Queen*'s Soho headquarters.

Mom's Knock 'em Dead hammer—ironic. Right?

The rest of tonight's plan was simple. Use Mom's alphanumeric to...

...avenge Mom's murder.
...save the who's who crowd at the V&A.
...save *ME*.

By my watch, I had one hour and twenty-nine minutes to do it.

My brain was spinning faster than a ripsaw as I slipped into Cranmont Tower and felt along the boulder wall. I wasn't expecting to find a light switch in this derelict tower. I definitely wasn't expecting the round dimmer switch my fingers pressed or the elegant wrought iron light fixture that lit up and cast a warm glow over the floor's smooth terracotta tiles and plush Oriental rug.

Geez.

Nothing derelict about the perfectly pointed mortar in the circular brick stairs that I sprinted up either. Even the cold metal rail I gripped was silky smooth.

I stuck to the outside of the wedge-shaped steps. I was in total darkness with the first full turn. I'd just made my third full turn when my pantaloons snagged on what felt like two planks crisscrossing a door-less entry. I peeked between the planks and was surprised to see the same Oriental rug from the lobby. In fact, it *was* the rug from the lobby. This particular room had no floor.

OK, so the building was a *little* derelict.

I looked up and was happy to see a ceiling. That boded well for a floor being up there too.

After twenty more dark steps, gusting rain smacked the side of my face but not because of another missing floor. I'd reached the arched window that Conrad and his cousin climbed through when playing

Sardines. Peering out through the rain, I could faintly see the top-floor nursery where those Sardines games used to start.

Moving on, I passed another empty room and began having doubts.

What if Nunchuck only mentioned the tower to get me out of the V&A?

But then Kurt and JJ wouldn't have sounded so worried about me heading to the tower.

Right?

Speaking of which, if they cornered me up here that would be bad.

"Know all your exits," I said, repeating one of Kurt's spy tips. I looked back down the stairs, by far my best option. The other, a metal ladder leading toward the roof, would truly suck.

Speaking of options, I had explosives. They'd make a great diversion. Although, to me explosives were on par with guns. Usually a no-go zone. Although if I found the master computer and Mom's alphanumeric *didn't* stop its countdown, I'd use the explosives to blow the shit out of that computer.

I darted my head through the very last doorway. I was relieved to see state-of-the-art equipment, perfectly pointed brick, and that super-long Snooker table I'd seen on those monitor's behind Old Mr. Albany's study wall.

This has to be it.

A blinking computer screen on a wooden drinks trolley across the room caught my eye and my shoulders didn't just tingle. They felt like a 220 volt wire had bored right into them.

Dropping my backpack and plumber's bag onto the table, I surged across the room. I bent over the trolley to examine the blinking dots and asked, "So are you the one that wants to kill me?"

"It depends," answered a male voice from the darkest end of the room.

Those two words made my heart pound against the cat puzzle in my bustier. I peered into the shadows. I was squinting down the long Snooker table when at the very end, lit by another computer screen, was a familiar face from the annex.

A *good* familiar face.

"Rock! What are you doing *here*?" I took one step toward him but was violently pulled back. I swung around with fists clenched, ready for a fight, only to discover that the splintered drinks trolley had snagged the ties on my bustier and wouldn't let go. Like a Chinese finger puzzle, the more I pulled the tighter the trolley gripped them. I would have used my knife except it was in my plumber's bag out of reach on the Snooker table.

And people wondered why I kept important stuff in my bra.

"Rock, have you got a knife?" I asked.

He shook his head and jangled handcuffs identical to the ones I wore at the V&A. His were threaded through the Snooker table's corner pocket.

"One hour, twenty-five minutes, and counting." Schott's jovial voice blasted the silence and I froze.

How the heck did he get here so fast?

Rock held a finger to his lips and pointed at his computer screen. Good thing I'd got stuck across the room, otherwise Schott would have seen me.

I watched his reflection in the glass cabinet behind Rock and recognized Esher High Street out his limo window. The limo was plowing through a crosswalk where pedestrians, who dared cross on the WALK command, hopped out of the Hookmobile's way as it loudly *ticktock*'d.

He was nearly to Cranmont.

"Rock, thanks to you, the Lord Mayor of London will very soon be on his knees and that high-and-mighty Lady Wolverhampton will swoon in the queue for swashbuckling lessons," Schott said with glee.

With renewed anger, I focused on freeing myself from the drinks trolley. If I unplugged the computer, I could roll the trolley to the snooker table and get my knife to cut my ties. I bent over and wrapped my fingers around the plug.

"It's a pity…" Schott said, in a quiet solemn voice.

Is that regret I hear?

Is Schott having second thoughts?

"…to not personally witness all those deaths," Schott said. "But it's the thought that counts," he added with a sinister cackle.

Schott showing regret? What was I thinking?

With that, I yanked the power cord from the wall and rolled the trolley, *with computer*, to the other side of the Snooker table. Schott's voice repulsed me so much, I was happy that he'd stopped talking.

"Sam, what did you do?" Rock asked in a mystified tone.

"What do you mean?" I asked as I cut my satin ties, jogged to his side, and stared at Rock's blank screen. "What *did* I do?"

"You made Schott disappear," said Rock.

"Cool" I said, but then noticed something not so cool on another of Rock's screens.

On it, a man was running along a dark, muddy tunnel with a heavy pack pounding his broad rigid shoulders. He leaped over a wide pile of something I couldn't make out and kept on going.

"Who the heck is that?" I asked.

"I don't know," Rock said.

"OK then, *where* is that?" I asked.

"Don't know that either," Rock shrugged as we both watched the man in near darkness, dodge puddles and slick spots. There must have been dozens of cameras in that tunnel because the camera angle changed as the man jogged left or right with familiarity and finally pushed away creeping overhead roots before pulling up sharply at a dead end.

Looking back at Rock, I asked, "OK. So why are you here?"

"Schott wanted me here in case of any last-minute snafus," Rock said. "He's going to kill me after all this."

"That's not going to happen," I said, hugging Rock's shaking shoulders.

I hoped not anyway.

"Why is Schott coming here and not watching people die at the party?" I asked.

Rock shrugged and said, "He's watching from here."

"Answer me this, if Schott's patches are programmed to kill everyone tonight, why do they need controllers?" I asked.

"The guy's a sicko. He wanted the option to kill his guests individually using their controllers," he said.

I scrunched up my face.

"I know," Rock said.

"I've got all the controllers," I said.

Rock looked like he didn't believe me.

"I stole them from the V&A," I said and turned to go grab the backpack. "I'll short circuit them and stop the whole process."

"No!" Rock stood, looking visibly shaken. "The controllers are controlled by the master computer. If you kill the controllers the computer might go ahead and kill the people."

"You're kidding me. Why?" I asked.

"The computer issues the final killing sequence. I know it sounds like overkill, because it is. Added safeguard in case the controllers didn't work," Rock said.

I pointed at the screen in front of Rock that I *hadn't* unplugged. It not only showed the 3-D V&A floor plan, like Kurt's, but it also had a 3-D globe with blinking dots in foreign lands.

"At the V&A when Schott said, 'I'd like to remember those who couldn't be with us tonight,' he wasn't talking about the dearly departed, was he?" I asked, pointing at the globe.

"No, he was talking about classmates abroad," Rock said, finishing my sentence. "Schott pre-patched those who couldn't come to his pirate party."

"Geez. So, is this the master computer?" I asked.

"I think so," Rock said and gave a hesitant nod.

"If I stopped it, would all the killing stop?"

He nodded again, but the way his freckly nose squinched up didn't fill me with heaps of confidence.

"OK. Well, let's try this first," I said, undoing the bottom of my bustier. I pointed a finger at the letters and numbers beside my tattoo.

"Your Mom's alphanumeric?" Rock's ecstatic face filled me with hope.

"Read it off while I'll type it in," I said.

Rock awkwardly tilted his head and finally laid it on the corner pocket to read the alphanumeric above my hip. "First there's a *K* and then a *2*. Next a *W*. No. Wait. I think that's an *M*."

I checked my watch.

01:22:06

"You think or you know?" I asked through clenched teeth. I backspaced to erase the *W* and then waited with my slightly shaking pointer finger hovering over the *M*.

"*W* definitely *W*," Rock stuttered.

After several more backspaces and deletes, we double-checked the two-inch-high alphanumeric that stretched across the screen.

K2W49MUEP>>>XXQ8U01BB57LF88

"Here goes," I said and hit ENTER.

A full minute later, with one hour and twenty-one minutes to go, the countdown stopped. One by one, the dots on the V&A map *and* the 3-D globe stopped blinking.

In fact, the whole screen went blank.

I'd expected something more dramatic to flash onscreen, like, "Game Over—Resume Life," taking a line from Conrad's Snood game. But hey, I could live with less dramatic.

Rock fell back in his chair and wiped his brow.

I didn't realize I'd been holding my breath until the used-up air burst from my lungs.

But a second later, I was holding my breath again as a horrible thought occurred to me. What if the dots *not blinking* meant that everyone had just died?

I frantically scanned the screen that showed the V&A foyer and breathed easy again. Partiers looked normal. Well, as normal as they could dressed as pirates and fairies with water up to their knees.

It seemed so odd that guests weren't jumping for joy about their lives being spared.

The lucky devils had no clue.

CHAPTER SIXTY-ONE

"Thank you, Mom," I said to the ceiling. This was a thousand times better than any demolition ever. "We did it," I added, as I looked down at Rock.

"With over an hour to spare," Rock exclaimed. He tried to low-five my hand but with his wrists still cuffed to the corner pocket that didn't work too well. Then he frowned.

"What's up? You should be ecstatic," I said.

"Schott will still be here any second," he said, shaking his handcuffs.

"You worry too much." I slapped him on the back. "OK. Let's get you out of here."

Poking around in my bag, I pulled out my mini hydraulic jack. Rock looked skeptical as I wedged it into the Snooker table's corner pocket.

"This baby could lift a Humvee," I repeated its marketing line and switched it on. The quiet ratcheting sound wasn't remarkable, but the way it ripped off the corner pocket impressed the heck out of me. Most importantly, Rock was free, albeit still handcuffed.

"Thank you, Sam," said Rock. His awkward hug felt good even with his handcuffs cutting into my neck. "It's the first time I've really been free in—"

"Get out of here. Go to my barn at the bottom of the hill and use the metal cutters in my workshop. You know where you're going?" I asked Rock, who was already halfway out the arched doorway. His quick nod wasn't convincing. Did it really matter?

"I'll meet you at the barn. I've got something to do first," I said.

As Rock's rapid footsteps receded in the circular stairs, I was so psyched I couldn't help talking aloud. "Mom, I solved your ultimate puzzle. It's over. I'm safe. Rock's safe. The V&A crowd is safe. Even Schott's traveling classmates are safe." Pause. "I'm so sorry I doubted just a little bit of the total brilliance of your plan."

I was still grinning when I slung my plumber's bag over one shoulder. *But* as I lifted Kurt's backpack onto the other, my warm and fuzzy feelings went right out the proverbial window. A quiet ticking sound was to blame. My shoulders stiffened. I surveyed the dim room, looking for a ticking clock, even a cuckoo. But only racks of Snooker cues and squares of blue chalk lined the walls. I shrugged and headed for the door.

That's when I realized the ticking sound was following me, *on my shoulder.* Rushing back to the Snooker table, I ripped open Kurt's backpack. Masses of ticking MedMaker controllers flashed at me. Worse than that, across the room, Rock's computer made a whirring sound like it was rebooting.

In the next miniscule slice of time, it was as if I'd been lifted and transported to the computer, because I didn't remember moving, but I was there. I watched horrified as, one by one, Kurt's dots and names reappeared on the V&A *and* 3-D globe images.

Worse than that, everyone's one hour and sixteen minutes of "time till death" had been cut in half, *including mine.*

Had the controllers gone haywire?

"Shit." *Sorry, Mom.*

If the clock was right, only thirty-eight minutes remained.

I unconsciously reached for that spot above my hip, worried I'd incorrectly copied the alphanumeric from the back of the cat puzzle. *Double-check it.* I ripped the duct-taped cat puzzle from my bustier and was horrified once more. Its inked letters and numbers were now smeared in my cleavage.

Darn. Darn. Darn.

Maybe I got Mom's alphanumeric right and it just didn't work.

I dumped out Kurt's backpack, hoping something in there could help. I lined up all the controllers across the Snooker table. Moving from left to right I read their labels. Nothing jumped out at me until the second to the last one. My hand faltered as I picked it up and dragged my thumb across the part of the label that read, "S. Albany."

And then I heard, *Ticktock. Ticktock.*

Schott's Hookmobile sounded from somewhere near the front gates.

Shoot. Shoot. Shoot.

Think Sam.

Maybe this wasn't the main computer. What if there was another one where Mom's alphanumeric *did* work?

"Mom, I need more help here," I pulled out my slightly soggy cheat sheet.

~~Mom's Wood Gift Box~~
~~An eye for an eye~~
Dansnurmur
~~Xenan~~
~~Cats are an Puzzle~~
~~Mom's MedMaker chip~~
~~Metal Disc from Mom's safe~~
~~Polyporphyrin Balls~~
~~IMd~~
~~Plastic kid's Cat Puzzle~~

Only *Dansnurmur* was left and I'd had no luck figuring it out so far. Things were looking worse and worse.

Ticktock.

Ticktock.

Schott was rounding the manor.

If he trapped me up here, no amount of clues would help. I began stuffing controllers back into the backpack at a furious pace. This time, they didn't all fit. The last couple I put into my plumber's bag, along with the S. Albany one.

That's when, *honest to goodness*, the explosives, in my bag, spoke to me. *Blow up that damn computer,* they said.

Really, they said *damn*.

I knew nothing about explosives, but I decided that one-quarter of what I took from the beach house would do the trick.

I knew I could detonate using my phone so tested that first *without* attaching the wire. I typed *###* on its keypad and hit ENTER. Immediately, the word *kaboom* flashed across the detonator's small screen.

I took that as a good sign and pushed the detonator and explosives into an intact corner pocket beside the computer.

Then I got out of there. I was flying down the circular stairs. I was going so fast that as I heard *ticktock, ticktock* right outside the small arched window, I was three more steps down before I could latch onto the metal handrail and stop myself. That's when I heard and felt metal hitting metal. Either Schott's sword and/or Nunchuck's gold gun were hitting the railing. I was not in the mood to see either one, and definitely not both.

Damn.

A shot of adrenaline rushed through me. Bizarrely, it brought on the most amazing clarity about Mom's final unsolved clue. *Dansnurmur.* I knew without a doubt that it would tell me where to find the master computer.

"Dans" meant *in*.
"Mur" meant *wall*.
"Nur" meant *nursery*.
In nursery wall.

As in *Conrad's* nursery wall on the manor's top floor. Coincidentally, I'd just glimpsed lights shining through its window.

Too bad my moment of clarity hadn't included running like all get-out. *Because* next I saw a flashlight, the top of Schott's plumed hat, and Nunchuck's shaved head only ten steps below.

Hugging my plumber's bag and Kurt's backpack to my chest, I raced back upstairs but not into the computer room. Getting trapped in there would be suicidal and, come to think of it, probably homicidal.

The ladder to the roof was my only option.

So much for clarity.

By the time Schott and his sword reached the top landing, I was perched in the shadows on the ladder's top rung with shoulders pressed against the roof hatch. I was breathing like a maniac, but between Schott's huffing and puffing and Nunchuck's squeaky Naugahyde coat, they couldn't have heard me.

They couldn't see me either for all Schott's plumes.

"Where is Rock? Where are my controllers? Where are you?" Schott screeched from inside the room without taking a breath.

Go to Schott. Go to Schott. Go to Schott. I telepathically urged Nunchuck inside but he just cradled his gun and stayed rooted to the spot. Obviously, he hadn't told Schott about the controllers going missing *or* who took them.

Finally he moved inside but it was too late for me. The man from the tunnel was charging up the stairs.

With a feeling of despair and only thirty-three minutes left, I pushed the hatch open and crawled out onto the dark flat roof. Wind and rain hit my face like a power washer. Couldn't see a thing. I stretched my arms out in front to feel for scaffolding poles. One step…reach…another step…reach…another step…

It felt like forever. Forever I *didn't* have.

With step five, my palm finally smacked a horizontal rain-slicked pole. Then hand over hand, I moved along it. I knew I was getting close to the roof's wall because a strong vertical wind lifted my soaked hair. I also knew because a halogen light popped on behind me and lit up the roof.

I had to dive behind a wet stack of roofing materials, ripping my pantaloons and my knees.

"Ms. Samantha, I know you're here," Schott's sugary sweet voice oscillated in the rain. "Dearest, you really should come in out of this horrid weather. We'll chat."

I could tell he didn't know exactly where I was because he was talking to a spot way to my left.

Good.

I snaked further to the right and was looking straight out the newest three-foot gap in the tower's wall. *Surprise. Surprise.* My long-lost crowbar was lying beside it. No doubt used to pry out that boulder. I slid it into my plumber's bag thinking I might need it later.

Without any warning, lightning crackled overhead like Fourth of July fireworks. It occurred to me that I was holed up in a veritable lightning rod forest of metal scaffolding poles. I needed to get off this roof. I could climb out one of the missing-boulder gaps but there was that pesky bottomless ravine if I fell...

"Ms. *Demolition Queen*, I want my controllers," Schott bellowed over the howling wind. His voice had not a hint of faux sweetness this time. "Don't be like your friend Max and die trying to stop me," he said while moving further away from the door.

Schott had one thing right. I was not going to die. Not if I had anything to do with it.

Still hidden by roofing material, I inched past scaffolding poles and toward the door. Kurt's backpack and my sopping wet plumber's bag slowed me down, but as Schott looked the other way, I was ready to make a break for it.

I probably would have made it too, but my damn emergency foghorn ringtone sounded. As Felicity shouted, "Sam!" a shadow fell across my bleeding knees.

"A paging service? How splendid." Schott sneered as rain dripped from his nose like an eye-dropper.

"How else would you find me you loser..." I stopped short as my heart felt like drywall screws were starting to work their way into it.

"Oh goody. It's started," Schott said, as I clutched my chest. "In a very short while, you will suffer a massive heart attack. Quite fitting." He paused to watch me with bright eyes. "Like mother, like daughter."

Like mother, like daughter.

Exactly.

Because, like my mom, I had a brilliant backup plan. *A humdinger.*

I shielded my eyes to keep the rain out, but more importantly to spot the guide wire between the tower and the nursery.

Keep him talking, Sam.

"I can't believe you're killing off those people at the V&A," I said. With one hand still on my heart, the other located the zip wire acsensor in my bag. "All this time I thought you were a random-acts-of-kindness kind of guy."

"I go way back with those scurrilous sods, and believe me, getting rid of them *is* an act of kindness," Schott said. His loud chuckle ended in a hysterical wheeze.

"So your school prank vendetta is true? How pitiful is that?" I laughed at him.

"I like to call it proactive," Schott said, wiping raindrops from his eyes. "You know, for such a pretty face you've certainly been more trouble than I would have thought possible."

I heard a laugh behind him.

"Obviously, you don't know her as well as I do," said Kurt smugly, as he climbed out of the roof hatch and closed it.

Of course. Kurt was the man in the tunnel.

"I am so very glad you could join us," Schott said.

"I found the controllers hidden downstairs," Kurt said and then casually glanced at me.

Was I delusional?

I felt for the bags at my side. They were still there and with the controllers inside.

Please don't tell me there's another set.

"We've replaced a shorted-out board, so we're ready to roll," Kurt said, shaking rain from his spiky hair as he waved Schott over.

"Excellent," Schott said, excitedly clapping his hands and walking toward Kurt.

With his back turned and blocking Kurt's view, I wasted not a millisecond.

I jumped onto the tower wall, I clamped my zip wire acsensor onto the guide wire, and I looped my wrist through its strap. All was good until out of the corner of my eye I saw the hatch re-open.

Nunchuck was climbing the last bit of the ladder as he stuttered, "She…she…she's getting away." Then he tripped, fell, and dropped his gun.

As his gun slid out of reach along the slick roof, I thanked the heavens that talking, climbing, and gun-aiming weren't in Nunchuck's repertoire.

Then I hit my acsensor's warp-speed button. Knowing that it would whisk me away at four feet per second, I felt cocky enough to tap my bag and say, "Bye, boys. Thanks for the controllers…"

Not so. The damned acsensor was putt-putting along at *snail*-speed. I was only nine feet from the tower as Schott screeched at Kurt, "Get my controllers."

Nine feet should be out of Kurt's reach I thought as he sprinted to the wall. I was wrong. He catapulted over the void and headed straight for me, wearing an excited hell-bent expression. When he latched onto my waist, my pruney fingers strained in the strap and arms practically tore from their sockets.

"Are you crazy?" I screeched at his head that was pressed against my cold, wet, bustier-encased ribs.

Kurt merely did a chin-up on my body. We were chest-to-chest. His cheeky grin to my pissed-off frown. His hot breath felt incredible on my cheek. But no time to enjoy it.

Nunchuck had retrieved his gun. Over Kurt's shoulder, I saw the flash of metal under the halogen lights. I tensed waiting for his shots. But when he and Schott instead sped toward the hatch and disappeared down the ladder, I was sure they were headed back inside to kill everyone right then.

Sam, blow up the computer. Now.

Looking straight into Kurt's eyes, I whisked out my phone and pressed *##*.

Immediately, a low rumble came from behind Kurt. A bit like thunder, but different. I looked around Kurt's head and saw just how different. A huge orange cloud poofed out around the tower, like an A-bomb cloud. It sent alternating waves of light and heat that warmed my rain-soaked clothes. The computer was definitely blown up, but from the looks of it so was the tower.

"Samantha Albany using explosives? I'm shocked. Isn't that against your demolition creed?" Kurt grinned at me even as another huge explosion rocked the wire.

Boy was I glad I hadn't used more explosives. Especially as my acsensor halted for no reason and left us swinging above the bottomless black ravine.

"You're grinning when I just blew up your friends," I said.

Then what I'd just said sunk in.

Ohmygawd. Schott and Nunchuck had to be dead.

Dead. I couldn't believe it.

Their killing spree was surely canceled now.

V&A guests were finally safe. So was I.

Yippee.

Kurt must have taken my smile as an invitation because he wrapped his legs tight around mine like some new Kama Sutra pose. Steely thighs sent heat through my damp pantaloons. His stare was all too much. It seared my crotch, flipped-flopped my stomach, and…*wait for it*…slammed the center of my chest. His lips were a breath away. His two-day-old beard even scratched my chin. Our bodies pressed together. They even vibrated.

Wait.

I got that wrong. Romance hadn't vibrated anything. Kurt's backpack was the source, which meant the controllers were still counting down. I took a quick peek at the countdown on one. *Twenty-six minutes.*

Twenty-six minutes might be all the time I have left on this earth…*with Kurt...*

Darn it, girl, pull yourself together. I gave myself a mental slap.

"I can't believe you're helping Schott kill all those innocent people," I shouted. I so wanted him to deny it.

"I don't think Schott's doing much of anything anymore," Kurt said, pointing at the flaming tower.

He didn't deny it.

He made a joke of it.

Kurt's a murderer.

Disgusted, furious, and murderous myself, I wanted Kurt off me. I scissor-kicked at his legs. I kicked again so hard that his hands slipped from my shoulders and his arms were once again clenching my waist.

Another lightning bolt crackled overhead and threw ghoulish shadows on his upturned rain-drenched face, as he asked, "How do you know those people were innocent?"

"Well I know my mom was innocent, and you had no problem killing her." I pushed down on Kurt's shoulders. His arms slipped to my calves. My wet black pantaloons were slapping his face.

"Now, that's kind of not true." He shook his head and spat the wet fabric from his mouth. "Sam, could you not do this?" He sounded so casual, as if asking me not to change the TV channel.

"Which part wasn't true, Mom being innocent or you killing her?" I didn't want to hear his response. I wanted him off me *now*. I kicked with all my might and felt a sudden lightness. I looked down at my feet where Kurt hovered for one beat. I thrust my hand at his, not sure whether it was to save him or catch the backpack he'd just snatched from my shoulder, but I was too late. His backpack, his chest, and then his head disappeared. His outstretched arm went last, sinking into murky darkness. I noticed an odd brightening of the air below as I shouted, "Kurt!"

But I quickly forgot about that as an even larger explosion rocked the tower and my wire flew up like a giant jump rope. Hanging on for dear life, I was at the top of its arc one second and dipping low the next.

All this time, zipping away from the tower, I'd kind of forgotten I was also zipping toward the massive and *very hard* manor.

Next, my wire jolted once more then went slack.

Now what?

I looked over my shoulder to see why.

Cranmont tower was *gone*.

I wasn't only zipping. Now I was falling *and* swooping too.

With this sucky combination, I calculated that I'd go splat halfway between the second and third floor windows in about ten more seconds.

A new Tambour headline flashed before me.

Sam Albany Makes a "Dent" in Cranmont Manor's 500-Year History

No way was I giving that sleazeball any more material. I hit my acsensor's power boost with everything I had.

"Come on, baby," I yelled.

It strained. It groaned and at finally pulled me up two measly feet so that boots first, I rocketed through ancient window glass, across the dining room, and into the far wall.

CHAPTER SIXTY-TWO

Dazed, I looked around Cranmont's dining room. I heard Felicity's voice talking like a newscaster, but I couldn't see her. It took me a minute to realize I was hearing the feed from her head-cam. Hitting the wall must have made my phone dial its number.

So now, I heard Felicity say, "We're here at the V&A, where at least a hundred guests have fallen ill while attending a private party…"

Fallen ill?

Dammit. That meant my WD-40 *hadn't* worked on everyone.

Although, she'd only said *"fallen ill."*

I'd take that over fallen *dead* any day.

Felicity continued, "Not thought to be food poisoning, it could be a highly contagious flu. We're keeping the dignitary-filled crowd as comfortable as possible. As this illness has not yet been identified we are under an indefinite quarantine."

I needed to keep moving. The tightness in my chest was still there but otherwise I was feeling OK. Nothing seemed broken. I couldn't say the same for the crooked wall before me. I hooked a finger around its edge, pulled it open, and realized I was staring at a hidden passageway. This floor's dumbwaiter was there too with its doors already open.

Cool.

I quickly checked the miniature "S. Albany" controller. *Yep. Still counting down even though…*

> The tower and computer were decimated.
> Max was in that man-sized tureen at the V&A.
> Schott, Nunchuck, and Kurt were dead.

So, who was keeping the countdown going?

JJ, the chocolate sharer?

Doubtful.

My next thought hit me like a sledgehammer.

What if no one was running this operation?

What if it was on autopilot?

If it was, that definitely supported my theory of another computer. "Dansnurmur," I whispered.

In the nursery.

Checking my watch, I had twenty-four minutes to get there, find that computer, and enter Mom's alphanumeric. *Simple.*

I bounded into the dumbwaiter and pushed the TOP FLOOR button. Like last time, one door rose from the floor and the other dropped but their rubber seals didn't gently kiss. They sucked shut with a *slurp* and the dumbwaiter took off like a rocket. It shot past Old Mr. Albany's study but then stopped so abruptly at the between-floor "Storage" slot that my feet left the floor.

I pressed the TOP FLOOR button over and over but all I got was a rattling sound. It was coming from the waist-high grate. I bent down, expecting the same trickle of water as last time. Instead, hot water gushed out with such gusto it flung me against the opposite wall. It covered my black boots in seconds. In less than a minute, it reached my knees.

I couldn't risk my phone or the controller getting wet so quickly tore off a strip of silver duct tape and climbed onto the bench. I was taping them to the dark wood ceiling when another startling pain cramped my chest. *Oh my gawd.* Moving made it hurt like hell but not moving would be way worse. Grabbing my mini jack, I managed to wedge it between the back wall and glass doors. Then I revved it up.

"You can do it," I said, urging it on at the exact moment the water surged and the jack went *phitz.*

My jack had died. My heart felt like it was being stomped on. Water was within a foot of my phone and controller. That meant my air supply was rapidly shrinking too.

"I am not drowning…in…a…friggin'…dumbwaiter," I shouted through gritted teeth.

I gulped three huge breaths and sunk below the surface to hand crank my jack. My lungs already wanted to burst. *One, two, and three…*I silently counted cranks to keep me going…*four, five, six…*I was about to pass out…*seven, eight…*and the glass shattered.

Huge silvery bubbles floated past my face. Water belched out the broken doors. I was free but as I ripped my things from the ceiling, pulled off the duct tape, and caught a glimpse of my phone's timer, I wasn't feeling so celebratory.

00:18:11

The demonic dumbwaiter had taken four of my precious minutes. I briefly paused to put a small bit of duct tape back on the controller. *That might come in handy very soon.*

Grabbing my drenched plumber's bag, I extended one leg through the jagged glass door opening. As I did, my damn pantaloons pulled glass shards free that clattered to the basement without missing a pipe, threshold, or beam. If someone *was* in the nursery and didn't know I was on my way before, they sure did then. *No more pantaloons for me, ever.*

I climbed into the shaft above the dumbwaiter and pulled myself up into the linen closet. I crawled through the fireplace and then out into the nursery. With plumber's bag dragging along behind, I moved to the center of the dark wood floor. My bag left a wet trail which glowed orange from remnants of the fiery tower remains, barely visible through the soot-streaked terrace doors.

Time till death was getting uncomfortably close, so I was psyched to find no one in the nursery. I didn't need any more disruptions. Although, if I was going to die, I was going to die happy. I pulled out my champagne bottle, popped it open, and took two quick swigs. Then I thought about the secret Conrad's cousin had told me at the wake. "Our favorite hiding place was a hidden compartment in the nursery."

Dansnurmur.

In nursery wall.

"OK, so which wall?" I whispered as I placed my bottle beside my bag and grabbed my Knock 'em Dead hammer.

The room was so dark, much darker than the first time I was here. So it took a while to scan the walls for indentations, seams, or anything. I halted on the frolicking stallion wallpaper between the terrace doors. Someone had 'stabbed' each and every horse with a drawn-on fluorescent dagger. Wide-eyed, I studied the jagged, gruesome constellation. *How twisted is that?*

But, I noticed something even more disturbing over the Albany blanket chest. Last week two tasseled crisscrossed swords hung there. Now, one was missing. I silently hoped the housekeeper was giving it a *right old polish* and not the alternative. Someone hiding in the nursery about to use it on me. I didn't need any more time wasters.

Ignoring the new tingling in my chest, I climbed onto the nearest sleigh bed to tap the wall with my hammer. I'd just found a hollow-sounding spot when an even more unbearable pain gripped my chest and I slumped against the curved headboard, gasping for air.

Oddly, in this shutdown state, I noticed things that hadn't registered before. Such as, the nursery lights that I'd seen from the tower weren't on anymore.

Plus, Vivaldi's staccato violins were playing. Ironically, at that moment I'd have much rather heard Led Zeppelin than Conrad's favorite. I tried to get up. I wanted to see where the music was coming from, but another sharp pain, *not* in my chest, forced me back down. This pain was in my side. It was coming from the tip of that tasseled nursery sword I'd wondered about.

Next, something knocked my hammer from my hand, and I heard it skitter across the room.

I saw the brim of a wide black pirate hat above me and heard, "Darling, don't get up."

I didn't.

Not because of the pain.

Not because I was shocked to hear his voice, because I *wasn't*. I'd figured out he was the Boss.

I didn't get up, because I was staring at the painting of Winchester's Grand Day. It was lifting like an awning on a camper van, perpendicular to the wall. Behind it was a narrow alcove, lined with computer screens, just like the ones behind Old Mr. Albany's study wall.

The largest screen at the back had hundreds of bright multicolored taunting faces like the "game" Snood from Conrad's computer. It also had red blinking foot-high numbers.

00:15:27

I finally looked up at the smiling face of the Boss, shadowed under the hat.

"I knew you wouldn't let anyone else run this little operation," I said to him. "Snood was your cover for communicating with Schott, wasn't it, Conrad?" I asked my *husband*.

I was trying to sound intrigued not accusing. Pissing Conrad off never did anyone any good.

It worked. Conrad looked pleased and impressed as he nodded.

"And Cranmont Tower was just a decoy that you devised so that Schott thought he was running the show, right?" I asked.

This time Conrad smiled and tapped the tasseled hilt of his sword against the bed as if to say, "Bully!"

"Very clever," I added. "You faked your death in the steam room so well too. Let me guess, you had your own MedMaker chip that you programmed to slow your heart rate enough to appear dead. Then when I pushed the steam room's emergency button, *that you'd rigged*, it alerted your handpicked medic. He appeared. He pronounced you dead. He was also your minister. Correct?"

Conrad nodded and smiled again.

His plan was brilliant, *sick*, but brilliant.

"So you were not surprised to see me?" He tried to stroke the top of my head.

I could pretend to play nice, but Conrad touching me was too much. I pushed off the sleigh bed. I held on as I rounded its footboard, trying to look steadier than my impending heart attack was making me feel.

"At first you fooled me. I thought for sure you'd died," I said in a chirpy tone. I quickly frowned to try and cover my tone. I was too late.

Conrad's lips twitched. He began to pace too. From bed to terrace doors and back to the bed he went. He only hesitated long enough to kick my champagne bottle out onto the balcony.

OK, so I pissed him off. Playing nice is out.

"Tell me." He tapped his sword against his open palm. "I am *dying* to know where I slipped up." He emphasized "dying" the same way Schott had at the V&A. Same cynical tone too.

I was pretty sure he didn't really want to know, *so* I told him. I wanted him off guard. I knew pacing alongside would tick him off too, so I did that as well, my long legs matching stride for stride.

"Let's see. There were so many ways. It's hard to know where to start," I said and flicked my hair over my shoulder.

I reached the bed and turned, happy to see that what I'd said made him stop by the terrace doors. If the glare in his cement-gray eyes was on laser, I'd have been vaporized.

I still had the floor, so I said, "First of all, you accessed your computer on the day of your own funeral." I'd guessed that from Kurt's and JJ's comments. But Conrad's surprised expression confirmed I'd been right. "That wasn't too smart." I rolled my eyes. "Plus the extra labels you slipped into Mrs. Party's pile were *your* friends—or rather, your enemies." I paused. "And you stole Mom's Matisse. Very bad taste, I might add." I shook my head. "A huge risk for only a fake. Mom knew you were up to something. She'd already switched out the real Matisse with the fake in the guest room."

His bug-eyed surprise was so gratifying. I wanted to see that look up close and paced back to the doors.

"Others could have done that," he said, in a tight but close to bursting voice. He slapped his sword against his hand so hard he grimaced.

Perfect. Just the mood I was going for.

I'd never seen him this flipped out.

"Whatever," I said with a smile. "Then your cologne left purple fingerprints all over Mom's and Max's office too. Not to mention your own study."

"Max—"

"Yes, it could have been Max, but if he went rifling through your desk, he sure wouldn't leave his birth certificate behind." I let that one sink in. "Ironically, I found one of the most convincing clues in the tower tonight."

One eyebrow arched, and his lips pursed as if he didn't believe that was possible.

"Has to do with DNA, my boy." I emphasized "boy" because I could. "But you probably know more about DNA than me these days."

"Yes, I guess I do," he said.

He looked sad as he pulled from his breast pocket one of my thin black fan belts. The one I'd stupidly left during tonight's annex visit. I shrugged, casually took it, and pulled my hair into a ponytail, out of the way for later.

I expected him to gloat, so when he angrily pointed at the fan belt, I was thrown off guard. "Schott got your DNA tonight from one strand of hair off that thing. So he knew you'd been at the annex and hadn't died yet," he shouted. "Samantha, how idiotic could you be?" Next, Conrad sighed. "I tried protecting you as much as I could." His anguished tone confused me. When he rested his forehead on the side of my head, I was gobsmacked.

"My darling Samantha, I would have given you anything," he whispered, caressing my forearm. "But you wanted him. You went straight back to *him*." His hand tightened, squeezing my arm to bits.

I wrenched my arm away and rubbed it to get the blood flowing again. "Geez. My life would be so much easier if my ex-partners *stayed* dead," I said.

Conrad's face transformed. The soft lines around his frowning eyes and lips lifted. A jagged laugh started in his throat and cackled through rigid smiling lips. They looked like the Joker's lips in *Batman*.

OK, that's disturbing.

"At least you got half your wish tonight." Conrad pranced to the balcony doors and kicked them open. "Somewhere at the bottom of my ravine is your Kurt or Jake, whichever name you whisper into his ear."

My fingers automatically moved to my frowning lips.

In one lightning-swift move, Conrad flicked my hand from my mouth. "I never understood that look until I heard you talk about the love of your life and this matching tattoo," he said. Then he lowered his sword to the bottom of my bustier. Like a needle scraping my side, it began to lift my bustier. I pushed it away and sidestepped so he wouldn't see the alphanumeric.

"Shame, really." Conrad's voice turned light, almost gossipy. "Kurt and I had much in common. Women, for starters, or should I say *woman*? In addition, as you pointed out, neither of us really died when we 'died,' *except,* for tonight," he said with a maniacal laugh that started and stopped in one breath. "I never had a chance. Did I?"

It wasn't really a question. More like an accusation.

Then he actually beamed.

It was hard to keep up.

"I am pleased you found my secret passage." He paused. "Mother never guessed. She locked me in here, and a split second later, I would ride the dumbwaiter down to the basement kitchen and race through the tunnels." His smiled disintegrated. Shoulders dropped. His narrowed eyes went wet-cement-gray. "I almost lost Cranmont when Mother drained its accounts. Most likely her plan," he said and pointed at Winchester's portrait.

I peeked at my watch.

00:11:48

Conrad's longwinded explanation was going to kill me, *literally*.

"That painting was Mother's constant reminder to me of how I murdered her precious baby. He didn't deserve to die," Conrad said, and swung his sword in its direction.

I was about to sidestep in case he swung back in my direction, but what he said next stopped me cold.

"But Mother did deserve to die. That part was easy," Conrad muttered his murder confession. "She never loved me. Never!" he screamed and then shrieked in what I guessed was his interpretation of his mother's voice. "You were supposed to stay in your room."

Geez.

I was worried he might mistake me for dear old Mum and kill me right then. I didn't realize I'd been backing away until my legs hit the blanket chest. Good thing too. He'd begun slashing at an invisible attacker.

He's loony tunes...

And then, just like that, he was back, saying, "Your Mom was in here several times during that week she stayed. Behind the wall in my study too. The last time was during the fundraiser."

Aha. So that's where Mom went.

"She tried to fool me by switching surveillance tapes that night, but she botched it up. Hers had no balloons. I used the dumbwaiter to follow her." Conrad looked over his shoulder at the fireplace and then marched toward it, saying, "Like my old Sardine days, I watched from over here."

He was loving this.

While his back was turned, I silently went for the second sword. But the man had eyes in the back of his head. I'd barely taken it from the wall when he spun, charged, and slapped his sword against mine.

I was ready. I even smirked, "Oh, by the way, sorry about your tower." I nodded toward the door. "But you won't need it anyway."

He paused. He looked puzzled, not angry. "Excuse me? What are you thinking?"

"If I was to be truly honest, I'd have to say I was thinking..." I paused for a second. "That I liked you better dead," I added as I thrust my sword at Conrad's chest.

I underestimated him. *Not too smart.* Using one of Silverblade's signature moves, Conrad knocked my blade aside and dug his into my ribs. He backed me up with it until the balcony doorframe hit me square between the shoulders. Then he wrenched my sword away.

OK, so maybe Silverblade was right about more boot camp.

"You know your social life is ruined, right? I'm sure the powers-that-be strip murderers like you of their in-line-to-the-throne rankings." I was trying to get him off guard again so I wasn't happy when he chuckled at that.

"Oh, I have given my reentry a lot of thought," he said. "First of all, tonight's murders were untraceable. That's the beauty of the MedMaker bioweapons. If questions are asked, Mrs. Party will take the fall." He paused, laughed and enthusiastically continued. "Plus, my life will be so much simpler without you," he said as he went to the balcony's thick stone railing and heaved my sword over. "You see I will explain that *you* faked my death, held me hostage, and stole my money." He paused. "I'm trying to decide if I should kill you right this minute in self-defense." He paused again to think about that. "Hmm. Everyone will agree that I am so much better off without my crazy, cheating, tattooed wife. Tambour's little stories about you have been invaluable in that department. Money well spent." He pressed his sword hard into my shoulder and sneered as I winced.

"OK, then how about Prunella? She knows what you did with her accounts. You going to kill her too?"

"As we speak," he said, pointing toward the alcove's V&A screen.

He must have become bored with the topic because he sliced the air twice and then took an en garde position. He also eyed the rain that hammered the balcony and splashed onto the nursery's dark wood floor.

I looked too, but not at the rain. I looked at what was between me and the rain. My sopping wet plumber's bag. It was sagging like a tired puppy in the center of the room. I took one small step in its direction. Conrad must have guessed I was up to something because he began circling me and my bag. I turned with him. I also slowly moved closer to my bag, until I was near enough to hook its strap with my boot.

"You know this whole bioweapon idea was mine," Conrad gloated. "I dropped anonymous hints about it to Max, and he became my unwitting pawn. Then I blackmailed his guilty little arse."

True confessions?

Not a good sign.

He must think I'm history.

Think again, bud.

"I kept Cranmont's creditors at bay with funds from Prunella's HFNC and MedMaker Corporation. My art sales helped too, but I still need the massive bioweapons payout to keep my precious Cranmont," he said calmly.

"Payout? Ha. Schott can't pay you now. He's dead." Expecting a panicked expression or at least a crestfallen one, I was unsettled to see his smirking smile.

"Schott? Schott's paltry payment was insignificant compared to what my new buyers are about to pay. Especially after tonight's little V&A demonstration," he said, checking his watch, "in only eight minutes and twenty-five seconds."

I waited until I was sure he was watching me, and then I moved the foot that I'd looped through the strap to pull open my plumber's bag. Conrad immediately spotted the S. Albany controller I'd put on top. He leaned down, and took it out.

"Who'd pay that kind of money?" I laughed at him, pretending not to notice he'd grabbed the controller.

"Several governments which are extremely tired of pouring trillions into money-devouring wars with nothing to show for them. MedMaker bioweapons are cheaper and much tidier," he said, then focused on the controller. "What have we here?" he asked, running a finger over the controller's *S. Albany* label.

He looked pleased, at peace even. So it was easy to snatch the controller away from him. I expected anger. I didn't expect him to backhand my cheek. It spun me away like a top. My hair wrapped around my face as I slammed into the rocking horse and landed by its creaking runners. I was raking it away from my eyes as Conrad stood over me and straddled my waist.

"Now be a dear and pass that controller up to me," he said. He also accentuated each word by tapping his sword on the skin an inch above my right breast. I held on tight. That was *until* Conrad leaned on his sword and his blade sank into my flesh. My hand involuntarily let go and moved to the warm blood pooling between my breasts.

"S. Albany?" Conrad read the controller's label once more as he buoyantly walked to the open terrace doors. "How serendipitous," he said. Even though the brim of his hat still shadowed his face, I knew he was smiling. "I need to get rid of you, and I get to push the button."

While he exulted in his good fortune, I did a backward crawl to my crowbar. I grabbed it and silently rolled onto all fours. Next, I reached for my Knock 'em Dead hammer, so that a second later, I smacked my crowbar against his sword along with a hammer chaser.

Unfazed and still sneering, Conrad slipped the controller into his breast pocket and riposted with a bored look. "You're using Silverblade's moves on me? My dear, this is a catastrophic waste of time," he said with a laugh.

"We'll see," I said. My crowbar's next parry thudded against the fine metal of Conrad's sword. He chuckled and responded with Silverblade's second attack and then added his own dig into my forearm.

"That worked beautifully. Don't you think?" He pointed at the blood streaming down my arm.

"Uh-huh." I nodded and tilted my head. My arm completely killed, but I smiled just to ramp up his anger. I also circled so that I faced the open balcony doors and he didn't. "But Silverblade liked me better. He'd never teach you this," I said and lunged. I swung my crowbar once under his blade and once over like in Silverblade's unbeatable move. Then I slammed my Knock 'em Dead hammer into his chest dead center. My attack, lightning swift and unexpected, sent Conrad pitching backward through the doors. He slipped *and* tripped on my champagne bottle and kept on going. He didn't stop until, straddling the wall, his arm hit the slick stone and his sword, just like mine, vanished in the mist.

His hat went too, so that rain splashed onto his black hair and ran down his cheeks. Heavy rain surrounded him like a dense steam, just like the day he 'died'.

Still straddling the wall, he pulled the *S. Albany* controller from his breast pocket. Hunched like a gargoyle, he sheltered it against his body. He squinted at me through the rain. Without even looking at the controller, he tapped in a password and aimed it at me.

"Darling, before you die, tell me, weren't you the slightest bit glad to see me?"

I tapped my chin with one finger as if I was really considering his question. Then with a light tone and a shrug, I said, "No."

"You ungrateful bitch!"

Conrad's venomous shout screwed up his face so tight I didn't recognize it.

"I should have ordered Kurt to kill you at the fundraiser like I had him kill your mother," he shouted and then gulped in the cold wet air and coughed. "But I get the last laugh, do I not? Your mother's brilliant invention will kill you now. Quite ironic."

He wiped rain from his eyes and then twirled his pointer finger to make a big deal about lowering it to the controller's activation button. He pushed it and looked up at me with an excited Cheshire cat grin.

However, when my expression didn't change, nor anything else about me changed, he angrily hit the box against his hand as if something was stuck.

With that, his left eyebrow arched. His entire body jerked like someone had just pinched his bum. His expression morphed from puzzled, to furious, and finally to nothing. Blank eyes rolled back in his head, and he slowly tilted away until his upper body fell below the top of the wall. He hung by one leg for a second. Then it was as if someone grabbed his arms and pulled, for his wing-tipped foot flipped up and sank out of view.

I ran out into the rain. I didn't look over the wall. Instead, I grabbed up the dripping blue controller. Then back inside the doorway, I dug my fingernail under the small rectangle of silver duct tape that I'd pressed on just to the left of the *S*.

Peeling it away now, I uncovered the name, *Conrad*.

I stared at the completed name, *Conrad S. Albany*.

"Conrad S. Albany done in by a bit of duct tape. Now *that's* ironic," I said, looking back to where he'd gone over.

The pouring rain was incredibly loud but I still heard a warning beep inside. I wheeled around. With an energy I didn't feel, I charged across the nursery and into the narrow alcove. My shoulders brushed screens on either side as I squeezed toward the last one at the back. The one whose tall red numbers, blinked…

00:05:48

A foot from the computer, an onscreen keyboard appeared. It floated below the blinking numbers and taunting Snood faces.

I could destroy this computer too, but what if *it* wasn't the master computer?

Mom had given me the alphanumeric for a reason and I was going to use it.

I pulled up the bottom edge of my bustier and examined the upside down alphanumeric I'd written above my hip.

My fingers tingled.

My nose twitched.

I angled my right side close to the screen to read it. Using the most careful, most deliberate strokes, I entered the whole code.

K2W49MUEP>>>XXQ8U01BB57LF88

I couldn't risk the countdown cutting in half again so I double-checked it.

Then I triple-checked it.

"Mom please, please, please let this be it," I said as my hand hovered over the ENTER key.

I felt its smooth curved plastic surface under my finger. I started to apply pressure, and then a bloody arm grabbed me around the waist.

"Hey!" I shouted as another arm reached over my shoulder and deleted Mom's alphanumeric.

As the arms dragged me out of the alcove, my shoulders bounced from screen to screen like a pinball until I stood between the twin beds.

"Would you just die already?" I screamed as Conrad grabbed my shoulders and twisted me around.

We stood bloody chest to bloody chest.

Except, it *wasn't* Conrad's chest.

It was *Kurt's* with what looked like straps of a mini-parachute still attached. *Aha.* The 'brightening' I saw below my feet as Kurt fell was a mini-parachute opening.

"Sorry to disappoint you, but what the hell are you doing?" Kurt shouted.

"Saving lives here. Now let me go," I said, elbowing his ribs.

"Your code won't stop the countdown." He pointed at my right side.

"That's what you'd like me to think." I smashed my boot onto his toes.

"Sam, believe me I am not the enemy," Kurt said, hopping from one foot to the other.

"The only thing I believe is that you definitely *didn't* kill Conrad," I shouted.

Kurt tensed and looked around the room.

"I hate to disappoint *you*, but he is not here," I said. "He's dead." *At least I hoped he was finally dead.* I nodded toward the balcony. "He said you killed my mom for him."

"And you believed him? Sam, Conrad did it," Kurt said, pulling at his hair.

"Prove it. Prove you didn't do it. The short version please," I said, checking the countdown.

00:04:13

"OK. OK. The day of the fundraiser, Rock sent electronic slides to your mom. They showed the virus that killed the Bolivian villagers. After one look, your mom knew the virus had been produced using her MedMaker gene technology. Someone had hijacked it and converted it to bioweapons. She was sure it was someone who knew her company inside and out, like Conrad or Max who first proposed the bioweapon option."

"This is the short version?" I raised my eyebrows. "Hurry up already."

"Recently I discovered that Conrad made controller #01A to override your Mom's MedMaker commands. The night of the fundraiser, Conrad realized that your Mom knew about the bioweapons. He knew it was just a matter of time before she confirmed he was behind it. So Conrad used controller #01A to kill her."

"Conrad was about to finish off Mom," I said to myself, vividly remembering Conrad's foul mood that night.

Kurt nodded. "Your mom knew that whoever it was would kill her. She wasn't afraid for herself. She knew her cancer was about to kill her anyway.

"She was so busy setting up clues for you she almost didn't go to the party. But then she received an anonymous threat on your life. She worried that by not attending, the killer, who we now know was Conrad, might panic and kill you anyway. Plus she desperately wanted to say goodbye."

"But you could have learned all of this from eavesdropping," I said angrily.

"OK, then what about this?" Sporting his best cut-the-crap look, Kurt kicked at my crowbar and flipped it into his hand. He executed six quick thrusts, parries, and ripostes to complete Silverblade's unbeatable move better and quicker than even Silverblade could.

"Where did you learn that?"

"Silverblade taught me," said Kurt.

Only taught one person, Silverblade had said before he taught *me.*

So that one other person had been Kurt?

"Impressive, but I need more," I said.

"Come on, *Sam,*" Kurt growled at me. "In Switzerland, I wasn't in that Zurich bar by accident. My agency was contacted by your mom. Because of MedMaker Corp's product development, she was worried about kidnappers and wackos like your Mousetrap Stalker. Who, by the way, was no wacko. Conrad hired him to 'stalk' you. Then Conrad killed him off in a way that implicated you. That way he could swoop in and clear your name for a murder you hadn't committed. You and your mom would be in his debt."

"You're enjoying this, aren't you?" I spun my hand in a circle to hurry him up.

"Your Mom also worried about the security of her technology. She knew that in the wrong hands it could be deadly. So as Jake, I went undercover to find out what if anything had been done to turn the MedMaker into bioweapons. I finally discovered what Max was up to *and* who else was involved. After that, I approached Conrad under the guise of helping him sell it. But I was there to find out how much further this had already reached. He insisted I prove my loyalty by first killing Jake. The murder you 'witnessed' in Switzerland."

Kurt talked so fast it was hard to keep up.

"If my mom trusted you so much, why didn't she just give *you* the codes?"

"Your mom thought you'd be safer if you held all the cards, or codes, in this case," Kurt said. She knew you'd figure it out.

I wanted to believe him, but something in me couldn't. I lurched around Kurt and dashed for the massive plasma screen. When the onscreen keyboard popped up, I typed fast and furious. I'd already input *K2W49MUEP>* when he said, "I know you took that envelope from my place marked *Sam.* The one with the photo inside."

Surprised, I looked over my shoulder at him.

"There was a letter too that I hid elsewhere. In it, your mom asked you, '*What was your most favorite puzzle ever?*'"

"The matchstick puzzle," I said without hesitation.

"Huh?"

"The matchstick puzzle on the Cracker Jack wrapper," I said, scrambling out of the alcove. "In Mom's will she'd said, *Sam, you crackerjack* but I stupidly ignored it." I paused to think. "How much time have I got?"

"One minute, forty two seconds," Kurt said as he moved out of my way.

"It's about soft focusing your eyes and moving words or, in this case, an alphanumeric closer and closer to your face, until your eyes cross. The middle letters then kind of go invisible. The crackerjack box puzzle was about two *U*'s coming together." I paused. "That's what Mom wants me to do with the alphanumeric. Make the letters between the U's go 'invisible'. We'll use only the letters and numbers between the U's."

00:01:14

Kurt looked confused.

I pulled up the bottom of my bustier to expose the alphanumeric. Kurt didn't even look surprised, as if he already knew it was there. "Are there any U's?" I asked, tilting my hip so I could see it too.

"Yep. Two of them."

Eyes darted toward the clock.

00:01:03

"Ok then, I'll read off everything except what's between the *U*'s," I shouted as Kurt rushed to the screen.

"Where's the keyboard?" he yelled.

Kurt's broad shoulders blocked the screen so I couldn't see what he was seeing.

"Quit kidding around," I yelled.

"I'm not kidding. How'd you make it appear?" he truly sounded puzzled.

"It popped on screen whenever I got close," I said then repeated Mom's words, *This one holds everything you'll need.* Kurt needed my knife.

00:00:50

"Kurt, catch," I yelled and tossed him my pink knife.

"We've got a keyboard," his ecstatic voice boomed from the alcove.

"You ready?" I asked.

"Go," he said.

"K-two-W-four-nine-M-U-U-zero-one-B-B-five-seven-L-F-eight-eight," I read.

"Here goes nothing," Kurt said. He pressed ENTER so hard the screen rocked.

I pictured Schott's V&A party guests *and* his dearly departed ones regaining consciousness. I could feel the euphoria of success starting to build inside. Kurt would turn and look at me, full of excitement.

But he didn't…

"It's still going," Kurt shouted.

"What? NO," I said and then added. "Please tell me the time didn't cut in half."

"Yes, it did," he said, giving me a queer look and then turning back toward the screen.

10...9...8...

"OK. OK. OK. Try this. Leave out the two *U*'s."

7...6...

"K-two-W-four-nine-M-zero-one-B-B-five-seven-L-F…" I said to Kurt but stopped short from completing the code as I felt a strange sensation near the stab wound on my arm. My eyes widened at a swirling, blackened patch of blood on my shoulder.

Shoot. Shoot and double shoot.

5...4...

"I need two more numbers. Sam!" Kurt barked.

3...2...

"Eight-eight," I screamed, ignoring the swirling blood.

Kurt typed and then pressed ENTER even harder than the last time. He had to grab the massive plasma screen to stop it falling over.

1...0

The blood which had reached the flat of my shoulder, stopped moving.

As Kurt leaned against the side of the alcove, I saw each and every onscreen Snood face morph into a beady red-eyed skull. Those familiar Snood game words flashed.

Game Over—Resume Life

Staring at the V&A screen, I willed those lumps to get up. I stood stock still. It felt like forever. Finally, one fairy wing fluttered. A sword rattled. Lump after lump started to stir. Felicity, who had not been affected, put a blanket around the Lord Mayor's shoulders. Lady Wolverhampton helped Prunella up. Silverblade was holding the Indian princess in his arms, *of course.* Mrs. Party, forever the partier, began handing out fresh champagne glasses.

I pictured those charging cells in Max's flat and wondered if they had sunk to the bottom of his Venetian vase.

I flopped onto the bed.

Kurt limped back out of the alcove and flopped onto the opposite bed.

"Sorry I doubted you about Silverblade teaching you his unbeatable move," I said.

"He didn't," Kurt grinned as he rolled onto his side and sat up.

"What? Then how did you…?"

"Remember when James drove you to Silverblade's? That really was me, disguised as James. Your Mom had died. You were a mess. I was worried about you, so I stuck around and watched." Pause. "How in the world did you figure out Conrad was still alive?"

"Max told me Conrad was a thief. When I finally believed it, I couldn't figure out who was running this show if Conrad was dead. Things didn't add up. When I dumped out your backpack full of controllers in the tower tonight, I found one for Conrad. I was guessing that Schott wouldn't have made one for a dead person. I also figured Schott didn't need Conrad after tonight so could save millions if he killed Conrad" I said.

"I'm impressed," Kurt said.

"Thank you and I also assumed that Conrad was the only one who knew to rig the gushing water in the dumbwaiter, so that clinched it."

"What?" Kurt asked.

"Nothing," I said and eyed Kurt/Jake. *Why was I talking about evil Conrad when Kurt/Jake was alive and a good guy? And oh-so-handsome.* But I didn't say anything nice.

"Your exit strategy sucked," I said, in a furious tone.

Kurt gave a matter-of-fact nod and said, "Yes, faking my death on a cliff side was bad, but—"

"Bad?" I reached over and slapped his cheek so hard he rocked backward.

"Yes, I deserved that." Kurt straightened and rubbed his cheek. He took a deep breath and stared at the ceiling as he said, "Once the whole Conrad/Schott crisis pulled me in there was no turning back. Best I could do was work with your mom and try to protect you, *against* your best efforts," he laughed. "Oh, and prevent the spread of the MedMaker bioweapons," he added and then took a deep breath. "It didn't help that you were more like me than anyone I ever knew. You unnerved me. You even made me fall in love with you," he said, grimacing. "I'd have given anything to avoid putting you through what you went through. I considered defying your mom and contacting you after I 'died.'"

"My mom?"

"Your mom told me to leave you alone," said Kurt.

"My mom wouldn't interfere like that." I thought for a second and tilted my chin down. *Or would she*?

"If it would make you feel better, slap me again." Kurt closed his eyes and leaned toward my bed.

"You do deserve another slap, but you sure as heck don't deserve this." I grabbed his shoulders and pressed my lips to his.

His lukewarm response, as in, *no* response, was disappointing, to say the least.

"Geez, nice kiss," I said.

I pulled back and saw his face. It was whiter than the pillowcase behind him. I barely pushed his shoulders, and he fell back onto his bed. I aimed a reading lamp at his left leg *and* the growing patch of *non-swirling* blood soaking into the light blue duvet. Slipping my knife blade under his jeans, I ripped until I exposed ruptured skin from knee to hip. I sopped up the blood with a dry corner of the duvet. I also gently removed a couple small shards of green and blue Chihuly glass, relieved to see his injuries weren't as bad as they first looked.

"When was the last time you slept?" I asked, studying the rings under his eyes.

"Night before Denmark," Kurt said with his eyes half-closed. He rolled onto his side and held up his arm for me. "You?"

"Something like that," I said, leaving out my Gatwick Express 'nap' and collapsed beside him. I barely felt his arm hug me before I was out.

CHAPTER SIXTY-THREE

"I found them," I heard Rock's unhappy voice call to someone from somewhere near foot of the sleigh bed. I didn't have enough energy to open my eyes. Kurt's arm was still wrapped around me, and I was vaguely aware of a cool breeze on the skin above my bustier and near my hip.

"Do you believe these two? Up here fooling around while I've spent the last hour trying to get these off," Rock said and then rattled his handcuffs.

"Come on, I think you should cut Sam and Kurt some slack. Sam was implanted. She was going to die of a heart attack," I heard JJ say.

"No, she wasn't," Rock said.

"Yes, she was," JJ said, and I pictured him glaring at Rock.

"No, she wasn't. *I* programmed her patch to give only enough heart attack symptoms so Schott wouldn't get suspicious," Rock said.

"You didn't think to tell her that?" JJ asked, sounding exasperated.

"I had a lot on my mind," Rock said.

"Well, how about everyone else?" asked JJ.

"*They* were going to die. I'd made theirs before I knew I was working for the bad guys," said Rock.

I heard footsteps moving around the bed toward the alcove.

"And how did I miss all this?" JJ's voice came from inside the alcove.

"What happened in here?" The housekeeper joined in.

Geez. It was like party central. All we needed was Mrs. Party. Not.

"I'd say *they* happened," JJ said with a smile in his voice.

I felt Kurt move. His hip hit mine. Our tattoos must have matched up because the housekeeper said, "Blimey never seen tattoos do that."

"How about we let them sleep?" JJ said.

I felt a new soft duvet lowered over us, and tuck in by our shoulders. I also felt Kurt's arm tighten around me, and that was it.

CHAPTER SIXTY-FOUR

The next morning I woke to a bizarre and wonderful sight—Kurt smiling down at me. I felt happier than if I'd just wrapped a *Demolition Queen* episode *and* solved Mom's clues all over again.

Kurt suggested we head straight for his Grindelwald chalet. I didn't want to go, I was sore and tired, but that wasn't the reason. Kurt's injuries didn't have anything to do with it either. In fact, he bounded out of bed first thing. Well that wasn't the *first* thing he did before getting out of bed.

Cue fingers to lips.

I didn't want to visit Grindelwald because to me it was still where Jake had "died."

Not that I could have gone that day even if I wanted to. Or the next. There was too much to clear up.

Kurt disappeared that morning. Of course, he'd told me where to find him when the time was right.

Preliminary investigations into the bizarre goings on at the V&A and Cranmont took a while. Finally, Silverblade reported that the whole V&A incident was caused by an odd temporary flu brought on by a bacteria in the water leaked from the radiator system. *Ha.*

When I was finally deemed a no-flight risk, I headed straight for Kurt's chalet.

***

When Kurt and I finally hiked up the mountain above Grindelwald where we first met, it was a glorious day. Sparkling sun. Snow only on the highest Jungfrau peaks. Paths were nice and clear.

Not a Nunchuck in sight.

Perfect.

Holding Kurt's warm hand was pretty perfect too. Especially as we rounded that last set of boulders and I saw the sheerest side of Jungfrau. The one from my nightmares. With Kurt/Jake standing and breathing right beside me, I was able to push those horrible dark bloody images of Jake right out of my head.

"You know our last day together when I followed you up here?" I asked.

Kurt nodded and squeezed my hand extra tight.

"I wanted to tell you how I really felt. It scared the bejeezus out of me. You were the first person who really got *me*," I said and paused. "I lied to you about something, and it's time to come clean," I said, studying his serious expression. "I'm sure I'm going to regret telling you this…" I paused. "…but you're even better looking than before." I smiled and kissed his cheek.

He flashed his best cut-the-crap look, but his grin gave him away.

"So is Foster-beer-can-blue your real eye color?" I asked.

He nodded.

"Cool." I moved away just a little so I could 'drink' them in. "But, I'm still ticked off about that treatment you gave me at your flat. When you went into the shower—"

"*Not* ripping off your clothes and carrying you in with me was probably the hardest thing I've ever done. Don't know how you missed the arctic blast from my cold shower." Kurt laughed.

"Geez, I've missed *you*," I said, laughing too and then pressing the front of *all* of me against the front of *all* of him. The deep kiss that followed was stunning. I could have stayed like that for hours.

"Get a room," JJ called.

I looked around Kurt's shoulder as Felicity and JJ trudged up the path, carrying a half-assembled hang glider.

"Who invited you guys?" I laughed and kissed Kurt again anyway before he moved away to assemble our tandem glider. I'd opted to go tandem today, not wanting to let Kurt out of arms reach on *this* mountain.

"Nothing but good news here," JJ said, smiling. "Good to see you two finally together."

"JJ has photos to show you," Felicity chimed in and elbowed JJ. She playfully grabbed his phone, as if they were long-lost buddies. "Look what JJ found in the tunnel."

I squinted at the small image on JJ's phone and saw a pile of something. Felicity zoomed in and I could make out my canary yellow pocketknife and several others.

"My knives?" I threw my arms around their necks. "Thank you. Thank you," I said, pulling back as my phone pinged with a text.

"It's Silverblade," I said then read his text out loud:

Thanks for the Switzerland invite. Sorry I couldn't make it. Damsel in distress needed my help!! Boot camp next week? Silverblade

"Boot camp? The man's a broken record," I said and typed my response. *Ha-ha. See you soon. Sam.*

"Where's Rock? I thought he was coming too," Felicity said.

"Guess," I said.

"Hunting virus?" she asked.

"Hard to believe," I said with a nod.

"Wasn't sure we'd ever be back here together," said Kurt. He'd finished assembling our glider and walked back over to put an arm around my shoulders.

"Tell me about it," I said, hugging him tight. "You know what? It's so beautiful. I'd love to film a *Demolition Queen* episode here."

"Really? If you love this, you'd love filming at my Danish beach house." Kurt said and then paused. "Oh wait. I don't have a beach house anymore."

"Oh? That's a shame," I said, giving him my own cut-the-crap look.

"Any chance you're as good at building things as tearing them down? I could use a new one," Kurt said.

"Building's not really my thing," I said, shrugging into the harness he held up for me.

As Kurt hooked us into the glider, I watched Felicity get ready for her first flight ever. She adjusted her Chanel headband, checked the zippers on her Gucci boots, and then switched on her camera. As she patted JJ's shoulder I noticed how good they looked together.

"OK, we're off," Felicity said with a giggle but as she and JJ ran off the cliff to soar over the open void her bloodcurdling scream echoed off Jungfrau.

Kurt and I ran off the cliff next. While Kurt steered, I had time to think. I reviewed my manic, insanity-filled weeks. In a crazy way, I was grateful for them. They'd helped me not think about losing Mom.

I was also grateful that MedMaker Corp's enemies were finally gone. I'd be stepping in for a while to make sure Mom's MedMaker got properly launched. Something that wouldn't have been possible if not for Silverblade. Right or wrong, he never shared the evidence that made the MedMaker appear faulty.

Kurt and I flew up near blinding white clouds and I felt like Mom was right there with me. I couldn't resist talking to her.

"That hunt was amazing Mom. Your clues were great. We had fun, didn't we?" Tears welled up and the wind pushed them off my cheeks. "I'll always be your biggest supporter," I added and then swallowed the lump in my throat. "I never got to say good-bye like you did but I understand. I just miss you so much."

Wind was whistling through our glider but Kurt must have heard me sniffle because he asked, "How you doing down there? You OK?" he shouted at the top of my head.

"I'm OK," I said, pushing my hands into the pockets of my goose-down vest. Something inside poked my cold fingers. I pulled out a note card engraved with the MedMaker logo. This *was* one of Mom's old vests so I wasn't surprised to see her handwriting. At first I thought it was one of her old grocery lists but then I noticed how odd a list it was.

> *Bananas are ripest at midnight*
> *Mykonos on my mind*
> *Sour pickles*
> *Schrödinger's Mouse*
> *I get no kick from champagne*
> *Lovely mangos*
> *Checkout time: 8:00 p.m.*
> *Fireflies forever light*

I stared at it. I wasn't sure what it was, but it wasn't a grocery list.

"Did you put a card in my pocket?" I shouted to Kurt. He shook his head no.

"This almost looks like..."

...clues.

I grinned the biggest grin ever.

If my suspicions were correct, we'd be going on another clue hunt. Maybe I didn't have to say good-bye to Mom just yet.

"Thanks, Mom."

THE END